Shard

Book One Of *Aetherworld*

Second Edition

Jane Senese

Contact the author in care of Trafford Publishing.

Printed in Victoria, Canada

Visit the Aetherworld website at http://www.intotheaetherworld.com/peri_scope

National Library of Canada Cataloguing in Publication Data

Senese, Jane, 1981-
Shard
ISBN 1-55212-789-3
I. Title.
PS8587.E549S52 2001   C813'.6   C2001-910822-2
PR9199.4.S46S52 2001

TRAFFORD

This book was published *on-demand* in cooperation with Trafford Publishing.
On-demand publishing is a unique process and service of making a book available for retail sale to the public taking advantage of on-demand manufacturing and Internet marketing. **On-demand publishing** includes promotions, retail sales, manufacturing, order fulfilment, accounting and collecting royalties on behalf of the author.

Suite 6E, 2333 Government St., Victoria, B.C. V8T 4P4, CANADA
Phone 250-383-6864   Toll-free 1-888-232-4444 (Canada & US)
Fax 250-383-6804   E-mail sales@trafford.com
Web site www.trafford.com   TRAFFORD PUBLISHING IS A DIVISION OF TRAFFORD HOLDINGS LTD.
Trafford Catalogue #01-0189   www.trafford.com/robots/01-0189.html

10 9 8 7 6 5 4

To Erin,

For Absolutely Everything

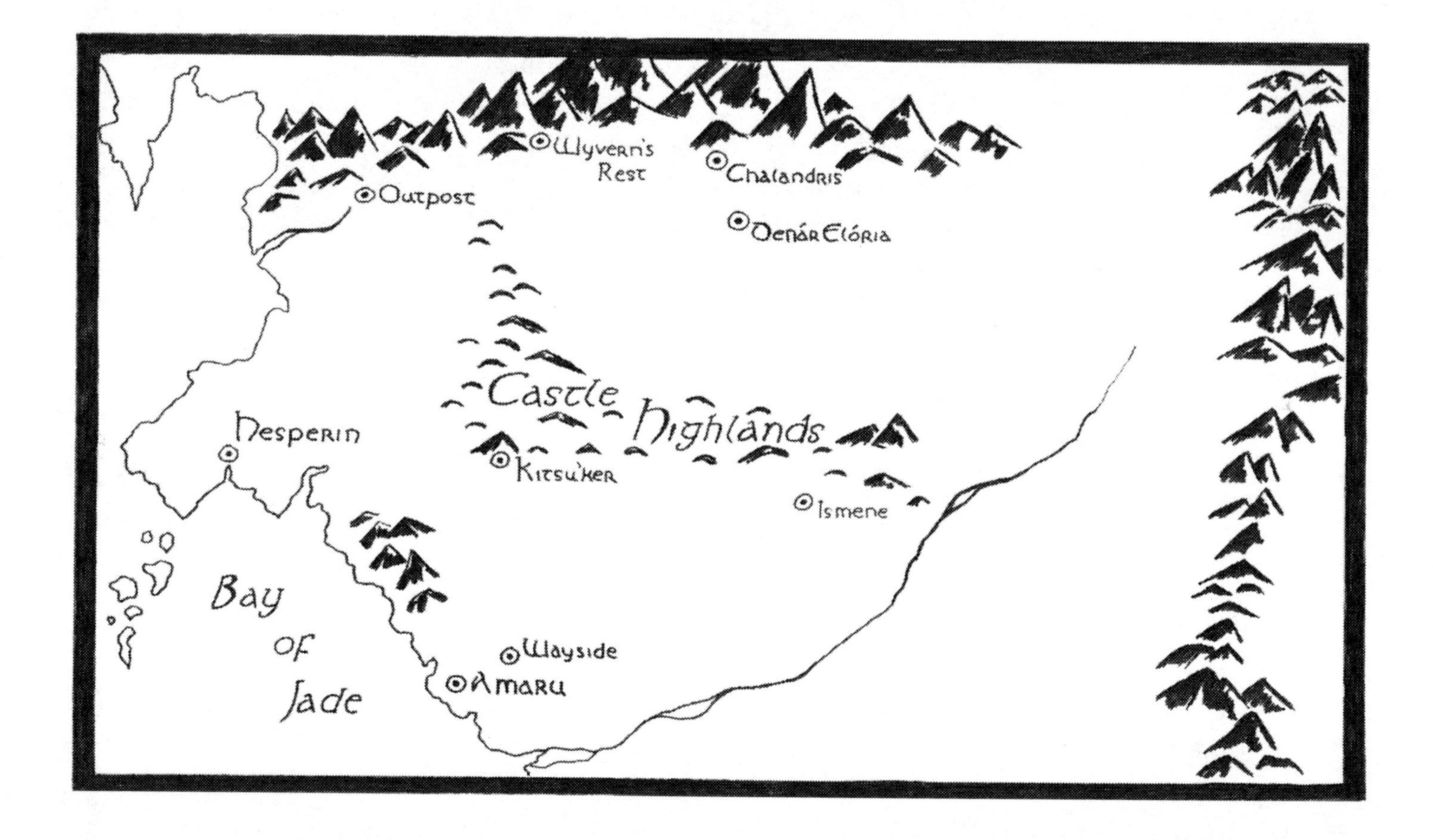
Wyvern's Rest
Chalandris
Outpost
Denár Elória
Castle Highlands
Hesperin
Kitsu'ker
Ismene
Bay of Jade
Wayside
Amaru

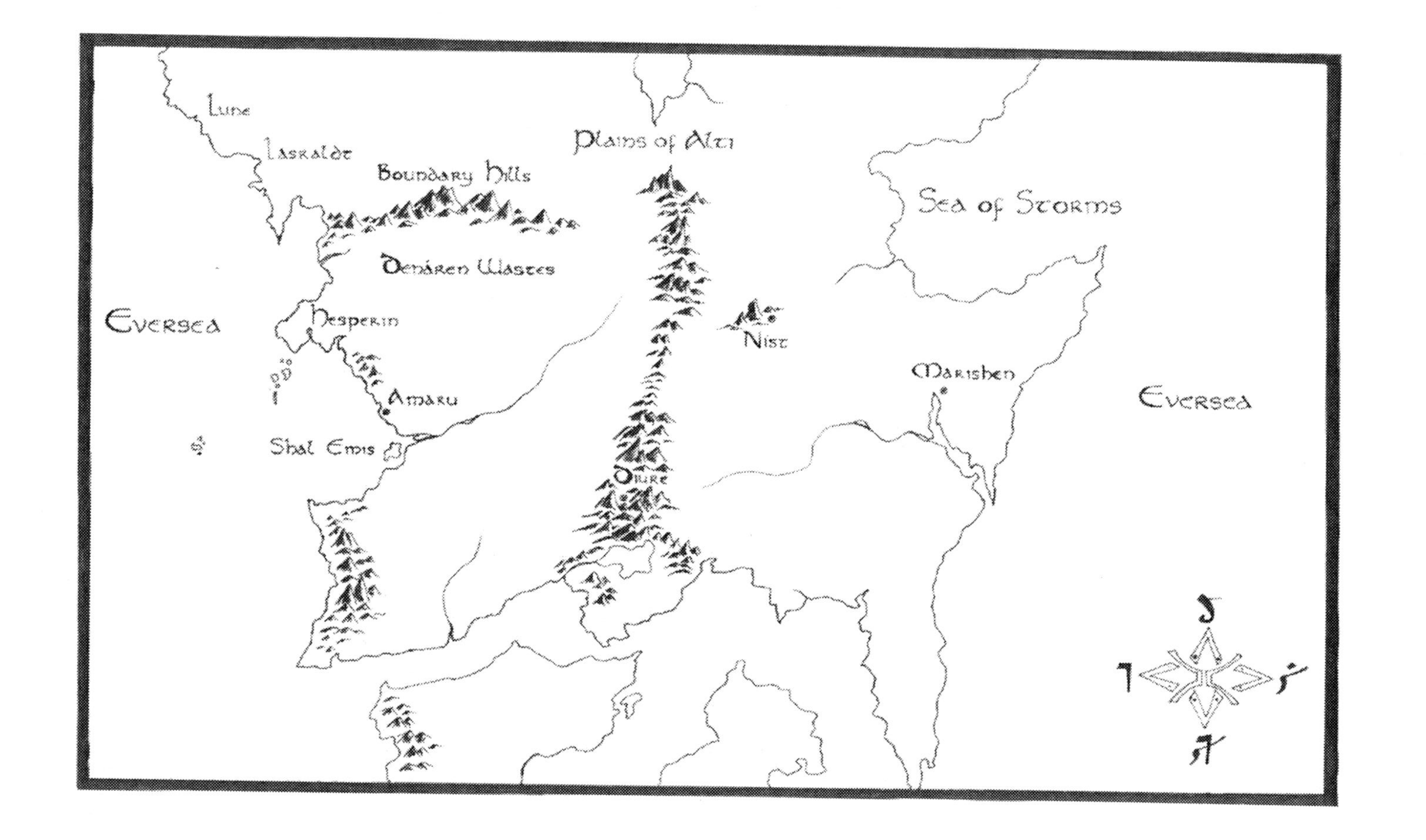

Lune
Laskaldt
Boundary Hills
Plains of Alti
Sea of Storms
Denaren Wastes
Eversea
Hesperin
Nist
Marishen
Eversea
Amaru
Shal Emis

Dramatis Personae

Celaeno tal Amaru: Dynast of Amaru, Empress of Nations
Kemuri tal Hesperin: Royal Consort of Celaeno
Sintaka tal Amaru: Celaeno and Kemuri's daughter
Yósha tal Amaru (Stargazer): Celaeno and Kemuri's son
Shard: Celaeno and Kemuri's adopted son

Murren tal Kitsune: Matriarch of the Kitsune House
Arjin tal Kitsune: Murren's son
Aerin tal Kitsune: Murren's daughter, Stargazer's consort

Shiori tal Tora: Matriarch of the Tora House, Celaeno's bodyguard
Ceih tal Tora: Shiori's eldest son, Arjin's consort
Mindrin tal Tora: Shiori's younger son, Sintaka's consort

Terrays Onmyóji: Golden Age sorceress
Sim Onmyóji: Golden Age sorcerer, Terrays's twin

Larien: Satrap of Chalandris
Varron Lehs: Larien's lieutenant
L'al Darhis: Alteri bounty hunter

The fireflies danced overhead, glimmering white-green balls against the dark canopy. The baby watched them entranced, his tiny hands outstretched. Above him he could see the cool hues of the forest canopy, and through the trees, the faint blue glow of the starlit sky.

Dimly he remembered a time when he had been elsewhere, when the green flickers of the tiny stars had not danced above him. But it seemed only a distant dream. And so he was not afraid, all alone in the forest, with only the rustling of birds for company. He was content to watch the fireflies, to reach up in the hopes of catching an bouncing ball of light.

He heard a crash through the bushes, followed by a loud explosion of laughter. Indignant, the baby began to cry, his eyes squeezing shut with anger and distress, his fists clenching tight.

"Mindrin!" the girl laughed, stumbling through the bamboo, kicking her legs free of the tangle of vegetation. She glared down at her companion who had collapsed into the underbrush and was now regarding her with a playful expression.

She jumped back as he dove for her legs again. Once again he missed and rolled over into a patch of moss. The peri maiden placed her hands squarely on her hips, delivering him the disapproving glare she had seen the Palace Matriarchs affect with great success. But the crimson-haired youth only gave her the same wide smile, and she could not help but laugh again at the sight of him, sprawled on his back in a bed of thick moss, his good clothes wrinkled beyond recognition, his head craned back as he inspected his would-be prey with a puzzled gaze.

"You're upside down," he remarked.

"You're impossible," she exclaimed, extending a hand. She yanked him to his feet. "Shiori will kill you," she reprimanded, dusting the stems and shreds of plantlife from his tunic. "And you, meant to be protecting the Lady Heiress."

She stepped back and spread her arms wide. "Honestly, what sin have I committed, Great Powers?" she asked, turning her golden eyes to the heavens. "That I, Sintaka tal Amaru, daughter of the Dynast, Lady Heiress to the Wonder of the Seven Worlds..."

Mindrin ran a hand through his hair, narrowed his blue eyes, and determinedly fixed his sights on the Heiress. But she was still ranting, oblivious to the new attack being planned.

"...Should be cursed with such a mate: tactless, mannerless, infantile, common, *common* little gardener!" she looked back at him just in time to see him lunge forward.

Her exclamation ended in a squeak of surprise as they both toppled over into another patch of flowers and ferns. Laughing together they rolled deeper into the thicket of dense moss, Sintaka pummeling him with ineffective blows, Mindrin jestingly trying to pin her arms to her sides.

Their brief struggle ended, their limbs entwined, bodies locked together in a close embrace. "Well, this is unexpected," Sintaka murmured, raising an eyebrow before leaning further into the embrace and covering his mouth with her own.

She meant to pursue the kiss, idly wondering how long they could stray from the rest of the party, but then she heard a faint but unmistakable sound and swiftly pulled away.

"Mindrin? Did you hear that?"

He nodded, his brow furrowed in bewilderment. "That.... I'd swear it almost sounds like a baby."

Sintaka rose, slowly turning around, trying to place the sound. "I think it's coming from over here."

"Is it?" he followed her as she moved off deeper into the forest. "I could swear..."

"You don't think it is a baby, do you?"

"Do the Powers really leave babies in the forest?" Mindrin asked.

"Min," she swatted at his puff of crimson hair.

"We have been thinking about kitlings. Maybe it's for us."

"Yeah, with a little note – 'to Sin and Min, love from the Powers of the Overworlds,'" she teased as they wound through the green bamboo leaves, searching for the source of the sound.

Celaeno tal Amaru ran a soft hand over her dragon's short horns, trailing her fingertips down the side of his lion-like face. Her mount purred appreciatively, then set his head down on his massive paws and dozed lightly. A half-dozen other dragons lounged in the shade, their long bodies in shadow as they awaited their next command. They could be nocturnal if forced, but they far preferred the daytime, and had little wish to join their riders in exploration of the isolated wood.

Celaeno was a delicate woman, her short stature belying the commanding presence she carried about her. She wore a long riding gown of rich blue, heavily embroidered with the emblems of her kingdom. Soft locks of silver hair framed a delicate round face; her thick mane fell unbound down her back, and swept the ground at her feet. The Seal of Amaru, the mark of her authority, was carefully tattooed on her forehead.

She turned, gazing up at the stars glimmering through the verdant canopy. The bamboo fronds parted overhead and she stepped forward to catch sight of the starshower above her. The meteors had been streaking through the sky day and night for the last few days, heralding the solstice. It was a relatively rare occurrence, and Celaeno watched the starshower in awe. The meteors fell across the sky, burning their bright blue trails behind them before they were swallowed up by the dark heavens. Such showers were believed to bear fragments of Old Magic.

"Beautiful night, isn't it, Mistress?" Shiori murmured. "One could almost believe the legends of old."

"'And down the shards came falling,'" Celaeno quoted the old ballad softly. "Do you think we'll find our own shard tonight?"

"Old Magic... from before the Dark Age," Shiori breathed. "Galen Minyami speaks of such things, doesn't he? The old sorcerers' magic, cast into the stars during the Great War, only to fall to the earth years later."

The Dynast paused, cocking her head to listen to a faint sound. She recognized it instantly. The Amarin Vastwood stretched across the lowlands and plains of her kingdom, and she knew well that there were no settlements nearby. She had specifically chosen such an isolated wood for the family's excursion. What on earth was an infant doing here?

"A baby," her son murmured softly, looking up at her with wide silver-blue eyes.

"Yes."

Shiori tal Tora drew near to the Dynast's side, her arm unconsciously reaching for the dagger concealed up the long sleeve of her white robe. Celaeno raised her hand, stilling her *ani*'s instinctive action.

"Sounds upset." The boy drew closer to the Dynast, squeezing her hand as he retreated against the folds of her long gown.

"He does, doesn't he?" she whispered. There was no reason to suppose it was not simply the crying of a little kobold, the child of some travelling peasants, his teething tears uneased by his mother's comforting arms. Yet there was a tone to the cries, a desperate pitch that raised the hairs on the back of her neck.

She could not ignore her mother's instinct. "Come, Yósha," she said, tightening her grasp on her son's hand. "Let's go find him. Shiori, stay here in camp." The bodyguard hesitated, then nodded obediently and silently withdrew.

The little boy hurried alongside her, eager for another adventure. The evening had already yielded such exploits: a flight to the secluded corner of his mother's kingdom, a picnic under the midsummer moons, and a dark forest to explore under the lights of a starshower. Now they were going even farther from the little glade where their mounts were tended, venturing deeper into the dark wood. He hardly noticed where he stepped, his eyes tracing the path of the meteors above. At his side, Celaeno picked her way through the thick carpet of wild grasses, unhampered by the long robes she wore.

Mother, a cool voice echoed in her head. *Mindrin and I... we hear crying. A baby...*

I know, Sintaka, Celaeno replied, returning the mindspeech. *I can hear it too. Stargazer and I are trying to find it.*

"I can hear him," Stargazer darted ahead, tearing his hand from his mother's. The three-year-old scampered ahead, his disordered puff of crystal-silver hair disappearing in the shadows. He wove through the fluttering bamboo fronds, a silhouette against the pulsing lights of the phosphorescent wildflowers. Even with her large owl eyes, used to the darkness of night, Celaeno lost sight of him almost immediately. "Stargazer!" She quickened her pace, lifting the embroidered hems of her riding gown. "Be careful!" The solstice nights were strange ones, when the moons aligned and the magic lay heavy on the air. There had been starshowers the night Stargazer was born, three years before.

She stumbled through the last wall of brush, almost running her son over. Little Stargazer stood still, spellbound, hardly aware of his mother's presence. Celaeno gasped at the sight. It was a idyllic picture: a glade of bright blooming flowers set against the cool green fronds. The entire vista glowed under the light of the fireflies.

And there, in the center, lay a baby.

He was clearly abandoned, left with nothing but a wrap. Not even footprints disturbed the pillowmoss surrounding him, Celaeno realized, as she moved towards the little blanket wrapped about the kitling. Her robes, which had previously been so cooperative, tangled about her legs.

She sank down on the grass. The baby had ceased his crying now, and only blinked in confusion at the face peering down at him. Where he had twisted and kicked against his crimson blanket, now he was peaceful and content. Celaeno smiled down at him. He was no newborn, but nearly a month old by his size and the clarity of his stormy violet-blue eyes. He kept his eyes on her a moment longer, then, as if bored, turned back to the glimmering lights above him.

"Hello, hello," she whispered to the child. "Do you like the fireflies?"

Stargazer appeared at her side. "Is he all right, Mother?" he asked in a hesitant voice.

"Oh, he's a good baby, aren't you?" Celaeno gave him her warmest maternal smile, reached down and scooped him up from the moss. "Who are you, hmm? Who left you here?"

The baby coughed once, and gave a little sleepy murmur, but did not cry again as she clasped him against her. "Shh, shh," she whispered, rocking him softly. "We'll set this right, little one," she promised.

Stargazer was edging around the two, his eyes warily focused on his mother and the child. He wasn't entirely certain what to make of this little baby they had found together. As Celaeno shifted the infant, the blanket slipped from his back and Stargazer caught sight of something dark against his skin. "Mother, look!"

"Shh, you'll scare him. What is it, Yósha?"

"His back! He's got something. On his back."

"His back?" Celaeno frowned, carefully turning the baby around, biting her lip in dread of some deformity that would explain his abandonment.

The blanket fell away and by the faint light she could see two intricate designs stenciled on the infant's back. Sprouting from his spine at his shoulder blades, they arched up and then dipped down his back, ending in fine tips below his waist.

Wings. A pair of wings, with individual feathers carefully outlined. Like an expert tattoo - but who would mark such a little child? Stargazer reached out a hesitant finger and lightly touched the fine lines. "It doesn't come off," he exclaimed.

The baby began to fuss at being held away and gave a faint warning cry. Swiftly Celaeno clasped him close anew, lifting the discarded blanket and wrapping it about him once more. "There, there, it's all right. I'm not going to leave you. See? Who are you, little one, hmm? Are you one of those shards we sing about?"

A loud crash of rustling brush and Celaeno looked over her shoulder to see her daughter belatedly stagger into the clearing, Mindrin close on her heels. Celaeno smiled softly at their rumpled clothes and Sintaka's silver hair, even wilder than usual.

"Is it... is it all right?" Sintaka asked, echoing her brother's words.

Celaeno glanced back at the infant, his eyes slowly sliding closed, a soft yawn escaping him. "Yes, I think so."

"I wonder where he came from," Mindrin mused, peering at the baby in the Dynast's arms. The infant had fallen fast asleep, his little hand curled around a few strands of Celaeno's hair.

Mindrin's mother moved behind him, peering uncertainly at the infant. "A kobold, maybe? A half-blood? I've heard of peri girls abandoning babies by kobolds."

"Oh no, no," Celaeno murmured, careful not to raise her voice and startle the child. "He's far too delicate. Look at him, Shiori, he's pure peri. And well born by the looks of this blanket."

"He's healthy; he's not sick," Mindrin frowned. "Anyone who could afford that blanket is rich enough to raise him. They went to the trouble of putting those wings on him."

"Unless he was born with them," Sintaka mused aloud.

Mindrin straightened, turning back to her. "You think?"

The bamboo rustled softly. "I had a feeling this midsummer would be a special one," a soft voice spoke. Celaeno glanced up to see her consort inspecting the infant. His golden eyes seemed distant, as if he were looking at something far away.

"Kemuri," Celaeno extended her hand as he knelt down beside her. "Can you sense anything from him? Anything to tell us where he might have come from?"

The dreamseer stared at the child at length, then slowly shook his head. "Only that he's powerful. Very powerful for his age," he added, his voice briefly fluttering above its customary whisper. "He could be a dreamseer."

"He was crying when we found him, but as soon as I reached him he was quiet. Watching the fireflies, like he belonged here. Look at him. Powers know what he's been through, but he's sleeping peacefully."

"*I* found him," Stargazer piped up.

"I don't think anyone'll come back for him," Sintaka sighed sadly.

"Maybe his parents were afraid," Mindrin suggested. "Maybe they could see he has a lot of magic in him and... and they didn't want him anymore."

"Maybe." Celaeno looked back at the baby, then lifted her eyes to meet her soulmate's. "Someone will have to take care of him." A hesitant smile tugged at her lips.

Kemuri returned his softest smile. "Someone will."

Celaeno lifted her hand to tenderly brush back a strand of the dreamer's long platinum hair.

Stargazer looked from one parent to the other, trying to decipher their expressions. "Are we going to keep him?"

Kemuri laid a hand on his son's shoulder. "What do you think, Yósha? Can we fit a little brother into the nursery?"

Abroad grin spread across Stargazer's face. He looked ready to erupt with delight, and Mindrin swiftly swept him up into his arms. "Sorry, sprout; looks like you won't have me all to yourself anymore."

"I think you could bear to share yourself between two little brothers," Sintaka laughed, ruffling his hair.

"What will we name him?" Kemuri asked.

Celaeno was silent a moment, examining her new son from under thick silver-tipped lashes. "Shard," she whispered at length. She looked up at her consort. "His name is Shard."

Kemuri smiled again. He tilted his head to the side, gazing at the kitling with a dreamy expression that betrayed the extent to which he was already smitten. "What are you going to be, Shard?" he breathed, his fingertips lightly grazing the child's cheek.

The newly declared Lord Heir of Amaru opened his eyes again with a tiny yawn, blinking once, his eyes clearly asking what all the fuss was about, before he settled back in his mother's arms, returning to sleep.

1

The Bluestar had set several hours before, and the sky shone brightly with silver and blue. White Moon was a faint crescent just beginning to wax, signaling the beginning of the Lovers Moon, a half-turn before midsummer. Aerin tal Kitsune stood on the metal staircase of the observatory, staring up at the starlit sky through the wide door in the dome. Beside her the immense telescope lay idle, pointed at a distant speck of light.

Even with the lights on in the metal dome of the observatory, she could see the Well of Stars, a snake glittering with countless dots of light. The old chronicles from before the War spoke of intrepid explorers who fashioned wings and flew up to the stars, who dove into the Well to emerge on the other side in the Overworlds.

She wondered if there was any truth to the old tales. The Golden Age was said to be a time of powerful magic and heroic feats, when palaces of crystal had stood over great cities stretching across horizons. She couldn't say she had much interest in the legends, one way or the other. The War had destroyed such fantasies and scarred the land forever. Peri who could live forever in peacetime were slaughtered as children and the stars were darkened for a thousand years.

She glanced at the metal telescope, marveling that when her mother had been a child such a commonplace fixture as the observatory would have been an unheard-of miracle. It had only been three hundred years before, when Amaru was reclaimed and the five kingdoms allied, that the Dark Age ended and the new calendar began. Her brother had told her countless stories of the years that followed, when the new palace was built on the ruins of the old, when the great observatory was raised above the cliffs. But to an infant of her age, a mere nineteen, it seemed as if the observatory and its surroundings were as old as the fabled Golden Age itself. She could hardly grasp that the great palace, Wonder of the Seven Worlds, had once been a sprawling ruin.

Aerin leaned on the railing of the staircase, sweeping her gaze across the floor of the observatory. Pages were scattered across the floor, some blank, some scribbled with sketchy drawings and covered with nearly illegible notes.

A tender smile touched her face as another flurry of paper fluttered off the desk.

"This place is a mess," she informed her companion.

Stargazer looked up from his desk. "Is... is it?" he stammered, rearranging his reading glasses which sat slightly crooked on his nose. "I... oh it's not that bad. I... I was meaning to clean it up a little later..."

"Sure you were," Aerin sat herself on the metal banister of the staircase and slid down its curve to the floor.

"I was! Anyway... it's not that bad. I've just been busy lately."

He was always busy, ever since his father had given him a desk beneath the telescope fifteen years before. Now he was twenty, and Kemuri had never again gotten more than a fleeting glimpse through the telescope.

"So, what are you working on?" Aerin asked, walking over to the desk.

"Oh, oh, nothing," Stargazer stammered, spinning about to face her, blushing nervously. Aerin struggled to keep the smile off her face. He looked so adorable in his rumpled tunic, his glasses slightly askew, his long silver-white hair starting to slip out of its thick braid.

He used to let her watch over his shoulder as he worked, his ever-present shadow. But lately he was growing more and more uneasy around her, especially once the sun set and she showed no intention of retiring for the night. She supposed it was because of their advancing age; they could not play as little children forever. Surely he noticed by now that maidens who had once patted his head were now slyly appraising the young lord, just as she was quite aware that her fellow knights were paying her far more attention than once they had given the fire-haired sprite.

Stargazer turned, opened a drawer swiftly to check inside, then closed it again just as quickly. He must have notes of a most important nature in there, she decided, for he had been furtively checking the contents of that drawer for the past month or two now.

"So!" she declared loudly, startling him.

"So," he spun back to face her. He fumbled with his glasses, taking them off and folding them carefully. He rolled the glasses in his hands a moment, then hastily set them down on the desk.

"Is... is your mother still planning that... get-together of the kingdoms?" Aerin asked, knowing full well the answer.

Stargazer nodded. "In two months, more or less. A state of the empires conference – to make sure we're not sliding into the Dark Age... or whatever. Another diplomatic function – *augh!* I'd rather just stay up here." He glanced down at the floor, then back at Aerin, his blue-gray eyes suddenly brighter. "Hey, you can stay up here with me. We could hide out together."

Aerin forced herself to keep her smile light. "Well, I'm sure they'd miss the Heiress of Kitsune." It sounded like nothing more than an idle flirtation. She should know better than to let her imagination run untempered.

"You're probably right. Price of being aristocracy."

Aerin nodded readily. "Powers forbid I forget my place and start carrying on like–"

"Like your brother."

Aerin laughed. "Exactly."

Stargazer chuckled at that. A moment's silence passed, however, and suddenly he was shy again. "So, do... do you want to go up and see the eclipse?"

Aerin shrugged gamely and they walked over to the metal staircase. She cast one last glance at the drawer and the mystery it contained. It was probably nothing. Strange though, usually he was always trying to impress her with his latest discovery. Trying and succeeding, for she was spellbound by his every word. But it seemed even that had changed lately.

Aerin considered the grim possibility that, since their days as children, they were drifting apart. Had he forgotten? Surely he had. They had been five and four, little kitlings playing in Mindrin's gardens. Suddenly he had knelt down before her and asked her to marry him. Little games of foolish children, she knew. But she had never forgotten it, even as they grew to teenagers and it became increasingly clear that he saw her as nothing more than a friend.

They reached the top of the staircase, at the lens of the telescope. With White Moon's crescent shimmering in the background, Silver Moon, half its size, waited in the sky, its lightly scarred surface a glowing cloud-gray. Before it, Red Moon, the smallest of the trio, slowly moved into eclipse. Its size and shadow were not enough to hide its mate, but they would hang together in the sky, lovers embracing, before Red Moon moved on. Red Moon sped through the sky, going through a full turn of its face in nine days. It eclipsed the slower Silver Moon every two months, roughly, when their paths through the sky crossed. Tonight the spectacle was stunning: White Moon reduced to a faint sliver, the light of the two eclipsing moons doubly brilliant.

Stargazer had once likened the moons to the two of them: Silver Moon, soft, mysterious Aurin, patron deity of all astrologers, and Red Moon, fiery Chaiya, emblem of the Kitsune knights. The association was never far from her mind; seeing Red Moon once again catch its mate, she wondered whether Stargazer would ever learn to slow down like Silver Moon, and let himself be caught.

"Perfect," Stargazer murmured, his breath stirring her hair. She hadn't realized how close he was standing to her. Against her best attempts to repress it, she felt a blush begin to creep up her cheeks. Before she quite knew what she was doing, Aerin edged up the stairs away from him. A moment later she cursed herself. If he hadn't been there she might have kicked herself too.

She kept her attention pinned on the moons, telling herself to focus only on the skyscape, until the constriction in her throat subsided and the knot in her stomach eased. At length her legs felt sturdier and her breathing relaxed.

She watched the moons a long time, until Chaiya began to edge away from the embrace, reluctantly continuing on through the sky. She would set after midnight, and rise again some time in the morning, dwarfed by the aurorae of the rising sun.

Aerin turned then, only to find Stargazer near his desk again, pacing restlessly. As Aerin slowly began to creep down towards the floor, he turned, striding purposefully to the desk, and pulled the drawer open once again. Hiding from view behind the telescope, Aerin descended, stealthy as a cat.

Her boots touched the floor as she watched him carefully. He paused, rubbing his palms together, worry written across his face. Aerin inched closer, craning her neck to see over his shoulder.

She stepped on a ball of paper, which crackled loudly. In the silence of the domed observatory, it was loud as a explosion. Stargazer slammed the drawer closed on instinct, letting out a yelp of pain as it caught his finger.

"Oh, Star!" Aerin was at his side in a moment, her hand closing over his before she could stop herself. Surprised at her sudden action, her eyes darted up to meet Stargazer's. For a moment they only stared at each other, uncertain in their gaze.

Aerin laughed lightly, lifting his hand and dropping her head to bestow a quick kiss on his injured finger. "You should be more careful–" she began, raising her head. Her words died in her throat when she met his eyes anew.

Her legs were taking on that distinctly watery feeling again.

For an instant they only stared. Then, surprising them both, Aerin leaned forward, her lips brushing across his in a soft, timid kiss. Just as swiftly she drew back, a flustered smile on her face. She glanced back at Stargazer reluctantly, her cheeks flushed with embarrassment.

Then Stargazer darted forward impulsively, casting his arms about her waist, kissing her fiercely. Aerin froze at the sudden turn of events. She recovered her senses a moment later, winding her arms around his neck, deepening the embrace.

Aerin awoke the next morning just before dawn. Sleepily, she looked over at her new soulmate, fast asleep next to her. His hair was undone from its heavy braid, something he allowed few people to see, and lay in long silver strands across the bedcovers. His face seemed even younger, framed by his disordered locks, peaceful and contented in sleep.

He was dreaming, she realized instinctively. Snatches of images, as cryptic as her own dreams, fleetingly passed through her mind. She smiled contentedly; their soulbinding was still so recent, she could read his thoughts as easily she could her own.

She remembered the mysterious drawer and she sat up, gazing across the room at the desk, a dim silhouette in the near-blackness. She cast a quick glance at Stargazer, then rose, slipping to the floor, wincing at the feel of the cold floor on her bare feet. She took a step forward, then, suddenly feeling self-conscious, turned back. A sheet had slid nearly entirely off the bed and she scooped it up, wrapping it around her body.

As quietly as she could, determined not to wake Stargazer, she padded across the floor from the little bed to the desk, taking care not to step on any treacherous sheets of paper. She hesitated a moment before she slid the desk drawer open, breathing a silent prayer that it didn't squeak.

Inside lay a little black box, sitting primly atop a stack of blank paper. Aerin lifted it out and held it up, frowning as she tried to decipher its meaning. Carefully she opened the lid, gazing within at the mystery he had so long kept from her.

A beautiful ring lay inside, which she instantly recognized as from the Amaru house by its distinctive design. White, yellow and red gold twined in an intricate pattern, swirling around a delicate fire opal. Even in the dim lightning she could see the fine workmanship in the minute details. It was a ring meant for royalty.

That was when she realized it; he had never forgotten.

2

The fireflies danced overhead, glimmering white-green balls against the dark canopy. The baby watched them entranced, his tiny hands outstretched. Above him he could see the cool hues of the forest canopy, and through the trees–

Shard awoke with a start, his heart racing. As always. He never slowly drifted out of sleep in a hazy peace – his dreams invariably shattered in explosions.

He sat up bed, running a hand through his short hair. It was a glossy ebony, forever tousled in thick locks, shining like black quicksilver in the sunlight. The merest attention was all it required before it fell into its daily style. Shard liked to keep things simple.

A glance through the heavy curtains revealed it was just before sunrise. Faint starlight and the glow of the palace lanterns filtered through and he closed his eyes at the intrusion. Preferring the gloom, he drew the curtains once more.

Magic books lay on the floor surrounding his bed, his black cloak draped over a chair. Large metal clockwork sculptures sat in the corners, old gears from obsolete contraptions he had saved from the melting furnace. Shard smiled at the way faint light bounced off the metals – "elegantly chaotic" was his mantra in life.

Yawning, he peeled off his shirt, casting it behind him on the floor. Landar would probably sneak into his room later and hide his pyjamas away in so strange a place as the closet. Running his hands through his black locks once more, he paused at the large floor-length mirror he had set among the more eccentric of the castaway machine-works. Turning around slowly, he came to face the small mirror he had painstakingly hung on the opposite wall.

He inspected his back's reflection, the large wings spread over his skin. They hadn't known what to expect, his parents, when they had watched him grow up. Would his wings stretch and fade and distort as he grew, like a drawing twisted out of shape? But they had grown with him, and they had all observedwith fascination and a little bit of fear as new knifepoint-thin black lines began to appear over his skin, filling in the contours of his wings, the detail growing more precise as he aged.

The last year they had slowed their growth, as had he. It seemed he would grow no taller – a fact which annoyed him to no end – and the wings seemed complete. They sat in perfect detail, feathers gently curving as if about to spread wide at any moment, sloping down his back until the edges disappeared under the waistband of his pants.

Shard didn't know what to make of them. He had yet to decide whether he hated them or not, whether he fancied the idea of being a spirit child who had materialized into the world on midsummer's night, or whether he preferred to believe he had normal peri parents who had simply abandoned an unwanted baby.

They celebrated his birthday on midsummer. His birthdate was listed in the records as fourteenth of the Lovers Moon. Some days they even believed he had not existed before then. Maybe he hadn't. Maybe when Stargazer built a powerful enough microscope they might find his blood was nothing like theirs.

He didn't know what he would prefer.

FIRE! he commanded, staring at the remnants of last night's fire in the large fireplace. A flurry of minute orange-red sparks danced in the air before the charred wood caught. Shard scooped up a handful of dried broom from the wicker basket and tossed it on the newborn flames. The flames greedily devoured the broom, and Shard placed a log over the growing fire.

He pulled on his clothes: black jacket, black trousers, black boots. He pulled the drapes over the glass doors wide open and silver light spilled into his room. It was not yet sunrise. He had time yet.

He stepped out onto the balcony, then climbed up onto the stone parapet. He reached up to measure the distance and steady himself, then leapt up into the air, flipping over backwards to land on the sloping roof of his apartments.

Sitting down on the edge, his legs drawn up before him, he turned to the east where the first rays of the aurora were beginning to edge over the horizon. Within minutes the black sky was alight with sweeping arcs of blue-green light. They snaked upward in waves, glinting silver-tipped whiplashes, sparkling with dancing violet bands, like an acrobat's banners.

The dancing lights rose higher into the sky as the first rays of the sun itself began to peek over the horizon. Bright blue beams glittered, and then the disc of the star appeared, and the aurorae were prodded into a frenzied dance. The sun slowly rose, smaller than the smallest moon, its size belying its power. Rays of light spread across the sky, magnified by the aurorae, and soon the entire eastern quarter of the sky was lit up, the Well of Stars outdone. A misty blue film blanketed the sky, shot throughout with colour, from white silver to deep black where the aurorae ebbed to reveal the sky behind.

Shard closed his eyes, tipping his face towards the rising sun, feeling the creeping warmth of daylight on his cheeks. At length the glow ebbed away and he opened his eyes to see the aurorae retreating down to the eastern horizon, withdrawing their tendrils of light. Soon the Bluestar climbed higher. Once again the sky was its pure black. The Well of Stars was as bright as ever, and the moons glowed with renewed light. The show was over until sunset and the sun itself appeared little more than a large star, its light now a universal glow that lit the earth while leaving the sky pitch black.

"Good morning, Mnemsyara," Shard murmured, before he stood and began to pace along the roof. From his vantage point he could see most of the City Mount: the high vaulted ceiling of the throne room and the cavernous banquet hall already being feverishly prepared for the feasts to come; beyond it, the library, where he could while away countless hours during the idle summer days; the imposing black temple of Herasis, the cult serpent, and next to it, the cathedral to Myrddin, the horned avatar of the kobolds. The city sloped down from the ornamented pagodas and temples of the High Town to the grid-planned homes and warehouses of the guild quarters. The gobletplum trees were in their second flowering of the year; the streets were lined with pink blossoms. He could even see a glimmer of the harbour where the warships and trade galleons were anchored, and beyond it the islands in the Bay of Jade, Amaru's own portion of the Eversea.

Behind him the caravans were bustling in the streets of the city. The tripartite East Gate was being polished to a sheen, ready to be opened to receive the royal dignitaries during the coming days. The Lord Heir was to be married. Guests from the entire Continent were arriving to pay their respects. It was to be a joyous occasion, a day to be remembered forever.

Shard smiled softly. And judging by his calculations, all hell would be breaking loose in about five minutes.

"*ARJIN! You lazy troglodyte! Get your ass out here this minute!*"

Again she received no reply, and Aerin lost all patience. No longer content to wait, she stormed down the hallways, crossing the chaste sitting room of ornate chairs and antique tables. Too late she noticed the row of golden temple bells strung across the archway, just above the floor. She tripped over the string, setting the bells jangling discordantly sending her face down into a pile of cushions. She kept her face buried in a pillow to muffle the loud kobold swears she unleashed, then leapt to her feet. The immense hanging bed in the center of the next room was heaped with silks and woolen blankets, the trailing edge of a rich crimson cover spilling onto the floor.

"Arjin!" she barked, one final demand. The heap of sheets and blankets stirred once, shrugging in reply. Then it settled once more, unmoving. Her patience gone and her indulgence worn thin, Aerin gave no further warning. Marching to the bed, she delivered a sharp kick to the frame. It swung wildly on its hinged supports, and the pile of sheets dissolved onto the floor. A sharp curse sounded and two figures tumbled out gracelessly.

"Aerin!" Arjin wailed, his long disheveled hair hiding his face. Sleepily, he tried to toss it back, but only managed to muss it up further. A moment later his companion appeared, slowly getting up on his knees, rubbing a sore forehead. His shiny dark red hair was much shorter than Arjin's, but just as disordered. He slowly tried to sit up, but seemed too uncoordinated to move, and collapsed against Arjin.

"Do you mind?!" Arjin snapped, still trying to push the auburn strands from his face. His companion managed to sit up and, chuckling, assisted him in tucking his hair behind his ears.

"You knew we had a meeting!"

"Did you have to come barging in? We could have had a woman in here."

"Yeah," his companion readily agreed. "Or... or two!"

"Or three!" Arjin insisted.

The two paused a moment, smiles crossing their faces as they both stopped to consider the idea. "*Three...*" they nodded in unison, slow smug smiles spreading.

"As if either of you has *ever* had a woman in bed! You couldn't fit one in there if you tried," Aerin growled. "You're both too much in love with yourselves."

"I think you mean 'each other,' dear," Arjin corrected her sweetly.

Aerin smiled just as sweetly. "No, I don't."

Slowly it dawned on their sleep-drugged brains that they had been insulted, and the two knights pouted in unison, prompting Aerin into a flurry of laughter. She could never stay mad at them for long. Ceih and Arjin, knights of the realm, Lords of Amaru, in their mint-green and powder-blue pyjamas, respectively; both overgrown kitlings able to melt even the hardest hearts. They had been bondbrothers since they were children, and were as inseparable two hundred years later, still acting as if they were no older than nine.

Arjin leaned against the edge of the bed, stopping its swinging. "Why are we doing this again?" he yawned.

"Because Mother says so."

"Why can't she say so a few hours later?" he muttered.

"Arjin," Aerin growled menacingly, the temper of the Red Knights flaring to life.

"The sun's not even up yet," Arjin whined.

"I'm sleepy," Ceih protested drowsily, wrapping his arms about his soulmate, burying his nose in his neck.

"Like hell you are," Arjin pushed him away, sending the now-laughing knight to the floor. "If I'm going you're going."

"Arjin," Aerin smiled sweetly. She bent low. "Arjin, my dearest, sweetest brother. I... am getting married in nine days. Ambassadors from all the kingdoms in the civilized world are coming to see the daughter of Kitsune join with the Lord Heir of Amaru. This is going to be beautiful. This is going to be the wedding banquet I always dreamed of. And I am *not* going to let my *idiot delinquent overgrown, overblown, oversexed idiot brother screw this up for me, UNDERSTAND?"*

Arjin thrust his face up into hers. His gray eyes narrowed. "What are you going to do?" he taunted.

"Let me go! Damn you Aerin, *let me go!*"

Celaeno shared a secret smile with the couple standing before her throne. A more mismatched pair would be hard to find: a somber palace healer in his dark robes, and a firebrand of a Matriarch, her scanty black costume baring her long limbs. Tiryn and Murren: trusted counsel and good friends, if only they could keep from killing each other long enough to offer advice. Celaeno smiled inwardly as she recalled the sparks that had flown the day the old enemies had first met; she could still see Tiryn's look of utter horror when he realized the lingerie-clad harlot before him was actually the Amaru warleader and his direct superior.

Was it any wonder then, that they produced such children, who thought the customary show of affection between siblings was a battle to the death?

Aerin strode into the empty throne room, her brother's bare foot in her hands as she dragged him in on his back. Arjin, still in his nightclothes, was thrashing and fighting, trying to twist free from her vicelike grasp. Behind him Ceih followed, fully dressed in his warrior's tunic and trousers, struggling to keep his smile as polite as he could.

"You could help!" Arjin shot at him.

Ceih shrugged. "I'd rather not."

"I'll make you pay for this, Aerin," Arjin raged. "Damn you, let me go, you *demon peri bitch from hell!*"

Aerin threw him free, and he spun on the newly polished floor. The Dynast stepped forward, sweeping her long silver and blue gown to her side. "Well now," she smiled. "Now that you're here..."

Arjin sputtered, staggering to his feet, his eyes shooting daggers at his sister.

From his vantage point high above, Shard watched the show. One never needed to look far for amusement in Amaru; the Royal House was as much of a ship of fools as anyone could hope for. Right now Murren was harshly instructing Arjin and Ceih not to repeat their wild behavior at Sintaka's wedding, over a century before. But even from his position high on the ceiling, seated on the great stone arches high above the throne room, Shard could see the smile tugging at her lips. Where else had Arjin gotten his mischievous humour from? Not even Tiryn could bring himself to reprimand his son. Ceih even dared to slump at the edge of the dais, until his mother Shiori swatted his hair lightly and spurred him to his feet.

Shard watched the meeting as slowly it grew more lighthearted and Arjin was let off lightly. He pouted and fretted like a kitling and then ran to Ceih to be comforted.

At length Celaeno laughed, a clear silver laugh that rose to fill the vaulted throne room, and shooed the knights away. Aerin chased after them, her short flame-red hair bouncing about her ears as she followed, no longer intent on Arjin's murder – yet. Murren and Tiryn swept off silently, and Celaeno breathed an audible sigh of relief when they left the hall. Massaging her forehead lightly, she waved her leave to Shiori.

Hello, little one, she mindspoke as she sat back in her throne.

Shard paused, startled. **I need a better hiding place.**

Very few hide who don't want, in the end, to be found. Come down and sit with me a while, Shard. She looked up at the tiny figure high above her. A distinctly motherly smile touched her lips. **Try not to break your neck.**

Quick as thought, Shard dropped down from the arch. He leapt to a thin decorative ledge, then moved to the tip of the large royal seal raised in relief on the wall. He proceeded from one foothold to another, hardly pausing to take breath, until he dropped down to the marble floor.

"You know I hate it when you do that," Celaeno shook her head. Shard merely smiled and Celaeno sighed with defeat. "Have you seen your brother yet?"

"I just came here from my room."

"Climbing over roofs and through the rafters all the way I'm sure." She raised her hand to his cheek. "What a strange little thing you are, Shard."

"Wish I wasn't so little," Shard glanced away, lacing his hands behind his back. "You'd almost think I have kobold blood in me."

"Oh, Shard," Celaeno swept out her arms and pulled him into her lap before he could resist. "You aren't *so* short. And besides, if you were tall as Arjin or your father, would you be able to climb like you do?"

Shard smiled a little despite himself. "I suppose not."

"Oh, you can do better than that," Celaeno hugged him close with one last squeeze before he slipped out of her grasp and danced back a pace. "Look at me," she stated, holding out her hand. Shard took it and bowed in exaggerated formality, to help her rise. "Have you ever heard anyone say: 'She can't be the Empress of Nations. Why, she's barely five-foot-four'?"

Shard's smile grew, just slightly. Celaeno swatted at him with her kimono's sleeve and he allowed his grin to widen. "Ah, I'm getting old, Shard," she lamented. "Yósha's soulbound. Sintaka has a little daughter of her own now. I'm a grandmother already. A grandmother! Stay close to me, Shard; you're all I have left now."

"Don't worry, Mother," he assured her, smiling truly now. "You'll always have me. I'm not going anywhere."

His face was honest and open. But as Celaeno stared into his stormy eyes and sensed the restlessness within them, she wasn't as sure of it as he was. There was something in her youngest son, something beyond his mysterious origins and the wings emblazoned on his back. There was something in his eyes, in the magic surrounding him like a cloak.

Unable able to resist, she drew him near once again and hugged him fiercely. "Come on, little one," she told him. "Let's go see if we can't find your brother somewhere."

He offered her his arm with a chivalrous grin and they left the throne room, striding down the marble floors of the cavernous hallways. Silent as a shadow, the ever-present *ani,* Shiori fell into line behind the Dynast as they glided over the dragon and phoenix inlay on the polished floors. Courtiers bowed and nodded with respect as they acknowledged their ruler. Shard left his mother's side to scale the eight-foot-tall marble lion statue, only fall back into stride a moment later.

They emerged into bright summer sunshine to stand overlooking one of the large courtyards in the inner court of the palace. Some held fishponds and floating gardens meticulously tended by Mindrin and his army of gardeners. This one was bare, a flat floor of brick surrounded on four sides by elegant porticoes and red-tiled rooftops, their eaves sweeping up and inward. Several other balconies on lower levels faced the courtyard, and tables sat in wait of guests.

Two silver-haired peri stood in the courtyard: one a slender youth armed with a longsword, the other a tall muscular woman, her wild hair held back with a headband. Shard could just catch sight of Mindrin holding his little daughter up to watch the training.

"Not a half-turn to the wedding and still in training," Celaeno smiled proudly.

Shard watched his brother carefully, leaning on the balcony railing for a better view. The sword moves played out like an intricate dance speeded up beyond reason: Sintaka's thrusts, Stargazer's evasive parries, his attacks, her withdrawal. His blade angle was perfect, his thrusts and parries exactly timed. What precision it took – Shard would be lost within moments. Their mother was right, by his twenty-first birthday Stargazer would be an Arashi knight, with all the battle skills and mental discipline of the ten-thousand-year-old school. As was his birthright, Shard acknowledged bittersweetly, pride mingling with jealousy. The Red Knights of Kitsune had founded the school, and though the discipline had spread throughout the known world during the Golden Age, it was the Amaru and the Kitsune who best exemplified the art of Arashi fighting.

"Do you wish you could be down there with him?" Celaeno asked softly.

Shard looked back, shaking his head. "I don't have the willpower to be an Arashi knight, you know that."

"Do you wish you did?"

Shard shrugged, but the disappointment showed in his face. "It would be incredible, to be able to move like that, to fight like that. But the meditation, the exercises, the drilling – I just don't have the head for it. Not in my blood, I guess."

Celaeno laid a comforting hand on his shoulder. "True, you've never been able to align a crystal for long, and you have little head for the drilling. My little scatterbrain," she ruffled his hair. "One moment's notice and you're climbing the walls with your head in the clouds."

She looked back at her children sparring. "To be an Arashi is all about faith. One can have the greatest technical skill and be defeated by one's own doubts. Sintaka has grappled with that more than once. Her training was slow, difficult – more than once she demolished a training ring and stalked off leaving everyone but Mindrin afraid of casting a shadow about her. But Stargazer... he has the faith, the conviction of become one of the greatest Arashi warriors Amaru has seen in ages." She smiled admiringly. "You know your brother. 'We are peri and we are invincible. We can dream nothing that we cannot accomplish.' Such faith in his own dreams will serve him well. Watch, Shard."

Stargazer's blade met Sintaka's over and over, the clashes of metal singing. "If you believe you can only walk, if you are content to stay on the ground, then you will and know nothing else. But if you convince yourself it's possible..."

Sintaka swung her sword at Stargazer's torso, and the youth folded his arms over his chest, vaulting into the air. Shard watched, spellbound, as Stargazer somersaulted high in the air, rising effortlessly against gravity. He flipped backwards, executing one somersault, two, three, all in flawless slow motion, before landing on the curving eaves of the roof with all the grace of a bird.

"You can fly," Celaeno finished in a soft voice, before stepping to the edge of the balcony and applauding her son's feats. Stargazer looked up, puzzled at first, then broke out into a broad grin, saluting his mother before slumping against the roof, exhausted from the morning exercise.

Kemuri stood as the guards ushered the kobold into the large study. The room was lined with bookshelves along one wall and decorated with intricate maps and starcharts on another. A little dwarf-tree sat in its pot in front of his desk, and several meditation crystals sat on pedestals around the study.

The kobold bowed low at the waist. "Lord Kemuri," he beamed as he straightened.

"It's been too long, Bys," Kemuri smiled his warm ghost of a smile, his glowing eyes revealing the extent of his joy at seeing his childhood friend once again. Then his smile faltered. "You said you have urgent news. I take it it's not good."

"Not... not exactly, no," he shook his head. He glanced at the guards questioningly, and they in turn glanced at the Royal Consort for orders. He nodded and they withdrew; Kemuri motioned for Bys to sit in the large armchair in front of the desk.

The kobolds were the miners and farmers of the lands, the peasants who populated the forests and hills between cities. They stood on average a foot shorter than their cousins the peri, and were of a sturdier build. They were by no means rough and plain workers, but possessed all the beauty and charm of the peri, albeit beauty of a simpler, more earthy sort. Their eyes were a fraction larger than those of the peri's, for theirs was the way of darkened caves and tunnels, and they possessed a speed and grace belied by their short compact stature. In the cities they lived in basement dens, connected by subterranean avenues; in the country they made their homes in large hives and molehills dug into the rolling hillside and under the forest floor. They were carefree creatures, and they gladly left complexities of government to their trusted peri leaders, preferring to spend their days in pursuit of a simpler fulfillment.

Bys was a rarity: a kobold of the courts, the mining overseer of all of Hesperin. His responsibilities were numerous, as he governed all the extensive mining that went on in the countless caves and pit-mines of Kemuri's native country. But he had always tackled his daunting tasks with the inborn joviality and enthusiasm all his folk possessed. Only now he seemed unnaturally somber, his brown eyes clouded with worry.

He sat down opposite Kemuri. "The men have been having some... problems in the northern mines," he confessed. "In the Boundary Hills region, which, as you know, was your bride-price to Dynast Celaeno."

"Why not take this up with Celaeno?" Kemuri asked.

"Technically, they are her property, but their practical governorship falls to you. And, to be honest," he blushed, "I feel more comfortable talking to you. You're a Hesperin – you're one of us. We've known each other for years. Your soulmate... she's a little too rich for me."

Kemuri nodded uncertainly. "I'm not good at this," he murmured. "Celeano usually handles these things." He took a deep breath. "What is it, Bys?"

Bys reached into the utilitarian leather sack he had set on the ground. Though he wore the silks and linens of the court when at the palace in Hesperin, Bys preferred the homespun cloth and leather clothing of all kobolds. He withdrew a painstakingly folded map which he carefully opened and set out on the table. It showed the outline of the Hesperin coast above the Illay Peninsula, with markings for the many mines lining the contours of the Boundary Hills at the far north of the kingdom. Hesperin was the smallest of the five Pentagram lands, but its rocky terrain held a wealth in metals and precious stones. By all rights the land that had once been part of Amaru should have fallen in the countless wars of the Dark Ages. Yet the kingdom's rich treasury had held firm against a thousand years of warfare until Kemuri's marriage, when Hesperin had allied with its once-master and ended the Schism.

"Here." Bys pointed to a cluster of circles at the far edge of the map. "In the last few years, we've found poaching inside these tunnels. Now, we thought it was nothing more than snatching an emerald or two. At the same time several teams of scouts disappeared. We decided the supervisor sent novice kobolds to scout tunnels – we charged her with neglect and thought that would be it. Scouts die mapping unexplored rock – it happens. But then, about six – seven months ago, their bodies turned up; I think you know what happened to them, poor bastards. They didn't deserve that kind of death. At the same time, some of the perimeter scouts caught sight of activity out on the Denáren Wastes. Mining out on the flats. Within Hesperin borders, in your Dynast's own mines. Little camps, heavily armed, guarded by troglodytes and kobolds. The camp formations, the poaching style, even the way the scouts were murdered – it all stinks of the same thing: ferals. If I didn't know better, I'd swear they were remnants of Larien's old slave packs."

"But Larien's been dead for four hundred years. All his slaves were freed long ago."

"And a lot of those slaves went mercenary," Bys pointed out. "Some of my men think they might have turned rebel. Not everyone was happy when the Schism was repaired. A lot of those slaves weren't exactly thrilled to come home only to find out we've allied with the land we'd spent one thousand years vilifying."

"It's been four centuries, Bys," Kemuri reasoned. "I can't imagine it's rebels resisting the alliance; not after all these years."

"No," Bys sighed. "You're right. Before the Great Alliance, maybe, but now – you and your Dynast got us into the Pentagram! Hesperin says "frog" and the world jumps! Only a fool would oppose that. No, thinking it disgruntled nationalists – it's a sloppy answer. Damned sloppy – I don't like that lazy kind of thinking, but I have to say, sometimes it's tempting. I don't know, Kemuri. It gets my hackles up, knowing my folk are in those caves, running the risk of ambush from those... beasts."

"What are they after? Are they poaching the emeralds?"

"I wish it were that simple. They are taking them, certainly. For the official record that's all they're taking. I think we've pushed them back from our best tunnels. Their main camp is so far east, just on the border: most of my men don't even think it's worth the risk to launch a large-scale assault. You know our eastern border only exists on paper – once you're in the Denáren Wastes, all bets are off. But we've found chambers they've opened up – chambers in low-grade, ordinary rock. There are no emeralds there, no crystal veins. Not even decent stone."

"What are they after then?" Kemuri asked. Bys was silent and a moment later Kemuri understood, his eyes widening. "No... no they couldn't possibly be looking for that."

Bys nodded slowly. "I think so."

Kemuri shook his head. "Hesperin wasted centuries looking for it. No one has ever found any sign of it. I don't think anyone really believes in it anymore."

"I do. And so do they, I think. And I also think they're getting close. Their digging's getting more and more localized each time reconnaissance catches sight of them. This last camp they set up is tight, concentrated, hiding Myrddin knows how many warriors and miners. They're driven."

"Wyvern's Rest. The Treasury.... If they do find it..."

"If it exists, and they uncover it, all hell's going to break loose on your wife's New Age."

3

Varron Lehs drew his cloak more tightly about him as he waited with growing impatience. To his left was a large window, and through its tinted glass he could see the land of Níst sweep out below the citadel. It was a dark land; it always had been, even before the *yúgure* and the Winter of a Thousand Years had ravaged the world. Humid forests and murky swamps hugged the base of the jagged black peaks. The Fang Ridge ran across the land like a scar, rising nowhere as menacingly as the peak upon which the citadel was built. A light shudder ran through him; he felt his symbiote's tentacles tightening within his skull in apprehension. This was a land forged of blood and warlords, spies and conspiracies. He appreciated the kinship of these people, but he had no wish to linger any longer than he had to.

A silent man glided out of the shadows. A chimera, a sorcerer's creation - once peri, no longer. A heavy ridge ran over his eyes, dipping down to the bridge of his cat-like nose. His cheekbones were pronounced, the grayish skin pulled taut over them as they swept down to meet his jawline. His eyes were a fearsome red, glowing in the shadows. He beckoned with a long black talon, and Varron followed.

The ghoulish creature led him through vaulted corridors and down deep stairways, past doorways guarded by black-robed spectres, their cowls framing a faceless black void. Varron avoided looking at them. He had heard stories of those who looked too long at the spectres, and though he discounted them as fiction, he was in no hurry to be proven wrong.

At last they reached a gaping maw in the wall, the stairs disappearing into a darkness untempered by lanterns or candles. The majordomo motioned for Varron to proceed alone. The man hesitated a moment, then grudgingly brushed past, turning a corner almost immediately as the spiral swept him deeper into the castle.

He proceeded down the stairs, his eyes scanning the shadows for ambushes. His last visit to Níst had been decidedly unpleasant. Winding down the stone steps, he kept his cloak drawn about him. The golden glow of the private chamber beckoned him forward.

An ugly little form leapt out at him and he recoiled despite himself. The gremlin bounded on the floor, his scraggly head just reaching Varron's knees. Laughter burbled up to greet him. Varron scowled at the little vulture-like creature, potbellied and gangly-limbed. The gremlin cackled. Varron kicked at it and it went scurrying for safety.

He turned the corner, stepping at last into the large chamber. Rich colours and fragrant perfumes assaulted his senses. The room was dimly lit by low-resting lamps burning a faint incense, periodic sparks cast by the little fires. A thin wisp of smoke hung in the air. Before him an immense dais spread the length of the farthest wall, draped in silks that would make the richest despot blush. Gold chains dripped from the lamps, and jewels sparkled from the corners. An Alteri woman reclined on a set of cushions, her scanty body armour revealing the intricate tattoos wrapped about her limbs. Nearby, a nobleman arrayed in rich robes sat cross-legged, his hand protectively clasping his water-pipe. Kobolds huddled around the elaborate pillars, their little faces glowing in the light as they him pass. A chimera woman lounged across the silks, her features those of a leopard, her cat's eyes watching him intently. Peri maidens in wispy gowns clustered against the walls.

A large divan sat in the center of the dais, next to which rested an immense bejewlled hookah. Seated on the cushions at the foot of the couch was a handsome peri dressed in costly garments, an ornate collar about his neck, a thin golden chain leading from it up to the couch. And draped across the divan throne lay the Empress of Níst.

She wore a long indigo gown that swept to the floor of the dais; the skirt was slit high on one side to reveal a shapely white leg. Iridescent black hair fell in thick waves around her. A long black serpent wound about her wrist, disappearing into the folds of her gown. Gold jewelry dripped from her body; finely wrought chains encircled her waist and throat; her fingers were sheathed in long golden claws. She proudly wore the Scorpion Seal of Níst on her forehead.

She hardly acknowledged Varron's presence as he slowly stepped forward, preferring to gaze off into space. When he stopped short paces from the couch, she slowly turned towards him with a bored expression. Varron stared back, and she raised one eyebrow slightly. Slowly, deliberately, he sank to one knee, keeping his eyes defiantly locked with hers. Then, swallowing his distaste, he bowed his head low.

"Varron," she spoke at last, a charming laugh issuing from her throat. "It's been too long a time. Last I heard you were a half-mile underground."

Varron smiled back tightly. "I have kept myself busy."

"Still have that... *worm* wriggling about in your head?" Seiren asked. She drew on her water-pipe, then blew the smoke directly at him. "Why are you here, then?"

His face darkened, but he was undaunted. "My spies are as reliable as yours, Seiren. I hear Celaeno's little son is to be married. I hear you have even sent your daughter Athyr to lead the Níst delegation to Amaru for the wedding."

Seiren shrugged, stretching cat-like. "I wish to offer the young couple my best wishes. I want Celaeno to appreciate the friend she has in Níst."

"Níst never used to concern itself with 'friends.'"

Seiren rolled her eyes. "The same old refrain, Varron." She glanced over at the silent man at her side. "It really does grow tiresome, doesn't it, pet?" she asked, drawing on the chain attached to his collar. She bent her head down and kissed him long on the lips, an embrace he did not hesitate to return. She slipped her arms about his neck, and the snake slithered out of her sleeve, gliding down the man's back to disappear into the cushions. Varron struggled to keep his face emotionless, but a little sniff of scorn escaped him and a little muscle by his lips twitched once.

The little gremlin, perched in the lap of a buxom peri maiden, cackled with delight.

Reluctantly Seiren pulled away from her slave and lay back on the couch, taking another long draw from her hookah. "The Dark Age is over, Varron," she continued, winding the gold leash about her wrist, tugging the obliging slave nearer once more. "Chalandris is a shamble of ruins. Your followers are dead; your master has not been seen for four hundred years."

"Your brother understood our ways."

"My brother is dead," she informed him coldly. "I rule Níst now."

"And you make treaties with the Amaru. You breed *diplomats!* Hairath's daughter has fallen from her proud heritage. Don't you ever long for something grander than these petty schemes of negotiations and alliances? Don't you look back on the old days and long for true power?"

"You're a fool," Seiren snapped. "Your 'true power' as you call it, was nothing more than the brutal dreams of small minds, fools afraid of their own shadows. Favoring short-term solutions and power-mad reveries over rational strategy."

"Like your brother? Was he such a fool as I, Seiren?"

"He stood in the way of progress, Varron," she explained. She glanced back at her "pet." "And I don't much care for those who stand in my way, do I, now?"

"Then perhaps I have made a mistake by coming here."

"Perhaps you have," the man at Seiren's side spoke for the first time.

"Now, now, Jinn," she reprimanded lightly. "Varron Lehs would never make a fool's errand, would he?" She fixed Varrion with a glare. "You didn't come all this way just to reminisce."

The entire entourage, peri, kobold and demon alike, leaned forward in anticipation.

"What would you say if I told you I knew a way to regain my power? What would you if I told you that I intend to recover all I lost during the past four centuries? Would Níst take me so lightly then?"

The Empress frowned. "Your armies are gone. Your kobold slaves rebelled and ran free. You have nothing but a handful of assassins and bounty hunters.

What could possibly return all you've lost?" She lay back, slowly turning her long pipe in her hand. "You've said nothing to convince me that we have anything more to say to each other."

"I only wish to serve Níst, Your Glory," Varron spread his arms wide. "You are quite right," he brooded darkly as he began to pace. "My master is gone, and I have lost much. But I don't intend to stay beaten down much longer. Soon I will be in a position of great power. The kobold slaves that my men managed to hold for me are hard at work in my mines, and soon they will have uncovered for me a treasure from the Golden Age itself, a treasure which will purchase me the heart and soul of every warlord and bounty seeker in all the known Aetherworld."

"What?" Jinn scoffed.

"The Treasury of Ravanor."

Seiren's eyes widened. "Ravanor?" She sat up, then shook her head. "You'll never find Wyvern's Rest. Peri and kobolds have searched for it for over two thousand years. I'm not even convinced it was ever anything but a myth-"

"Oh, it's no myth," Varron interrupted her. "All the riches of Ravanor's decadent satrapy, the wealth of five hundred years of plunder and destruction, still lie undiscovered. They say he sealed six of his consorts in the tomb with his wealth, burying them alive, so their spirits could guard his riches. They say the jewels of his Great Consort Kishca alone are enough to sink three ships with their weight."

"No one has ever found it."

"I have already found it."

Seiren sprang from the couch, and in an instant was floating an inch above the floor of the dais. The sudden movement yanked Jinn up on his knees. Openly disgusted by both Varron and her own impulsive reaction, Seiren shook the chain from her wrist. "You have found... the Treasury of Ravanor?" she hissed incredulously, rage in her eyes. The sycophants clustered about her slowly eased back, recognizing that look all too well.

"Oh, not the main chamber. No... but my men have uncovered the first of the antechambers." He drew something from his robe and the Alteri was on her feet, her hand darting for her dagger. Varron held out his hand, opening it to reveal an exquisite gold brooch, in the shape of a roaring tiger's face, the reddish hue of the metal and the expert hand of the craftsman identifying it as from the Ravanoran Dynasty.

"Intriguing," Seiren smiled, her eyes gleaming with greed. Then she tossed back her head and laughed. "You've still failed to convince me," she explained, her mirth only heightened by the rage she saw in his eyes. "Men have been uncovering 'antechambers' for years. True, your pretty little pin there seems to be from the right period at least, but it's a long way from the Treasury itself."

"This is only the beginning! As we speak, my kobolds are digging further into the rock, unearthing more and more treasure. Consider my offer carefully, Mistress. Even a small fraction of the rumoured wealth of Ravanor would be more than enough to tempt all the warlords in the land to my side. The Garthan Raiders themselves would be my personal bodyguards for the wealth I would promise them. Consider this, then, a gift," he reverently placed the brooch on the edge of dais as the Alteri watched him closely. "A promise, of what I could offer Níst, if it chooses to accept my aid."

"And if it sends men to die in your mines? And feeds your fat friends and supplies them with playthings when one appetite is sated and another demands sustenance?"

"A small price to pay for such an offer. Are you content with your little 'sister Celaeno' being the Silver Queen, the Empress of Nations? Wouldn't you like to see the world order tip in your favor? Wouldn't you like to stand in the central vault of the Treasury and see the fortune despots and tyrants died for?"

"You're a fool, Varron." With a flourish of her claws, she floated back onto the couch. "A tired, broken little man. You'll never find it. And whatever trinkets your slaves unearth will never be enough to buy back the respect you lost when your slaves sealed you in your own mine." She blew a lazy smoke ring towards the ceiling, then set the pipe down, turning back to Jinn. "Still, he intrigues me, pet. What do you say? Oh, I forgot," she laughed lightly. "You were enslaved under him, weren't you, dearest? Why... I bought you from Varron himself. What did he say? 'That meat's not worth it'... why yes, that was it exactly!" She glared at Varron. "You were so weak you could barely walk for nearly a half-turn!"

Jinn too stared at the warlord, his copper eyes fierce with remembered pain. Varron felt the first flickers of panic, and his throat tightened against his will.

Seiren slid to the floor of the dais next to Jinn, and he handed her the end of his golden chain, their fingers interlacing. "Shall I kill him for you?" Seiren purred, one golden claw tracing a line down his cheek. She cast one satisfied look at the now decidedly nervous Varron, before turning back. "Would you like that, my pet?" she asked, nuzzling his neck.

"No," Jinn kept his eyes pinned on the warlord. "I think I like him like this."

He knew Varron had failed in his mission long before the man had cast himself to reveal the news. The peri sat back in his old throne, settling in the musty old fabric, aged and frayed with the passing of time. He ran his hand over the worn black metal armrests, scratched and tarnished. He had been asleep too long.

It had been four hundred and fifty years since the kobolds had taken his satrapy from him. Four hundred and fifty years since he had been forced into exile, forced into sleep.

Far too long.

He held his right hand into the faint light, gazing at the blood-ruby ring on his gnarled finger. Lightly his finger traced a circle around the perimeter of the gold-rimmed gem. He would have his lands returned to him. He would see his satrapy thrive as it had in the glorious days of the Dark Age. More, he would see it grow, until it spread across the land and enveloped the known Aetherworld. He would have all the wealth of the world in his hands. And at last he would have the pleasures and the peace he had butchered so many in the hopes of finding.

Everything was proceeding according to plan. That halfwit cow Seiren's refusal hardly even mattered in the long run. He should have foreseen her rejection; she was weak, too easily wooed by her slave-mate and her addle-brained courtiers. But no matter. It only meant less power to share between pawns until his vision was achieved.

Even the pawns would not matter in the end. He had his own plans for them.

He was cold; the draft in the ruins ate at his flesh and chilled his bones. His joints ached, his breath came in short gasps and he huddled inside his black cloak to keep warm. But it was only to be expected. He was four thousand years old, after all.

He was not yet at full strength. The sleep had done that to him. He had not managed a safe hibernation. Dreams had haunted him, wearied him. But he would soon grow strong again. He laid his hand protectively over the red jewel, which began to pulse lightly, a rhythmic palpitation within the opaque gem.

"Soon..." he murmured in a raspy voice. He raised his hand to his lips, laying a soft kiss on the gleaming ruby.

4

Shard slipped through the open window, gracefully alighting on the floor of the library mezzanine. He straightened his jacket and proceeded towards the staircase. The Great Library was immense, encompassing six floors in all, each one containing several additional mezzanines and balconies within it. Innumerable books sat snug on the tall shelves surrounding the young heir; tall step-ladders attached to the side of each of the bookcases.

He slid down the banister, stumbling to the floor at the bottom of the stairs. "Hello, Shard," came a vaguely annoyed voice from behind a large tome propped up on a nearby table.

"'Morning, Galen."

Galen Minyami stood up, adjusting his glasses, which had slid down his nose, and gave Shard his usual shy smile. Shard marveled at the scribe, as innocuous as ever, his tall frame covered in simple trousers and a button-shirt. He seemed to go to great lengths to appear little more than a humble librarian. A passerby would never know he was the Royal Scribe of Amaru and nephew of the Empress Seiren herself. Yet his graceful cat-like figure and his delicate oval face betrayed his aristocratic blood, and his long inky-black hair spoke of his ties to the Níst Imperium. Shard sighed inwardly with more than mild envy; as if it weren't enough, Galen stood a full seven inches over the Heir's head. Little wonder Shard couldn't help but feel like a clumsy kit around him.

"Good walk today?" Galen asked, closing his large book.

"Pretty good," Shard nodded. "I went over the west wing this morning: you know, along the blue tile roofs over the Tora apartments. Where's Jax?" he asked, turning his eyes to the stacks.

"Oh, she's up there somewhere," Galen took off his glasses, setting them by his book. "I think she was looking into something on the Rhopisad satrap–"

"Ha-*hah!*" came a cry from above. A young peri woman appeared a moment later, her arms filled with heavy hardbound volumes, her long ocean blue hair tumbling down about her knees. Behind her Stargazer followed, meek as a lamb, carrying another large stack of books.

Jaxa stumbled down the stairs, trying to see her feet – impossible with the stack in her arms. "Galen!" she called out. "Wait 'til you see what I–" she misstepped, and stumbled, the top book in her arms sailing off the pile.

It stopped in midair a moment before hitting the ground. Jaxa released her breath. "Thanks," she sighed in relief.

Galen floated the book up to his hand. "You read this book already," he remarked.

"So?Oh, thank you, Shard," she smiled as he raced to her side to take the heaviest books as she walked down the last few steps. The young lord made no secret of the deep infatuation he had held for her as a child. Stargazer shot him a wry glare as he struggled down the steps alone.

"You're one to talk," Jaxa continued, "You read through the same chronicles over and over and over and over..." she dumped the books on the side of the table and wrapped her arms about her soulmate, giving him a tight squeeze before tipping her head up to receive a soft kiss.

"*The Worship of the Great Herasis in Rhopisad, in the time of Ducalo the Great,*" Shard read the title of one of the books. "Broadening your horizons, I see;" he chuckled.

"I have a duty to study. It's a thankless chore, but such is my destiny. As the High Priestess of Herasis, I need to keep and guard the traditions of the past."

"Funny, I thought you made it up as you went along," Shard chuckled, wincing a moment later, a tingle burning at the edge of his mind from Jaxa's painsend.

"Atheist," she sneered, her amethyst eyes burning indignantly. She tossed her long mane of hair, then glanced back and shared a smile with the heir. Their teasing and sparring never lasted long.

"What are you reading?" Shard peered over the edge of the table at the book Galen had just closed. "The Treasury of Ravanor? Why?"

"Father recruited us," Stargazer explained as he set his own books down next to Galen. "He met with the mining overseer from Hesperin a few days ago. Rogue kobolds are raiding the mines in the Boundary Hills, and the Hesperin think they might be looking for the Treasury."

"But the Treasury is a myth," Shard laughed. "If Ravanor did seal all his fortune in his tomb somewhere in the Boundary Hills, it certainly wasn't the wealth the stories talk about. Hesperin kobolds have been searching for Wyvern's Rest ever since the stories started, but no one seriously thinks it's there anymore."

"These kobolds think it's there," Stargazer ruled. "And they're willing to kill to find it. And if the Treasury is there..."

Shard whistled appreciatively.

Jaxa smiled, greed sparkling in her eyes. "I *have* thought about updating my jewelry. I have to present an image, after all. Galen," she batted her eyes with obvious exaggeration. "If *you* found the Treasury would you give me

Kishca's jewels?"

"Of course I would," Galen assured her, blushing slightly. He brushed a strand of her deep blue hair out of her face and tenderly tucked it behind her golden headband. "Even if they wouldn't do you justice..."

It was Jaxa's turn to blush fiercely and hide her face in the shoulder of his white shirt.

Shard leaned across the table, averting his eyes respectfully from the couple - he knew how shy Jaxa was behind her flamboyant façade. He ran his finger over the edge of the old book, stirring a little cloud of dust from the seam. "The Treasury of Ravanor," he murmured. "In *our* emerald mines. Now that would be something."

Stargazer chuckled, but he seemed too weary to manage much cheer. He yawned softly, raising a hand to his mouth before shaking his head and rubbing his eyes.

"You should go, I can handle the research for a while," Galen offered. "You're getting married in six days; you shouldn't have to worry about this now."

"I'd rather hide out here. *Augh*," he wiped the sleep from his face. "All the delegates arrive tomorrow. I'm either being fitted one last time for my robes or meeting with some Matriarch or other, or making sure all the bride-price is gathered," he heaved a sigh. "I hope I'll still be awake when it comes time for the banquet. I haven't gotten close to my own soulmate for *days* now. She's making sure the dress is perfect – won't let me see it until the banquet. Her parents are trying to get everything ready, and Powers know her brother isn't helping! I'm just about ready to tear my hair out."

"There's a thought," Jaxa flirted, sashaying over to him. "Make a good little rug with a mane like that." She leaned across the floor, fixing a predatory eye on the young Lord. "I should scalp you."

"I'll scalp you," Galen seized a large handful of blue hair and spun her around to face him. Laughing at his protectiveness, Jaxa wrapped her arms about him anew.

"Oh, don't worry," she instructed Stargazer. "It'll all be over in a few days, and even the worst indignities will seem funny as hell when you look back on it."

Shard listened with half an ear as Jaxa and Galen shared particular headaches from their own wedding. He had already decided that should he find a soulmate he would never have a wedding – useless ceremony, and what did it accomplish? He hated ceremony. Star and Aerin were already joined as soulmates and consorts – had been since their soulbinding. Marriage with soulbinding was a mere formality, a simple party to please the nobles; marriage without was nothing more than a political contract, devoid of meaning. Galen's own mother had been sold into such a worthless pact with the Lord Heir of Níst, and had hardly seen her so-called "husband" since Galen was born. She had her soulmate, he had his, and their marriage was now nothing more than a faded parchment.

"Why, when Galen and I were wrestling out the details," Jaxa laughed, "pulled three ways between my family, the Minyami *and* the Níst, each family with its own ideas of a proper bride-price and a proper wedding – I swear, we nearly eloped so many times!"

Shard flipped open the large book Galen had been reading to a random page. The scribe had underlined a passage. Shard frowned as he slowly deciphered the old script, running his finger along the text.

"*Shi'mia tal elsatór tsina úndao rhesváni ges Ravanor es'rìn firreral til'lal uldî kìnja Ki'mméria eos tal es yúgure,*" he read aloud in a soft voice. "'And one shall find... in the ill-gotten riches of the tyrant Ravanor, power and death as of Cimmerian's destruction, the *yúgure*.'" He frowned at the words. "*Yúgure...*"

The little girl raced down the pathway, squealing with delight, a redhaired peri in hot pursuit. "Run, Spark," her mother's voice followed her from a distance.

She raced towards the little tree, hoping to climb it to safety, but a moment before she reached it, her father caught her up in his arms and they both toppled over into a deep pile of pink blossoms at the base of the tree.

The girl laughed out loud, struggling in the sea of flower petals. Mindrin sank through the blossoms, soon swallowed up to the shoulders. Running to catch up with them, Sintaka gave both soulmate and daughter a disapproving shake of the head before summarily collapsing down next to them.

"Get it out of you while you can, Spark," Sintaka sighed. "Come tomorrow we'll both be in court dresses hating every minute of it."

Emrith tal Amaru sat up on her father's lap. "Why?" she frowned.

Mindrin ruffled her dark red hair, then picked out one of the bright silver streaks that ran through her mane. "Because, royalty doesn't know how to enjoy itself."

Emrith pouted sadly, then brightened. "But Nari'll be there, right?"

Sintaka smiled reassuringly. "Right alongside your great-grandparents."

"Nari – wouldn't have thought you'd be older than your great-uncle, would you?" Mindrin asked his daughter. "C'mere." He lay back in the blossoms, pulling the squealing six-year-old down with him. Sintaka laughed and proceeded to shove handfuls of the pink blossoms top on of them.

Father and daughter came up for air a moment later. "Mouse!" Emrith cried, holding out her hands as the catling leapt into her arms. The little pet squeaked in excitement as she scrambled up Emrith's shoulders, then tumbled back into her lap and began to scratch her long rabbit-like ears before springing off to chase the floating gobletplum blossoms. Mindrin released Spark to let her run off in pursuit of her pet.

Mindrin barely glanced up; deep within the palace court, a child had little to fear. "And you get it out of you while you can," Sintaka informed him, plucking a petal out of his hair. She traced her fingertip along the tattoo gracing his forehead: three golden diamonds, arranged like the petals of a flower. "I don't want you fidgeting at the banquet."

"And I don't want you complaining about your robes and intentionally tripping over your hems," Mindrin warmed sternly, before wrapping his arms about her and dragging her under the blossoms with him.

"It's not my fault they always cut them too long," Sintaka protested laughingly. "And they always make those halls too stuffy." She idly twirled a strand of Mindrin's hair about her finger. "I should have been born an Alteri. Wild forests... practical clothes..."

"Oh, but then you wouldn't have had such a *charming* palace gardener for an *ani,*" Mindrin teased, drawing nearer for a kiss.

"Mommy," came the little voice. Sintaka reluctantly poked her head above the petals. She saw what had caught Spark's attention. Above them, beyond the garden of gobletplum trees, loomed the old clocktower, one of the oldest structures on the City Mount. The immense clock at the top of the imposing stone tower was forever locked at a minute before three. And seated on the hour-hand, one leg dangling over the five storey drop to the garden below, was Shard.

"Why is he on the clock?"

"He says he likes the view," Sintaka explained.

"Why don't the hands move?"

"Because Uncle Shard pulled all the gears out so he could make his sculptures."

"Why?"

"You don't want to sit on a chair that moves, do you?" Mindrin teased, catching her about the waist and pulling the squirming, laughing kitling back to him.

Shard watched the family below with an envious smile as he sat on the clock, his back to the immense minute-hand. They were happy; they knew where they belonged. He supposed he had no reason to be jealous of them – it had taken them a hundred and fifty years to reach the state of simple bliss they had now. A lover, a soulmate, a quiet place to rest after a long day; there was more than enough time to find such things. He simply didn't think he had the patience for it. Even waiting a few years seemed impossible. Something within goaded him, compelled him onward. He felt his very being would fly away some days, so great was his restlessness, his painful anticipation.

The sun was behind him to the west but still high in the sky. He knew he had better get an early sleep, if he wanted to be rested for the next day. A long series of receptions awaited him. He hated these functions. He knew everyone was watching him, the little misfit of the house of Amaru. He wasn't like Stargazer and Sintaka and their parents. He didn't have the royal blood, the inborn patience of it all. He was the oddity who lived in old ruins and walked along rooftops.

He couldn't bear the impending misery that awaited him: a half-turn, maybe more, of pressed clothes and impeccable manners. Already he felt suffocated.

From his vantage point atop the clock he could see the north quarter of the city and the farmlands beyond it. The Vastwood carpeted the hills and vales of Amaru.

He felt so tired, so frustrated. He didn't want to get up at dawn and let Landar dress him in a fine silk kimono. He didn't want to force a smile on his face and offer a polite greeting to diplomats from Diure or Marishen.

He wanted to go.

The next morning Stargazer sought his brother out. The route to Shard's room was long and complicated, carefully planned to keep out unwanted guests. A walk along the roofs or a flight to the balcony by dragon was the fastest way. Stargazer marveled how Landar managed to surreptitiously clean Shard's room every day.

But then Landar had his methods.

Midway down an old hallway, the stone walls worn with age, cobwebs clinging to the corners, hung a large tapestry, depicting the military triumphs of Celaeno's mother, Aladar tal Amaru. Lifting the edge of the tapestry, Stargazer pushed lightly on the false wall, which easily slid aside, allowing him access. Letting the tapestry drop behind him and sliding the door back into place, Stargazer proceeded into an abandoned chamber. Dust motes danced in the air, illuminated by slim shafts of white light that peeped through the cracks in the rock. A decrepit spiral staircase led him up into the tower. Everything looked on the verge of crumbling decay, but Stargazer knew that was only an illusion Shard cultivated.

From the top of the old spiral staircase, Stargazer stood facing a large statue of a sphinx, flanked by two suits of ancient armour, like forgotten museum pieces left to rust in the tower. Easing his way around the statue, Stargazer found the steps hidden in a recess in the wall, and walked down into Shard's apartments.

He dropped to the floor from a little step and looked around for Shard. It was still a little before sunrise – Shard might still be in bed. Perhaps he was a little early, but he was too excited to sit still and wait for his brother. Besides, Shard might never come downstairs if not for a little brotherly persuasion.

He walked down the deserted hallway, entering Shard's bedroom. Odd, the bed was made, as if Landar had already been in, yet it was rare for Shard to rise so early. In fact the entire room was in eerie order. A feeling of foreboding rose in Stargazer as he stepped down from the doorway.

He caught sight of a piece of paper lying on the pillow, and his heart sank. Walking over to the bed he picked it up, lighting the bedside lamp.

Yósha, I'm sorry. I can't stay here now. I just can't. I'll be back in a half-turn. Don't be upset. I'd only be an embarrassment, sulking in my chair anyway. You and Aerin have the best time you can. I'll see you both soon.

Stargazer shook his head, letting the letter fall to the bed.

Mother, he called. *Shard's run away again.*

The reply was swift, all too immediate. *I know, Stargazer. Don't be so disappointed. We both knew this would happen.*

5

L'al Darhis sneered, wrinkling her nose at the pungent sulphur fumes that rose from the flats below her. The smell was the one thing she could not abide. Before her the Denáren Wastes spread out in all directions, a monotony of acidic fumaroles and seething hotsprings, the red ground caked and cracked, dotted with mounds and cones of burnt out geysers. From Chalandris Keep, high on the Devil's Rim mountains, she could see the vast wasteland of plateaus and plains, of eroding cliffs and sunken craters. A dried-up river bed coursed through the flats, creating deep fissures and valleys in the parched ground. The wind whispered over the rocks like a mournful song. An eternal cloud hung over the Denáren Wastes, glowing a faint orange from absorbed starlight and the reflected glow of volcanoes. Occasionally a soft ash, like gray snow, would fall.

To the south, a hundred miles distant, lay the northern edge of the massive caldera. Denár Elória. Once it had been the cornerstone of a far-reaching kingdom, the capital city of the entire Aetherworld. Until the war. Until the *yúgure*. The darkness within that cursed stone had reduced all of Elória's city to a smoking crater and had tainted the world, bringing about the Winter of a Thousand Years.

The rest of the world had recovered from the *yúgure's* powerful curse. But not the wastelands. They remained an eternal testament to the power of the crystal and the devil who had unleashed its darkness.

Darhis confessed she missed the forests of her youth, confronted with the barren sulphur flats of Elória. She was an Alteri, one of the many matriarchal warriors who inhabited the valleys and peaks of the Great Chain mountains. During the War the Alteri had been a formidable fighting force, and during the Lost Years they had been fearsome warlords, the mythic amazon women of legend. Now the majority lived in relative peace in their deep forests, while a small few sought employment and adventure elsewhere.

Even fewer, like Darhis, were outcasts, selling their services for a price, trading their loyalties with amoral ease.

She edged along the dried ridge, following the sound of infuriated growls and bays. She jogged down the sloping incline of the worn path, then slowed her pace as she approached the sunken pit. The walls were dug straight and vertical, and tall, at least thirty feet in depth. Below, at the bottom of the pit, the hellhounds paced restlessly, snarling and snapping, constantly challenging and baiting each other. Darhis's original catch, over the winter's hunt, had been twenty-five. Of them the strongest nine remained.

A dead ryyx, the bird-lizard of the Denáren Wastes, larger and fiercer than its southern cousins, lay on the edge of the pit. Freshly killed, it was partly skinned; the long rust-coloured feathers on its forearms and tail lingered, unplucked. Already the creature was decaying in the stagnant air; blood dripped down the side of the pit, driving the dogs into a frenzy. Scavenger hawks circled above, but did not dare risk the dogs' anger.

Darhis nudged the kill with her foot, and the ryyx fell. The strongest of the hounds snapped it out of the air ten feet above the pit's floor. Four other dogs fell on it, and the bird-lizard was portioned out by vicious combat.

"To think," Darhis murmured, watching the hounds with an appreciative eye, "once you were nothing more than huntdogs. Until the *yúgure* and its... *loving* corruption." The hellhounds were fierce creatures, wiry and long-legged, their dark-gray skin stretched tightly over bony shoulders and visible rib cages. Nothing of their ancient pedigree remained: only savage hearts and relentless hunger. Mothers would eat whelps, and mates would consume each other after copulation. Only the fiercest survived the ruthless pecking order. Some had escaped to the fertile lands beyond the *yúgure*'s reach, only to be picked off by the healthier packs of furbacked wolves. They had long since learned scarce food and brutal pack life was preferable and nurtured their own vicious code of honour.

Perhaps the Denáren Wastes were not such hell after all, Darhis reflected.

A voice rang in her head, summoning her, and she winced at the feeling. She did not like her current master, but the challenge he offered was irresistible.

She turned, marching back to the keep with a practiced walk.

"You should be careful, pretty," Varron taunted her. "A little morsel like you could get eaten up out there. You never know when those hellhounds will take a liking to you."

"Fiercer dogs in here than out there," she hissed as he motioned her up the worn steps to the audience chamber. The spicy smell of silken was rich in the air; the golden dust of the Alteri forests was highly prized as a heightener of a peri's senses and magic. She saw Morden was already there, the fat glutton, drumming his fingers on his stiff leather jerkin, impatiently watching the chair turned away from him that faced the large circular window. The man was a half-breed, a mingling of peri and kobold blood. Such a mating could result in children of exception beauty and strength, but in Morden's case it only created a pompous fool with all the arrogance and greed of a peri and all the self-indulgence of a digger.

"How goes the work?" the voice rasped from the chair. Now she could see his gnarled hand resting on the edge of the armrest. Still yellowed as parchment, but not quite so skeletal as the last time she had glimpsed sight of him. He was growing stronger. Still, she had not seen his face. The ring he wore continued to pulse with a life of its own.

"Oh, as decent as one can expect," Morden gloated. "I'd work much faster, my Lord, if you could supply me with a better crew of slaves."

"Slaves are in short supply these days. No matter, you'll soon have all the slaves you could desire."

"Yes, yes, whatever. As long as I get my reward," Morden reminded him. "You promised me. My cut from the Treasury, once we find it."

"Never fear on that count. You will have everything you could possibly desire, once you have completed your task and found me the Treasury. You will all be richly rewarded. Darhis: Is your mission completed?"

"Master," she flattered him with a little bow of the head. "My Alteri are already seeing to it."

"You are certain they are capable of the task?"

"I have complete faith in their abilities."

A long silence. "Very well," he hissed. "Return to your duties," he waved his hand, his ring glinting. "Hard work is the key to soft living. Report back when you have any news. I expect prompt results."

Morden gave a short bow and slunk out of the room. Darhis hesitated a moment. "You would have further words with me, Alteri?" the disembodied voice asked.

Darhis blinked once. "No." She remained one moment longer, then turned and left, her head held high.

"I don't trust her," Varron hissed as soon she disappeared down the stairs.

"She's willful," his master breathed.

"She needs to be broken."

"I need her intact." A moment later he hissed in pain, and his claw-like hand clasped his forehead.

"Master?" Varron inquired.

"Come here, Varron," he beckoned a claw-like hand. Varron stepped up to his master's side. He knelt on the floor before the throne, as the skeletal claws rose to the sides of his head, clasping his skull. "Is your symbiote still living? Ah... good. You must be my eyes and ears. It will be a time yet until I am strong once more. Until then you must be my strong hand. Keep the kobold filth in line and watch the Alteri witch carefully." Again he gasped, bucking in sudden pain. "Ah... only the wraith... crawling about in my mind. Like little spider mites... ah it's... difficult to concentrate sometimes. The price to pay for such a life.... If only I could.... *silence* this..." he gasped sharply, drawing in a painful breath. "*Silence!*" he cried out.

It was true what they said about him, Darhis thought, as she crouched at the base of the stairwell, quietly watching. He was mad as marshfowl.

Shard gazed down at the forest passing beneath him. It was nearly noon now. The City Mount had long since fallen behind him, and his blue dragon, Smoke, glided now over unbroken forest. She was a young dragon, only seventy years old and forty feet long, barely out of childhood. But they shared a close bond, and he wouldn't trade her for the fastest dragon in the realm.

She paused a moment, before scrambling up high into the sky, her four powerful legs flailing for a moment, before she found a more pleasing updraft and began a leisurely soar once again. Shard gave her a little warning tap on the neck, just above her shoulders, and sent her a soothing mindspeech to calm her nerves. She was nervous, as she always was on Shard's impromptu excursions, being so far from Amaru. He knew she would calm down eventually. She always did.

Shard looped his hand through the little handhold on the edge of his saddle and closed his eyes, letting Smoke set the pace for a time. Sitting on her shoulderblades, he was soon lulled in a gentle drowsiness by the rhythmic movement of her muscles beneath the saddle. He still felt a pang of guilt at fleeing – coward, to run away from his brother's wedding of all things – but he assured himself they would not hold it against him. It was hardly the first time he had run away.

He had considered landing at Wayside, the large kobold settlement that served as a crossroads on the large trade routes leading east. He could have bunked with Taki and the boys at the Peregrine: they would never begrudge him a bed and a mug of mead. But in the end he felt too brooding to find sanctuary in any civilized town. He wanted to be alone, to think without the oppressive pressure of life in the City Mount.

North, he commanded, and Smoke adjusted her flight accordingly. He wanted to get away from the carpet of green forests beneath him. He wanted to go higher.

The Castle Highlands.

The City Mount was alive with excitement and wonder as the processions of delegates each made their way in turn up the great street through the guild quarters into the Old City and the High Town. Already a satrap from the Broken Islands had led a troupe of men bearing the richest bounty of the Bay of Jade, and only the day before the royal procession of Diure had meandered up the streets with dancers and acrobats in tow, performing for the awestruck crowd. All of Amaru joined in the festivities, merchants dusting off their best wares, children squandering a handful of lidas to visit a fortune-teller or a street magician. Bold banners flew from every turret and spire of the towering palace, and the sky seemed to rain gobletplum blossoms in celebration.

Yósha? Aerin asked. *_Are you thinking about Shard again?_*

I'm all right, he nodded his head. *_I just... I_ know _he doesn't like the court, the functions, I know he likes to be alone. I just wish he'd stop thinking of himself as this outsider._*

She touched his hand lightly. *_I'm sure he doesn't. He... he's just shy. You know how he feels about the crowds. We'll go to the Peregrine and have a_ *traditional kobold wedding when he gets back.**

You mean the tradition where we get all our friends together and try to see who can handle the most mead?

Exactly.

Celaeno stood patiently as the procession of porters continued to carry the elaborate wedding gifts into the throne room. Servants of Níst in their impeccable black uniforms set gift after sumptuous gift before the royal family: jade phoenixes; caskets of blood-rubies; cedar chests of fine *rishti* silk; jeweled flasks of incense and ointments. For the Lord Heir the slaves presented ancient volumes of astrology and starlore; for his bride they offered a veritable arsenal of ceremonial weaponry. The Dynast shot a quick glance to her right side; Stargazer and Aerin stared openly with amazement, their young faces unused to the masks of formality.

At length the last group entered the great hall: four black-robed spectre guards, followed by eight men carrying a large veiled litter, four spectres bringing up the rear. Whispers and hushed exclamations of wonder spread through the crowd as the litter slowly approached the throne. **Nothing in half measures,** Kemuri sent, and Celaeno repressed the slight smile tugging at her lips.

The spectres moved to the side, and the servants set the litter down, two handmaidens swiftly flanked the crimson curtain concealing the occupant. The women took up the edge of the heavy veil, then, after a moment's hesitation, lifted the curtain. A beautiful peri woman rose from the lush pillows, her head bent, her straight black hair shading her face. With deliberate poise, she swung her legs from the litter and rose to her feet. She wore a long crimson robe, embroidered with a fearsome golden dragon.

She bowed low before the royal family. "The Níst Imperium extends its warmest greetings to the Realm of Amaru and offers its blessings to the Silver Queen and her family."

Celaeno returned the bow. "The Realm of Amaru welcomes the Níst Imperium and offers its blessings to the Black Queen and her family," she raised her head, unable to repress the smile any longer. "Welcome, Lady Athyr. I hope your journey was a pleasant one."

"The skies were clear," Athyr nodded. Her obsidian black eyes scanned the royalty assembled around Celaeno, methodically taking in the many faces she saw. "I hope the Powers have been generous to you, Majesty, and to the Lord Kemuri, since last we spoke."

"I have little cause for complaint," Celaeno said. "You will remember, of course, the Lady Heiress Sintaka tal Amaru and her Royal Consort Lord Mindrin tal Tora." Mindrin and Sintaka offered little perfunctory bows, Sintaka unable to resist fidgeting with the high collar of her robe. "And their daughter Emrith, whom you first met six years ago." Athyr caught sight of a little girl peering out from behind her father.

"And my son the Lord Yósha tal Amaru, who has sought the hand of the Lady Aerin, daughter of Murren tal Kitsune." Stargazer offered a congenial smile and little bow.

Murren stepped forward now, dressed in golden armour of a Red Knight. She bowed low to the Heiress of Níst. "My consort, your Highness, Tiryn Acallis. And my son, the Lord Arjin." A flicker of recognition gleamed in Athyr's eyes as Arjin stepped forward in his immaculate suit and offered her a gracious bow.

"My lord," Athyr raised an wry eyebrow. "It's been too long."

Arjin smirked back, and Tiryn gave him a sharp nudge in the ribs. Arjin remembered his lines a moment later and his smile brightened. "And may I present, your Highness, my esteemed sister, the Lady Aerin tal Kitsune, who has accepted the suit of his Highness the Lord Yósha."

His gray eyes sparkled with mischief as he brought his sister forward. Aerin's smile faltered. Before she could protest, however, he swung her forward and caught her in his arms, planting a decidedly lengthy and by no means detached kiss on her mouth. Stargazer moaned softly, and Celaeno sighed, raising a hand to her suddenly aching forehead. Arjin's parents seemed ready to murder him.

Arjin swung her away and set her back on her feet. Celaeno murmured a soft curse through her hand. Arjin only grinned, bowing before the assembly once more.

Athyr chuckled low in her throat, seemingly unfazed by his antics. She held his gaze for a long moment, before turning back to the ceremony at hand. She snapped her fingers, and instantly a handmaiden rushed forward, laying a beautiful enamel box in her hands.

"Níst blesses your bond, and prays it shall be smiled upon by the Powers."

Aerin, still flushed to the roots of her hair, nodded her thanks as she accepted the gift.

The Heiress of Níst cast a glance at the rogue Kitsune brother. She drew nearer, inspecting him with a wary eye. She flashed him a pretty smile as she turned back to the Dynast; her long robes concealed her motion as she stomped her heel into Arjin's foot. Arjin bit his lip to quash a cry of pain, and Aerin bowed her head to hide her malicious grin.

From the shadows of one of the large alcoves, a man clothed in the deep blue uniform of the Amaru guard watched the proceedings with intense interest. His eyes lazily scanned the entire court gathered about the throne, before his gaze rested on the elegant Dynast as she sat back in her throne, her hand instinctively reaching for her soulmate's.

He studied her carefully, as a hunter studies his prey.

Shard yawned softly as he stood surveying the terrain. He and Smoke had made excellent time after two days of flight. Already they had left the Amarin Vastwood and ascended into the wild moors of the Castle Highlands. The last kobold settlement had fallen behind them several hours before. No one beside the odd prospector and the occasional cleric ever tried to make a life in the

Highlands. There was simply nothing to do.

He left Smoke to keep watch over their makeshift camp while he went scouting. Not that their little shelter inside one of the mineral castles needed looking after – he doubted he would meet anyone in his sojourn on the moors.

The moorland lay dusted with broom and grass, guarded by the ancient stone formations that gave the Highlands their name. The great kobold guild Nahga had once ruled over the highland moors, crafting their homes not underground, but in large mineral castles, created by a complex process now lost to time. The guild had been exterminated during the Great War, and only the conical structures remained, silent testament to the lost wonders of the Golden Age.

Shard halted before a small cluster of castles. Turrets of pearlescent minerals rose from a central hive, several smaller mounds surrounding the central castle. The structure rose to nearly forty feet in height, and Shard could only guess at the number of careful tunnels built underground branching off from the main hive.

Stargazer... he attempted a call. No answer; he was too far away from the palace. He'd have to put himself a trance and cast himself if he wanted to talk to his brother. It was probably just as well. He wasn't sure what he's say to him. Maybe Stargazer was furious with him, ready to pin his ears back. Or worse, maybe Stargazer hadn't even noticed he was gone.

He wouldn't be too surprised if that were the case. He had cultivated his eccentric reclusiveness well during his seventeen years, perhaps a little too well at times.

A small creek ran through the tall sweetgrass, and Shard bent down to fill his leather canteen, scooping up a handful of water to taste and finding it delightfully cool and sweet. Only a few minutes' walk from his campsite, excellent for filling his little water pot or soothing a dry throat in the middle of the night.

He returned to the campsite to find Smoke fast asleep in the grass. He supposed he couldn't blame her; she had made such a long journey.

"Still... can't even count on you to keep me company, can I?" he muttered, unpacking his supper: some white rice and a little smoked shimmertrout he had poached from the Amaru storerooms. Slim fare for a growing boy – perhaps he should have stayed with Taki at the Peregrine after all. He supposed he could go hunting for a hare or pheasant, but he felt too weary.

He took out his water pot, filling it with the water from his canteen, then set about making a campfire. There was little wood to be found, but he supplemented it with some roots and tough grass stalks. In short order he had a little fire burning and the water was beginning to bubble inside the pot. Shard returned to the creek to refill his canteen. *Should have brought the pot with me,* he thought as he hiked through the grass. *Would have been easier – then, when do I even do anything the easy way? Could be eating feasts at the court, or drinking ale at the Peregrine, and instead I'm camping like a penniless prospector.*

He returned to his fire, canteen in hand, a few drops slipping from the cap, dripping onto his trousers. *Wish I could be more like Yósha. Peaceful, happy – he knows he's got a perfect life, he knows how to enjoy it. A new soulmate – and he's only* twenty *for Oracle's sake! Why can't I be like that? Why can't I just* enjoy *my life?*

"Always the hardest road, little one?" his mother gently chided him as she gently patted his bloodied knee with a moistened cloth. He was seven, and he had fallen from a tree, trying to reach a third-floor window.

Why was that? Why did he shun the easier path? Why could he never stop running?

He ate his rice and fish slowly, scanning the horizon as Smoke snuffled lightly in her sleep, her whiskers twitching in dreams. He stretched his legs, too weary to hike the two minutes' distance to the creek to wash the sticky remnants from the side of the cooking pot.

The pot bumped against one of the worn leather bags, and the sack tipped over, spilling the contents on the ground. Shard groaned, rising from his slouch against the gray rock. A length of smooth silky kobold climbing rope, about seventy lidas in small coins, and a seven-sided jade-green meditation crystal.

He held it up in his hands, resting his fingertips against the smooth surface. Why had he brought the damnable thing with him? An escape was supposed to be just that: a time to leave all the headaches behind. Yet he knew he was already deepening his stare, slipping into the meditation exercise.

The magical gem pulsed softly, glowing with inner light as he exerted his will against the gem. It was a simple exercise, to lose oneself in the structure of the gemstone, to focus one's energy and reach an inner peace, if only for a moment or two.

The sweetgrass stirred in the soft evening wind, and Shard was distracted, briefly, by the faint rustle. The crystal's pulsing lights broke their pattern, dimmed as his focus faltered. Shard turned his attention back to the gemstone. He would master it.

Shame burned at his temples. Stargazer had been able to align a crystal when he was six; but then his brother had been born with his mind in perfect alignment. Celaeno's Solstice boys; but Stargazer took after the still winter midnight, and Shard took after the restless summer thunderstorms.

His mind drifted once more, back to the countless lessons of his youth. "You just have to focus, Shard," his father's gentle voice told him. "Forget the outside world. Don't block it out – try too hard and you'll never find your focus. Just relax, breathe out, and let the world dissolve."

He saw himself, a little child of seven, biting his lip as his brow furrowed, his eyes boring holes in the crystal, the air around him crackling with his tangible frustration. "No, no, Shard," Kemuri's cool hands ran over his shoulders, brushing the tension aside. "You're fighting too hard."

Magic was not about fighting. It was about becoming calm, becoming tranquil. That was how his parents worked, how Stargazer worked. To be a magic-wielder was to harness the tangled threads of lifeforce turning through the air and weave them into a unified spell. To create order from chaos. To use magic in anger only created further chaos. The sorcerers in the Great War had created such chaos, and their spells had leaked through the world, creating dark pockets of stagnant lifeforce, twisted and dangerous. Uncontrollable.

Chaos was not inherently destructive. But it could not be easily mastered by a novice. Calm had to be established first; one needed to control oneself before one could control the magic. These lessons had been with him from the beginning of his training.

Why couldn't he accomplish such a simple exercise? He had the skill. Everyone could see that. He had the magic of the Solstice night in him. He was a firestarter, capable of producing combustion with a blink of his eyes. Occasionally, by mere chance, his powers would erupt, and a cup would suddenly fly across the room. Yet whenever he tried to harness it, his magic fizzled into nothingness and his frustrations defeated him once again.

"You're my little Solstice boy, you know that," his mother whispered in his ear.

The lights continued to flicker, discordant.

"It takes longer with some than others," Kemuri reassured him, his long hair brushing against the child's neck as he leaned closer to study his progress. "Don't be discouraged, Shard. I know it's in you. The magic's in you. You just have to find a way to let it out."

The lights dimmed, flared brightly, then died away again, their pattern chaotic, unordered.

"I hate it!" he hissed aloud, under his breath. The lights grew brighter, fueled by his anger. "I hate not being able to do this." *I've got the power. Father tells me I could have a talent for Old Magic, if I worked at it. He thinks I could be a dreamseer! But I can't* do this!

He knew the way the nobles looked at him: Shard the worthless magic-wielder. He glared at the crystal. *Shard who can't be a sorcerer, who can't be an Arashi, who can't be anything. She called me her Shard, that I'm a fallen star she found, full of the Old Magic the world's lost since the War. What a name that is to live up to!*

The crystal began to pulse angrily, the greenish yellow glow growing. *Everyone treats me like I'm part of the family, like I'm just any ordinary student. But they all know I'm... I'm not right!* An audible hum began, rising in pitch as the light throbbed faster and father. *If I had enough magic in me to topple the clock tower if I felt like it – then, then they'd think me an avatar. But now, what am I – nothing!* The crystal was pulsing with a furious, blinding light. *I hate this. I hate this. Why can't I make this thing work?*

The crystal shattered.

Shard fell back on the grass, staring aghast at the remnants of the crystal. Smoke croaked miserably as she woke up, then trilled quizzically at the glass-green shards and her stunned master.

"What's wrong with me, Smoke?" Shard sighed. The dragon gave no reply, and Shard moaned softly. He rose to his knees and slowly gathered up the larger of the crystal fragments.

His hand closed over a large fleck of clear jade green, vaguely diamond shaped: two straight sides and one smooth arc connecting them. Shard lifted it, taking care not to cut the tender skin of his palm on the edge.

An image flashed in his head. He saw a second diamond-shaped shard, not clear green but an opaque violet-blue, aglimmer with silver highlights. Dark, rich, like a black opal, the light glinting off its many overlapping hues. A light violet energy seemed to halo it, static electricity dancing in the air.

Shard shook the vision from his head. He looked over at Smoke, but the dragon merely blinked back with her lion-eyes. She unfurled her long red snake's tongue in a yawn. With a soft trill, she set her head down on her scaled paws and drifted back asleep.

6

Shard walked along the edge of the hillside, his little crossbow slung over his back, his leather bag and his canteen tied to his belt. The sun had just set on his third day in the Highlands, and he had eaten all his rice. No longer could he malinger in his little shelter; if he wanted to eat, he had to hunt.

"Every heir worth her riches should live like a rogue now and then," Sintaka had told him once, on their first excursion into the wilds. "A campfire, a warm bedroll, and good night under the stars is all a peri needs." She had shown him the way to live by his wits, to escape palace life and lose himself in the woods; he supposed she lived vicariously through her brother's exploits now that she was too old, too respectable to simply run away as she had in her youth. He had learned his lessons well, and if he could scare up a pheasant or a rabbit, he might have a chanceof shooting it down. Otherwise it was to be dry bread and some fruit he had raided from the pantry.

He caught sight of movement in the grass, and a moment later a plump rabbit leapt out of the brush. Unshouldering his crossbow, he raced after the rabbit, which was already fleeing between a cluster of tiny domes that reached to Shard's shoulders. The young peri scrambled up one of the ringed mounds and aimed his sights on the rabbit. The arrow flew and the rabbit disappeared into the broom. Shard hurried through the grass, pulling out his little sack. He could already taste that roast rabbit.

Stargazer was getting married on the morrow.

If he left immediately, and flew all through the night, taxing Smoke to her limit, sleeping on her back, he might just make it back in time.

He shook his head, striding forward with a confidence he did not feel. *No turning back, Shard,* he cautioned himself.

He found the rabbit, cleanly killed, lying in a patch of brush. Shard scooped up the rabbit and stuffed it in his bag. He stretched, looking back at Amaru in the west.The aurorae lit up the western skies as they withdrew to join the setting sun.

He felt something, a strange haunting sensation, like a far-off melody he could just hear. He frowned, closing his eyes and extending his senses, trying to pinpoint the vague sensation. Nothing, only the slight tingling at the edge of his awareness, raising the hairs at the back of his neck.

Smoke, he called. *Stay in camp. I'll be back... later. Don't worry.*

He heard the reassuring answer from the dragon; he could almost see her, napping contented in the shade cast by one of the smaller castles, her whiskers twitching slightly in a near-dream. Assured of her safety, he proceeded in search of the strange sensation. It was definitely magic, and old magic by the feel of it. It had an ancient, reverent quality to it, like some of the older monuments on the City Mount. But what kind exactly, he could not say. A beacon, perhaps, or a guardian spell. It was very faint, probably a peri of lesser magic would not be able to detect it. Reshouldering his crossbow and wrapping the ties of his bag around his wrist, he waded through the grass, passing another cairn of mineral cones.

He proceeded up a hill and through a cluster of small, stunted trees. The soil was too barren to support anything more than wild grasses and some hardy shrubs. No one was certain whether that was another effect of Cimmerian's *yúgure,* or whether the Highlands had always been so. A long wisp of aurora streaked high through the high, almost reaching the sky's zenith. Shard smiled at the sight, his search stalled for a moment. Fox Moon produced the best sunsets, lazy spectacles in the late summer evening, moments when the entire world seemed to stand still.

He could feel the magic again, as ethereal as the wisps of light in the sky, crackling slightly at the edges of his consciousness. Old Magic, the ancient breed from before the War, perhaps even from before the Golden Age. He continued through the broom, passing another cluster of iridescent-white mineral mounds. He crested another ridge and a gasp slipped his lips as he saw the ground level off into a gentle plateau, revealing an immense gathering of mineral hives. Like a cluster of old redwoods in the depths of the Vastwood, the monoliths were duller, older, the rings of their construction more pronounced, little veins of glimmering mineral sparkling in the sunset light. A large egg-shaped castle dominated the cluster, surrounded by several smaller domes of irregular shape.

He could see, with his mind's eye, the magic emanating from the rocks: broken, fragmented aurorae pulsing faintly in a kaleidoscope of sparking colours. Looping out in long arcs, trying vainly to unify itself in a cohesive pattern, too old and too weak, faltering and flickering across the spectrum.

Any passing peri, and certainly any kobold, never would have noticed it.

Shard raced down the hill, barely aware of the ground beneath his feet, as he hurried towards the largest castle. He laid his hand on the cool rock, closing his eyes as he felt gentle filaments of magic course through his nerves. He let his hand glide across the rock as he listened to the subtle melodies of the magic. A guardian spell perhaps, but something even older and frailer than anything Kemuri had ever taught him to recognize.

Slowly pacing around the circumference of the rocks, he listened, dulling all his other senses to concentrate solely on the play of forces at work in the rock. He let his fingers glide from rock to rock, until at last his hand was pressed against the central egg, feeling all the discreet contours in the stone. He focused, feeling for any little differences in texture. At length he found a patch of rock where the melody was discordant, fractured. Concentrating, he plied his own magic against the rock, slowly stirring the patterns. The currents resisted at first, unsure what to make of this new force exerting its will. Shard pressed further, forcing the filaments into a more unified pattern, as if slowly piecing together a fragmented puzzle. The resistance grew, but Shard would not back down; a challenge had been declared, and he would not let some obsolete piece of stone best him. Slowly the pieces began to fit together, the colours growing more uniform, the melody tempering. Beads of sweat began to dot Shard's brow as he pressed further, seeing the light pulse more brightly, the song rise in pitch. He *was* having an effect! He had actually assimilated something in all those tedious lessons with Father. He pressed his advantage further, like a victorious swordsman, forcing his opponent to the ground. The magic was uniform now, blazing brightly with the infusion of new talent. Shard smiled as he threw the last of his strength into the rock.

The rock wall gave way all of a sudden, and Shard tumbled into the void, collapsing on the hard stone floor before he realized what had happened. Swearing, he sat up, looking out at the turquoise-tinted valley behind him. It made no sense. The castles were frequently filled with cracks and doors, leading to tiny passageways within. Why would anyone bother to seal one up with a guardian spell? And who?

He turned back, looking into the chamber, and was surprised anew. It did not lead up into a tiny tunnel anyone taller than he could never hope to navigate, but down, into a large staircase hewn in the rock, descending deep underground. Shard hesitated a moment, but only a moment, before rising and starting down the staircase. Large and rough, about twenty steps deep, it lead him into a rock antechamber beneath the castle. Shard thought he spied a lamp hanging from an iron hook in the wall, but told himself not to arouse any false hopes – by the look of things, the lamp was surely too old to hold any oil. Yet when he picked it and shook it lightly, he thought he could heard a thick liquid sloshing within. The lamp was too old to have a sparkswitch inside, and he lifted the lamp to his eyes, staring intently at the wick. A moment later he heard a little sparking sound, and a tiny flame sprouted on the oil-soaked wick. Shard smiled to himself as he lifted the lamp high, looking around at his surroundings. Ancient carvings ran along dull red-brown walls, broken up at times like small panels depicting abstract designs of unknown origins. Shard thought it looked like a tomb.

He turned from the antechamber, cautiously advancing into the main chamber. It was much larger, the ceiling higher, the walls longer. The walls were of a lighter, higher quality rock, but still the feeling of a necropolis persisted. Shafts of light fell from artfully placed cracks in the ceiling, and faint beams pierced the warm gloom lit by the small lamp. Shard noticed that no dust danced in the light. Indeed, there were no cobwebs in the alcoves, no smell of musk and mold in the air. No air of decay anywhere. It was immaculately clean, which instantly unnerved him.

A firepit, long extinct, sat in the center of the terracotta floor. Shard absently let the rabbit in its sack fall to the floor next to the ring of stones. Along the walls stood old stone cabinets of some alien style and construction. A bed lay tucked along the walls in the corner, heaped with warm furs, another small lantern hanging nearby. Shard saw no sign of a sarcophagus, unless one of the foreign cabinets was in fact a burial casket.

At the far end of the room, next to the bed, rested a particularly long and ornate stone bier. Perhaps that was the sarcophagus after all, for Shard noticed that several of the shafts of light seemed to be illuminating that particular item; more, they were illuminating a small red enamel jar that rested on top of the stone. Approaching with a cautious reverence, Shard set the lamp down on the smooth surface of the sarcophagus, examining the jar. It seemed too small to be an urn, this little red container with a slightly domed lid, an intricate silver cap adorned with three tiny bells. Shard picked it up despite a pang of guilt telling him to set it back down and let the poor man's tomb be. Before he could stop himself, he was twisting the top, which was tightly pressed into the jar. It gave a musty squeak as he began to turn it, and suddenly the lid came off, startling him.

His astonishment was only heightened, for instead of dry gray ash, a dazzling light rose from the jar, a brilliant green ball of blinding intensity dancing into the air, trailing a little glittering dust behind it. Shard let the container fall to the ground, all his attention on the light ball of energy. The light pulsed once and seem to waver and Shard hesitantly reached up for it. Then it began to dance erratically in a frantic zigzag, as if about to explode, its light shifting and pulsing with a dangerous speed, and Shard abandoned all restraint, leaping up and reaching out.

He stumbled as his hands closed around the ball, and a bright flash blinded him as he tumbled to the ground. He landed hard on his tailbone, lights exploding under his eyelids, and suddenly he felt something heavy fall on his legs.

"Son of a..." he murmured, opening his eyes, blinking the flashes away. His curse died on his lips as he beheld the creature that had fallen into his lap.

A young man, a boy, surely no older than he, perhaps even a year younger, his eyes closed, his face pale, drained of all colour as if in death. He wore a long kimono of spotless white, a long beaded necklace around his neck, ending in a charm of a design Shard could not identify. His inky black hair was short, tousled in his sudden transformation, lying against his pale skin. Long black eyelashes brushed cheeks that were only now beginning to take on a hint of colour – or was it Shard's imagination?

He stared at the peri, his eyes wide with incredulity, at a complete loss. Was the boy dead? Or only unconscious? Was he even a peri, or a wraith or demon or – Powers help him - an avatar in the shape of a boy?

He stared in wonder at the boy's face, so peaceful in sleep – or was it truly death? He looked so innocent, so beautiful, like a priceless work of art – surely he could be no mere peri but a being of infinite powers. Unconsciously he reached out and brushed a lock of face away from the boy's cheek. So beautiful...

In what seemed like an explosive sound in the stillness of the crypt, the boy drew in a ragged breath, sudden colour rising to his cheeks. His head stirred slightly, and for a moment his eyelids flickered up, revealing deep emerald eyes. They struggled to focus, and for a moment it seemed he was looking right at Shard, before he collapsed back into unconsciousness.

Shard gently carried the unconscious peri to the bed and lay him down, drawing one of the furs over him to shield him from the chill beginning to invade the crypt. A low rumble in his stomach reminded Shard of the rabbit, and he walked over the firepit, examining the wood stacked inside. He found a few gnarled branches and a single log in the corner, and heaped them in the center, staring at the dried grasses and old kindling until they ignited.

He skinned and cleaned the rabbit as well as he could remember, and after much muttered cursing finally put the rabbit on the old metal spit over the fire. He only hoped the metal wasn't some toxic alloy that would poison them both – *if* his companion ever stirred.

He cast a glance at the peri, still sleeping, though now it seemed a more peaceful sleep, and his face no longer bore the colourless pallor of death but had warmed to a delicate rosy complexion. What was intended as a covert glance soon became a long stare, as Shard leisurely gazed at his phantom companion. Surely no normal peri could be so perfect, so innocently beautiful, looking all the world like a sleeping avatar. At length he shook his head, returning to the meal over the fire. For Powers' sake, he would turn into an adoring worshipper as easily as Jaxa if he went on.

He poked at the rabbit with a little stick. Almost ready. He wondered whether he should try to wake the boy. Perhaps the attempt would only interfere with the lingering spell. Perhaps it was better to let him sleep until he woke up on his own. A selfish flicker ran through Shard – just as well not to share dinner; he was starving, and the smell of the roast was driving him wild.

He heard a gasp, and looked up, to see the boy awake, staring back at him with the same wide eyes.

"Y-you're awake," Shard began clumsily, tripping over the words.

"*Demas ren?*" the boy demanded in a foreign tongue Shard could not identify. It seemed vaguely familiar, yet laced with melodic tones and accents he had never heard before. "*Tal islat melórin údlaon? Uddalia shem'as delèla tamalin es s'il tesif al'veu s'il jesr forirr ta?*"

"It's all right," Shard stood, holding up his hands. At his action the boy backed up on the bed, his eyes wide with terror. "It's all right, I won't hurt you," Shard explained in a soothing tone, accompanying the words with a mindspeech. "I won't hurt you."

"Than'thul? Sugash ven ti'l ryuu? Hè? Jensei da loa'ria gem se ten se damenra!" The boy's panic seemed to subside slightly, but his suspicion remained just as strong.

"It's all right," Shard reassured him, taking a step forward, continuing his telepathic explanation, hoping the boy would understand that. Mindspeech could often transcend barriers of language, but the stranger's tongue was so unfamiliar that he wasn't certain.

"*Nanyaaa?*" the boy asked warily, his voice trembling. "*Imya metalúne?*"

"It's all right," Shard repeated once more, slowly. "I'm not going to hurt you. I... found you here... in the jar," he pointed to the discarded container on the floor. "I... I didn't know you were in there until I opened it. I'm a friend," he soothed. "I'm not going to hurt you."

The boy seemed to relax, for a moment. "Who... who are you?" he asked in the Common Tongue, the faintest accent lingering on his words.

Shard smiled with relief. "My name is Shard," he spoke. "I'm from Amaru. I was exploring the Highlands and I sensed the guardian spell on these rocks."

The boy frowned, then coughed once. "You did? You" – another cough – "must be a very powerful sorcerer."

Shard shrugged. "Not really."

The boy coughed again, an intense fit. "Here, here, would you like some water?" Shard offered hastily, holding up his canteen. The boy raised his head and smiled for the first time, a beaming honest smile that Shard couldn't help but return. The boy nodded swiftly, and Shard rushed to his side to bring him the canteen.

The boy drank deep, taking another deep breath as he set the canteen down. He raised a hand to his forehead. "*Tiktu,* I've been asleep too long," he gasped. He looked up at Shard, waiting hesitantly at his bedside as might a nervous servant. "Thank you," he handed the water back. "I'm... I'm sorry about that..." he waved his hand vaguely to indicate his initial fear. "I... I'm always confused when I first wake up, disoriented." He bent his head, drawing several more deep breaths. Suddenly his head snapped up. "*Desheea maiya'narain?*" he demanded sharply, his eyes wide with panic. "What – what year is it?"

"It's... three-forty-two," Shard explained after a moment's pause. "New Age calendar," he added a moment later for clarification.

"Three hundred and forty two..." he frowned. "The last time I was awake it was... it was 1153 – by the Kistu'ker calendar. Uh.... Chalandris had just fallen... about a month ago, I think."

Shard did a swift calculation in his head. "That was over four hundred years ago. Chalandris fell in... in ninety-four, in the Old Calendar."

"Four hundred years," he sighed, rubbing his face. "I've been out of touch." He paused, sniffing the air a moment, before inhaling a deep breath, another wide smile breaking out on his face.

"Oh," Shard turned back to the fire. "I was cooking a little rabbit. I... I hope you're hungry."

The boy swung his legs to the side of the bed, standing up. "I haven't eaten in an eternity," he declared, taking a step forward before he stumbled, his legs giving way. Shard rushed to his side, wrapping his arm around his waist to support him.

"Careful," he cautioned. The boy blushed deeply.

"Sorry. I haven't used my legs for nearly half a millennium." He took a step back, straightening. He stood just an inch above Shard's height, a fact for which Shard was infinitely grateful.

He took a few uncertain steps, then leaned on the edge of the bed for support. "Here, you stay here," Shard offered. "I'll bring it to you."

"Thanks," he said, slowly easing himself back on the bed. Shard noticed the melodic accent had now left his speech entirely and he spoke the Common Tongue like a native of Amaru. Shard carefully lifted the rabbit from the fire and divided it up, placing several pieces of meat on the rabbit's skin. He carefully carried them over to the boy, setting them on the bed next to him. "Here you are....?" he looked at the boy with a slightly embarrassed questioning.

"Ohh. Sim. Sim Onmyóji."

Onmyóji? Was he perhaps related to the great Onmyóji sorcerers of the Golden Age? Shard bit his lip to restrain a wide smile. The Onmyóji were believed to have been eradicated during the Great War. Had a small branch of the family survived through the Dark Age? He stared at the boy in open awe before he remembered his rabbit and hurried back to the fire. He nearly stumbled, and cursed under his breath, especially when he heard a little chuckle from Sim's bed. He was acting just like the clumsy little kitling he had always accused himself of being.

Sim slowly removed his white gloves, laying them on the bed. He took another long breath, savoring the smell of the meat, but only took a tiny bite before he set the haunch back down. "Don't want to overindulge," he explained to Shard's questioning glance. "A body doesn't handle rich food well after a long famine."

Shard nodded; it made sense. He tasted the rabbit, then took a larger bite, assured of his handiwork. For a moment they ate in silence, Sim slowly tasting his meal, Shard trying to keep himself from rushing, all the while keeping his eyes averted from the bed.

"You must be wondering what I was doing in there," Sim spoke at length.

"A little," Shard understated. "I didn't want to pry."

Sim narrowed his eyes. "You aren't a bounty hunter or a mercenary are you?"

"Oh, oh no," Shard held up his hands. "I'm just a kit. A rogue courtier."

Sim seemed to relax. He laughed nervously. "I... I like to sleep," he explained. "It passes the time. I don't have anything else to do." His expression grew sad. "I wasn't always like this, of course. I used to live out there, live like any normal peri. But after the war... I didn't have anything else to do. My family was dead, my kingdom was in ruins. I didn't want to stay out there." He shrugged. "Sleep seemed the more merciful end."

"The war..." Shard frowned. A moment later his eyes widened. "Not the *Great* War?"

"That's what they call it now, isn't it?" Sim nodded. "It was just the war to us back then. We didn't have anything to compare it to."

"Then you are from Elória?" Shard stammered. "You *are* one of the Onmyóji sorcerers!"

Sim nodded sadly. "Alecta's own grandson."

Shard nearly fell back on his heels. "The court sorcerers to Dynast Nikaas Maleni? You knew the Dynast, and Lady Alsaya? Powers – did you know Cimmerian?"

"It was a long time ago."

Shard sat staring up at him, at a loss for words. Ever since old Larien had died it was thought that all the survivors of the War were long extinct. And yet here he was, facing the last living peri who had seen Elória standing. His belief that Sim was an avatar had not been far off then. The boy who seemed surely no older than sixteen was in fact over four thousand years old.

Sim saw his look of disbelief and merely nodded. "Now you know why I asked. One of the last survivors of the Great War - more than enough people in the old days would have liked to keep a curiosity like me behind glass. But... I didn't see the *yúgure,*" he explained, almost apologetically. "I went to sleep about thirty years before Cimmerian unleashed it. I'd wake up every few hundred years, for a few months at a time, to see what was happening, then I'd go back to sleep. Once I woke up after only a hundred and fifty years. Another time I was asleep for over a millennium. But this has been the first time anyone woke me up." He looked across the fire at Shard, tilting his head quizzically. "You *are* a powerful sorcerer, to be able to open that door. Where do *you* come from, Shard?"

Shard only shrugged. "Nowhere, really. I'm the adopted son of Dynast Celaeno tal Amaru; she found me in the Vastwood on midsummer. No one knows where I really come from."

"A Lord Heir of Amaru?" Sim mused under his breath.

"I.... My brother soulbound two turns ago. He's getting married tomorrow, and I couldn't stand all the diplomats and dignitaries who'd be coming – all the court ritual. So I took my dragon and came to the Highlands, just to camp out in a castle for a quarter-turn or so. Just until the palace was a little less crowded."

Sim nodded understandingly. "I don't care for crowds either. A Lord Heir," he marveled again. "Don't meet many on the Highlands. Celaeno... she had just reclaimed Amaru, when I last went to sleep. She was planning to drive the Garthan troglodytes further south – wanted to expand Amaru to the southern plains. Most people thought her mad."

"You've missed a lot over the last four hundred years," Shard smiled proudly. "Mother helped create an alliance between the five great powers. We call it the Pentagram now. Amaru, Hesperin, Níst, Diure and Marishen: all allied three hundred years ago. That's when the New Age began, by the current calendar. Almost all the continent is allied under the Pentagram, only the smallest, most outlying kingdoms resist the alliance. The Garthans are nearly all gone, pushed back into the southern deserts. There are a few raiders, a few separatist rebels in some of the outlying provinces, but other than that: peace."

Sim shook his head. "The peri have come a long way since I was last awake. Next you'll tell me your managed to settle the Wastelands."

"No, no the Wastelands are still barren, I don't think they'll ever be habitable. What was it like before they were wastelands?" he marveled. "Was Elória as beautiful as the legends say?"

Sim smiled fondly. "It was home."

"I have so many questions I want to ask you," Shard shook his head. Sim battled back a wearied yawn and Shard hastily amended, "But I should get back to my dragon. She's probably worried about me by now."

"Why don't you call her over here?" Sim suggested. "She could sleep just inside the door if she's not too big. You could stay the night down here."

"Oh, I wouldn't want to impose," Shard shrugged. "I've got a little campsite I was going to set up."

Sim picked up a large bearskin wrap and threw it towards Shard; it collapsed dully to the floor quite a distance from him. Sim blushed. "My aim's off," he murmured. "No, no, stay here," he persisted. "You wouldn't want to get caught in a thunderstorm – they can hit without warning on the Highlands this time of–" he paused, blushing again. "What moon it is?" he asked.

"Fox; it's the eleventh today."

"Then we *are* in the middle of thunderstorm season on the Highlands," he smiled, almost triumphantly. "You should stay here, you'll be safer." He blushed again. "I'd... I'd like you to stay," he admitted sheepishly. "It's been a while since I've had anyone to talk to."

Shard nodded eagerly, through with hollow protests. "All right," he offered diplomatically, absently wondering why it mattered to him whether he remained or not, why he had felt that strange rush of elation.

7

Sim Onmyóji awoke slowly the next morning. It was such a strange sensation, to slowly awaken in a warm bed, to feel a dreamy contentment at the edge of consciousness. He had almost forgotten the simple peace to be had in the normal sleep of most peri, that it could have almost the same cleansing effect as the drastic hibernation of a sorcerer.

He remembered Shard, his companion by a quirk of fate. He lifted his head from the blankets to look for him. The firepit was dying, only the dimmest ember still aglow. The bearskin wrap on the other side of the firepit lay discarded on the floor, the peri gone.

Sim slowly sat up from bed, swinging his legs to the side. With infinite care and patience not to tire himself, or incur another dizzy spell, he tugged on his soft white ankle boots, then rose on shaky legs to look for Shard.

Eagerness to find Shard: it was another strange sensation to a mind accustomed to an oblivious limbo. He couldn't remember the last time he had ever cared for anyone enough to spare them more than a passing thought.

No, that was a lie. He could remember exactly, and that was what gave him pause.

He could not deny that the young peri intrigued him. Such strength in one so young – surely he could be no older than fifty, yet he had enough power to open the complex guardian spell protecting the crypt.

He slowly crossed the chamber, pausing frequently to draw breath and to still the tiny tremors in his muscles, then ascended the staircase in the antechamber with the same care. The centuries of sleep had taken much out of him.

He exited the castle, into the warm sunshine. The stars were aglow above him, and the Bluestar was already high in the sky, a brilliant blue beacon against the soft glow of the Well of Stars. He slowly turned, taking in the view, all the while searching for the younger peri.

"Sim! Up here!"

He looked up, craning his neck to see Shard perched on the top of the egg, surveying the territory as might a satrap. "How did you get up there?" he called.

"I climbed up," Shard laughed at the naiveté of the question. "Come on," he held out his hand. Sim backed away, holding up his hands.

"I think I'd rather stay down here."

Shard shrugged and proceeded to slide down the egg's surface, gracefully gliding down until he landed on the ground a few feet from Sim. The elder peri shook his head. "You'll break your neck trying that."

"You're as bad as my mother," Shard scoffed.

"And you're as bad as my sister," Sim stated, before he caught himself and his eyes widened as what he had just said. Shard marveled at the sudden change. Where a moment before the peri had been smiling, belying his disapproving tone, now he was solemn, mournful, his eyes filled with pain. Shard took a step towards him, but Sim turned away. "I shouldn't have said that," he murmured, his hand rising to cover his mouth. "I should have..."

"Sim?" Shard asked. "What's wrong?"

He wiped what Shard thought was a tear from his eye. "Where's your dragon?"

"Smoke was hungry; I turned her loose to catch herself some breakfast. Maybe we'll be lucky and she'll bring us back something too. I'm less a hunter than I'd like to believe. Sim? Are you all right?"

"Just... bad memories. I'm... I'm going to go for a little walk, I need to stretch my legs."

"Can I come too?" Shard asked, backing up a little a moment later, regretting his eager tone. "Or would you... would you rather be alone?"

Sim smiled shyly. "No, I could use some company."

They walked in silence for a time, neither daring to speak. Shard watched the elder peri warily, several times stepping forward as if to venture a thought, each time falling back into the slow pace, hanging his head.

Sim's voice echoed in his head, startling him. **What are you thinking?**

Trying to decide how to talk to an avatar.

I'm hardly an avatar, Shard, he replied sadly.

The oldest living peri, you might as well be.

Sim paused. "The oldest...." he mused. "Then Larien is truly dead?"

"Did... did you know Larien?"

"I killed him."

He began to walk anew, leaving Shard frozen in amazement. At length he recovered his legs and raced to catch up with Sim. "You killed Larien?"

For a moment Sim continued to walk in silence. Then he paused, turning back to his companion. "I suppose history records that Larien's kobold slaves rebelled, aided by his peri servants and led by a phantom ringleader, probably one of Larien's warlords. They overthrew him and killed him, and enslaved all his surviving men." Shard nodded. Sim smiled tightly. "What history leaves out is who incited them to rebellion. Who the ringleader really was." He blinked once, then looked up at the sky, gazing at the constellations. "I watched them drive him into the canyon," he spoke, his voice soft and distant. "There were nearly three hundred slaves – many too weak to move, let alone fight. But together they were... a sea. I blasted a rock overhang, watched it fall down on him, crush him." Sim smiled grimly. "He saw me, a moment before the first of the rocks fell. He knew I was the one who had killed him. It took me over three thousand years, but I had my revenge.... For my sister."

"Your sister," Shard spoke, remembering how the mere mention of her had brought tears to his eyes.

Sim looked about, and moved over to a large rock. "I'm tired," he sighed, sitting down on the stone, running his hands over his legs. He paused for a moment, keeping his head down, before he slowly looked up to meet Shard's worried gaze.

"Terrays. She was my twin," he smiled sadly, his eyes briefly taking on their former light, before they darkened with sadness once more. "My perfect duplicate – if you saw us side by side you could never tell us apart – except that her eyes were bluer than mine - turquoise." Shard sat down on the ground next to Sim, listening. "We were born in the year 12,797, by the Elórian calendar. The war had been going on for..." he gazed down at the grass, trying to remember, "oh, for thirteen hundred years by then. There were still a few old peri from before the war, but most had only known fighting. The Maleni Dynasty was just at its end when we were born. Nikaas had been ruling for about six hundred years, and the Onmyóji were his court sorcerers. Our parents were killed when were only five – a sorcerer from Djedethra had poisoned our mother and killed our father in combat when he had tried to avenge her death. We were raised by our aunt, and given free rein in the palace as soon as we were out of the nursery."

A fleeting smile crossed his face. "We were perfect twins, you know. The palace healer, the midwife, the clerics, they all said we were special. We were supposed to be one child, not two. One Onmyóji child filled with power unseen in generations. We would have been an *alyha*. But something happened, no one knew what, and we were born as twins. A daughter and a son, halves of a perfect whole."

Shard stared up at the sorcerer, not entirely understanding his cryptic speech. All at once the ancient terms suddenly fell together, and Shard's violet eyes lit up. "You're a two-spirit!" Shard exclaimed, a broad grin of delight breaking out on his face. The rarest of sorcerers and shamans: a peri with a perfectly balanced energy, neither male nor female. Their bodies might be one sex or the other, but their souls were something else. A third gender, they possessed uncanny powers of healing and prophesying. Even with all the ambassadors and sorcerers passing through the court at Amaru, Shard had never seen one before.

Sim blushed self-consciously. "My ears don't point," he protested softly. When Shard frowned, Sim brushed back a wispy tuft of hair to reveal his ears. "They say powerful two-spirits have pointed ears – like the avatars. Terrays and I, we're rather low on the power scale, I'd imagine."

Shard shook his head in wonderment. "Are you a healer?"

"I'm healerkin. I can heal myself, and if paired with someone of powerful magic, I can heal others. But Terrays was the real healer. She got the lion's share of the magic – female two-spirits are the rarer ones. My powers are mostly... more ethereal in nature. More abstract. Terrays was the chosen successor to our parents – she was the older twin, the more powerful one. She fit in at court, while I hid in the background; she met with generals to discuss strategy while I stayed in my room and tried to forget we could all die at any moment. She was a powerful Arashi knight. Oh... senders could cast their essence farther with my help; floaters could lift huge blocks into the air working with me. And when Terrays and I worked together we could practically bring the dead back to life. But I wasn't a fighter, and I couldn't do what she could. During the war they needed Arashi and healers far more than they needed an abstracting two-spirit." He looked back at Shard. "Do you know why the war broke out?"

Shard bit his lip. "Oh... Denár Elória and Denár Djedethra were blood enemies. No one knows what first started it, but–"

"Mining rights," Sim interrupted. "A feud between kobold guilds over a strip of silver mines on the border of the two kingdoms. The kobolds started fighting over who owned the mines, the mine leaders went to the guild leaders, and the guild leaders went to the Dynasts. It was just a small border war, before Elória and Djedethra started to call in their alliance treaties with the other kingdoms. Within ten years full scale war had broken out across the Continent. The Armistice was declared after about a century, but it was broken before long, over more border raids. By the time Terrays and I were born no one cared what the reasons were any more. All anyone cared about was destroying the rival kingdoms and allied satrapies. The oral history of the Dark Age did its best to vilify Djedethra and Jaridan – you'd think Elória was fighting all the forces of darkness, avatars and demons alike. But we were just peri – stupid, arrogant peri. No darkness, no light, just a never-ending gray." He shuddered. "Elória was still pure, the city and the royal forests surrounding it. But outside – outside the world was torn to shreds: forests turned to mud and barren rock; the dead and the dying displayed on crosses – these horrid eight-pointed crosses – at every crossroads, left to rot as a warning to others; prisoners of war paraded down the streets; constant lightning storms from the dueling sorcerers' magic. But no one wanted to stop – we couldn't stop. Just to stay alive meant more slaughter – eat or be eaten." He glanced down at Shard. "You're sitting like a supplicant," he criticized lightly.

"I can't help it," Shard shrugged goodnaturedly. He leaned closer, placing his hand on the rock. "Please... tell me more about the war. About your sister."

Again he smiled sadly. "She would have liked you. She probably would have said you reminded her of me. We lived at court in Elória for nearly a century. It was a simple life. Terrays would go out on frequent missions. I would stay home and help the other magic-wielders, offer Nikaas counsel. I think he gloated a little, having two-spirits in his inner court. I think we were... seventy-eight, when she died. We weren't the only sorcerers at court, there were many, the best in the land, gathered together to help Nikaas. One of them was Larien. He was from one of the provincial satrapies. And he was powerful, a formidable Arashi. He had won many battles for Elória; he never made anyone doubt his loyalty. We should have. We should have noticed how he envied Terrays, the natural power she had. He was exactly a century our elder, but Terrays could best him in a duel any day, even when she was only a kit. But Larien could charm a nightadder; everyone thought he was Terrays's greatest admirer. Some Matriarchs even imagined he would propose to her. No one thought anything of the two of them going on a mission together, to scout the territory we had just taken from Jaridan."

Sim fell silent, would not go on. "He killed her?" Shard ventured.

"He murdered her. They had just caught sight of Jaridan forces – kobolds, on the hills. Terrays was standing on a ridge, overlooking the plains, trying to count how many they were. She was just... standing in the open; they were only kobolds, and she was far out of range of their crossbows. Larien... he was standing behind her. And he killed her. I was back at the palace, but I saw everything – twins, we're practically soulbound to each other, we could read each other so easily. I knew the instant she died, I could see through her eyes the moments he stabbed her. But he didn't just kill her, Shard, he.... *destroyed* her. He stole her power, stole her essence."

Shard shivered. To destroy someone, to rend their soul to pieces and suck up their liberated energy for one's own greed – it was a hideous crime, almost unheard of in the New Age. It was the rarest death, the worst, to completely annihilate a victim's essence. He would not endure as a spirit – he would simply *end*. Even during the War, the penalty for destroying a soul: peri, kobold or troglodyte, was one's own destruction.

"And I felt it," Sim went on, his eyes tightly closed against the memory now, as he doubled over at the remembered pain. "I felt her..." he drew his a ragged breath. "There are no words for it. I felt her... felt her very soul being torn apart... I nearly died myself, from the shock of it. For him... to do that to Terrays, whose only crime had been to be too strong...." his voice broke. "I'm sorry," he slowly straightened. "I can't..."

Shard placed his hand over Sim's. "I can't imagine.... It's all right, you don't have to say anything else."

Sim smiled wanly. "She would have liked you, Shard." He reached out to lightly brush away a stray lock of Shard's tousled hair. "A kind heart like yours..." he swiftly removed his hand, returning it to his lap, "was in short supply back then," he finished sadly.

"Larien..." Shard ventured cautiously. "He defected to Jaridan, didn't he? He fought on their side for the rest of the War, until the *yúgure* and the Imperial Rebellion."

"Jaridan's hero. He fought for their Dynast in the first years of the rebellion, until it was clear the Níst house was gaining ground. Then he cut his losses and left. Founded Chalandris Keep and set himself up as an independent satrap, fed his hunger another way."

"And you went to sleep?"

"I couldn't stay in Elória after what had happened: my sister dead, our supposed ally a traitor. I left the court within a year of Terrays's death, as soon as I recovered from the shock enough to travel." He looked up at the stars. "I don't know why I came here, exactly. The feeling of being higher, above the lowlands and the war. The Nahga guild had been obliterated nearly five hundred years earlier, there was nothing left here, everyone ignored the Highlands, for the most part. I don't know... the air..."

"Seems purer up here," Shard nodded. "I know."

"I made my tomb here; it's Terrays's tomb, really. And I went to sleep. It took me a few tries to reach true hibernation, but I couldn't stay awake, remembering how it felt to be torn apart every waking moment. I thought about killing myself... but if what they said about the souls of the destroyed was true, suicide wouldn't find Terrays for me, and then what would be the use? Sleep was the best compromise. When I woke up, about forty – fifty years later, the world was gone. Cimmerian had unleashed the *yúgure* and the entire Denáren valley was a wasteland. The sky was heavy with dust, ash was raining down, and the ground was poisoned. The grasslands up here had only barely survived, and even they were too withered to support anyone. You could see the Devil's Rim from here, the mountains were always aglow, this red haze on the horizon, constantly pouring lava onto the Wastelands and throwing ash into the sky. The few peri I met said they hadn't been able to see the stars since the *yúgure*. Djedethra had already fallen into civil war, and Jaridan was under constant attack from the Tagan barbarians. Eleusyne, Sanskre'e, Andiaen – even your Amaru – all were collapsing into disorder. There was nothing to do but go back to sleep."

"I'd wake up every few hundred years, just to see what was happening. Each time Larien was still alive, just out of my reach. Each time it was easier to sleep – I think I grew addicted to it over time. It can be a wonderful oblivion if you let it. But I swore I'd avenge Terrays's murder, no matter how long I had to sleep. My last time awake was my longest; I was awake for nearly three years, plotting with the Chalandran kobolds. I grew to hate the outside world during those years, but it was worth it, just to see his face again." He smiled bitterly, then sighed in defeat. "I thought I could move on, after I had avenged Terrays. I thought it would... lighten me somehow. But it didn't. The ache stayed. I tried to stay with the kobolds; they were ready to call me brother. But I couldn't. I was... I was just too tired. So I came back here. I've been asleep ever since."

His tale finished, he fell silent, and Shard sat at his feet in equal stillness. "What... what are you going to do now?" he asked after a moment's pause. "Are you going to go back to sleep?"

"I don't know," Sim shook his head. "I'm just so tired."

Shard covered the sorcerer's hand with his own once again. "Stay awake, at least for a little while. The world's a much brighter place since you were last up. You might not find it so painful this time. I think you'd like this world," he timidly ventured.

"If you're any indication of this world," Sim smiled shyly. "I can't say I've ever met anyone like you before. Peri when I was alive... they were so... so tightly closed, all except Terrays," he smiled fondly at the memory. "They would lock everyone out, keep themselves inside their masks. It was the only way you could survive back then. I don't think I've met anyone... as... *open* as you."

"Why don't you stay up, see how the world's changed?" Shard pressed, rising from the grass. "Maybe you could come back to Amaru with me, see the City Mount. Maybe... maybe if you see what we've become now, you might want to be alive again."

Sim nodded thoughtfully. "Maybe..."

It was cold, inside his fortress. He could sense all the minute cracks that let in the chilling drafts. The kobolds might be toiling in scraps of leather by the hot steam vents, but inside Chalandris Keep all he could feel was the cold.

His fists clenched tight as he relived his last moments before the sleep. The rocks, crashing down around him, the grit, the burning of the dust already blinding his eyes. The jeers of the kobolds rising over the deafening roar of the rockslide, as they howled for their former leader's blood. The silent spectre on the ridge, dressed all in white, silently watching his prey fall, not a hint of emotion on his young face.

The Onmyóji had played them all well. He had more of his sister's scheming than he'd ever admit.

A shiver of pain laced through his ribs and he groaned, closing his eyes against the shadows of the keep and the dull orange light of day. It had taken all his strength to transmute his shattered body to pure energy and to seek out his chamber, his receptacle, where he could safely sleep and recover.

They had shattered it, the cunning kobolds. The Onmyóji must have told them about that. His crystal urn, tinted blood-red, had lain in countless shards on the floor of the keep, several pieces crushed underfoot to mere powder. He had been forced to find shelter within the rocks that had crushed his body, to sleep interred in stone, until such time as he had gathered enough strength to rise again.

It had taken four hundred years. Even now he was little more than a walking corpse.

He drew in another deep breath, shivering at the pain that was brought with it. He was constantly coughing, suffocating, the dust of the Denáren air burning his throat and chest. Little wonder the world had given him up for dead.

The world had changed much. Amaru had been nothing more than a ramshackle collective of small keeps, ruled by a mere child. Now it covered the entire west coast of the land, from the arctic plains down to the Southern

Ocean. Now the world thought it could have peace. It thought the days of the warlords were over, that the iron-fisted rule of monsters like Larien could be supplanted by the mewling of women and eunuchs.

He would teach the world the folly of its ways.

A sharp pain at his temples, like cat's claws rending his flesh. He groaned. "Begone, wraith," he snapped. "Leave me be."

You know me better than that, Larien.

"I will not let myself be beaten," he gasped as he felt the fire-knives trace around his ribs. "I am the master. Not the flesh, not the sleep, not the pain. I will have control. I will have life."

Never.

"Silence," he hissed. The silvery laughter continued to ring inside his head as he rocked in his throne, his hand twisted over his ring, rubbing the smooth jewel furiously as if to wear it down. "Stop, stop, stop..." he implored of the empty room.

Larien...

"Larien?"

He spun his chair about furiously, his eyes falling on the short-haired woman who stood at the bottom of the stairs. A raw cry tore from his throat before he caught himself. It was only Darhis.

"What?" he demanded. "Has the Alteri nothing to do but spy on me?"

She carried her long metal staff in her left hand; in her right, she held a little leather bag. Larien's lips curved in a hungry smile. "Ahhh... now you see your worth to me, Alteri."

She edged up the stairs, her face twisted in naked revulsion. "Not quite as handsome as I once was, I'm sure," he sighed as she handed him the bag. "Wrinkled and skeletal, I must seem a corpse to one so young and lively as you. Ahhh..." he held the bag in one hand, loosening its drawstrings. He let a thin stream of sparkling golden power fall to into his open palm. Sighing, he closed his fist over the dust as it shimmered into his skin. He inhaled deeply, feeling his lungs grow stronger as the magic coursed through his veins. "More of this... and a little patience, and you might find me fit company after all, Darhis."

She made little attempt to hide her skepticism. "I hope you realize, Master, that there are some services which cannot be bought, not even from one like me."

He laughed, a dry, crackling utterance. "I have never before needed to *pay* a woman to stand at my side admiringly. I have no intention of starting now."

"Silken..." Darhis murmured. "I have seen the old witches of Alteri try to extend the dying's essence with it. It seldom lasts long."

He could hear the scorn in her voice. "Oh, silken is no substitute for a healer's power, to be sure. But for one recovering from a sleep, the stimulant is an excellent focuser – just the medicine I need to regain my strength."

Larien could see her doubt. She was no fool; no sorcerer needed so much silken as a focusing agent. She doubtlessly thought him an addict. He waved his hand and she left, casting him one last scornful glance. He would not let her judge him – she, a mere Alteri, probably an addict herself. He crushed the bag in his hands, weighing it, as with his heightened senses, he heard her leave.

"Wait..." he decided a moment later. "Darhis," he beckoned. "Come here. You have served me well, Alteri, since Varron recruited you last year. Captured my hellhounds, licked my assassins into shape... why? You care little for the money, that is obvious. I see Morden's eyes widen with lust at the mention of the Treasury. You... hardly seem to notice. You wish little of my power – you have already made it clear you will leave once our mission is completed. Why are you here? What do you crave?"

"The hunt, Master."

"No more?"

"There is no more."

Larien smiled. "An Alteri forever. Why, I wonder, are you not with your tribe, chasing the eternal prey?"

A flicker of bitterness swept across Darhis's face. "I will not speak of my tribe, for they will not speak of me."

Larien nodded. It only confirmed his suspicions. "I know you tire here, Darhis, languishing in your crypt, waiting for reports from your men in Amaru. Now, you and my dear Morden have precious little in common. However, I have always believed the best kobolds function under scrutiny – even half-breeds. How would you like a sojourn at Wyvern's Rest?"

"A wasted while at Chalandris, listening to Varron bait me, or a wasted while at Wyvern's Rest, listening to that hog-man bait me. A difficult choice."

"Perhaps a few of your puppies at your side might change your mind? A few hellhounds on guard may well be what we need to keep our dig site free of Hesperin meddlers. What do you say, Alteri?"

"Puppies in a pit make for a dull afternoon. Would I get a chance to let them stretch their legs?"

"Let's not get ahead of ourselves, my dear. But should the workers lapse in their proper work ethic, perhaps your pets could aid you in... *inspiring* them."

She smiled. "Wyvern's Rest suddenly possesses quite a... captivating quality."

"Then go see the kennelmaster and prepare for your journey." Larien waved her away. Darhis gave him a neat bow and practically skipped down the steps. Larien's smile fell. At least he knew bloodthirsty hellhounds could excite her passion, if he could not count on the usual bribes of wealth and power.

You didn't used to need bribes.

"Quiet," he hissed.

In the past your glance was enough to get any woman you wanted. Now you're nothing more than a joke to a jaded Alteri outcast. She mocks and derides you, when she's not merely disgusted by you.

"Don't you bait me."

How the mighty have fallen. Larien, Satrap of Denár and Chalandris, living off silken dust and focusing crystals, struggling to force a little more magic into your tired frame.

"I won't hear you."

Forced to bribe your motley crew to accept your feeble pretense *of power.*

"I won't hear you! You're nothing."

Poor, poor Larien.

"Silence! I made you all that you are. I am the master. You're nothing but a figment, a wraith, a madness of the sleep. I will not... let... you–" his voice rose in another pained howl as the pain continued, unabated.

8

"Jaridan kobolds," Terrays announced confidently, her feet firmly planted on the uneven ground, the spyglass held up to her eye. She heard Larien's breathing behind her, shallow, nervous. "Relax, Larien," she chuckled confidently. "We're far out of range up here." She lowered the glass to stare deep into the ravine below her boots. They were nearly seventy feet above and a quarter-mile removed from the little brown specks against the barren earth. The Elórians called the land *Maktû Heríadja,* the Blackened Earth. In truth it wasn't blackened, but parched a dull rust-red along a canyon separating the Elórian annexed satrapy of Kholat from the Jaridan Empire's rambling provinces.

"Has this land always been this... dead?"

"Since before my father's time."

"Are you all right, Larien? You sound a little... off, somehow?" She lifted the spyglass to her eye once more, scrutinizing the kobolds shuffling back, their pudgy little hands lifted to shield their eyes from the Bluestar's light, their postures betraying their fear and awe. *Look at them cringe,* Terrays gloated to herself. *They'll go running back to their men on the front lines screaming "Elória, Elória," staining their shorts and weeping like infants.*

"Just thinking of home," Larien replied distantly.

"I know what you mean. I can't wait to see Sim again." She felt Larien's hand on her shoulder, light, almost trembling. *Elória,* she thought dreamily, thinking of the green fields and the crystal spires, and the look of sheer joy mirrored on her brother's face as she raced towards him–

A little gasp, no more, escaped her as a searing pain tore through her chest. She bucked reflexively, a raw moan rising her throat as the blinding agony spread throughout her. Something salty, metallic touched her tongue, and she felt her warm blood trickling from her parted lips. Struggling to move, she bent her head to stare horror-struck at the sight. Larien's hand protruded from her chest, fingers curled inward slightly, as if grasping her very soul. The sunlight struck his ruby ring, a painful starburst. Her thick blood coated his hand, already beginning to smoke as if evaporating from fierce heat. Dark stains began to blossom through her dark tunic, steam boiling from her shirt as well. The burning pain had now spread through her every joint, her every cell. By all rights she ought to be unconscious, or dead, yet she endured, wracked with agony so intense she could barely think.

Several drops of blood dropped to the ground, only to evaporate, leaving dark scorched stains on the rock. Terrays felt as if she was floating, her legs dissolving, boiling away into nothingness. Darkness was edging into her eyes as she lost all feeling below her hips, below her waist, below her ribs. An emptiness loomed before her, yet the pain continued, unabated.

"Larien..." she croaked hoarsely, slowly turning her head to gaze up into his deceptively calm visage. A smug smile touched his face as he withdrew his hand roughly.

The last thing she saw was his calm, arrogant smile, his unreflective stare.

Sim awoke in a panicked sweat. It took him a moment to realize he was not in Elória, not in the midst of a war. He was in his bed, in his tomb, in the Castle Highlands. The year was... 342, by his recollection.

Shard?

Shard was still asleep, lying on the floor on the other side of the firepit, curled up under the fur wrap. His arm was contentedly tucked under his folded pillow, a faint smile on his face. Sim found himself smiling, despite the pain of his nightmare. How rare such a sound sleep was to him, and yet Shard didn't give it a second thought.

Shard's body twitched once, and his eyes snapped open, with almost painful speed. No trace of sleep clouded his eyes; his expression was one of complete alertness.

"Sim?" he asked, blinking in the darkness. "Is everything all right?"

Sim nodded. "I just had a dream, that's all. You?"

"Hm?"

"You just woke up, like you were in shock," Sim gestured.

"It's sunrise," Shard explained. When Sim frowned in bewilderment, Shard grinned proudly. "I always wake up about five minutes before sunrise."

"Not everyday, surely," Sim asked quizzically.

Shard nodded. "Every single day – ever since I can remember. I wake up with a start. Sometimes I go back to sleep. Sometimes I get up and see the sun rise." He grinned again. "What do you want to do?"

Sim frowned, still not entirely understanding. "I don't know."

Shard yawned sleepily. "All right. I'm going back to sleep, then, if you don't mind."

Sim nodded, and Shard smiled again and rolled over, drawing the bearskin with him. Within moments the steady rise and fall of his chest indicated he was fast asleep.

Sim shook his head in wonder. He lay back down, drawing the blankets over his chest as he stared up at the ceiling. He could still hear his sister's voice – or was it his own? – in his head. It would be a long time, he knew, before he could fall asleep again.

The great banquet hall was filled past capacity with Amaru aristocrats and visiting dignitaries from all over the Continent. Servants bearing trays of refreshments struggled through the sea of milling peri, as they awaited the command to take their seats. Already the aroma of the banquet to come was filling the air.

Ceih tal Tora shifted on his feet, scanning the crowd for Arjin. Late, as always, waiting to make a perfect entrance, or perhaps lingering on the other side of the room, attempting to seduce some noble's virgin firstborn and completely neglecting his soulmate. He ran his finger under the edge of his collar, grumbling to himself once again about the shortcomings of formal wear. A furious tiger – his family's crest – was embroidered on the back of his long cape, complementing his simple silk suit. He was a warrior born, far more at ease in the training yard in his loose knight's tunic than in the constricting suit of the court. He could take down a posse of raiders with several clean sweeps of his huge sword. What use did he have at court?

He ran his hand through his puff of chestnut-red hair, scanning the crowd with his cat's eyes. He caught sight of his brother Mindrin, arrayed in sweeping scarlet robes, conversing with their father, Raen. The vultures were already circling – diplomats and ambassadors appearing out of nowhere to curry favor with Sintaka's consort. Ceih smiled: what other gardener was such a spy, his empathic powers allowing him to sense the slightest duplicity in an ambassador's voice? Sharing a nod with Raen, Ceih continued to survey the assemblage, on guard for danger. He could see Alcyon, the Lord Kemuri's father in one corner, his consort Nadami at his side. Conversing with Athyr was the Dynast of Diure, his soulbound concubine on his arm, his political consort at home in the mountains with her own lovers. Light music filled the hall, mingling with the smell of the imminent meal. Galen's mother, Nereid Minyami, sat at her immense tetra-harp, her fingers producing a pleasing silky melody.

The sea of murmuring peri parted like the clouds for Cimmerian and Ceih gasped audibly. Arjin sashayed into view, twirling his swordstick with the maximum of aristocratic arrogance. He was wearing a new scarlet coat, fitted indecently tight, the coat's tails sweeping around his calves, his equally snug tailored trousers emphasizing his long legs. A wide collar about his neck led into the smart cut of the jacket, its fit secured only by an stunning brooch from the Kitsune family jewels.

"Hello Ceih." Arjin joined him, spinning his cane about with one last flourish before smartly tucking it under his arm. Ceih could only stammer a faint greeting, his gold-green eyes wide as moons.

"Ooh," Arjin pouted. "*This* is the appreciation I get! Here I go to *lengths* to dress appropriately for the evening, and my own *ani* can't think of a thing to say." He tossed his long mane of shimmering auburn hair.

"You look...." Ceih could only shake his head.

"Sin incarnate?" Arjin offered hopefully.

Ceih replied with a vigorous nod, his eyes only growing wider. Arjin began to pace about him appraisingly and Ceih straightened his jacket. "How... how do I look?" he ventured.

Arjin gave one last sweeping look down the lines of Ceih's suit and leaned close. "Good enough to eat," he whispered, his lips brushing his ear.

Just then a gong sounded, and Arjin sighed loudly. "Come on," he tugged on Ceih's sleeve, leading him through the slowly dispersing crowd towards their table. The royal family and the important delegates from the other four Pentagram nations were arranged at five tables around the central floor of the banqueting hall. Ambassadors and aristocrats from lesser houses sat at tables set back from the main circle.

After everyone was seated, the gong was struck again, and Celaeno and Kemuri entered from the wings, silently descending to take their seats at the table. The Dynast was dressed in what seemed like dozens of her finest silk gowns. Six handmaidens glided down in her wake: five white-robed girls and Shiori, resplendent in a formal kimono, her dark brown hair arranged atop her head. Everyone rose, and the sound of several thousand shoes against the marble deafened the guests momentarily. As the silence settled again, the Dynast turned, sweeping her hand up to indicate the two doorways opening onto the landing behind her.

The gong was struck once again, a pleasingly mild sound that reverberated through the hall, shifting tones as it grew fainter. From the left side Stargazer stepped out, clad in an elegant blue coat, upon which a dazzling dragon was embroidered in silver thread. His hair was gathered back into an immaculate braid, a bejeweled clasp securing it. Silver-white bangs framed a beautiful heart-shaped face, and whispers ran through the crowd, marveling how like his mother the handsome young heir seemed. He calmly strode out to the center of the landing, carrying a jeweled box in his hands.

Aerin stepped out a moment later, and a faint gasp spread through the assemblage. Her wedding dress was a scarlet red kimono, worn off the shoulder, its neckline precariously low, revealing her long white neck and delicate collarbone. Beneath the scarlet overskirt lay a train of golden silk, and beneath it, an underskirt of the finest white linen. A golden sash wrapped about her waist, securing at her back with a complicated bow. She wore no jewelry save for the gold ring on her little finger, and in contrast to her formal, complicated dress, her short red hair was as charmingly tousled as always.

Stargazer stared in wonder at his bride, struck mute with astonishment. Now two handmaidens had positioned themselves behind Aerin and waited patiently for the ritual to proceed.

Aerin raised an eyebrow. **Are you going to pick your jaw up off the floor anytime soon?** she teased.

Stargazer recovered his wits quickly, and bowed, offering her the jeweled box symbolizing the bride-price. Aerin received the box, bowing just as formally in ritual acceptance. She held the box out at her side and the handmaiden swiftly took it from her.

Aerin held out her hand and Stargazer bowed again, taking her hand and kissing it. He straightened and they stared at each other across the slim void for a long moment, before Aerin stepped forward and slipped her arms around his neck, drawing him down for a deep kiss.

Cheers and applause rose from the assembled guests as the marriage was sealed. Stargazer and Aerin did not part, however, but remained locked in a tender embrace, almost forgetting themselves. At length, one voice rose above the others in cheers, and they reluctantly parted. **Arjin,** they thought in unison, laughing softly.

They turned to the crowd, their hands clasped.

"The Lord Heir Yósha tal Amaru and the Lady Aerin tal Kitsune," Celaeno declared, and the applause renewed itself in congratulations.

"What is this, exactly?" Ceih asked, eyeing the plate before him with skepticism. He almost lost sight of the food itself under the veritable jungle of orchids adorning the plate and the sea of steamed rice.

"Grilled Milandran shimmertrout in spiced cream, my lord," the waiter explained politely as he moved on to the next seated dignitary.

"*Fish,*" Ceih sneered. He continued to inspect the dish suspiciously. "Saddest, whitest little thing to ever leave water. Too many flowers." He prodded at the garnish with a chopstick. Heaving a loud sigh of protest, he fumbled with his chopsticks, struggling to master the finger positioning.

Arjin regarded him curiously out of the corner of his eye as he deftly lifted a piece of fish to his mouth. "Not one word!" Ceih growled under his breath. "Not one bloody word."

Arjin shrugged agreeably, helping himself to a delicate mouthful of rice.

Ceih struggled to bite a piece of fish precariously balanced between his chopsticks, then swallowed with evident misery. He swiftly reached for his wine, downing a generous draught. "Powers, what I wouldn't give for a few hours at the Peregrine," he moaned, sinking onto his elbows. "A nice side of roast howlerboar..."

"You are *such* a barbarian."

"*Dripping* in fat..."

"You think you'd appreciate a little culture now and then," Arjin scoffed, clicking his chopsticks together with a flourish of the hand.

"With a *huge* mug of mead..."

"I swear, Ceih, you must have troglodyte blood in you."

"And a kobold wench on either arm."

Arjin couldn't help but smile wistfully at that. "Mm... you have a point."

"Dessert is coming, right?" Mindrin whispered to Sintaka. "I don't want to fill up on this... *stuff* too early."

"More than enough sweets for you and Emrith both, little bear," she whispered back. "I checked with the chefs myself."

That dress is indecent, Stargazer accused.

So tear it off my back, Aerin shrugged good-naturedly.

I might have to, Stargazer decided thoughtfully a moment later.

"Aww, damn it!" Ceih swore as he dropped his chopsticks again.

Seven courses and countless china plates later, the first of the guests, mostly aging Matriarchs, excused themselves, while others milled in a crowd once again, renewing old acquaintanceships with foreign visitors. Nereid Minyami at the harp was assisted by the assembling orchestra, which soon began the opening chords of the first song. The crowd withdrew towards the edges of the central floor, and Stargazer led Aerin to the center of floor for their first dance together.

"Why don't we have a wedding?" Arjin asked, his arms wrapped about Ceih, his head resting on his shoulder.

"It's hardly necessary, don't you think?"

"Ohhh...." Arjin pouted, disentangling his arms in abject disappointment. "But they look so happy out there. Why can't *we* have a wedding?"

"*Fish,*" Ceih ruled grimly, wrinkling his nose in distaste.

Arjin responded with a quick kiss on Ceih's nose, laughing as a heavy blush spread over Ceih's cheeks.

"Dynast..." Alcyon whispered. "I assume Kemuri has briefed you about the situation in your emerald mines."

"Not now," Celaeno objected in a hushed voice. "We'll have plenty of time for conspiracies and plots tomorrow." She turned back to her son and his soulmate. "Tonight's a night for celebration."

"Look at them," Sintaka breathed, her eyes on the couple. "Thousands of eyes boring into them, just *waiting* for them to miss a step. But they're loving every minute."

"They're in their element," Mindrin confirmed, shaking his head.

The dance ended, and the crowd rose in a thunderous applause for the couple as Aerin and Stargazer bowed to the assembled guests. Almost immediately the band began a new song, and the guests began to pair off and join the couple on the floor.

"One dance with the bride?" Arjin asked, favoring Stargazer with a modest supplicant's bow. They eyed him skeptically before Stargazer nodded his assent and Aerin crossed the floor to join her brother.

"Hands above the waist!" Stargazer called a warning. Shaking his head, he turned to find the Dynast standing before him, a hopeful smile on her face.

"Too old for one last dance with your mother?" she asked. Stargazer smiled warmly, then took her hand and led her to the center of the circle.

Good night? Celaeno asked with a mother's knowing smile.

Stargazer beamed, unable to contain his grin. "The best." He spun Celaeno about the central emblem on the polished mosaic floor.

"You're my dearest Solstice Yósha, you know that don't you?" If Stargazer hadn't known better, he would have sworn she was starting to grow tipsy on the sapphire wine. Confirming his suspicions, Celaeno suddenly stopped dancing, taking his face in her hands. "Sintaka's a hellion and Shard's a deserter," she whispered desperately. "You're Amaru's last hope," she giggled before dropping her head to his shoulder and throwing her arms about him in an unabashedly motherly embrace. "Oh... take care of Aerin, and let her take care of you," she advised him softly. "All my children are leaving me too soon. I'm becoming a fossil."

"No, you're not," Stargazer protested. "You're the Silver Queen, the Empress of Nations." He smiled warmly. "And I'll always be here. Sintaka fancies herself an Alteri T'Jara and Shard wants to fly to the ends of the earth. But I'll always be here. I can hardly imagine a world outside of Amaru. *They* can find the portal between worlds and track down Herasis himself. Give me the observatory and the City Mount" – he blushed – "and my Aerin, and I'll be happy." He looked up at the vaulted ceiling, at the familiar surroundings. "This is my home. I never want to go anywhere else."

"You'll stay behind and protect your aging mother from the terrors of the world?" Celaeno asked hopefully.

Stargazer cast a glance over at Arjin and Ceih, now mock fighting over Aerin, each with a firm grasp on one of the bride's wrists, ready to tear her between them if need be. "I'll protect you from him," Stargazer offered a compromise.

"Oh, you *are* a gallant one," Celaeno laughed, hugging him fiercely anew.

Aerin found herself alone all of a sudden. Her last dancing partner, an amiable man from one of the lower houses of Amaru, had just disappeared, and she was suddenly forgotten. She saw Jaxa across the room, in her shimmering silver-white gown, her arm laced firmly through Galen's as he conversed with his mother and her soulmate Kestrel. Mindrin danced with Sintaka, the two clearly recalling their own wedding by the wistful sparkle in their eyes. Spark raced across the floor, chasing the young heir of Hesperin through the crowd. A breathless, exhausted Nari hid behind his brother's long kimono. Aerin had to smile at the incongruous picture: four-hundred-fifty-year-old Kemuri, silent and graceful in his regal robes, and tiny Nari, short for his five years, resembling nothing so much as hyperactive cricket. Kemuri barely had time to ruffle the boy's silver hair before he bounded off, Spark in hot pursuit.

"Aerin," a voice whispered, and a hand brushed her wrist. Startled, she let out a little gasp as she spun around to confront her soulmate.

"Star," she laughed, an irrepressible smile tugging at her lips.

"Come on, before they remember who the party's for," he said, leading her out through the large double glass doors, into one of the many gardens within the central palace court. Aerin's smile grew at the tranquillity outside, and she stepped further down the tiled path to gaze up past the leaves of the trees. White Moon had already slipped beneath the high walls of the palace, and above them the square of sky was pure unmuted starlight. The large trees rose from the gardens, their trunks and branches ringed with countless tiny white lights, creating a phantom forest of earthly starlight.

"Is it everything you'd hoped?" Stargazer asked from behind her.

"Oh, it's been perfect, Star," she grinned, before her smile turned wry. "Even Arjin is behaving himself." They both flinched on instinct as they heard a loud whoop from within the banqueting hall. "Relatively speaking," she amended a moment later.

"I wanted it perfect for you," he murmured, laying a soft kiss on the nape of her neck.

"How could it not be perfect?" she asked, turning around as he slipped his arms about her.

"What matters to you?" Stargazer asked, growing solemn. "What's your life's mission?"

Aerin was puzzled a moment. She saw it was an earnest question, and gave it the consideration it deserved. "To defend Amaru from its enemies. To honour the Kitsune name and prove myself worthy of becoming a Red Knight. To live life as sinfully as possible." She traced a part in his bangs. "And to – on occasion – define my life solely through my soulmate's happiness. What about you, Yósha?" she asked softly, thoughtfully. "What matters most to you?"

"You," he spoke honestly, and she blushed as red as her hair. "And Mother and Father, and Shard and Sintaka. All of Amaru. Protecting my family and my kingdom... and becoming the best astrologer the land's ever seen. Oh Aerin.... You should be out with Ceih and your mother, running Garthan Raiders through on your swords and treasure hunting for the philosopher's stone. You seem... too *vibrant* to be locked up in my observatory."

"You're hardly dull," Aerin tenderly brushed a stray lock back into his bangs. "And I *hate* to camp outdoors."

"You're sure 'the demon peri bitch from hell' won't mind being a Royal Consort?"

She grinned. "The court's baby? I think I can manage. Just as long as you let me steal you away from the more tedious meetings," she informed him.

"Just as long as you let me beat you now and then at sword practice," he countered.

"Deal," Aerin nodded, stepping back a pace and holding out her hand. Stargazer shook it firmly, then pulled hard, drawing the laughing, stumbling Kitsune heiress back into his arms.

9

Aerin tal Kitsune leapt from the portico, a long wicked hook, over two feet in length, in each hand. Her skirt whipped about her legs as she dropped from above with a fearsome banshee's cry. Stargazer spun about, lifting his sword to take the brunt of the blow, bracing his feet on the stone to absorb the impact. Aerin's hook struck his sword hard, and she spun about, trying to trap his blade between her vicious weapons. Aerin's left hook rattled over the sword blade for a moment, then Stargazer freed himself and advanced upon her, driving her back. She kicked off the ground, holding her hands high above her head. She sailed slowly, leisurely through the air, before she gracefully dropped to the roof.

She stood perched on the tile, her tattered skirt of vivid scarlet blowing about her legs, held about her hips by a belt formed of rich gold ornaments. Her midriff was bared, her breasts covered by a slim strip of dark red silk crisscrossed over her torso and knotted behind her back. Black sleeves that seemed torn from a Matriarch's gown were held at her shoulders and elbows with gold bands, and her wrists were adorned with golden gauntlets and bracelets. Black boots encased her legs to the knees, decked with gold and ornamented with deep blue gemstones. The Bluestar overhead set her hair afire and she looked nothing so much like an avatar berserker as she confidently gazed down on her opponent.

"Come on, Stargazer," Murren tal Kitsune urged as she stood under the portico, watching the combatants. "Forget she's your wife – right now she's trying to kill you."

The young heir ran his hand through his hair, pushing back the disordered locks behind his ears, sweat beading his brow. *Bloody Kitsune!* Between his wife and matemother, he would be dead inside a month. They had been dueling for what seemed like hours under the hot sun, switching weapons at Murren's whim, yet Aerin had barely broken a sweat. Above him, she whistled lightly, twirling the hooks in her hands.

Stargazer tore his tunic over his head, tossing it aside to Aerin's delighted laugh. He rubbed his hands on his trousers, then adjusted his hand on his sword. He raced up against the wall, bounding off the brickwork, and flew up onto the rooftop.

The long thin blade of Stargazer's sword met the curved metal of Aerin's dueling hooks, and they danced about the tiled roofs in a flurry of moves. Aerin leapt back, floating up to the higher step roof, jumping back down before Stargazer had a chance to judge her attack. She flew over his head, alighting on the roof behind him. She whirled the hook high, aiming a blow for his head, and Stargazer parried. He drove her over the edge and Aerin fell backwards, flying through the air. She let her weapons fly, catching herself on her hands, performing two more handsprings to land on her black boots. Stargazer dropped to the ground, ready to resume the battle.

"They're formidable," Athyr ruled as she watched from the balcony above. "The Lord Heir of Amaru and the Heiress of Kitsune, family lines to be reckoned with. Educated by the scribes and bards of the Minyami house, instructed in combat by the best knights of Amaru. They will make excellent Arashi."

"It will be two years until Aerin's of age to be knighted," Celaeno nodded. "Yet already she can best seasoned Arashi warriors."

Aerin had charged Stargazer and leapt for his sword, and the two were locked in a struggle, their hands on each other's weapons, their legs seeking to trip each other. Stargazer broke away and staggered back. They leapt into the air, hanging above the courtyard as they spiraled about, trading blows. Stargazer pushed away, somersaulting in midair to land back on the stone courtyard floor. Aerin dropped down a moment later.

"Swords, dueling hooks, quarterstaffs, spears, fighting clubs... they are exceptional with every weapon," Athyr admired.

"You should see Aerin with her axe," Celaeno smiled.

"A valuable asset to Amaru. Especially if the rumours I hear are true," she added slyly. "We all know the Lady Sintaka, for all her skills in battle, lacks the subtleties of a Dynast."

"You think I will overlook the matriarchy and name Yósha my heir?"

"He does take after you more than Sintaka or little Shard. And with the Lady Aerin as his soulmate – is it rare in this day and age to find a woman who can disarm an opponent in three moves and speaks over thirty different tongues. The rumours are not unfounded, I think."

Celaeno only smiled coyly. "Mere whispers. As a matter of fact, I intend on living forever. Shiori: drinks." Shiori made a subtle gesture to the handmaiden standing just inside the doorway to the palace. The white-robed girl stepped out into the sunlight, carrying a heavy tray of refreshments.

"Thank you, Bria," Celaeno smiled as the peri set the tray down on the table. "Athyr, this is Bria, Shiori's latest project since Tírsa left us to marry Lord Ismene."

"You must be honoured," Athyr replied with a polite but guarded smile. "It's not everyone who becomes one of the Dynast's handmaidens."

"Lady Tora has been patient with me," Bria exchanged a soft smile with Shiori, then bowed, returning to her position just under the archway.

"Here you are, Athyr," Celaeno handed one of the slightly smaller cups to Athyr, and the second to her soulmate. "Aged caprisan nectar." Athyr regarded the nectar curiously, a calm smile forming at the corners of her mouth.

Kemuri felt a cold chill run up his spine. Something wasn't right. He could sense it nearby, a cold darkness, a thick cloud, slowly, sluggishly reaching out from the white walls ringing the courtyard. A murderous intent lurked somewhere in the air.

Below Aerin leapt at Stargazer. He ducked and she slid down his back to land at his feet. She turned around, delivering him a teasing slap with the flat of her hook, and Stargazer spun about indignantly. His leg swung out and he managed to trip her; Aerin dropped her hooks with a cry as she fell onto the hard ground, and Stargazer dropped on top of her, straddling her as he pinned her hands down above her hand. "Hah!" he declared on a ragged breath.

Aerin surged upwards and rolled him under her. He tried to rise but she pushed him back down, pinning his own wrists to the ground. "*Hah!*" she countered triumphantly.

Celaeno indicated for Athyr to taste the nectar and lifted her own, larger goblet to her lips. Kemuri fought for a greater clarity, trying to pinpoint the exact source of the disturbance. A sense of urgency overwhelmed him and he struggled to focus on the churning cloud, far closer than he had originally perceived. It turned the clear pink nectar into a thick mucilaginous poison, spreading a black death throughout the unsuspecting host.

The goblet.

His hand shot out instinctively, closing about Celaeno's wrist just as the gold rim touched her lips. "Celaeno!" he whispered fiercely. She stopped instantly, gazing to at her soulmate. Beneath his wispy platinum bangs his golden eyes glowing fiercely, his pupils now slit, catlike. "The wine's poisoned," he breathed, still locked in his trance. A moment later his eyes reverted back to the normal state and he blinked once, letting out a slow breath of relief.

Celaeno nearly dropped the goblet, then clasped her hands tightly around it, for fear of spilling the poison within it. Athyr, her own glass just at her lips, looked down slowly as the colour drained from her face.

"Shiori," Celaeno whispered as she handed her goblet to her waiting *ani*.

"Mine?" Athyr asked in a tiny voice, the first time either peri had ever seen her flustered. Kemuri stared at it intently.

"No. Nor mine. Only Celaeno's was poisoned."

"Bria!" Shiori snapped, her voice suddenly tight and severe, a great contrast from her usual liquid tones. "Did you pour these yourself?"

"No... no. They were given to me already filled by.... by..." she frowned. "I don't think I know her. But then I've just advanced."

Celaeno rose slowly, her face as pale as Athyr's. "Shiori," she nodded. "Summon Murren. Take Bria with you. There's an assassin in the kitchens somewhere. I want her found."

Shiori nodded business-like, marching over to the girl in the doorway. "You have some lessons to learn, handmaiden," she hissed as she lead the servant away.

"Mother!" Stargazer scrambled up the wall to the balcony, alerted by the wild emotions above. "Are you all right?" Behind him Aerin followed, her puff of flame-red hair peeking over the rim of the parapet.

Celaeno? Kemuri asked. He noticed her hands were shaking slightly, and he covered her hand with his.

As well as can be expected.... Powers, that was too close.

"It was nightadder venom. Colourless, odorless, nearly untraceable. And slow-acting enough for the assassin to flee."

"It wouldn't have killed you for several hours," Athyr nodded, recovering her wits. "The assassin would have more than enough time to flee. Nightadder venom... that's an *Alteri* method."

Stargazer stood high above the courtyard where he had so innocently sparred the day before. The wedding was barely two days past, and already the spectre of death loomed over them. He hid in the high tower, watching the bats flit about the ramparts. It calmed him. He would often be found thus, when something disturbed him.

Yósha? his mother called gently. **Could you join me in my armoury?**

He left the parapet and the winged mammals, smartly striding down the twisting staircase. **Have they found her yet?**

Not yet; don't worry. Murren will. I have the utmost confidence in your matemother.

Stargazer said nothing in reply. His mind was still in too much turmoil. He was glad Shard was gone; he did not want his brother to suffer the same torment of dread anticipation.

His mind drifted back to a memory, a comforting remembrance, which gave him strength in the darker hours.

It was a clear day, he remembered, in the summer month of the Lovers Moon. Only a handful of wispy clouds concealed the starscape above the brightly lit land. Stargazer was eleven, Shard had just turned eight a quarter-turn before. They were playing at the seaside, their mother's retinue abandoned on the beach as the Dynast and her sons waded in the warm water. Just down the coast to the north Stargazer could see the masts of the tall ships anchored in the great city's port.

Shard raced through the gently washing surf in his shortpants, laughing as Celaeno chased him, her long kimono skirts trailing behind her in the ankle-deep water. She sank down on her knees, crawling through the surf, her silver hair floating about her. But Stargazer stood fixed, silently staring out at the tall ships. Their sails were black; their flags flew at half-mast.

"Yósha?" Celaeno sat back on her heels, the front of her dress soaked, her hair clinging to her face in thick wet locks. Shard tried to climb up on her back, then slipped off, splashing back into the water.

"What is it?" she asked, crawling through the soft sand towards her elder son.

"The funeral ships," he murmured.

Celaeno nodded. " Lady Akaiya. Her funeral was yesterday, remember? Everyone from all over Amaru came."

Stargazer nodded solemnly. He turned back to his mother, worry written across his features. "Why do we have to die?" he asked.

She frowned at the question. "Why, we all die, someday. You've been lucky, you haven't lost anyone in your family yet. Half a millennium ago, you might be an orphan by now. But everything dies eventually. Even I will die someday."

"No!" Shard cried, stumbling through the surf towards her. "Mother! You can't die! Not like Lady Akaiya. You're – you're *Mother!*"

Celaeno smiled gently, lifting him in his arms. "But I will, Shard," she murmured tenderly yet firmly. "Death is part of life. It's all a cycle." Shard began to sniffle, tears appearing in his deep violet eyes, and he cast his arms about her, hugging her fiercely. "Oh, Shard, don't cry. I won't die now. Not yet, don't worry." She glanced back at Stargazer to find him staring at her accusingly.

"*Why* is death part of life?" he demanded. When she stared at him, no answer on her lips, he pressed: "Why? Who says we have to stop living?"

"We don't *stop* living, Stargazer. That would be impossible. No, we simply live somewhere else. This earthly life ends, and we ascend there," she pointed to the Well of Stars, "to the stars, to the Overworld. We join the avatars, and Powers, and all the lifeforces of these worlds. Death isn't an end, only a change. You're too little to be afraid of it."

"But why does it have to change?" Shard wept, now shivering with dread, clutching his mother's dress tightly. "I don't want you to go, I don't want you to die!"

Celaeno gave Stargazer a reprimanding look for so upsetting his brother, but Stargazer was unaffected. "Why do we have to die?" he went on. "Why did Lady Akaiya die?"

"She was old; she was ill. Tiryn could only do so much for her. She was tired. She wanted to rest–"

"But she could have kept living," Stargazer continued. "We aren't like dragons, like dogs or catlings. We don't die in the winter because we're too old. Galen – he said peri never died in the Golden Age. They could live three, four, five thousand years, even longer. Some would have lived forever if there hadn't been a war. We could live forever if we wanted to!If there's no war, no plague, nothing a healer can't fix – who can tell us we're too old? You don't get gray hair like a cat or a dog, Mother. You don't grow rot like a tree."

"The Amaru may worship me as an avatar, Stargazer, but I'm a mortal peri, like everyone else. Nothing can last forever. Not even the Golden Age, the Reign of Ten Thousand Years."

"Maybe it could have. Maybe your New Age will."

"You'll have to see to that for me, Stargazer," Celaeno smiled.

"No!" Shard wept. "No, you'll see it. You'll live ten thousand years. You're our mother, you can't die! I won't let you die."

Stargazer stamped his foot in the surf. "Who tells us we have to die? The Powers? Does Oracle come down and kill us herself if we live too long?"

"Yósha! Stop this now! You'll only give Shard nightmares. It's all right, Shard. Don't cry, little one." She rocked her son gently, afraid to wipe his tears and brush seawater in his eyes.

"We don't have to die," Stargazer insisted hotly. "We had to before, because of the war, because of the Dark age, because of the *yúgure.* But that's over now. When do peri die, Mother? When they're six hundred? – Aerin's mother doesn't look old. When they're seven hundred? – Grandfather Alcyon doesn't look old. When they're a thousand? Two thousand? Has anyone stopped fighting long enough to see how long they can live if they want to?" He kicked at the surf, swearing in kobold. "Why does everyone love death? Why does everyone want to fight, want to kill, want to die?"

Celaeno smiled gently. "Oh, come here, Yósha." she gathered him close with her other arm. "I want to see our kingdom grow strong and safe. I want to see peri and kobold live long, peaceful lives. But nothing lasts forever."

"Why? Has anyone tried?" Shard asked. "You say we can do *anything* if we want it badly enough! Why can't you live forever if you want to?"

Stargazer watched her closely for an answer. Shard looked up at her with his wide eyes. At length Celaeno could only smile helplessly. "I don't know, Stargazer. Maybe they did, long ago, in the Golden Age. Kitlings like you and Shard and Sintaka – you were born into peace, you knew nothing but life. I can still remember the Dark Age. The fighting, the hunger, the knowledge that death was always only a step away. We had to accept it; we had no other choice. A kingdom could fall in a night. A war could be waged in an afternoon. Nothing lasted. My mother, your grandmother Aladar; she always said: 'Drink your life down quick and hard, you never know how deep the glass might be.'" Celaeno hesitated, staring out at the sea. "I wonder sometimes... did she drink it down faster than she needed to. I was hardly much older than you, Yósha, when she died. And I asked the same questions. Why? Why did we need to drink our life so quickly? What is this in our blood? Why do we burn out so swiftly? My nurses and my *ani* had no better answers for me than I have for you."

Stargazer looked down at the surf sadly. Shard continued to sniffle, fighting back further tears. "I don't want you to go," he whimpered softly.

"And I don't want to leave you, oh, I don't want to leave you like my mother left me." She hugged them close. "My little boys. I would live forever for you."

"Why can't you?" Stargazer asked, his blue-gray eyes overflowing with the tears he had struggled to hold back.

Celaeno looked up at the sky, at the seagulls flying overhead, white dots against the black starlight sky. She could see the bright glow of the Bluestar to the south. At length she smiled gently. She set the boys back in the surf, lowering her head to gaze at them. "Let's make a pact, then." Stargazer and Shard both stared at her, not understanding, yet with hopeful glimmers in their eyes.

"I will not die," she vowed solemnly. "Ever. I promise you both. I will live forever. And if ever I falter, if ever I grow tired and want to stop, you tell me about today, you tell me about our pact, and I will get up, and I will go on. And you, my boys, you promise me this. Promise me you will grow up strong, strong enough to protect everyone you love. Promise you will always fight against your enemies, against those who would want the old ways, the fighting and the death, against peri who say there are things even we can't do. Promise you will both do all you can to ensure this New Age lasts all long as the Golden Age before it. Longer. Recover the lost secrets of the Old Magic and keep the Aetherworld strong and united. And when someone tells you to stop, to catch your breath, to rest and let someone else shoulder the load, tell them about today. Will you both promise this?"

Stargazer nodded eagerly, holding out his hand. Shard hesitated, unsure of that was being said, of what was being decided, and Stargazer took his hand too, holding it out towards their mother. "It's all right, Shard," he assured his brother.

Celaeno clasped her hand over her son's, holding their little hands tight in her own. She closed her eyes, bowing her head reverently, and they bowed theirs as well. "This we pledge, this we vow with all our beings. Body, heart, and soul," she touched her forehead, her heart, and swept her hand out to seal the vow. Shard and Stargazer pledged themselves in the same manner.

"Body, heart, and soul," they mumbled in hushed awed tones.

Celaeno opened her eyes, and the beginnings of tears shone in them. She held out her arms and her sons rushed into them. She gathered them up close, and she laughed as they fell back in the surf, sending new splashes of sea water into their faces and hair.

"My little Solstice boys," she smiled, gazing into their beaming faces before hugging them close anew. "You're right, Yósha," she whispered, kissing their foreheads. "Why should we stop? We're peri," she vowed intensely, "and we'll never let them stop us."

I remember that day. Again he heard Celaeno's soft voice in his mind. **I've never let myself forget that promise.**

Stargazer entered the Hall of Vigilance, the Dynast's personal armoury. Coiled knots of serpents decorated the marble floor, and lacquered columns held the ceiling high above. On the walls hung axes and daggers, greatswords and dueling hooks, glaives and halberds. Some weapons were ancient ornaments, liable to crumble in actual combat. Others were regularly sharpened in anticipation of a battle to come.

Celaeno stood at the far end of the armoury, her eyes on a large lacquered cabinet sitting on an ornamental table. She had changed from her formal robes into a long blue gown edged with gold. A lounging gown of the late afternoon, worn as if nothing was amiss in the inner court.

"Come here, Stargazer," she beckoned when he hung back. He approached, drawing up alongside her as she kept her eyes on the cabinet. "You know what's in here, don't you?"

Stargazer nodded.

"I wanted to wait until your knighting in the winter. But now is as good a time as any, I think." She opened the doors, revealing a beautiful sword sitting up on its metal rests. She lifted it, turning to face him. It rested inside a scabbard of tightly woven leather, lacquered in countless coats and strengthened with fine metal ribbons laced throughout. Dragons and phoenixes were stitched on the sheath in silver thread.

Celaeno grasped the delicate hilt and withdrew the sword. Its engraved blade hummed as it quivered in the air. "The North Star," she pronounced. "The Amaru ancestral sword, over a thousand years old. When the Amaru people were at their lowest state, starving and terrified, our ancestors wielded this sword and inspired them to rise and fight once more." She stepped back, holding the sword high. "It's light and maneuverable, but its strength's found in its many layers. It was used as the model for all Amaru Arashi swords after it. I carried it when I reclaimed our home, when I liberated our land from the Garthan Raiders." She swung it about in a complex maneuver, her fingers twirling about the handle as if she were a gymnast playing with a baton. She kicked the train of her robe aside as she assumed a defensive posture. She twirled the sword effortlessly about her body as she went through the motions of Arashi sword-drilling, the humming blade becoming an extension of her arm. It was the intricate, flawless dance of an Arashi Master. "Arashi fighting has always being about war, about combat. But our ancestors understood, even in their darkest moments, that it is about art as well." She spun about, her slippered feet lifting off the ground as she spiraled effortlessly into the air. She ascended to touch the very ceiling before she crumpled like a dancer bowing, falling back to the ground. She flipped in midair, her robes whirling, her hair a silver maelstrom, until she came to rest directly in front of her son.

She picked up the scabbard from the table and slipped the North Star back into its sheath. She held it out to Stargazer and he backed away, as if afraid. "No, no," he held his hands up. "It should go to Sintaka. It's her right."

Celaeno shook her head gently. "Not to Sintaka. To you. You have the inborn gift for the dance, the instincts of an Arashi. Sintaka would be the first to agree. Take it." Stargazer tentatively received the sword, sliding the blade midway from its scabbard before hesitantly tucking it back in once more. "Come here whenever you like. Hold it, feel it. Practice your drills with it. It will be yours, someday."

"Am I a fool to dream of such things, Mother? That peri can outlive mountains?" He gazed at her imploringly. "You can tell me now; I'm old enough to take it."

"Never doubt yourself, Stargazer. It's your strength, your protective instinct, your determination. Faith has always been enough to move mountains and break the strongest of despots. What is our magic but our strongest faith? The ancients might have said no peri could fly like the birds, but I've seen you soar over the rooftops. Have faith now." She took the sword from his hands and set it back in its stand. "The North Star will be waiting for you when you need it." He looked down, and she took his chin gently, turning his face back to hers. "We'll fly forever, you and I, you'll see."

The sun had set and the moons had risen without sign of the assassin, the Lady Heiress reflected grimly. Usually assassins were swiftly flushed out by the palace forces. Four hundred years of threats to the Silver Queen had made such searches a practiced routine.

"Sintaka?" Mindrin asked as they slowly paced through the tall, narrow corridors of the lower levels of the palace. To think..." he laughed uncomfortably. "My ancestors were born down here. Who'd have thought a *Tora* would get into the Heiress's bed."

Sintaka mumbled an inaudible reply.

"We should go home," Mindrin put his hand on her shoulder. "Spark's waiting for us. Murren and Mother have checked all these passageways already; I don't think you can help pacing around here."

"I know," Sintaka sighed glumly. "And it's not as if it's anything new. Assassination attempts happen all the time. They've tried to kill Mother, Father, even me and Stargazer now and then. I should get used to it."

"Do you want to go to the old towers? Look at the bats? It always helps Stargazer."

Sintaka shook her head.

"We could go for a walk in the garden. I think I could find you a lantern rose bloom still in season."

"I don't think that'll work."

"Why don't I take you to the kitchen and we'll steal a little dessert?" he suggested, slipping his other arm about her shoulders, leading her down the hallway. "Sugar can fix anything, Sintaka."

"Why not?" she offered with a wan smile. They took a side corridor that branched off from the main hallway. The corridor was poorly lit, and the few glowlamps cast great pools of shadow. A superstitious peri might think he had wandered into a ghost story. The mood was only heightened by the efforts of that anonymous servant who had long ago dubbed the kitchens the Forges of Hell.

"Hey!" Mindrin stumbled over something in the gloom. "Why can't these kobolds keep their bags–"

His voice died off as he looked down. It was not a discarded bag of supplies but a peri, very still and very cold. Her brown curls slipped from her kitchen hat, framing her blanched face.

Sintaka bent down to feel the throat for a pulse. Instead she felt only the chill of death. "Nightadder venom." She pointed to the pronounced blue veins around the mouth and throat. She tugged the collar of the woman's kitchen clothes down to reveal a knot tattoo at the woman's collarbone. She next rolled the peri's left sleeve up, exposing the distended veins at the wrist. Another tattoo was on her arm, its design distinctive.

"Alteri," Sintaka ruled coldly. At her side Mindrin let out a breath of relief.

10

"Maybe this isn't such a good idea," Sim murmured weakly, clutching the handholds at the sides of Shard's saddle while Shard rode in front of him, one hand firmly through the leather thong at the horn of the saddle.

"Come on," Shard laughed. "Don't tell me an Onmyóji sorcerer is afraid of heights."

"It's been a long time since I was last on a dragon–" his words were cut short as Smoke ducked and dove through the air, and Sim tensed, a soft startled yelp escaping him as they fell. "Is this how you treat your elders?" he wailed, his eyes still tightly closed.

He was torturing the poor peri, Shard realized, though he had to admit it was hard at times to remember Sim was an elder. His fierce adoration of the sorcerer had hardly ebbed in the past quarter-turn as they had gotten to know each other better; only now he saw him as less an avatar to venerate but an shy agemate he needed to charm out of his shell.

He commanded Smoke to level her flight and soon they were soaring calmly. Sim was still rigid with discomfort; Shard could feel him at his back, muscles tensed, head bowed. Gradually Shard felt him relax, and at length Sim straightened. "You won't let me fall?" he asked cautiously.

"Smoke's never lost a rider before," Shard called back over the gentle rush of the wind. "Don't worry."

I wish you hadn't said 'before.'

The land below them was rippled with slight rises and soft valleys, peppered with settlements of ancient kobold castles. From their height the mineral domes were no longer randomly scattered landmarks, but part of an intricate web laid out on the moors. Thin wisps of fog and small dark clouds passed beneath Smoke's belly; above them the sky was clear; White Moon was full and bright. Shard closed his eyes, let the wind rush against his face and stir his hair. He need only nudge Smoke downwards slightly and he was freefalling. If he held his arms out, he could forget he needed a dragon to fly.

Don't ride with your eyes closed.

His eyes snapped open. "How could you tell?"

"I could tell." Shard heard the smile in his voice.

They soared over open moorland for a time, and Shard pointed out several landmarks to his gradually relaxing companion. At length Shard spied a path of forest climbing up from the valleys, intruding onto the otherwise sparse Highlands. They set down deep in the forest, in a small clearing guarded by hardwoods and peppered with slim bamboo trees. "We could have dinner here," Shard suggested as Sim staggered off the saddle, stumbling onto the rough ground. He bent over, hanging his head to help the lingering nausea subside.

Sim straightened, looking up at the sky. "Where are we?"

"Somewhere," Shard shrugged. "Don't worry, we can find our way back to your cave. If we can't, Smoke can. She remembers everywhere we go."

Sim looked back, smiling apologetically. "I'm a little nervous. I don't like to be far from... I suppose it *is* home to me. I've always been... 'a little nervous,'" he admitted.

"I thought two-spirits were supposed to have unshakable calm."

"I just affect it," Sim admitted. "I think Terrays got that out of the bargain as well. We're really only one two-spirit split in two."

Shard motioned to Smoke and she stretched, yawning wide to reveal her sharp dagger-like teeth. She shook her head, tousling her mane, then took off, claws digging into the air. Shard gathered some small branches from the surrounding underbrush. He returned to their makeshift campsite, keeping his head bowed over the wood. The elder peri had already set up a small ring of rocks in the center of the clearing, and Shard arranged the wood inside the circle, topping the small pile of sticks with a handful of moss and dried grasses.

FIRE! Shard commanded, and the dried grass lining the kindling burst alight.

"A firestarter," Sim marveled. "I've heard of them, but I've never met one before."

"Just a little trick I have," Shard tossed another thin branch into the growing flames.

"You're a mystery, Shard. You can unlock guardian spells four thousand years old and start fires with your stare. But you carry yourself as if you're nothing more than an ordinary peri."

"I can't do much," Shard shrugged. "My father... he's tried to teach me, you know, a few tricks. How to heighten your mindspeech, your telepathy, how to call a weapon to your hand... how to raise a basic shield... I'm terrible at it."

"You feel you could do more," Sim offered.

"Everyone's been telling me I'm full of magic. So why can't I even levitate a book? And my brother and sister, Arashi knights..."

"You're not giving yourself enough credit, Shard. The power's in you, I can tell. You just need more time to let it grow. You can't expect to be a perfect sorcerer in.... How old are you?"

"Oh," Shard looked down. "I'm..." he shrugged. "I'm only twenty."

He was a terrible liar, and Sim cocked his head to one side skeptically. Shard looked up, his storm-violet eyes dark with frustration. "All right, I'm... I'm eighteen."

Sim continued to eye him questioningly.

"Well, I will be in a few months," Shard amended. "Nine months," he finally admitted in a tiny voice.

Sim couldn't hold back a good-natured chuckle, and Shard shot him a venomous glare. "I wouldn't mind being so young if I thought I'd get taller in a few more years, but I don't think that'll happen either. I feel like I'll explode some days, I'm so frustrated. They tell me to relax, to have more patience... more... *introspection*," he sneered. "What short seventeen-year-old boy has patience?"

Sim rose from the rock across the growing fire and walked around the pit to sit next to Shard on the large decaying log. He slowly removed his gloves, holding his hands over the fire. "It's getting cold for the middle of Fox."

He glanced up at the stars. **'Restlessness is the awakening,'** he quoted. At Shard's bemused expression, he turned back at the boy. "Old Elórian proverb. Terrays hated it." He laid a hand on Shard's shoulder. "I wouldn't call firestarting a very *introspective* piece of magic. Next time you want to explode, go ahead. Don't try to hold it in. You might surprise yourself."

Shard smiled softly, nodding, though he couldn't say he completely understood. Yet there was something about Sim Onmyóji: his calm and quiet ways, his soft voice, that seemed to soothe Shard's most frustrated moods.

"I wonder where Smoke is," Sim mused, looking up at the sky. He then paused, rising from the log. "Something's coming. Can you sense it?"

"No," Shard shook his head, rising as well. "Wait: yes," he breathed as he heard the intruder with his heightened hearing. Something large, cutting through the bamboo, rustling the feathery leaves.

"Tiger, I think," Sim stated, his voice as calm as ever, but possessing that grim edge as when he had spoken of Larien. Shard felt a slight chill as he realized the danger in that tone.

Smoke! he called. **Come!** To Sim he asked: "A tiger wouldn't hurt us... would it? They only hunt the deer and the wild pigs – the – the only tiger I ever saw face to face in the Vastwood barely sniffed me before it left."

"Something's wrong." Sim's eyes were closed now, as he extended his hidden senses. "It's making too much noise. I think it might be wounded... or sick."

Suddenly the noise stopped, then receded. Shard shivered. **Smoke?** he called again, sensing the dragon still some distance away. "Where's the tiger?" he asked. "Did he leave?"

Sim let out a slow breath. "Maybe..." He began to turn back towards to Shard.

The brush exploded in a flurry of orange and white. An immense maned tiger, nearly twice the size of its southern kin, flew from the bamboo, limbs outstretched, claws bared. Shard froze in terror while Sim swiftly dropped to one knee.

Sim bowed his head, his eyes closed in concentration. He gathered his arms close to his chest. A golden energy wind shimmered about him, swelling and gathering strength.

"Sim!" Shard shouted as the tiger reached the kneeling sorcerer, fangs gleaming in the moonlight.

Sim's spread his arms out as a conduit for the fierce energy as the tiger towered over him. The magic lanced out, striking the tiger straight in the head, knocking it back. Shard gasped as the golden energy expanded to form a wide dome over the sorcerer. The shield shimmered for a moment, then dissipated.

The tiger lay on its side, its hind legs twitching in one final spasm. With the softest exhalation, the tiger fell still.

Sim sat back on his heels, letting his arms fall slack at his sides. "What was *that?*" Shard gasped, rushing to his side.

Sim looked up, his eyes clouded with exertion. "Blastshield," he breathed. He rose with effort, inspecting the dead cat. It was old, its pelt dulled, its furry ruff shot throughout with white. One paw seemed vaguely deformed. "Poor thing," he stroked the tiger's mane. "He's old – nearly forty, I'd guess. Came down from the mountains early – usually you don't see them until Sphinx Moon. Just as well we got him," he mourned. "Never would have survived the winter."

Shard continued to stare wide-eyed. "I've never seen shielding like *that* before!"

"It's... a very old spell. Powerful. Anyone can cast a shield for a moment or two. But it takes a trained sorcerer to cast one of these." Sim laughed weakly. "I'm... a little out of practice."

Shard stood silent, marveling at the power he had just witnessed unleashed. A maned tiger of that size usually required a full hunting party of kobolds on horseback to bring it down. Sim had done it with one powerful blast. A spell which could defend and attack at once – a prized talent. Shard understood, for a fleeting moment, the extent of the power wielded during the Great War. Countless sorcerers, trained in devastating spells even more powerful than Sim's blastshield, had laid waste to the entire continent.

Shard turned his gaze from the emaciated tiger to the Onmyóji sorcerer. How innocent he seemed, his hair tousled from the energy wind, his cheeks flushed with exertion and embarrassment at the extent of his spell. Yet once again Shard saw a glimmer of the ancient soul behind such a deceptive mask, and the power behind such disarming green eyes.

L'al Darhis scowled at the dirty kobolds in their sweat-drenched rags. They had been working themselves to death, and yet had uncovered nothing but false chambers littered with trinkets and trick walls. The rough walls of the hollowed-out room dripped with the remnants of the burrower slug's acidic saliva. The pungent smell hung thick in the air, as slaves carved out the now-weakened rock with their crude tools. Still the work progressed too slowly – Morden was using immature burrowers, and his kobold slaves were tired and weak, incapable of the demands Larien placed upon them.

Darhis hated the dust and claustrophobia of the diggers' mines – her Alteri nature longed for open skies and the rich smell of the deep forest. In the excavation shafts the sulphur fumes lingered and the walls themselves seemed to constrict about her. Hundreds of yards behind her the tunnel opened onto a barren ledge, the rust-orange clouds shrouding the wastelands in eternal gloom. It raised her hackles; she felt like a penned wolf. People *died* when she was this frustrated, she hissed to herself as she wrung her hands nervously.

"I didn't know Alteri had such frayed nerves." The hog-man was examining a set of maps rolled out before him on a low wood table, comparing them to various yellow parchments scrolls written in several old tongues.

"What's this," she picked up a piece of parchment and inspecting it. A diagram displaying a central rune with four glyphs at the four cardinal points lay on the frayed scroll.

"Ravanor." He pointed to the central rune. "His warlord Harbath," he indicated the north rune, "his warlord Lothgar," the south rune, "his son Parthaxan," the east rune, "and his mateson Habradar," the west rune. "There are four subsidiary tombs built around Ravanor's."

"I thought the Treasury was entered by the south end?" Darhis demanded, perching on the edge of the table. "Here," she lifted up a decaying scroll. "'Ye fools who crawl from the west and die with the setting sun, churls who rise with the Bluestar and never live to see noon: know now only by seeking the zenith shall you be enlightened.' The south. We should be on the other side of the peak."

Morden shot her a sharp glare that told her exactly what he thought of her opinion. "Yes, long-legs, by all means. Let's go in through the *south* end. Let's *find* the tomb seal, somewhere on the face of this forsaken rock. Let's find it, break it, and amble right into Ravanor's death traps. You can meet an ancestor or two down there, or whatever's left of them." He snatched the map away. "Ravanor set countless pitfalls, sinkholes, cave-ins, and all manners of inventive *death* for anyone trying to raid his Treasury. When he died they left more than enough workers to keep those death traps company, but they needed someone alive to seal the tomb up. Not out the main door: that's for the tomb robbers. This way. Upwards and northward, through their secret escape shaft. Peri – they love their pretty buildings and their expensive tombs, but they leave all the thinking to their squat-legged slaves. How you ended up the dominant species, I'll never know."

Darhis sneered, idly tangling a length of cord about her fingers. "What kind of traps?" she asked at length.

Morden chuckled, leaning across the table. "Oh... trap doors, sunken pits, falling rocks, swinging blades. Vats of boiling oil, kept afire under intense pressure, only to be triggered by unsuspecting tomb robbers." He leaned further on his hands, a lascivious smile on his thick lips. "Mechanical vipers, tripped by movement on stones, shooting blinding venom into the raider's sightline." He hovered an inch before her face, his intent gleaming in his eyes.

Darhis yawned. "You're too fat, Morden." She pushed him aside, and the kobold fell off balance, slamming his jaw on the table. The slaves laughed, and the large slavemaster shouted his displeasure, tearing one digger out of the line and cuffing him sharply on the head before shoving him to the ground.

A shivering kobold girl approached, dressed in the tattered robe of the camp servants. Her black hair was dulled by dust and bluntly cut at a practical chin-length. "Hey! Careful with that!" Morden shouted as the girl stumbled, nearly spilling the two mugs of mead. "That brew's worth more than you are! Here," he swept the two mugs from the tray, handing one to Darhis. "Drink – to the great Morden Mantalore – champion among tomb raiders!" Darhis wrinkled her nose at the pungent brew as the slave girl dusted the table with her grimy rag. Morden caught her wrist and forced her to turn out her pockets. "Slaves, can't be trusted," he sneered, letting her retreat. He downed his drink with one swift gulp. "So..." he leaned closer, flirtatious once more as the alcohol began to dull his senses. "Is it true the Alteri castrate their men to keep them nice and docile?"

Darhis rolled her eyes; yet another lecher spellbound by whispered rumours and female-domination fantasies. "Only the fat ones," she pronounced disdainfully. She yawned again as Morden joined the slavemasters in bullying the emaciated diggers. Nursing her own mug, she hiked up the sharply angled corridor. Coughing as her footsteps stirred up renewed dust, she shaded her eyes as she exited into the sudden light of the wastelands. Even the shaded sunlight seemed bright compared to the darkness of the cave. Below her a ragged set of bound ladders led to descending ledges and the main dig crews on the north col. To the west she might see the farthest settlements of the Hesperin kobold, if she lifted the spyglass to her eye. Straight before her, to the north, the Boundary Hills continued, dozens upon dozens of perfectly identical mountain peaks surrounding them.

She glanced to her side and saw the pretty kobold slave leaning against the rock, hesitant to climb back down to the valley. The girl immediately cowered in dread, holding her wooden tray before her as a shield. Darhis slowly ran her eyes up and down the slave, appraisingly.

"What is your name?" Darhis asked in a low voice.

"Ci- Ciilet," the girl stammered, blinking in apprehension.

A predatory smile touched Darhis's lips as she tossed her mug of mead over the cliffside, then advanced on the slave girl.

Smoke lay dozing in a thicket of long sweetgrass, now ripened to a soft gold. Shard had helped Sim scale the large castle egg and they sat on the top of the dome, gazing out over the western horizon. They could clearly see the divide as the moors of the Highlands descending sharply into the forest-carpeting of the Vastwood.

"I wish I could tell you more about the court at Elória," Sim apologized. "I can hardly remember more than a handful of faces. Court was Terrays's pet. She could manipulate the strongest of ambassadors and hold diplomats in the palm of her hand. All my faults were her strengths, all her aversions were my skills. We were only ever complete when we were together, and then... then no one could stop us." He reflected on that thought for a moment. " But everyone knew she was the one who'd go far in the world. I was the paler twin. I'd make a great scholar, a perfect counselor, but Terrays, she was a history-shaper. If she had only lived long enough, your books would be singing of her, not of Larien or Cimmerian."

"I wish I could have met her."

"You'd have loved her. Everyone loved her. You'd think I would have been jealous, but I was happy to be the less noticed one. Terrays was meant for something... something special. She wasn't supposed to die. She was supposed to live on, to have her own satrapy, to be a powerful sorcerer, to be soulbound to a perfect man," he chuckled a little bitterly at that. "A better man than I could ever find."

Shard frowned in confusion at his speech, looking at him quizzically until Sim gave him a little smile. "Oh...." He found his face growing warm, and the reaction puzzled him; of course Sim preferred men – he was a two-spirit, after all. Shard had not grown up *so* innocent.

"Yeah," Sim nodded, blushing. "No... I was always happy to hide in the shadows. It was simpler that way." He looked down at his gloved hands in his laps a moment. "There was someone... once. Daethin Imi. He was a cleric, a bit of sorcerer himself. He and I..." he looked back at Shard and blushed again. "We weren't soulmates... we never thought we would be. But he was good to me." He sighed bittersweetly at the memory. "He died. In the war. Everyone died sooner or later. After Daethin, I never wanted to get close to anyone, not even as friends... because I was afraid that they'd die too. And after Terrays... I just couldn't reach out to anyone. It was too painful, too hard. The fear... of losing anyone else." He hung his head sadly.

"It's all right," Shard offered gently. "I understand."

"After the war, during the Dark Age... everyone was like that. I had almost forgotten there could be peri out there who still *cared* about anything beyond staying alive and settling old scores." He turned back to Shard. "It's... confusing, suddenly caring about getting out of bed in the morning. I wonder why I don't want to go back to sleep – it's easier, really, that way. I feel.... It's almost like hope," he marveled. "I never thought I'd feel that again."

Shard touched his shoulder. "I was... thinking of going back to Amaru, in a day or two. The equinox is coming soon, and Aerin and Stargazer are probably going to celebrate with the kobolds. I know they'd want me there for their kobold wedding, if not for their royal wedding." He halted, unable to find the right words. "You'd like Amaru," he finished weakly.

Sim looked out at the Bluestar beginning to sink towards the western horizon and nodded once. "I think I would."

"Master?" Varron inquired as he stepped into the darkened chamber. He saw Larien's shadowed form, swathed in several heavy cloaks, sunk in a deep chair, his eyes on the glowing embers in the fireplace. The heavy odour of silken dust hung in the air. Varron cast a swift eye to the made bed in the corner, and the untouched food he had set on the desk the night before. Did Larien ever eat or sleep anymore?

"Jilah is dead," Larien stated firmly. Varron noticed his voice carried a certain strength to it now, a deeper pitch than the dull rasp of the previous months. "Darhis should have chosen better. Jilah was too weak. She killed herself when the first plan failed rather than stepping back and planning anew."

"A coward's tactic," Varron agreed. "But Darhis has one man in the palace yet. Perhaps he will succeed where the girl failed."

"In an ideal situation, perhaps. But events are moving faster than I had anticipated. Jilah has been dead three days now, and her companion has done nothing. Celaeno lives still, and unless a distraction is swiftly arranged, Amaru and Hesperin both will continue to interfere with our plans in the Boundary Hills. I want you to go to Amaru, Varron. Tomorrow. I don't want to worry about a rogue Alteri interfering with our agenda. Deal with Darhis's man. Finish the job yourself."

11

The world had changed much, Sim Onmyóji reflected. When he had last been awake, Amaru was known as a "plucky" nation state. He had been astounded to see the large map adorning the library wall; Amaru effectively controlled half the civilized world. The woman he had before known only as Shard's mother was the Empress of Nations, who controlled vast expanses of satrapies and provinces, and who could influence the course of kingdoms with a mere raise of an eyebrow. Her court was peopled with magicians and dreamseers and healers and all manner of diviners. Her armies were ranks of peri and kobolds enough to give even Elória pause. Even the quiet manner of her Royal Consort couldn't conceal the power he held in his golden lion-eyes. Yet she carried herself with a peaceful, benevolent presence that could melt the hardest of hearts. She had only to touch his face lightly and smile her heartbreaking smile, wishing him all of Amaru's honors in her sweet voice, and the Onmyóji was lost in love.

During their audience, as the ageless sorcerer had been reduced to an adoring child, Shard had merely stood to the side, wrestling amicably with his brother, beaming with simple joy to be home again.

Shard introduced him to everyone, from a taciturn healer to a silver-haired heiress dressed in rumpled robes. He met Stargazer, Shard's astrologer brother, and he marveled at the temperate, nurturing energies that flowed from the young man, so similar in tone to the Dynast's. Sim smiled politely when presented to Stargazer's young wife Aerin, only to stare in complete incredulity when she introduced herself in the Old Tongue of the Golden Age.

"*Shiralli djoroli toratal i'ima fuulariis Onmyóji szintsi aoru sanda melórin údlaon tesif al'ven Aeoren tal Kitsune ryui siornajsen*," she smiled, then asked in nervous Common Tongue if her pronunciation was accurate. Shard and Stargazer only grinned when Sim gaped in astonishment and Aerin nearly skipped with glee at the Onmyóji's reaction.

Who was this strange boy who had unknowingly given him life anew? This peri who professed to be nothing important, yet who was the son of the most powerful woman in the known Aetherworld and her formidable dreamseer.

He almost wished himself back into his crypt in the Castle Highlands, so overwhelming, so painfully alive was Amaru. Yet the young Amaru heir had a powerful hold over him, keeping him captive when he wished to flee, forcing him to confront so terrifying an experience as living.

The eternal revel at the Peregrine was already in full swing by the time the party from Amaru reached Wayside. The long tunnel bored into the side of Bearcreek Mountain was aglow with rich torchlight, filled with the music and shouts from below. The intoxicating aura of abandon permeated the air, beckoning them towards the orange glow of the firelight.

Music assaulted their ears and aromas of all manners of exotic foods flooded their senses. A step down a small flight of wide stairs and they stood in the mezzanine, overlooking the floor of the tavern. A ram-horned troglodyte stood guard at the doorway, ensuring that all patrons, humble miner and royal lord alike, left their weapons behind.

Ceih and Arjin grudgingly handed over their weapons, arguing with the guardian as the rest of the party hurried down the stairs towards the bar counter. The tavern floor stretched from one end of the huge cavern to the other, clustered with benches and tables, open spaces already filled with kobold couples. Garlands and ornaments celebrating the autumnal equinox were strung from the balconies, and kobolds in carved wooden masks danced to the hypnotic music. A carved wood statue stood guard in one corner, depicting the graceful alien figure of Myrddin, the personification of White Moon, and chief avatar of the kobolds. Behind him stood the statue of his consort, the Hidden One, the woman's face concealed behind a long veil. At the feet of the avatars lay harvest and metalwork offerings to honour the deity and celebrate the beginning of fall.

An entire howlerboar slowly turned over the roaring fire, joined by a veritable aviary of pheasants and three-feathers. Kobold wenches in revealing peasant dresses circulated throughout the crowd, serving drinks and flirting with their customers. Rickety staircases led to the upper balconies, for those desiring a greater privacy and some comforting shadows.

"Aerin!" Taki called as the young peri skipped down the staircase. "Or should I say Your Highness? Arjin, Ceih, get down here! Mnemsyara!" he laughed as Jaxa hurried down the steps, Galen in tow. "How's the Serpent today? We're going to have a full house tonight, by the looks of it. But I told Garrowar up there to close the door early. The Peregrine is yours tonight. Tess!" he called. "We're having a wedding tonight! I want as much of our second-cheapest swill as these long-legs can drink!"

The petite brunette nodded, skipping to the barrels of mead, opening the taps to fill the mugs. "Come on, snap to it," Taki urged his other workers. "A pitcher of caramel-malt for the priestess. Get out the sugarcakes and the chocolates for Mindrin. And save the best of the howlerboar for Ceih and Arjin."

Taki was a charming young kobold endowed with stunning beauty and brilliant golden hair – a rarity among the dark-haired kobolds. He stood taller than his kinsmen, matching Aerin's height to stand a few inches below Shard. An influential figure in the town of Wayside, despite his young age of fifty-three – still a child by kobold reckoning – it was rumoured he had a satrap's worth of gold in his hoardholes from the Peregrine's profits, and had heard more than his share of secrets from the tavern's shady clientele.

"Any new gossip?" Aerin giggled, leaning over the counter conspiratorially.

"Nothing you haven't heard already," Taki leaned into their conversation. "I hear there are feral diggers up in the Boundary Hills, looting the Dynast's emerald mines. Some say they're old kobolds nationalists who've never gotten over once being under Amaru's control. Some say they are the remnants of Larien's slave packs. But they aren't after the emeralds; they're looking for the Treasury. And from what I've heard from the Hesperin guildsmen who pass through here, they're willing to wage war for it."

"The same old story," Stargazer hung his head in despair. "How many wars were started over the Treasury?"

Taki raised an eyebrow, and Aerin stepped in. "My Lord Yósha's been indulging in more depression than is good for him. It's not nearly as bad as that. When has Hesperin ever been sure what's happening beyond their outposts? Larien's slave packs couldn't find their own heads if they lost them, and kobold nationalists? – Please! It wasn't the kobolds that started the Schism that broke Hesperin from Amaru. Isn't that right, Taki?"

The bartender nodded in confirmation. "See? You worry too much, Star." Aerin continued. "Your father and his parents will take care of it, and if they don't, your mother will."

"It might be connected to the assassination attempt–" Stargazer began, but Aerin cut him off. "Lots of people hire Alteri mercenaries. You always assume the worst, Star; you have to learn to relax more." She slid closer to him, wrapping her arms about his neck, bringing her face up to his. "*Relax,*" she purred, covering his lips with her own when he opened his mouth to protest.

Arjin and Ceih offered loud hoots of approval for Aerin's methods, and Sintaka slapped her brother on the back as Aerin left him reeling. "She's right; it's your wedding tonight; we can always worry tomorrow." She leapt up on a barstool. "Hey!" she called out to the band. "Pick up the pace a little, would you? This isn't a funeral!"

The kobolds laughed, and instantly complied; a louder, fastpaced harmony filled the room, set to a frantic beat on all manner of percussion and accompanied by the enthusiastic flutists. Sintaka dropped from the stool into Mindrin's waiting arms and the crimson-haired peri swung his soulmate out onto the dancefloor.

Shard laughed at the sight. He glanced back to see Sim shifting uncertainly from one foot to the next, scanning the crowd with an wary eye. The Onmyóji had traded his long kimono for a long, close-fitting coat and trousers, edged with fine gold embroidery. Just as blindlingly white as the sorcerer's robes and just as out of place in the wild revelry of the Peregrine.

Shard gestured encouragingly as Sim nervously approached the bar counter, easing himself onto a stool. "Now… how do we expect to get back to Amaru once we're all drunk?"

Ceih clapped him firmly on the back. "We're not going to go back tonight!" He gave Sim's hair a playful tousle, then leaned in front of him on the barcounter, giving him a heated look. "Why do you think they call this an inn?"

Arjin leaned in on Sim's other side, smirking wickedly. "What – you want us to spend all evening getting into this... *mood* and then waste it trying to get home?" He leaned closer across the bar, an intent gleam in his narrowed eyes, and brushed by Sim's face, almost as if to kiss him. "Silly."

"So!" Ceih cornered Sim on the opposite side. "You're a two-spirit, are you?"

Before Sim could reply, Arjin was back. "So, you basically... started with a girl's soul but somehow... ended up born a boy?" He leaned closer. "That's so *hot!*" he murmured, his lips a fraction from Sim's, before he pulled away abruptly and raced off onto the dancefloor, Ceih in hot pursuit.

"Don't mind them," Shard chuckled, sitting down next to Sim. "They just like to warp the newcomers before anyone beats them to it."

Sim cast a wistful glance at the two knights. "They do have... a magnetism," he reflected.

Shard laughed again. "You're too easy. You should see them go to work on a challenge. I've seen them turn the roughest, toughest, most skirt-chasing knight into paste with a few of their *looks*. But don't worry, get a few pints in them and they'll forget everything but each other. So, what do you think of this place?" Shard asked. Ceih and Arjin's advances aside, the Onmyóji seemed speechless with awe, his eyes wide as he struggled to absorb the sensory overload, naked joy written across his features.

"I can't remember when I was ever in a place quite like this," Sim marveled, scanning the room. In one corner a pair of Alteri women surveyed the partygoers as potential prey; in another a heavily-armed bounty hunter flirted with the scantily clad dancing girls. A trio of gentlemen salamanders kept to the shadows, their reptilian claws wrapped about their water-pipes, their long tails twitching in tune with the music. Troglodytes gambled over copper coins and gremlins messily devoured their plates of mash.

"I never thought things could change this much. That kobold and peri could mingle without any resentment or bitterness for the countless wars. Or that... there could be so much... so much joy." He looked over at Sintaka and Mindrin. "A Lady Heiress marries a man of servant class, even if aristocratic servant class, and no one even blinks. A girl like Aerin is free to think of nothing but the joy of the moment." He laughed. "Knights like Ceih and Arjin... well, we *never* had anyone like them before." He turned back to Shard, his gaze intense. "I don't want to go back to sleep. I want to see more of this world. I want to know how it became like this."

Shard smiled broadly, making no effort to conceal his delight. "I was hoping you'd say that."

Varron tightened the glove on his hand. Deadly and beautiful at once, it was an intricate pattern of thin metal plating and supple leather. Each finger was capped with a little metal claw, dipped in devilsblood poison. He gazed down scornfully at the body of the royal guard, his helm removed, his face pale in death. No more mistakes from Darhis's Alteri geldings. This time he would succeed.

He felt the symbiote tighten its coils in anticipation, and a rush of endorphins raced through his blood, making him catch his breath. He moaned softly, shaking his head to overcome the dizzying intoxicating fog of surging strength and building confidence. The symbiote not only connected his mind to Larien, it endowed him with endurance and strength, physical and mental alike, beyond that of ordinary peri. It was the only thing which had saved him during those four centuries in the mines. The symbiote and his rage.

He looked up at the high towers and spires of the palace, ringed with sapphire and emerald tiling, glowing from within in the darkness of night. *So, some little girl-sovereign think she will take the world from the powerful, does she?* Varron growled inwardly. *Enjoy yourself, pretty, and have your last thrill under that cursed dreamseer of yours. I don't plan on being discarded so easily by your new world order.*

"And then.... then they actually *dragged* the ambassador, out onto the dance floor. Mother looked ready to pass out from embarrassment. Sintaka didn't mind – she and Mindrin were in hysterics." Shard laughed. "I wish I had been there to see it."

He paced along the wall, his hands extended at his sides for balance. Below him Sim walked in silence, the multi-tails of his coat brushing against his legs, the same unflappable presence about him. Yet there was a subtle change in his bearing now; a timid smile would grace his face on occasion, and when he averted in eyes it was more in quiet amusement than in sadness. Only two days in Amaru and already Shard could see him slowly emerging from his shell. By the end of the festivities at the Peregrine, Sim was noticeably fascinated by the new world he had encountered. By the next afternoon when the others limped out of their snug kobold dens mortally hung-over, the party's after-effects had the opposite reaction on the two-spirit. While Ceih and Arjin leaned against each other for support, Sim was eager to return to Amaru, hungry for more discovery. By that night the initial exhilaration still had not faded. Sim bore it modestly, hiding behind a downcast gaze and a shy smile, but Shard could see it in his eyes. He was slowly waking up.

Shard followed him everywhere, relentless. He loved to see the look of delight on Sim's face each time he discovered a new experience. He had guided the two-spirit through the fish ponds and hanging gardens of the inner courtyard; he had showed him the armouries and the museums, the menagerie and the library. He had proudly led Sim up the treacherous path to his room in the clock tower. He had even charmed him to step one foot onto the clock, before the Onmyóji's fear of heights won out, and Sim ducked back into Shard's room.

"That sounds like Ceih and Arjin," Sim remarked.

"Ohh, get the swing music playing and they come alive; then no one's safe. They like you, you know," he added.

"I never would have guessed," Sim smiled wryly. His expression softened, grew wistful. "I liked *them,*" he confessed in a quiet voice, blushing profusely a moment later. "What have you done to me, Shard? I never thought I'd ever leave my jar, my cave, my patch of the Highlands. I didn't want to! Now... now I'm mingling with lords and drinking in taverns and flirting with knights, and even *thinking* about...."

"Most people do," Shard remarked dryly.

"Ohh, if Terrays could only see me," he buried his face in his hands.

"Why are you apologizing?" Shard asked, dropping down from the rock wall. "Why are you afraid of living again?"

"If you only knew... how long. I was used to it. I liked it. It was everything I knew, everything I was. I never thought about ever having anything else. There was nothing else. And within the span of one half-turn, I'm suddenly living again." He hung his head. "Death can be comforting if you let it be," he admitted, ashamed. "It can be preferable."

"Don't say that," Shard took the sleeve of his coat. "You told me you wanted to see more, to learn what happened to the world while you slept. Don't turn back now."

Sim looked up. "Why do you care so much? How can you have so much... *life* in you?"

"I... I don't know," he shrugged. "I don't want to sit still. I always want to move. I want to see what's over the next mountain, and I want to see how different the world looks from atop a taller roof, a higher spire. I can't even stand still long enough to learn any magic, how pathetic is that? I only know I want... I want to run, I want to fly. I feel so restless, like I'm drugged, like I'm floating." He grinned. "And I never want to stop."

Sim smiled tenderly. "You *are* one of those shards they sing about, come down to earth to give us back what we lost." He reached up, a gloved finger lightly tracing a contour down Shard's cheek. "I swear, I wouldn't be surprised if *you* turn out to be the avatar among us. And don't tell me you're nothing special," he insisted when Shard glanced away, embarrassed. "I'd still be dead if it weren't for you."

"I just let you out of your jar." Shard averted his eyes, but Sim gently lifted his face until their eyes met again.

"You did a lot more than that. Trust me."

Kemuri dozed lightly, just on the edge of consciousness. He was vaguely aware of his surroundings, of the stillness and safety of the bedroom, of Celaeno deepin slumber beside him. For a moment he extended his awareness, exploring the room with all the senses of a dreamseer, almost waking as he felt Celaeno's soft breath against his neck. Then he slipped towards a deeper sleep, lulled into dreams by the mild aura in the darkened room and his soulmate's reassuring presence. Her fingers twined about a lock of his hair in her sleep and she snuggled closer, a long sigh escaping her lips as she stirred momentarily in dreamsleep. Kemuri unconsciously tightened his arm about her in a protective urge.

He slept deeply, for a few hours or only a few moments, before the darkness appeared, flickering like a black flame at the corner of his mind's eyes. Approaching slowly, stealthily, it drew closer to the sleeping couple, spreading its poison through the charged air. Kemuri watched, still not entirely aware, as the black tendril extended towards them. The dreamseer felt a dark wind run over his spine, and the dream haze dissolved suddenly.

"Celaeno!" he cried out, waking up instantly. A black shadow loomed over his mate, an arm already descending as her own eyes snapped open. A flash of metal glinted in the twilight.

Kemuri's reaction was pure instinct. A shockwave instantly materialized, knocking the assassin backward as Celaeno screamed in fright. The metal claws came down; they missed her vulnerable throat, scratching across her shoulder instead, leaving four lines that immediately drew blood.

The stumbling man was hardly affected by the shockwave. He raised his arm, a spring-loaded gauntlet propelling a knife at the Dynast and her consort. Kemuri raised his hands before him and an invisible shield snapped up, deflecting the knife mere inches from his face.

Celaeno writhed on the bed, her hand clutching her wound, her face twisted in fear and agonizing pain. "*Guards!*" she howled. Kemuri unleashed a second, more powerful shockwave, and golden energy shimmered in the room as the man was thrown back against the far wall. The force of such an attack should have killed him, or at least incapacitated him, but amazingly the man rose.

The doors crashed open as four blue-robed guards rushed inside, their wrist bolt-bows already aimed at the man. Four lethal metal darts flew through the darkness as the assassin leapt out the open window, disappearing into the night.

"Celaeno!" Shiori appeared in her white nightgown, carrying a robe to cover the Dynast, who shivered in the cool air. Raen hovered in the doorway, watching the proceedings with worried eyes.

"Get Tiryn," Kemuri whispered harshly. "She's been poisoned." Celaeno continued to shudder, her hand held tightly over her bleeding wound, tears streaming from her tightly closed eyes.

"Find him... *find him!*" she shouted, her voice raw with pain.

Stargazer sat bolt upright in bed, as if physically struck. Aerin awoke in an instant, rising at his side. "What's wrong?" she demanded, sensing the tension in his limbs, seeing clearly, even in the dim light, his horror-struck expression.

"Mother!" he gasped, cold sweat already dotting his brow. He threw the covers aside, peeling off his nightshirt as he stumbled to the chair where his clothes were draped. Aerin sat up taller in bed, holding the blanket against the thin *rishti* gauze of her nightrail as she watched him hurriedly dress. A moment later Aerin heard the sirens begin in the courtyard far below their tower apartments. She lowered her eyes sadly; she knew the grim routine all too well.

Sim and Shard heard the commotion from the courtyard below, long before the alert siren began. Before the sorcerer could stop him, Shard began scaling the portico. "Come on!" he called as he scrambled up the tiled roof and leapt up to catch hold of the ledge above. "It's coming from Mother's rooms." He hauled himself up on the ledge and began to run along the roof. **Come on, Sim.**

"Maybe we should let the guards handle it."

Mother's been hurt, Shard called back, and Sim knew nothing would stop him. Sim watched the lithe youth disappear into the night's shadows as he scaled another balcony to rise another storey higher up the palace wing. The Onmyóji bit his lip; he was no climber, and a long tailored coat no dress to be rockclimbing in. But a child was no match for whatever he would find up there. Without further hesitation Sim followed him, scaling the inclined tiled roofs in a swift, agile motion.

He soon lost sight of Shard and found himself blindly ascending without a plan. He searched with his hidden senses for Shard's vibrant presence. Gritting his teeth against the reeling sensation of vertigo, Sim continued to rise. *Not bad for a ghost,* he reflected wryly as he pulled himself up onto a pagoda roof, marveling at how fit he was even after centuries without a body.

A new presence touched the edge of his mind, not Shard's bright flame, but a dark shadow.

"No..." Sim breathed. *No, it can't be.*

Varron collapsed on the side of the roof, breathing in deep, ragged bursts. He tore the mask from his face in anger. *Curse her whore!* He hissed inwardly. *Blasted sorcerer broke some ribs, I'm sure of it.*

The symbiote pulsed inside his skull, urging him on. All that mattered now was escaping, and living to strike again. **It was not my fault, Master,** he sent fervently, cold sweat already dotting his brow as he contemplated what Larien would do to him.

The guards were coming; he could hear the sirens wailing. Panic welled in him until the symbiote repressed it. He leapt across the chasm between rooftop and spire, and edged around the ornamental lion's statue, before he slid down the sloping base to race across another rooftop.

A young man was waiting for him.

Varron's lip curved back in a snarl. It was not a guard, but a boy. He was dressed in rumpled clothes, his waist-length hair whipping about his face, the colour of moonlight.

"Out of the way, pup!" Varron hissed, scrambling to his feet on the edge of the rooftop.

"You hurt my mother."

"Varron's eyes lit up. "Oh, it's the little heir, is it?"His hand shot out and he released his last spring-propelled dagger. Stargazer raised his sword in a defensive gesture and a bubble of shield energy rose around him. The dagger glanced off the shield, tumbling away into the darkness.

Varron reached behind his back and withdrew the sword from its scabbard. "One Amaru's as good as another. Your dreamseer can't save you as easily as he saved your wretched mother."

Stargazer charged him. Varron parried the uncoordinated thrust and shoved him back, thrusting with his sharp-edged sword. Stargazer parried, lunging forward to catch Varron's wrist. He forced him back, towards the edge of the roof. But Varron pulled him around, catching his wrist and flinging him off the eaves. Stargazer disappeared below, and Varron turned, limping away. "Useless pup."

A shockwave hit him hard in the back, knocking him to the rooftiles. He groaned, struggling to rise. Glaring over his shoulder, he saw Stargazer high in the air, somersaulting towards him with precise control. An Arashi apprentice, well-trained.

"Ah, better balance than I thought, pup?" He staggered to his feet, to face the Lord Heir. He saw the boy's right sleeve was torn, his arm scraped badly and beginning to bleed. "Run back to Mother, boy, and have her lick your wounds."

Stargazer attacked with a force that stunned him. Varron staggered back, his ankle throbbing, his ribs searing with pain as the young man advanced, delivering blow after blow. Varron leapt, catching hold of an ornamented eave and scrambling up onto another building's roof. Stargazer simply *flew* through the air.

They were training Arashi with greater attention to the old ways, he realized as he was forced to parry more blows. The Arashi of the Dark Age had been little more than glorified mercenaries. But this one was a child nonetheless.

"Need... more... *training*, I think," Varron parried the last thrust, and reached out, catching Stargazer's beige tunic. He threw the boy over his shoulder, grimacing at the pain that laced through his ribs. Stargazer went flying, skidding along the rooftop before falling off the cathedral. Varron sneered as Stargazer righted himself in midair. He landed on a sharply angled roof of the choir below, then ran along the nearly perpendicular roof, unaffected by gravity's pull. With a leap he spanned a chasm to catch himself on a lesser spire.

Varron moved to challenge him, then thought better of it and retreated. He climbed up the cathedral roof, then scrambled over to the adjacent temple rooftop. He raced across an inclined roof, looking back over his shoulder once to see Stargazer gaining ground, a silver-lit figure in the distance. The boy raced like a phantom, crossing wide streets with great leaps, running along walls before flipping himself upright onto another roof. Damned Arashi – like locusts they refused to fall. Varron hurried with a growing panic. The temple of Herasis was to his left; he must be atop a smaller cathedral to a lesser avatar. Perhaps even the temple to the Horned One, for all the towner kobolds. He needed to go east. He would be safe soon, if only he could keep his calm about him.

Something tackled him from above, slamming him onto the rootop. Swearing, he fought against the force on his back, pressing his face into the hard tile. Had the *boy* caught up with him already? With a raw cry as the symbiote constricted and another rush of adrenaline pumped through his veins, he shoved his attacker off and rose swiftly, a hand instinctively lashing out in a panther's swipe. The claws lashed only air, and Varron whirled about as he heard the scuffle of feet.

He found himself staring at a peri with the face of a child and the eyes of an elder.

"You!" Sim gasped, his voice low and dangerous, his eyes narrowing. "I thought the kobolds finished you off at Chalandris."

Varron buckled once as another rush of energy flooded his limbs. His head snapped up, and his mouth opening. But it was not his voice that spoke.

"Onmyóji..." Larien hissed angrily.

12

“Onmyóji...” the man rasped, his voice no longer the gruff baritone of Varron, but a low, vicious serpent’s hiss, countless tones blending in his voice, like a thousand bass whispers at once. The man’s eyes shimmered, flashed, seemed almost to blink within his open eyelids. Sim’s face drained of all colour as he took a step back.

“So... you live still...”

“You’re dead,” Sim accused, his voice a faint thread of a whisper. “I killed you. I destroyed your receptacle.”

Varron’s hand shot out and caught Sim about the throat. “Yesss, you interfering brat,” Larien rasped. “And you condemned me to four centuries of limbo within the rocks that destroyed my body. Only my great powers saved me from eternal disembodiment. Even now, my body back at Chalandris is weak and feeble, unable to regenerate completely.”

“It’s a better fate than you deserve, you murdering, treacherous–” Varron threw Sim back and the sorcerer slid across the smooth roof. He held out his sword and Larien sent a bolt of blue lightning that crackled off the tip, aimed at his enemy. Sim held up his hands and a shield rose to repel the lightning.

“You’re a persistent annoyance, Onmyóji. Terrays’s boastful ramblings never did you justice, I fear.”

“Don’t speak her name!” Sim snapped, unleashing a shockwave. His five coat-tails whipped frantically in the wind as the vicious energy blast swiftly manifested itself. Larien met shockwave with shockwave, and the combined spells canceled each other out with a bright crackle of light. Varron raised his hand, and Larien sent a bolt of lightning through the conduit’s arm.

Sim raised both his hands and the spell was deflected. With a roar of fury, Larien forced the conduit body to raise his other arm, and two flashes of blue lightning flashed out at the sorcerer. Sim’s shield began to falter under the power, and he dropped to his knees, gathering his arms close as he struggled to keep the shield erect about him. Lightning highlighted the protective dome’s surface, tendrils of light trying to punch through. Golden energy began to whistle about Sim’s arms as he fought to maintain his power. Varron’s lips smiled as Larien advanced on the fallen Onmyóji.

Sim's head snapped up and he threw his arms out, and his spell hit Varron's chest dead center, throwing the man back, flinging him a full fifty feet to slam into the wall of the tower at the far end of the roof. Varron hissed, and his body buckled once, but then Larien forced it to rise once more. Sim stared in horror. The man's black shirt was burned; his reddened flesh was visible through several charred holes. A flushed burn began to blossom on the side of his face, and he rasped painfully. He coughed once, and blood appeared on his lips. But he lived still.

"You didn't think it would be so easy, did you, boy?" Larien laughed, and he threw Sim's own spell back at him. Sim cast a shockwave against the approaching spell, but Larien could cast a blastshield with a mere flash, and the energy blast tore through the shockwave to strike Sim hard in the chest.

Stargazer appeared on the cathedral gable, staring down at the scene. His shirt was torn, thin streams of blood was trickling down his hand. "Sim?" he called, aghast. Varron stood over the fallen Onmyóji, but Stargazer sensed something was wrong. It was Varron who stood there, and yet it was not.

"Sim!" he bounded across the cathedral roof. Varron raised his head and blinked once, as if in curiosity. Stargazer cried out as a shockwave struck him hard, propelling him back against the roof. He rolled aside, semi-conscious.

Varron raised a hand, and Larien smiled. He parted Varron's lips as if to speak, then shook his head sadly. Sim heard the energy crackle as the lightning formed about his fist. He winced in anticipation of the pain he knew would come.

Larien cried out as Shard tackled him from above, dropping from the tower spire to land square on his back. "What–" the distorted bass voice roared as the slim boy was cast aside like a limp rag.

"Shard!" Sim cried out a warning.

Shard rolled across the roof, recovering swiftly. The tall man approached him slowly, his lips drawn back in a sneer. "One of Sim's boys, are you? He always did pick the wrong side to get in bed with." Lightning shot from his hand and Shard rolled away, just avoiding the burning energy. It plowed instead into the polished stone of the tower, scorching the smooth surface.

"Shard, run!" Sim called, dragging himself to his knees. "It's Larien! He's too powerful for you, *run!*"

"I can see the wheels spinning," Larien laughed as he continued to stalk the petrified peri. "You can't believe it, can you? I was dead, wasn't I? Killed four hundred years ago." He leaned forward, and a shining black film flickered across Varron's eyes once. "Look closely, infant. The devil has arisen from Hell."

He set another bolt of lightning at Shard and the youth raised his hands to cast a shield. The defensive gesture was only half successful, and the unabsorbed remnants of the bolt caught Shard's side. He cried out, his back arcing against the painful current.

"Hey!" Stargazer flew through the air to land on Varron's back. He dropped his sword, throwing his limbs about Varron's body in an instinctive effort to stop the sorcerer's lightning burst. "Get away from my brother!"

"*Off, whelp!*" Larien roared in a crackling bass tone, casting the heir off his back.

"Shard!" Sim cried out, staggering to his feet. "*Larien!*" he held out his hands and his own lightning shot towards the sorcerer. Larien merely waved his hand and a shield absorbed the blast.

"Shard... is it?" he asked, drawing near the staggering boy. "Not Celaeno's adopted mongrel?" Shard held up his hands to cast a shockwave, but the air barely shimmered with the weak distortion, and Larien laughed as the feeble vibration passed through him. "Is that all you're capable of? You're far less amusing than his previous pets."

"Shard!" Stargazer called his sword back to his hand, raced towards them both. Larien merely gestured and Stargazer staggered back, blue lightning burning his skin.

Sim raced along the rooftop, intent on tackling Larien, but even as he was gathering energy in his hands for a strike, Larien turned back. The sorcerer struck him with a powerful shockwave, nearly as strong as a blastshield.

"Sim!" Shard started forward, and Larien spun back, flicking a finger and unleashing another bolt of lightning. Shard gasped and crumpled over.

"Be quiet," Larien scoffed, closing a gloved hand around Shard's throat. He cast a glanced back at the unconscious Onmyóji, then easily hefted Shard up to his feet. "Weak little thing, barely grown. A child. How unlike you, to involve a child in such matters." Shard stirred weakly, moaning softly, his eyes hazed with pain. "Ah well," Larien dragged the semi-conscious boy to the roof's edge. "I am a merciful devil, child. No reason for you to live to see what I have in store for your land. Pity, with a little discipline you might have shown some potential." He held Shard's limp body over the void. "Ah well."

"*Shard!*" Stargazer screamed, staggering to his feet.

Shard's eyes snapped open. Surprising them both, a shockwave shimmered to life between their faces. Yet it did not strike Larien as planned, but instead seemed almost to pass into him. Shard's eyes widened as he suddenly sensed two presences joined to his, as if in a moment of mindspeech: the host body's faint and submissive whisper, and Larien's raging fury. Larien's mind pressed back at Shard's as if shooing away a pesky fly, and Shard reacted on impulse, pushing back as he had against the guardian spell, driving against Larien's will.

Impossible! Larien's mind screamed as Shard forced him back, first a fraction, then by great strides. The painsends that crackled at the periphery of Shard's mind only spurred him on further. He advanced against Larien mercilessly, driving by sheer instinctive will. Before he realized it, countless images and sensations flooded his mind. He could sense the nuances of Larien's fury; he could read his thoughts. Within the sorcerer seethed great anger and frustration, greed and ambition. He had been subdued once and the humiliation alone was enough to drive him mad. He wanted vengeance, he wanted to rule again. He hated... everything with a passion that almost overwhelmed Shard's probe: Celaeno, for sparking a new order; Empress Seiren, for reforming Níst and denying him an ally; Sim, for surviving and existing to challenge him still; his own body, for being so frail, so weak; the world itself, for daring to be prosperous.

He wanted to destroy it. He wanted to call back the Dark Age.

He wanted to live forever...

He wanted magic. Old Magic.

Shard...

Larien's mind writhed in indignation, and a mental scream threatened to deafen him. Varron's hand tightened about his neck, and Shard hissed in pain as the claws punctured his neck and the poison burned his blood on contact. But still he continued his attack, delving even deeper into Larien's soul, pushing past the desperate barriers. For a split second the shields gave way and Shard saw what lay beneath, and for a split second he thought he sensed something else, distinct and unique, fighting within.

Larien roared in wounded fury, and shoved Shard backward. The contact was severed instantly and Shard was locked out just as he was on the verge of understanding. Stargazer surged forward, but he was too far away. The floor beneath Shard's feet vanished and he reeled in the open air. He heard Sim's anguished scream as he fell backward, and he saw Larien retreat behind the roof's edge, disappearing into shadow.

The fall was brief; the impact silenced his perceptions almost instantaneously.

Shard returned to consciousness with a weak moan of abject misery. His entire body throbbed with pain, from the roots of his hair to the soles of his feet. He felt on fire; his very blood burned with pain; he could feel the veins at his throat pulsing with heat. A fiery pain spread across his ribs, and his head ached fiercely.

His eyelids flickered, and he almost sank back into sleep. "Shard?" a gentle voice pulled him back. He felt the soothing cool of a moistened cloth on his forehead, washing down both cheeks. "Shard, can you hear me?"

He opened his eyes slowly, squinted in light that seemed far too bright for him. He blinked a few times as a face slowly materialized out of the blurred expanse. "S-Sim?" he asked, a faint smile touching his bruised lips.

"Shhh," Sim soothed softly. "Rest."

He blinked in disorientation. He smelled the various unguents and ointments in one of Tiryn's many rooms. The tingling healing magic still lingered about him, at his head, his chest, his arms. He was stripped to the waist, he realized, a constricting bandage wound about his ribs, another about his neck. Dimly he could see Tiryn in the corner, the low light glinting off the ruby teardrop imprinted on his forehead, the mark of a Hesperin healer.

"Here," Tiryn motioned to Stargazer, leaning in the shadows, clutching his cut arm. "Let's see that."

"Is Shard..."

"I've done all I can for him; let me see that arm." Stargazer reluctantly lowered his arm, and Shard saw the dark stain covering his long beige tunic.

"Stargazer..." he breathed.

"He's fine," Sim murmured. "He just scraped the skin off his arm, catching himself on the roof. You're the one we were worried about. You're lucky you landed in the shrubs."

Shard could almost hear the golden hum in the air as Tiryn placed his hands over Stargazer's long shallow cut, his healing magic quickly sealing the wound. The dark shapes in the shadows withdrew as Tiryn led Stargazer into the adjacent room, and Shard let his head fall back on the pillow.

"Shard?" Sim urged gently. "Do you remember what happened?"

"Larien... did we actually fight Larien? Unh.... The roof, he pushed me off the roof. Powers, I feel like I'm dying. Am I dying?"

Sim shook his head, smiling gently. "No, you're not dying, Shard. But you broke two ribs, and you have a fever from the devilsblood in your wounds." Shard raised his hand to his throat, and Sim caught his hand. "Don't touch – we had to bind your neck. Tiryn has healed your ribs and driven out most of the poison, but your body has to purge the rest itself. Don't try to move," he cautioned when Shard stirred again. "You'll be in bed for a few days until the fever passes."

"What – Mother!" Shard tried to rise again. Sim pushed him back gently once more.

"She's fine, she's already on her feet again. She only received a flesh wound. You took the brunt of it," he informed him, again lightly laving his face with the cool cloth. "What were you thinking? You're just a child, what made you think you could fight someone like Larien?"

"I had to help; he was killing you,"

"I'm an old man, Shard. You shouldn't risk yourself for me."

"No you're not," he protested weakly. "You're just a boy, just like me. You've just begun living." His eyes drifted closed, and Sim decided not to contradict him, continuing to brush the wet cloth over Shard's fevered skin, cooling his face and then his bare shoulders, careful to avoid the linen bandage about his throat. Shard tensed for a moment, murmuring something inaudible, before he relaxed again, too tired to do otherwise. His eyes drifted to the ceiling, glazed and unfocussed.

"Larien?" Shard asked weakly.

"Gone; he overpowered us and ran off over the roofs. He knew we'd go to help you. I imagine Varron's halfway back to Chalandris by now."

"I thought... he was dead."

"He survived, somehow. Managed to stay in this world until he could reconstitute himself. He's really at Chalandris right now; he was casting himself into Varron's body through the symbiote Varron has in his brain. Larien's true body is weak, frail. It will be until he gets his strength back."

He smiled grimly. "I think we took a little wind out of him, if nothing else. If I hurry I might be able to stop him before he's up to full strength again."

Shard had relaxed on his bed during Sim's speech, but at his last words surged up again, clasping both hands about Sim's wrist. "You're not leaving, are you? Please, Sim, don't leave me," he implored weakly, his eyes slipped closed as the fever overwhelmed him again.

"Oh, Shard," Sim's voice was rich with emotion. Shard felt a hand brush against his damp cheek. "I'm not going to leave you, don't worry."

Shard sank back into his bed, his breathing shallow. His eyelids fluttered for a time, then his eyes slid closed and his breathing slowed, growing more regular. Sim continued to gently brush Shard's fevered skin with the damp cloth, running the cloth over his shoulders, his collarbone, and down his arms. Shard's right arm had fallen slack at his side once more, but his left hand was still tightly clasped around Sim's sleeve. The Onmyóji tried to withdraw his sleeve, but Shard held it tight in his sleep. Sim smiled softly as he lifted Shard's hand and slowly slipped his sleeve from his grasp. Shard's fingers at length released the fabric, only to curl about Sim's hand instead.

Sim's smile grew ever-so-slightly. He lifted Shard's hand, pressing it to his cheek. "All right, Shard, you win," he murmured, patiently sitting back in his chair, keeping Shard's hand clasped in his own.

The sun had not yet risen; only the faintest aurora began to warm the eastern horizon. The bats continued to flutter about the high towers, one last stretch of their wings before they denned in their cracks and hollows for a long day's rest. Stargazer leaned against the old stone wall of the ancient towers, watching the black shadows dance in the pre-dawn gloom. Below him the palace was bustling; lights usually dimmed in slumber were burning as the household struggled with the latest crisis.

"Yósha?"

He looked up. Aerin stood in the archway, watching him. "How is Mother?" he asked.

"She's fine. Up and about and reviewing security down in the throne room, trying to figure out what went wrong."

"And Shard?"

She shook her head. "Asleep. It'll be a while. He's beaten up pretty badly."

Stargazer looked back at the fluttering bats. "Did they send you to find me?"

Aerin flinched. "No one needs to *send* me to find you," she spoke softly, drawing near. "I was worried about you; I'm allowed to be, aren't I?" She tenderly brushed back a silver lock that had slipped from his hastily plaited braid. "Star?"

"I'm... I'm all right," he breathed shakily. "After all... these things happen. People have been killing people since before the Golden Age. Mother's been stalked since the day she was born. I've been stalked once or twice. We... have to get used to it, is all."

"No, we don't."

"It's just... Larien? It turns out that the man who broke into her room was Varron Lehs, Varron Lehs we all thought was long gone, and – and now Sim Onmyóji's telling us he was – what, channeling? – Larien himself. That Larien's not dead. That he's alive. Larien! Larien, Warlord of Chalandris. How am I supposed to take it?" His voice grew more tremulous, his pace faster as he rambled on, tripping over his panicked words. "But... but how can we believe that? And who is this Sim, anyway? He says he's a two-spirit, he says from the Great War, he says he's an Onmyóji sorcerer, but why should we believe him? Sure, he's old, you just have to have to brush minds with him to know that but he doesn't need to be *that* old – he –"

"Yósha," Aerin touched his shoulder lightly and he whirled about, burying his face in her hair to hide his tears. "It's all right," she soothed, stroking his hair as he wept in frustration and pain.

"I wasn't made for this, Aerin," he confessed, his face red with shame. "I know I should be stronger. But... I can't; I can't accept that we're supposed to *expect* death around every corner, that we're supposed to live in fear because we're royalty. I can't make myself accept that every time I say goodbye to Mother it might be the last time I see her again – Oh *Powers!*" He sobbed at his own statement, and he crushed her more tightly against him, kissing her fiercely. "Or you!" he kissed her again, tangling his fingers through her hair. **Or you! Or Shard! Or Sintaka or Spark – little Emrith, she's too little for this! We all are. We're peri. We're not supposed to die.**

Aerin held him tightly, stroking his hair and kissing his tears away. At length she stepped back, drawing a tremulous breath, pressing her forehead to his. "We will, we will," she assured him. "We haven't lost yet. Celaeno's not dead, and neither is Shard. They'll recover, they'll be strong again, and they will find Varron Lehs and hand him his *lungs* for what he's done! Don't ever doubt that, Star. What did your mother tell you? 'We're peri, and we'll never let them stop us.'"

"My soul," Stargazer whispered fiercely, framing her face in his hands, gazing deep into her eyes. "My strength. I don't think I can go on like this. Mother wants *me* to carry the North Star. I hear the nobles whisper that Mother should make me the heir instead of Sintaka – that *I* should be the next Dynast. But I never wanted anything more than an observatory. I don't want kingdoms and wars and assassins; I just want my stars. And you. And my family."

Aerin smiled, sadness and joy at once in her eyes. "You'll always have me, Yósha, always." She kissed him again with all a newlywed's passion, clinging tightly to him until the tremors of fear gently eased in them both.

Celaeno sank into the mineral waters of the hot springs, inhaling the pungent vapors deeply. Glowlamps cast light against the steaming waters, causing shimmering reflections to dance across the stone ceiling. The Smoking Waters was an ancient hotspring, long predating the Golden Age. While Shiori had urged she relax within the safety and comfort of her apartments, Celaeno had insisted on the subterranean hot springs far beneath the City Mount. The mineral-rich steam could effect the greatest healing of body and mind.

She released the pins that held her hair high over her head and her silver locks pooled thickly on the water about her waist. Celaeno closed her eyes and ducked under the water, kneeling down on the smooth bottom, enjoying the sudden heat against her bare skin. Surfacing, she eased herself to the side of the pool where a natural ledge allowed her to sit underwater. The steaming water came up to her collarbone; the lapping waves brushed against her wound. She glanced down at her milky skin, the four gashes left by Varron's claws an angry red. Gently she cupped water in her hand, letting it flow over the injury.

Celaeno sighed, setting her head back on the rock rim, letting her limbs float in the buoyant water. She felt so slow, such an invalid, the wound itching like a goldstripe sting, the residual devilsblood draining her energies. She closed her eyes sadly. She didn't even have Kemuri to comfort her; he was busy tending to others, now that the Dynast was temporarily incapacitated. She splashed her fingers in the water lightly, dreamily recalling the many hours they had whiled away together in the hot spring.

Almost instantly she dozed, lost in the sleep that was not sleep. She opened her mind's eye, and saw a shadowy visage before her: a darkly beautiful woman, with black tresses framing her face, and a Dynast's seal tattooed on her forehead. "Your Glory," Celaeno spoke.

"Majesty," the image bowed its head. "My sister soul. My daughter has already informed me of the shocking attempt on your life. The second one in only a quarter-turn – I must say I am amazed."

Celaeno's ghost smiled slyly. "I must commend your spy network. It has barely been a full twelve hours."

"Níst is nothing if not... thorough. But tell me, it is true that your assailant was Varron Lehs?"

Celaeno nodded. "A surprise to be sure. I thought he had been killed years ago."

The Empress averted her eyes. "Unfortunately no. But I must say I am not overly surprised."

"Seiren?"

"No, that contemptible wretch paid me a visit not a turn ago. Fresh from the kobold mines, ready to rebuild his empire. He was spouting nonsense about finding the Treasury of Ravanor, promising riches to Níst if I joined him, threatening to bring destruction on my family if I refused. I threw him out, of course; my Jinn made me forget about him by sunrise as only he can. But..." she cocked an eyebrow. "I hear the Hesperin mines in the Boundary Hills are being looted, and just now, Varron resurfaces, and attempts to assassinate the Dynast of Amaru. Naturally, I felt compelled to alert you."

"You didn't see fit to tell me earlier?"

"Annoyance, sister? Your Kemuri's people are so secretive, I only learned of the lootings a few days ago. But now..." she smiled. "I don't suppose a simple raid on the ruins of Chalandris Keep would yield fruitful results?"

"Keep your hounds leashed, Seiren," Celaeno admonished. "Varron has surely moved on by now. And as the Alteri say: this hunt is mine."

"Well, I hope you will keep me informed of the situation, Dynast. Our combined partnership has brought down empires, and I hope you will continue to regard Níst as a trusted friend."

"Amaru will always value the friendship Níst offers," Celaeno bowed diplomatically. "And as a token, I have some news for you, Seiren. Would it interest you to know that Varron's master may not be the ghost he appears to be?"

Seiren's ghost shimmered once. "Larien? He's alive?"

"That's not a certainty yet," Celaeno admitted. "However-"

"If it's true..." Seiren breathed. "I *trust* you agree with me, Celaeno, that he is a dire threat to our kingdoms. Varron Lehs I counted as nothing more than an annoyance until last night – without Larien to pull his strings he's as weak as a mewling baby. But if Larien lives, he must be dealt with."

"*Most* swiftly. You can be assured I will deal with this situation decisively."

"Níst would be most appreciative of your efficiency in this matter, Celaeno." Seiren seemed almost to shiver with combined rage and fear. "You've never given me reason to doubt Amaru ruthlessness and so I leave the matter in your hands... for now. Larien must not live to endanger the Pentagram. And should you trip over Varron Lehs in your endeavor, my Jinn would be most appreciative of his head offered on a plate."

Celaeno bowed once more as the dream image shimmered away as she could dimly feel the hot water on her skin once more. "That he shall have, sister," she vowed. "No one threatens my family and lives long to boast of it over a mug of mead."

"Oh, sister..." Celaeno heard Seiren's admiring voice retreat as she opened her eyes. "I would not have you as an enemy."

"Shard... Larien... looking for... *Sim!*" Shard cried, startling awake. He sat up in shock, his heart racing.

"Shard," Kemuri reached out laying his hands on his son's shoulder. "It's all right." He gently guided Shard back down onto his bed.

"Where's Sim?" Shard asked weakly, blinking in disorientation.

"Sleeping. He's exhausted – he stayed up all night watching over you. You mean a lot to him." He softly brushed the black locks back from Shard's fevered forehead. "It's not everyone who can inspire that kind of devotion in one who's seen as much as he."

"Father," Shard coughed once. "I... I locked minds with him. With Larien. I know what he wants. He's behind the raids on our mines."

"You're very strong to be able to force a mindlock with someone like Larien." He smiled proudly. "I always knew you had it in you."

"No..." Shard struggled to rise again. "He's after the Treasury of Ravanor.

He's the one who's looking for it. But he's not after the gold, the money inside the Treasury. He wants something else."

"Shhh, Shard; you should rest. You've been through a lot."

"He's looking for magic. He think he'll find it inside the Treasury. That's why he's willing to kill Mother to keep her out of his way. He's looking for a shard. He's looking for the *yúgure!*"

13

Stargazer set the antique metal globe on the table, and examined the hinges on one side. The globe was made up of seven flat planes, growing smaller in size towards the bottom and top of the schematic sphere. A network of hinges on one edge allowed the globe to be opened and the planes to swing like pages in a book. The royal family clustered about the astrologer expectantly. Galen and Jaxa waded through several large books at the far edge of the table while Shard scrutinized his own tome, keeping his head bowed to hide the strain of exhaustion on his face. Frequently he paused to draw breath, fighting the fever-sweats which still lingered even after days of bed rest.

"Now," Stargazer began, righting his reading glasses on his nose. "Tradition holds that there are seven worlds, stacked one of top of each other, each containing a different component of the total existence. We are the fifth world: the Aetherworld." He flipped the top two planes over their hinges;.a map of the known world was engraved on the dulled bronze of the plaque, showing all the major lands and seas.

"Above us is the Auranworld, and above that, the Overworld of the Powers." He flipped the sixth and seventh plaques back into place over the fifth. "Now, below us is the Fulcrum, the center of our seven worlds, the flashpoint of all magic. And below there..." he trailed his fingertips down the plaques, "the Underworlds. We don't really know anything about them, but it's said their magic becomes more and more chaotic the further down you go, until you reach the Underworld itself, where the First Fires still burn." He opened the globe to reveal the smallest world, engraved with the myriad symbols of Chaos. "It's said the *yúgure* came from Underworld, or perhaps a fracture between worlds." He closed the globe once more.

"Fractures hardly sound healthy," Sintaka quipped, her arms crossed over her jacket. "Isn't that what happened when Cimmerian unleashed it?"

"Exactly!" Stargazer's eyes lit up. "At its heart, the *yúgure* is a focusing crystal, no different than any focusing crystal used for ritual magic. But it's Old Magic, from before the Golden Age, maybe even before our world itself.

It's magic from another world, inherently unstable in our own. And when Cimmerian used it he fractured the very essence of our worlds, and the other worlds, the magic currents and barriers that hold all the worlds in perfect sync. It's like dropping a pebble in a pond and watching the surface ripple. Only we *stand* on that surface; we *breathe* that surface. And when he unleashed the power in the *yúgure*..." he ran his fingertip down the edge of seven planes, "everything was affected."

Mindrin wrinkled his nose. "I thought it was," he shrugged, "well... *pure evil.* Aren't focusing crystals impartial?"

"Impartial," Stargazer chuckled. "I like that, Min."

"Everything in this world depends upon balance, Mindrin," Kemuri spoke thoughtfully. "If magic is in proper balance, there is no evil, no good, simply law and chaos, each with the potential for either good or evil, each with the power to balance the other. But if the magic-wielder is unbalanced himself, there can be no equilibrium."

"Right," Stargazer said. "That's why the War was so disastrous – all the world's sorcerers filled with nothing but ambition and hatred, destroying everything they saw, and that trickled down throughout all the seven worlds. The balance was destroyed long before Cimmerian. It's little wonder the *yúgure* had a special talent for amplifying dark thoughts."

"I still don't understand," Sintaka frowned. "The *yúgure* was destroyed, with Cimmerian, wasn't it? The... the legend of the shards, that's just poetry."

"Someone would have found it by now, surely," Aerin argued. "It's been four thousand years. No one would leave something capable of sending shockwaves through *worlds* just *lying around*, would they?"

"Aha!" Jaxa cried, looking up from her book. "Here is it. 'And Cimmerian, the Black Griffin of Djedethra, stood aloft the highest tower of Elória, the Lady Alsaya at his side, his unwilling bride. And from his perch he called forth the Darkness-Which-Shall-Not-Be-Spoken, the Twilight, the *yúgure*. And the wrath within the crystal shattered outwards, setting the very air with its dark fire. The ascending waves of destruction rose high to the Overworld itself, then collapsed back on itself, triggering a fearsome shockwave the likes of which even the Powers themselves had never seen. Cimmerian and Alsaya were incinerated instantly, joined at least in death, if life would not allow them their destructive love. The citadel was flattened, and Elória burned - burned with searing darkness as cold as ice and as hot as Hell's own inferno.'" She paused in her reading, scanning ahead, her finger tracing her path along the lines. "Ah. 'The *yúgure* itself fractured into five shards, which were hurled to the farthest reaches of the earth.'" She looked up. "That's it."

"What do you mean *that's it?*" Sintaka demanded.

"It changes the subject to talk about the first of the survivors and how they coped. And I have to say, this is only text I've ever read about the *yúgure* surviving the blast."

Shard continued to flip through the thick tome that sat before him. "I know it's in here. I read it only a month ago." His fingers swam through the thin paper, turning chapter and section one after the other until he found the familiar crease in the pages. "Here, here it is: 'And one shall find in the ill-gotten riches of the tyrant Ravanor, power and death as of Cimmerian's destruction, the *yúgure*.'"

Galen moved to his side, lifting his glasses to his eyes to scan the lines. "I'll be damned," he breathed. "I must have read that passage a hundred times. I never thought it more than a figure of speech, a metaphor for the wars fought over Ravanor's wealth. You think this is what Larien is using?"

Shard nodded grimly. "If it's this or another text, or maybe hearsay – Powers know he's old enough to remember when the Treasury was first built – it doesn't matter. He thinks the *yúgure's* there. And he's willing to risk everything to find it."

"What more can you remember?" Celaeno gently urged.

"I don't know. It all came in a rush. Images and images, too many to understand at once. I'm still trying to sort them out." He put his hand to his forehead.

Sim was at his side in a moment. "Do you want to go back to rest?"

"I'm fine. Just tired." Shard shook his head. "His thoughts – I hardly expected them to be ordered, but..." he frowned, at a loss. "You know, when you're in mindspeech with someone, there are always background thoughts, like whispers? When I linked with Larien – it was all whispers, of differing pitch, intensity, each one whispering something different. I'm only now managing to sort some of it out now. I wouldn't be surprised if he is completely mad."

"Why don't we just send our army into the Wastes?" Sintaka asked. "Haven't Bys and the others been spying on them ever since they found the camp months ago? We send in the troops, raze their camp to the ground, and go home. Sim's said Larien's still weak. So, let's wipe him out before he gets any stronger."

"I have no objections," Aerin nodded, her eyes gleaming with anticipation.

"We don't even know if the *yúgure* is really there," Mindrin objected.

"Larien thinks it is," Shard ruled. "I may have skipped over parts of the Dark Age history, but I know Larien tal Chalandris *motivated* is a dangerous thing."

"He's right," Sim spoke up. "That Larien even believes in its existence is enough to be worried. I've seen him driven by questlust before, and I've seen what's he's left in his wake."

"Let's go to Chalandris," Sintaka said. Deal with him like you dealt with the Garthans, Mother."

"You are Aladar's own grand-daughter, aren't you?" Celaeno sighed. "Things aren't always so simple."

"He'd see us coming miles away," Sim sighed, defeated. "And if we killed his body he might just find a place to sleep again, or jump into Varron's body through the symbiote. And we'd be right back here again."

Shard sat down at a chair, exhausted. His head still ached from the lingering fever and the brace for his ribs itched under his shirt. He didn't like to hear Sim so grim, so defeated. The Onmyóji was just beginning to emerge from his self-imposed exile; it was the world's cruel humour to force him back into his shell again. He wished he could say something to cheer him, but he knew it was hopeless. Sim had cause to be concerned. They all had cause to feel hopeless.

You're hopeless...

It's hopeless....

Death.... what hope is there... only yúgure. *Never find it. Damned fool... not in time. Hopeless.*

You're hopeless, Larien.

"He's dying," Shard blurted out.

"What?" All eyes turned on him.

Shard sat erect in the chair, his eyes wide and clear. He laughed, a weak, strangled chuckle. "He's dying. He won't get better. Not without the *yúgure.* That's what he wants its power for. Sim, when you destroyed his receptacle you *did* kill him. He just isn't quite dead yet."

"Ohhh." Sim let out a long breath of air.

"Well, the crystal could certainly do it," Stargazer ruled, removing his glasses and folding them in his hands. "What else it would do to him, I haven't a clue."

"A wounded animal is the most dangerous predator," Celaeno declared in soft voice. "He's intent on the *yúgure*. We stand in his way. He knows we will move to oppose him."

"We're forgetting something even more crucial," Kemuri said. "Who among us has ever tried to cast a spell with a flawed focusing crystal?"

Slowly, reluctantly, the hands rose. Stargazer, Jaxa, Sim, Galen, and even Celaeno sadly admitted their mistakes. Kemuri lifted his own hand, blushing slightly as he recalled that day. "Hardly a pleasant recoil, was it?"

"Had a headache for four days," Galen admitted.

"Nearly turned my hair white," Sim confessed. "And it only had the faintest crack in it. I was just a kit – I thought I could handle it."

"Even the slightest flaw in a crystal's matrix will render its power inherently unstable," Kemuri nodded. "If Larien finds the shard, it will have all the power of the original *yúgure*. But it will be degraded, flawed. Even if he tries to use it to turn the Denáren Wastes into a rainforest, he could easily duplicate the devastation Cimmerian realized."

"Then we're dead either way," Sintaka murmured.

"I've decided," the Dynast spoke. "I will address the Matriarchs this afternoon. I will tell that I am sending a royal delegation to Hesperin, to meet with Dynast Alcyon and discuss possible solutions to the mining problem. But you will not go to Hesperin's palace. You will go to the Boundary Hills. Meet with Bys Mantalore. I want to know what is happening there. Your mission is to stop Larien from endangering Hesperin and the Pentagram itself in his quest. I want a safe plan to find and crush Larien's forces. I want this threat eliminated as swiftly as possible."

"Who'll go?" Aerin asked.

Celaeno paused, weighing the importance of her choice. "Sintaka: you know Hesperin, and you know how to defend our land should it come to battle." She turned next to her mateson. "Mindrin," she smiled warmly. "I know I can't send Sintaka without sending you as well. Kemuri and I will watch over Emrith; you look after my headstrong firstborn."

Sintaka's objection was expected. "It was one thing for him to be my shadow when we were kits; it's another now! Emrith needs her father."

"And *you* need your soulmate," Celaeno interrupted calmly. "Anyone can raise a child if the worst should come – you can go to battle safe knowing your father and I will protect our grandchild with our very souls. Sintaka – no arguments," she raised her hand to halt her daughter's protest. "He is your shadow, and you his. I cannot afford to alter that now, with so much at stake."

Celaeno turned next to her son. "Stargazer: you know the legends as well as Galen himself. You know the stars, and you've learned your lessons well. Aerin, you've wanted a chance to prove you're of the same mettle as your mother. It's time to see how if the blood of the Red Knights flows as strongly within you as we've hoped. Lord Onmyóji... I can't order you to go, but no one knows Larien as you do." Sim nodded his acceptance and Celaeno bowed slightly in gratitude. Her gaze fell next on her youngest child.

"Shard," she smiled softly. "I'd love to keep you here with me in Amaru. But you've seen Larien's thoughts. You know his intentions. I need you to lead the mission." Shard leapt up from his chair, shaking his head violently, his face frozen in shock.

"*Mother!* I... I can't lead them. I'm just a kit. I've never been in combat; I've never been north of the palace at Hesperin itself. I hardly have any magic in me–"

"You had magic enough to invade Larien's mind," she corrected.

"I don't know anything about being a leader."

"No one does, at first." She walked about the table to place her hands on his shoulders. "I was two years younger than you when I became Dynast. I didn't know what to do. I had no skills, no experience. But I trusted those around me, I knew when to listen to advice and when to stand alone, and I had faith in my own capabilities. Shard, I could make Sintaka leader, but she has no knowledge of the darker magic Larien may wield. I could make Sim leader, but he knows nothing of the world as it is today. You know what's at stake, and you know what has to be done. No one is better qualified to lead this mission."

Shard blinked in fear and confusion, swiftly scanned the room at the expectant faces, encouragement and uneasiness mingling in their expressions.

He nodded weakly, not trusting himself to speak.

"The time for waiting has past, it seems," Celaeno ruled sadly. "To tell you the truth, Stargazer, I had hoped this day would not come for a while yet." She opened the cabinet doors to reveal the North Star, awaiting its next use. "It's time to put your Arashi training to the test, Yósha." She handed the white-faced youth the sword. To his fearful stare, she smiled bittersweetly. "Faith," she reminded him.

Stargazer nodded wordlessly.

"We should change your bandages," Sim said as they returned to the ground-floor room where Shard had been resting since his fall. The boy had been strictly forbidden to climb again until all his wounds had healed, and by the stunned look of complete disbelief still firmly fixed on his features, he would not wish to climb for some time.

Sim fetched a roll of fresh linen from the bedside table and sat Shard down on the bed. The daylight through the windows was enough in which to see, and he decided Shard was too dazed to deal with artificial light. Shard's short-sleeved shirt had a simple neckline that did not impede the bandages around his neck, and Sim carefully unraveled the linen binding the wound. The puncture wounds had shrunk to tiny red dots, little more than insect bites to the naked eye. Given the extent of the poison and the depth of the wounds it spoke highly of Tiryn's healing magic to purge such an infection. Satisfied, Sim lightly applied a cool salve to the wounds, reprimanding his patient lightly when Shard flinched at his touch. But Shard could not even muster a strong objection to the treatment he usually loudly denounced. Still he sat in silent shock.

"Why me?" he finally breathed as Sim began to wind the fresh bandage about his neck.

"Your mother's right. You are the best choice."

"I'm a kit! I'm clumsy, I'm sloppy, I haven't a speck of responsibility in me! I can't even keep a shirt unwrinkled for five minutes. I don't want to lead, I don't want the responsibility, I don't want the pain. That's for people like Mother. I just want to be free, to do what I want, in my own time, without being afraid. I haven't nearly enough experience, or magic, or common sense to be a leader. She can't do this to me. She can't force me to be their leader." He leapt to his feet, leaving the linen half bound, a long tail extending down his back.

He began to pace furiously, his panic increasing. "Powers! What if the shard is there? What if Larien's right and we find the *yúgure*. How can I think of anything to do? How can I be expected to know what to do? The world itself could be destroyed! Larien laid waste to the land from the Boundary Hills to the Milandra River without any focusing crystal – what will he do with it in his hands? Sim, I can't do this. I know I'll just–"

Sim caught him by the shoulder, arresting his pacing. He pulled him close and crushed him in a tight embrace. Momentarily stunned, Shard found himself collapsing against the Onmyóji sorcerer, hugging him back fiercely, relieved to have his support. "You doubt yourself too much, Shard." Sim held him back, staring deep into his eyes. "You need the confidence you had when you attacked Larien to save me. You need the strength you had when you forced a link with his mind. And you have it; it's in you, Shard. Everyone can see it but you."

Shard stared back, breathing gradually beginning to slow. "R-really?" he stammered as soon as he could find his voice.

"Really. I believe in you, Shard. Everyone does."

An instant smile rose, and Shard's tension dissolved into a giddy relief. His eyes were still wide, only now with sheer joy. He didn't care that he seemed like an adoring kit begging for a mentor's approval, nor that it was obvious to Sim that "everyone's" faith meant little to him compared to Sim's.

"Let's – let's go to the Boundary Hills," he declared on a dizzying rush.

Sim smiled fondly. "Let's fix your bandage first," he indicated the dangling strip of linen, then moved around to Shard's side to secure it. "It's healing well. By tomorrow I think we can leave it off."

"Good," Shard breathed, laughter still in his voice. "It itches when I try to sleep. And this brace feels like its choking me."

"It's just to protect your ribs if you bump into anything. Tiryn only knit the bone three days ago: the new bone's still fragile. Here, take off your shirt."

"What?" Shard looked over his shoulder, his cheeks instantly reddening. Sim couldn't help but blush as well, even as he struggled to maintain a professional demeanor.

"I want to see how the bruising's coming down – unless you'd rather have Tiryn's apprentice come in tonight and see for herself."

Shard swiftly stripped the shirt off over his head. He had no wish to submit to that woman's pestering and accompanying pokes and pinches. "You should take her place," he said, tossing the shirt to the ground. "You've got healer blood in you. Your bedside manner alone puts you ahead of Nidel. Tiryn would train you, I'm sure."

"Maybe," he considered it thoughtfully, undoing the loose ties securing the soft brace against Shard's left side. He did not need to add "if I stay;" the uncertainty in his voice was clear. A silence fell as he undid the final slipknot and the brace fell to the ground. "You never told me about your wings," Sim spoke at last.

"Oh," Shard looked over his shoulder at the pattern. "Those. I forget about them sometimes."

"Is it true you've had them all your life?"

Shard nodded. "They grew along with me, like a cat's stripes. No one can explain it. I think I like it unexplained. I don't know if I want to find out that it's just some kind of magical tattoo, or that I'm actually a chimera grown in a sorcerer's lab."

"Sounds sensible," Sim inspected Shard's ribs, where once a vicious purple-black bruise had flourished. Now it had dulled to the faintest yellow hue, already fading back into a healthy pink. "Tiryn's a good healer. Did it hurt, raising your arms?"

Shard obligingly lifted both arms high over his head, stretching his skin taut over his ribcage. "No, fine. I feel great, Sim. I really don't need the girdle back on." No reply from the Onmyóji and Shard anticipated an argument. "Sim?" he pleaded in his weakest, most imploring tone that never failed to move his parents.

Sim slowly considered the situation: Shard standing before him, extended arms emphasizing his slim lean chest, tensed with anticipation of the battle to come. There was really only one thing to do. Sim caught Shard in his arms and ran his hands down his ribcage, instantly provoked a high pitched laugh as Shard struggled against the tickling.

"You little *bitch!*" Shard exclaimed, still laughing despite himself, breaking free as Sim too began to convulse with laughter.

"I'm sorry, Shard, I couldn't help–" Shard picked up a pillow from the head of the bed and gave Sim a swift beating about the head. Sim struggled to wrest the pillow from his grasp and the two twisted about in a brief furious match. Abruptly Shard released the pillowcase and Sim went tumbled forward, collapsing on the end of the bed before sinking to the floor. Shard deftly scooped up his shirt and threw it over his head, tugging it into place as Sim spun around, his hair hopelessly mussed, his white coat sporting the first wrinkles Shard had ever seen. "Sorry, Sim," he chuckled, shrugging helplessly. "Couldn't help it."

For a moment something akin to adolescent lust for vengeance flashed in Sim's eyes, and then he laughed again, marveling at his own actions. He threw his head back, leaning on the bed as he stretched his legs out before him, looking for all the world like a boy of Shard's age. Shard sat down on the trailing blanket next to him, pulling down a little more of the cover to sit on.

"Pillow fights," Sim marveled, and Shard thought he saw a glimmer of a tear of laughter in his eye. Sim rubbed the blush from his face then threw his arms down at his sides. "Oh, Shard..." he laughed breathlessly.

Their hands brushed lightly as Sim let his arms drop, and something electric ran up Shard's arm. He frowned inwardly, wondering at the sudden heat he felt, the renewed tightness in his throat. Why had a new knot twisted itself in his stomach, and if he was suddenly so tense, why did he feel like flying?

He gazed at Sim, who leaned on the bedframe, his head tipped back on the blankets as he studied the ceiling, his breath slowing as the flush of delight reluctantly left his cheeks. Shard studied Sim's beautiful features, his wide innocent eyes that seemed far too deep, far too clear for one of such a bitter past. He had always known there was a young, vibrant soul under the years of loneliness and exile. And now that it was emerging his heart leapt with joy. He knew he would do anything to keep Sim at his side, forever smiling his shy hesitant smile.

Sim sensed Shard's gaze, and looked back at him. "Shard?"

"Nothing," Shard swiftly looked aside, lest Sim see the flush creeping at his cheeks or read his thoughts in his eyes. Once again the tension was knotting in his stomach, and his felt his heart race furiously. But it was a pleasant sort of panic, an exhilarating terror, one he would not trade for anything.

14

Larien opened his eyes and straightened to gaze out at a misty dreamscape. Surface and sky mingled into one cloudy expanse, only the faintest colours of swirling smoke brought light into the gray expanse.

He looked down at his hands, hands that only a night before had been gnarled with age, the skin yellowed and dry, stretched painfully over hollow bones. Now they were strong and healthy with rejuvenation, and a surge of adrenaline replaced the groaning pain when he flexed his fingers. The ruby ring on his right hand was gone now, he realized.

He lifted his hands to his face, and felt no wrinkles, no dried parchment, only smooth skin over a strong bone structure. In a rush of dizzying joy he stepped forward into the light that was not light.

A movement caught his eye and he turned to see a figure in the distance. A peri, all arrayed in flowing white, a white cloak covering his head, dancing as he slowly, gracefully drifted through the smoke. Larien's lips drew back in a predatory sneer.

Onmyóji.

He marched through the ascending mist over the dreamscape floor, bearing down on the phantom who continued to drift serenely, oblivious to his approach. His hand descended, clamped over the Onmyóji's shoulder and spun him around roughly. Oddly, Sim's eyes showed not the faintest surprise at encountering his enemy. He did not shudder, or swoon, but simply gazed up at the intimidating sorcerer with the same enraging Onmyóji calm. "Hello, Larien." The same soft, almost melodic voice he had heard torturing him in his slumber for four thousand years. It only provoked Larien to greater rage. He tightened his hand on the boy's shoulder, squeezing more and more tightly, waiting to hear the bone's snap, waiting to see the child's face contort with pain, waiting to feel the warmth of the boy's blood flow over his skin. But Sim only stared at him serenely, unaffected. "What are you doing here? You can't think you'll win, can you?"

"Demon!" Larien threw him back, but the boy didn't even stumble. The white kimono settled gracefully about his ankles, and the cloak slipped from his head revealing his pure black hair.

Larien swung his fist, leveled a furious punch at Sim's face, intent on feeling the delicate bonework of his cheekbones shatter. But his hand was only engulfed by smoke, and passed through the child's face without impact. Sim did not even blink, but stood motionless as his form rematerialized in the wake of Larien's blow.

"What are you?" he cursed. "Why have you come here to torment me further?"

He shook his head gently. "Still you think the world revolves around you. I thought I had taught you humility by now." Sim blinked, a slow methodical action, gradually lowering his eyelids before opening his eyes anew.

They were blue.

"You!" Larien hissed, drawing back as if burned.

"Did you think you could escape me so easily?" Terrays demanded, advancing with perfect composure as Larien staggered back. "Did you really think you could find rest *here?*"

Larien held his hands before him, fingers crooked to repel attacks. "Back, harridan. I'll not suffer your games tonight."

She laughed scornfully. "You're not the master, Larien. I thought I had taught you that, at least. He'll stop you," she promised, lowering her head to glare at him through her wispy bangs. "You should have played the ghost, Larien, and let him think Varron worked only for your memory. Now he knows. He'll stop you."

"You place too much faith in that wretch, you always have!"

"He's your downfall and we both know it. You can't deceive me, Larien. You might be able to fool Varron and your little hired help; you might even be able to lie to yourself, from time to time, but not to me. You didn't escape him, finding sleep in the rocks. It killed you, each day you spent locked in sleep." She began to pace around him in a wide circle, like a stalking cat. "You can barely maintain your form, and you know it will only get worse. Your diet of focusing crystals and silken, your reliance on the ring more and more – it only prolongs the inevitable. You're dying, Larien. You have a month, two at most, before your form shatters to pure energy and your molecules are scattered to the ends of the earth." She paused. "I've heard of sorcerers who die like that, who tax their powers beyond all earthly endurance, then fly apart with exhaustion. Some say it's as bad as being destroyed. Some say it's worse."

He glared at her. "You'd love that, wouldn't you? But you forget. My death is yours."

"If you die I am free."

"Or perhaps destroyed with me, your existence snuffed out as it was meant to be four thousand years ago. Are you willing to take that chance? It's not everyone who can claim such an... *intimate* joining to a devil of my standing."

"It's not everyone who would accept such a joining."

"Aren't you bored by this constant struggle?" he continued silkily, advancing on the white-robed woman. "Have you forgotten the peace, the contentment of a simple rest. Don't think I don't know how taxing it is for you to continually fight me. Can't we come to an arrangement?" he drew closer, clasping her forearm, lightly, almost tenderly. "We've been together for so long, Terrays – nearly soulmates, we. Were you to be my aid and not my nemesis, the rewards could be great." He drew her against him, but not roughly, one hand rising to stir her hair. "Would it be so bad to be a modern-day Alsaya? We could be much, together, you and I. We could live forever. We could be as avatars."

Terrays smiled at that, but it was a closed smile that did not match her eyes. "Such an honour. But your dreams taste too sour to me, and I have no wish to play Alsaya to your Cimmerian." Her smile turned deadly, and she withdrew the sharpened dagger from the folds of her gown, thrusting it through the tender flesh of his throat, driving the point into his brain.

Larien awoke with a start, gasping for breath, his leathery skin dripping with sweat. He jolted up from the bed and was rewarded with sudden pain screaming from his aching joints and feeble muscles. He threw off the ragworn covers he had wrapped about himself for warmth and staggered from the bed on shaking legs to the single shaft of light in the darkened room. He clamped his fingers over the ring, pulling and kneading, but the circlet would not move. He twisted at the ring, working furiously, until finally with a cry of desperate pain, he released it.

Cursing and gasping, his breath coming in desperate erratic pants, he picked up the small doubled-edged knife that lay just in shadow. *Now, don't be foolish, Larien,* the voice taunted him.

Larien held the knife over his ring finger with his left hand, the blade quivering in his shaky grasp. Biting his lip until he drew blood, Larien pressed the sharp blade over his skin, fighting against an invisible barrier that drove the knife back. The blade shivered, drew the thinnest line of blood above his knuckle, but would cut no further. He gasped as the knife finally fell from his trembling fingers.

Did you really think it would work? How many times have you tried? How many times has Varron tried? You can cut it, you can burn it, you can stick your entire hand into a hellhound's jaws. You won't be rid of your Alsaya so easily.

"Silence, harridan!" he cried out, throwing his head back with anguish.

We'll stop you, Larien. Sim and I.

"Sim thinks you're dead! He thinks you were destroyed. He'll kill me without a second thought and you with me."

I will be free. It's all I ever wanted.

"Or you may find life without me less palatable than you thought. You may find that without me, you'll have nothing but the oblivion your spirit should have found years ago."

I would gladly take oblivion over you!

"And so you shall. When I hold the shard in my hand I will purge your damned essence from my mind once and for all. Then I'll live to rule Denár and more as I was always meant to, and you, my unwanted soulmate, will not even live to see me kill your precious brother."

He had failed.

Varron Lehs huddled against the treetrunk, hissing with each breath as he tried to straighten against the pain in his ribs. The symbiote had been working without rest since the attack, and even now he was not yet healed. The fight with the Onmyóji and the Amaru boy had broken three of his ribs, cracked his spine, and drained him of precious energy. The symbiote could grant him incredible strength and endurance, but even it had its limits. Without proper rest the symbiote's attention would simply destroy his body in its attempts to heal the malleable flesh. It took a strong body to endure the constant overload from the creature; little wonder the symbiotes had been outlawed for nearly five hundred years, even before the New Age and its cowardly rulers.

Larien had not spoken to him since the fight. He had fled Varron's mind the instant they had dropped out of sight, leaving Varron battered and beaten in enemy territory, utterly alone. He had been forced to mount his dragon and flee to the Vastwood, to find shelter in a cool glade. After a quarter-turn of slow travel he had made it no farther than Hesperin's eastern mines.

Master? he called desperately. *_Master? Answer me, please,_* he begged.

Larien had turned his back on him, Varron knew it. He was even now turning to L'al Darhis and her insidious Alteri ways, making her his right-hand man while Varron wasted away alone. He had served Larien faithfully for over six hundred years, he had been the only one strong enough to receive a symbiote and live to tell of it, and now he was being spurned for a little amazon.

He could see her in his mind, the arrogant wretch: her short black hair, streaked with three auburn tiger's stripes; her cold gray eyes, flat as dull glass, or else sparking with silken and sadistic lusts; her lips curved in an arrogant smile. She would replace him in Larien's heart, and should the bitch worm her way into Larien's bed as well, Varron would surely be obsolete. She wouldn't touch him now, not as the Master was, his flesh still parched from the grave. But once he regained his strength, his sinister beauty – would she still refuse him then? Could she? Could anyone refuse Larien?

No, he would limp home to Chalandris and find her waiting for him, hellhounds at her side, dagger unsheathed and hungry for his blood.

Master! his subconsciousness wailed, too wounded to care how desperate he sounded. He needed to feel Larien's presence, to know he was still wanted, to know he was still worth something.

What do you want, Varron? You have not yet healed. Trouble me again when you are strong enough to serve me.

It was not my fault! Varron implored. *_I did my best to follow your orders, Master. I was wounded for you. I bled for_ you! _You cannot leave me like this._* No answer greeted him and Varron's anger blazed. *_Has_ she *eclipsed me so swiftly? Has that Alteri witch so enchanted you to make you forget your loyal servant? She failed to kill Celaeno as surely as I. I was the one you sent to clean up her mess.**

Silence. There are more important forces at work than your petty grudges.

Varron considered it. There were indeed many forces. The Onmyóji, that infernal meddler, and the strange creature who accompanied him now, the boy with the power of an ancient spellcaster. Were they the ones Larien was thinking of, or was it the wraith in his mind, driving him further towards the precipice?

They needed to find the Treasury soon. That much he knew.

So the wheels turn in your dull mind after all, the voice snapped scornfully, and Varron winced at the disdain he sensed. But at length his Master's mood softened. Larien's voice returned, newly contemplative. **You are a loyal one, Varron. Such help is in short supply these days. Where are you, Varron? Hesperin – yes, good. Then you are indeed in the perfect place to serve your master. I want you to journey north, to that hovel in the mountains. Outpost, they call it. If the Onmyóji filth intends to seek me out, we will see him there.**

I should be in Chalandris, at your side.

Silence. I am not old man in need of a nursemaid. Go to Outpost. Blend in with the local rabble, and listen for travellers. The Onmyóji sorcerer can only bring us grief at this late a juncture. I want him dealt with swiftly. And I want that boy of his – alive.

The connection broke off abruptly, and left Varron reeling, gasping raggedly as the withdrawal hit him hard. The endorphin rush ebbed. The symbiote's coils loosened around his brain. Varron nearly wept for the sudden emptiness as Larien locked him out of his mind, the connection severed.

Morden let out a cry of sheer delight, followed by a jubilant exclamation in his native tongue as the heavy floor panel dropped away to reveal a large chamber underneath the tunnel. "We've found it!" he cried, reverting to the Common Tongue. "It's ours! This *must* be it."

Darhis squinted at the bright light as the glowlamps of the tunnel reflected off the expanse of pure red gold beneath them. Morden snapped his fingers and one of his men, a tall crossbreed like himself, dropped down into the chamber below, landing on the hard granite slab they had pushed through the vault's ceiling. Darhis coughed at the dust. "Are you sure?" she inquired doubtfully.

"Look at the riches down there, woman. That's not false room. It's one of the main antechambers, I'm sure of it." He blinked, and his smile faltered. "I'm sure of it," he repeated, mopping at his fevered brow with the edge of his grimy shirt. "Damahn! All clear?"

The man disappeared out of their view, proceeding deeper into the antechamber. "All clear, Mord–" A swift hiss of unsheathed metal and Damahn was abruptly silenced. A dull thud was heard, followed by a heavier rattling collapse. Darhis thrust her face down into the chamber, hanging upside-down by her legs, as she inspected the source of the sudden noise. "Ahh," she smirked, her legs releasing their hold on the rock as she flipped over in midair, dropping to the floor. A pendulum blade continued to swing back and forth in the air, Damahn's head lying still on the floor a good two feet from his body. Already blood was staining the rich carpet of gold.

"Dead," she called up.

"Ah... oh, well," Morden sighed.

Darhis picked up a large scepter-cap fashioned of gold and pearls, and threw it to the ground, skipping it like a stone across a pond. It bounced by the kobold's still body without triggering further death-traps, and Darhis cautiously advanced down the carpet of gold coins.

"There shouldn't be more, eh?" she called up.

"Just one, maybe two, to give any robbers a second thought," Morden leapt down to the floor. "Poor Damahn. It gets and harder and harder to find a volunteer every time."

"Ohhh!" Darhis rounded on a large pile of gold. She reached into the coins and swore as her fingertips hit a hard surface. She scraped away a layer of thin gold drekks to reveal a solid stone surface. "A trick!"

"It's only the first of the five main antechambers, leading down to the Treasury itself. They can't afford to spend all the riches at once."

"You don't seem particularly worried about your cut in this little enterprise," she glanced over her shoulder.

"Not. Oh, I was at first. But now... ohhh, half of this would outdo my father's entire life's worth, and this is only the first." He rubbed his hands together. "Remind me to thank our master next time we see him."

"Just don't turn your back on him – hello, what's this?" she turned as she caught sight of a skeleton crumpled in a corner. The peri's bones had long been picked clean by microbes and parasites, even in the hermetically sealed environment of the crypt. But his sumptuous robes had survived untarnished. The man, whoever he had been, lay slumped against the wall since the day he had fallen, his bony hands cobwebbed by spiders, long-dead themselves. A gold tablet lay in his hands.

"The sacrificial priest, left to keep evil sprits at bay. Probably a Hokabalh cleric – what do you mean about Larien?"

"Let's just say I know my oral history," Darhis murmured. "And my gut as well. And a half-dead Larien tal Chalandris spiced out of his mind on silken is not the most trustworthy Tejar to have."

"As long as he pays well. I'm not coming in here and leaving empty handed."

"Hmm," Darhis pried the tablet free from the dead man's grasp, smiling as the bones dissolved to a fine powder. "'*Y'yimagh alhlad'h gh'desri taak ta'laa yihad...*' you read it," she passed it to Morden. "My Hokabalh is a little rusty." She reached down and ripped a priceless necklace off the man's throat, shaking his skull askew. Her hunter's eye noted the dried blood on his clothes: the stains the mites had not managed to consume. His throat had been ceremoniously slit. "Pretty way to go," she murmured.

"Ah..." Morden began to translate in earnest. "'Welcome, denizens of the most accursed darkness which shall from this point on never be'... ah, boring meaningless double-talk... here we are, 'know then that you have transgressed on the hollowed resting place of the Butcher of Sharazen, the Unholy One, the mateson of the all-powerful Ravanor himself," – his face fell abruptly, but his lips continued to form the words as he rambled on – "Habradar of Ghothli, consort and master of Dhiwen, fifth daughter of Ravanor the Great, and sire of Pathrein the Magnificent, here buried alongside his great mentor the all-powerful –" he broke off abruptly hurling the tablet aside.

Darhis began to chuckle, holding her hand to her face as she watched her companion's face molt in shades of crimson and fuschia. A low laugh built deep in her throat, tickling relentlessly.

"It's... the... wrong... tomb," Morden gasped, a tick flickering at his left eye. "It's... the... wrong... all-holy... mother-poking... sister-whoring... *tomb!*"

Darhis burst into unholy laughter, hugging her stomach as a fierce tremor ran through her. Morden let out a howl of pure rage and threw himself at the skeleton of the priest, rending robes and crushing bones into dust, all the while screaming kobold obscenities.

"*Hantma, chiga* wrong worthless *chiga-men igatin tantal TOMB!*"

Darhis fell to her knees, coughing as the laughter continued to rock her. Morden next picked up a jeweled scepter and began clubbing the pitiful remnants of the priest's bones, continued to rage in foreign tongues. Darhis rolled over onto her side, clutching her sore ribs, unable to stop. At length Morden released the scepter, drawing in pained breaths as he fought to regain control. Suddenly he paused. "Wait, *wait!*" he raced to recover the discarded tablet. Darhis sobered herself, stretching her limbs as she watched the kobold's frantic search through heavily-lidded eyes.

"Hah, *hah!*" He held the tablet aloft, triumphantly. "Look, look at this. "'Buried here alongside' Ravanor. Habradar was buried one mountain over from Ravanor. We know we're in the right place now. We just need to dig one mountain-peak over. Look at this, long-legs. See..." his pudgy finger traced a line of text.

She yawned. "I'm afraid you've lost me. What's your point, exactly?"

"Don't you see it, you stupid girl? Look." He began to draw in the dust left by the remains of the priest, creating a triangle with the tip of the scepter. "This is us, right here," he made a dot inside the pyramid. "And this, is the east slope of the mountain," he made a second peak, sloping off the side of the triangle. "Don't you see? If this tablet is telling the truth, this is one of the four subsidiary tombs off Ravanor's main chamber. All we have to do is tunnel east. We'll break through within a month, less, if I flog them hard. Don't you see? We have found it!" he laughed, blinking at his own words, betraying his own doubts up to that precise moment. "I found it. I found the Treasury of Ravanor. I found the *Treasury of Ravanor!*"

He leapt at her, casting his arms about her and planting a wet kiss soundly on her mouth. Darhis reeled, too overcome by shock to protest, though she wiped her mouth with the back of the hand the instant he skipped away.

"Urga'h! Send a runner to base camp! Tell them we've found it. I want the best brew pulled out of the stores. To hell with the mead – get me the sapphire wine – the fifty year one. Tonight we toast the great Morden Mantalore!"

An answering grunt came from the troglodyte above, and Morden threw up a handful of gold coins. "Not so fat now, am I, long legs?" he crowed.

The Treasury of Ravanor...

"You'll sing another tune now, won't you?"

They had found it.

"Garn! You up there? I want the best troglodytes we've got on guard. No half-breeds either! I want pure trog muscle guarding this crypt. No one comes in 'less I say so!"

That filthy kobold had *done it!*

"Alteri? Are you deaf or something? Don't you realize what we're sitting on top of?"

Tejar, she sent a call out to Larien, honouring him with the Alteri title. The mindspeech rose, carried on her rejoicing ambition. **We've found it. We've broken through. The Treasury of Ravanor is ours.**

15

"Welcome to Outpost," Bys Mantalore announced jovially. "Gateway to the Wild North and shithole of the civilized world!"

The air was dry, stagnant, and the faintest hint of sulphur and other loathsome elements clung cloyingly in the atmosphere. The clouds that shielded the starscape were darker, reddish in hue, mirroring the iron-rust mountains that hugged the little town of Outpost. The forests their dragons had soared over freely had shifted to spartan plains thirty or forty miles southwest. Unnoticed by the kobolds, a mild charge hung in the air, like a brewing lightning storm. There was no mistaking that they stood on the edge of the Denáren Wastes.

They paced through the streets of the town, captivated by the colourful sights. With the exception of seasoned Sintaka and Sim, the Amaru gaped at their surroundings with innocent eyes. Trios of seven-foot troglodytes argued in their loud guttural speech, shoving each other back and forth to emphasize their points. Dirt-faced kobold miners roamed the streets in packs, looking for the next saloon to attack. Horses and terrapins, armoured reptiles the size of small elephants, carried their loads through the streets. Performers acted out folktales and bawdy skits for the crowd. Large carts of coarse fabric and soft wool blocked intersections, as all manner of products were cried out in countless dialects.

Aerin's bright eyes darted from one dark corner to the next, as she sensed countless eyes on her revealing warrior's dress. Her hand tensed on the long handle of her wickedly curved battleaxe in warning and she sensed the voyeurs withdraw.

"Not quite the High Town in Hesperin, is it?" Bys laughed. "It started as nothing more than a dump two hundred years ago, and filth attracts filth. But it does its job. We haul out the raw minerals here, and process them enough to ship them down the Eluen River to the seaports, where the cargo ships can take them down to Gale Point, Demini, Thalatta and Hesperin."

Stargazer rubbed his stiff neck as they paced through the streets. It had been a long flight to Outpost; for four days they had flown from one city to the next, journeying above the jasper forests of the Oroön Mountains to the Hesperin border, then jumping further northeast as the city centers of the coast gave way to smaller kobold mining towns.

"We're going to stay *here?*" Mindrin asked as an overpainted courtesan batted her eyes at him and lifted her skirt high to reveal a generous length of leg.

"Hah! You wouldn't last a full day in a place like this. No, you're just going to bunk the night at the Guildhearst. Let your dragons take a stretch. Day after tomorrow I'm taking you all up to my keep, at Dragon's Jaws."

Shard followed Bys obediently, instantly touched by his father's friend. Despite growing up at court, Bys had the simple straight-forward manners of any kobold, a charmingly blunt style Shard preferred infinitely to the fussing of noblemen. The kobold wore the simple garments of his race: a long patchwork coat over practical leather clothes, his close-cropped black hair covered by a rough green hat, topped by a set of battered miner's goggles. He stood about average height for a kobold at four-foot-five, precisely twelve inches below the top of Shard's head.

Shard liked him.

"I have to say, when Kemuri sent word that you were coming, I never thought he'd be sending me all three of his children," Bys continued. "So, you're the leader of this troupe, eh? Well, I hope everything your father said about you is true. They've slacked off on our mines – they're more focused now, only going after one mountain side. But they're still close enough to our own emerald tunnels, and we're still losing scouts to those animals. Feral kobolds – lower than troglodytes. I hope you're up to it."

"So do I," Shard breathed.

"How old are you? Eighteen?"

"Seventeen."

"Whew. And your father let you out of the nursery? My own son's nearly twice your age, and he's still playing with his toy pickaxe. But then you peri can afford to grow like weeds – you can never get more than two or three kits out of each of you, can you? Kemuri's over four hundred by the time his brother comes along. Me? Secondborn of seven children. Hah! We little folk need to waste years as kits, or the tunnels would be overflowing with babies. Ah, here we are."

They rounded the corner, wading through the congested thoroughfare, to face a sprawling three-story building erected of sturdy rock brick. A six-foot-tall rock wall surrounded the Guildhearst, keeping out the street rabble who huddled around the wall, shouting out their wares.

"We'll put you up on the third floor – after four days of flying over Hesperin you must just want to fall into bed. Just ring whenever you want to eat, cook will make you anything you want – long's it's not too fancy." He nodded to the guards, who held open the iron-rod gates. "Sleep in as long as you like, build up your strength. It's a long ride, but not a hard one, to Dragon's Jaws. Faster as the eagle flies, but we've got packhorses to worry about." He nodded to the peri as they passed through the gate.

Shard stepped up onto the walkway, striding through the empty courtyard towards the double doors of the Mantalore Guildhearst. He cast a glance back at his comrades to see Stargazer yawn and Mindrin rub the sleep from his eyes. For peri used to nothing more strenuous than a day in the library being tutored by Galen or a grudgingly accepted session with the Matriarchs, merely sitting still on dragonback for hours on end wore them out. Only Sintaka seemed to be enjoying herself, out in the open air after an eternity shut up in the palace.

Yet the long journey had not wearied Shard. In fact the restlessness that plagued him was only heightened by the travel. He awoke each sunrise with a start, ready to run to the ends of the earth, and spent each day itching to break away. Not even the rush of spurring Smoke into the rolls and plunges that drove Sim to distraction could ease his anxiousness.

You're hopeless, Larien.

I will *find it; don't you question me.*

Hopeless...

When I hold the shard... when I have it, I WILL *have it.*

Shard stumbled, his hands rising to his temples, clamping tight on his skin to block out the sudden rush.

"Shard?" Sim rushed to his side. "What's wrong?"

"I'm... I'm fine," Shard staggered back on the path. The voices were already subsiding. Bys was at his side now, looking up at the peri with a baffled expression. Sim's hands were on his shoulders, steadying him. He nodded to Bys and the kobold frowned, leading them into the building.

"I'm fine," Shard insisted as they escaped the dull sunlight under the shaded doorway of the Guildhearst.

Sim's voice was low, almost harsh. "That's three attacks you've had today, Shard. You're not fine."

He blinked. **I... I didn't know you noticed.**

Sim shook his head, a faint smile brightening his stern gaze. "You're a terrible liar, and a worse actor. You've had eighteen psychic attacks since we left Amaru. I noticed every one."

Shard blinked again, before an answering smile graced his features. "I had nineteen," he murmured, turning to follow Bys inside.

Mindrin yawned, stretching out on his back before the great fire. "I ate too much," he lamented delightedly, patting his stomach. "Sintaka," he leaned his head back on the ground and looked over his bangs at his soulmate. "You're not going to let me get fat, are you?"

"Oh, yes, all that firm, lean, sculpted '*fat!*'" Aerin mocked. She dropped from her seat at the little table, digging through Mindrin's worn leather sack. "Where are your crystalsweets?"

"Hey, I brought those for me!" Mindrin protested as Aerin dug out a long orange stick. In annoyance, he fished out his own candy stalk, sticking it firmly between his teeth. "They probably don't even sell crystalsweets up here," he grumbled.

"I need some comfort right now," Aerin said, taking her seat anew, staring dismally at the long string of captured gamepieces. Stargazer had already taken the first two games of stratagem, and Aerin held little illusion about the third.

Sintaka sat up in her armchair. "Maybe if you laid off the sweets, you wouldn't be so fat," she teased.

Mindrin stuck his tongue out at her. Sintaka laughed.

"Mm." At length Mindrin withdrew his crystalsweet stalk, inspecting the point he had sucked it down to. He bit off the point, crunching on the hard sweet candy, before gesturing with the stalk. "Where'd you get that... that amulet thing?"

Aerin looked down at the dark red jewel, a circle rimmed with gold, suspended upon her breast by a thin silk ribbon. "Jax gave it to me, just before we left." She smiled fondly, recalling her friend's gesture. "The Eye of Herasis, she calls it. It's a focusing crystal, supposed to bring me luck. I don't know what spells I'll be casting with it, but it was a sweet gesture. Hah, I could always take out a trog or two with it," she hefted the weighty crystal.

"Your move," Stargazer smiled. Aerin shot him a withering glare.

"Did she give you a reading?" Mindrin asked. "Jaxa reads the sibyl cards, you know," he explained to Sim a moment later. "She's very good at it."

"No, I didn't ask for one," Aerin fingered each of her gamepieces in turn. "Her predictions have a way of coming true, and if we're all going to burn up in a well of Old Magic I figured I'd rather not know about it beforehand."

Unfazed by her cynicism, Mindrin munched on his crystalsweet contentedly, before he remembered his commander. "Shard? You want a crystalsweet too? You hardly ate anything for supper."

Shard shook his head. Sim looked at him questioningly, and Shard averted his eyes, sinking deeper into the large armchair, his legs drawn up, his hands about his ankles. His head still ached from the constant flashbacks to the mindlock with Larien, but he had trained himself to ignore the pain. He was no leader if he spent his time fretting about his own problems. He lowered his head, peering out through his bangs until he saw Sim look away, returning his gaze to the fire. The Onmyóji sat back in his chair, slowly removing his white gloves.

For a long moment Shard kept his eyes on Sim, before he reprimanded himself sharply. *What am I doing?* he asked of himself helplessly, lifting his head. Lately he could not keep his eyes off the Onmyóji; his gaze followed him everywhere since they had left Amaru. He had done his best to be subtle about it, but he was certain at least *someone* had noticed his adoring smile whenever Sim was near. Everything about the Onmyóji captivated Shard, from his smile and his calm stride to the way his green eyes shone when he spoke, to such things as the slow methodical way he would remove his gloves, easing them off one finger at a time.

He had the most *perfect* hands...

He was lost, Shard admitted miserably, continuing to gaze surreptitiously at the Onmyóji. He couldn't help but lapse into long lovesick contemplation, be it treasuring the lyrical bird-like speech of the Old Tongue on Sim's lips as he chatted with Aerin, or watching him stride through the streets of Outpost in his slim white coat.

Sim glanced up and their eyes met across the room. Shard felt the colour rise in his face, and desperately wished to look away. Yet he was spellbound, caught in Sim's stare. The Onmyóji wore an amiable, almost casual smile, yet his steady, unfluctuating gaze filled Shard with the most intoxicating unease.

Sim continued to stare across the room at his young companion, the same mild smile on his lips, the same dreamy intensity in his eyes. Shard was compelled to match his stare, unblinking, the energy to maintain such a gaze taxing his limited powers, his self-control only weakened further by the strange stirrings within him.

Sintaka slipped to the floor, reaching out for Mindrin's crystalsweet. Pure terror flashed in his eyes at the prospect of losing his sweet and he held it high above his head. Sintaka leapt up and snatched it away from him, sticking it in her mouth and smiling around it.

"Come on, take her!" Aerin encouraged as Mindrin caught his mate in a headlock and they rolled over together onto the floor laughing.

Sim? Shard mindspoke before he was aware of it.

Mmm?

Please blink.

Sim blushed and chuckled softly, averting his eyes. He rose now, and bid the group goodnight, retreating to one of the small, snug bedrooms built off the main hearthroom. His eyes met Shard's once more, before he glanced away, almost sadly.

Shard hugged his knees tighter, barely listening as Sintaka knelt to watch the stratagem game and Mindrin continued to devour his candy stash. His feelings for Sim puzzled and perplexed him to no end; never before had he ever considered any attraction to men. Yet in all honestly he had never been particularly attracted to the palace maidens. His heartfelt kitlove for Jaxa or Murren had long since faded in adolescence; now he never paid a girl anything beyond a long glance one might pay an attractive work of art: sincerely appreciative but lacking in all passion.

But with Sim... with Sim, he thought, lowering his head to hide the lovestruck smile on his face. With Sim he acted like a little kit, sick in love, falling over himself with clumsiness where before he had been agile, struck dumb where words might have come freely, caught in long gazes where a mere glance was enough.

He was torn, ready to run to Sim, to confess everything, convinced Sim already knew, yet terrified of acting, of speaking, of even *thinking* too loudly for fear he would betray himself. What was this strange feeling assailing him? Probably no more than kitlove, mere infatuation plaguing him, completely understandable in one so young. An aberrant emotion appearing in the midst of adolescent turmoil, an experiment of his unconsciousness, not to be treated with any seriousness. That was the rational explanation; yet every instinct told him this was no mere infatuation.

He rose and excused himself as well. No one questioned him: they probably attributed his weariness to the added burden on his shoulders.

What if he went to Sim, if he had the courage to admit his feelings? Would he only realize that it was nothing more than a passing phase in his adolescence, and confuse and wound his dear friend? Worse, would he know the feeling was genuine, only to be rejected by Sim? Sim might not believe him, might rule it a youth's fleeting fever, or would believe but reject him all the same, viewing him as no more than a friend, and a completely incompatible love.

The sting at his temples returned, and once again he felt Larien's self-loathing and pained ambition. He was too young to have sustained such a mindlock, Sim had told him. His mind wasn't sufficiently disciplined to endure such a psychic onslaught.

He closed the door to his room and surveyed the spartan, yet comfortable surroundings. A small bed laden with thick woolen bedding and warm furs, across from a simple chair and table, facing a tiny wood-burning stove glowing with hot embers. On the table he had lain his precious bundle: a large piece of spinner's web. The shimmering silver cloth was a muting force, blocking magic energies as surely as focusing crystals magnified them. So long as it lay wrapped inside the woven mesh, the *yúgure's* rampant energies would be neutralized. Shard picked up the bundle of cloth, running his thumb over the slick threads. Setting it down once more, he glanced at the low-hanging windows. If he parted the shutters he could look out over the lights of Outpost and catch sight of the cargo ships heading down the Eluen River to the sea.

He eased himself into the chair, covering his eyes with his hands. He yawned, feeling the exhaustion catch up with him at last. He laid his head down on the tabletop and closed his eyes for a moment. Almost immediately the images returned. He saw tatters of ancient parchment maps and heard countless voices alternately whispering and screaming in his ear, thousands of voices overlapping as they urged encouragement or shouted disapproval. He saw a young woman's face, her feature's twisted in fear as her pale blond hair whipped about in the intense wind. He heard an ancient spell chanted in a foreign tongue that resembled Sim's lyrical speech. He witnessed a tremendous explosion racing across the land; and at the center of a dark vortex, a large round gemstone, like a brilliant black opal, shattering into five separate shards. He felt Larien's lust and greed in his mind as he watched the shards fly in all directions, destructive emotions overlapping as if part of his own psyche as Larien made him reach his hand out to the nearest *yúgure* fragment.

He saw Sim's face before him, only the Onmyóji looked different somehow. Sad, mournful as he had been a lifetime ago at their first encounter.

He opened his eyes and Shard saw they were a brilliant turquoise.

"Shard!" Terrays screamed with Sim's voice.

He sat up in his chair, nearly crying out in shock.

"Shard?" It was Bys standing in the doorway, his childlike face peering into the room. "Are you all right?"

"Just tired," Shard breathed. He sat up and ran a hand through his hair.

Bys carried a package in his arms. "Long day's travel, huh? I just wanted to give you something, before you went to sleep."

Shard rose, walking over to the door. "Magic stuff, right?" Bys asked. "You mindlinked or whatever you call it with that Larien. Stargazer told me. I don't know about magic – glad we kobold never have to worry about that. Enough telepathy to soulbind with our sweethearts and scream for help if it comes to that. Everything else is more trouble than it's worth."

Shard smiled wanly. "You might be right about that."

"Here, I got you something," Bys laid the package on the bed, and began to unwrap it. "Now, you might just be a kitling, but you're a leader now, and being a leader's all about having a leader's mindset." He withdrew the garment and held it up. "Try it on."

Shard slipped it on over his jacket. It was a black leather greatcoat, smartly cut, hanging cleanly off his shoulders and falling straight to mid-calf.

"Perfect," Bys decided, checking the cuff length as Shard gazed at his reflection in the mirror. "I got the measurements from one of my men – frighteningly tall for a kobold. You've got a good frame on you, Shard. Your father's wonderful and all, but," he shook his head. "I swear he'll hit his head on the sky someday. You, you look just about right for a peri."

Shard smiled at that.

Bys smoothed the coat over his shoulderblades. "That's a leader's coat. Now you look ready to lead your troop into the mountains."

Shard studied his appearance. How different he seemed from the little kit who had run off into the mountains one month before. His eyes looked steadier now, clearer, more violet. They lent his face an older, more commanding appearance. The delight he knew he should have felt at that did not reach him; instead he felt more melancholy, feeling as if he had lost a part of himself.

"Cheer up," Bys patted him on the back, stretching to tap his shoulder. "You look like you're going to your own funeral. That's no way to inspire your men."

Shard blinked, nodded once. He couldn't afford sadness now. He was no longer a child with the leisure of his own melancholy to comfort him. He had to lead the others. They believed in him, for some unknown reason: his parents and his siblings. Sim believed in him.

He cheered at that.

He stood taller, rolling his shoulders back, holding his head high. His gaze turned resolute, almost grim, as he stared challengingly into his reflection's eyes. *You can do this. You will do this!* he commanded. *They believe in you – for some reason, they believe in you. You're not going to disappoint them.*

You're not going to disappoint Sim, *damn you. You will do this, or I'll break your short, scrawny little neck!*

Bys pounded him on the back. "There you go," he grinned encouragingly. "Those are a leader's eyes."

Varron Lehs hovered in the alleyway, his roughspun cowl hiding his face. He had little fear of being recognized by the common street rabble, yet a gnawing anxiety persisted that he would bump into a kobold he had once enslaved. Not yet noon and already three whores had propositioned him: two peri wenches and a young kobold boy with a face too innocent for the dangerous profession he was in. Pickpockets swarmed the alleys, and fights were breaking out everywhere; he had little doubt he would miss the Onmyóji or the Amaru rabble among such company. A sound caught his ear and he turned to see the lights flicker inside the nearby tavern. He heard crashes as heads met tables and bodies met walls. Some damn fool had just overdrunk his credit.

A kobold went flying out the open doorway, nearly knocking over the harlot who waited for a taker. Two trogs staggered out a moment later, their long manes streaming behind them. "Apologies, apologies, lady," they stammered in their native tongue as they scurried into the shadows with atypical cowardice.

Another loud crash, and two swarthy peri rogues went running from the bar, swearing indignantly as they nursed their cuts and bruises. A moment later another peri strode out, and the onlookers retreated in instant terror.

Varron drew nearer, captivated. It was a girl.

She was pretty morsel with short fire-red hair and a delicate white face. Her visage was that of a Palace flower, but she wore a skimpy warrior's dress that bared long slender expanses of milky-white flesh. She was petite, slim-boned and delicate like a sylph, her tiny hand clasped about a vicious long-handled claw-footed battleaxe. *Who are you?* He wondered. A bounty hunter, perhaps, or an Alteri mercenary like Darhis.

A wide-eyed young man staggered out the tavern to join her side, his pride a long tail of braided silver hair. He was dressed in an sleeveless tunic, practical warrior's trousers and boots, yet he ornamented his outfit with fine leatherwork belt and gauntlets out of place in the impoverished town. A long half-cape fell from his shoulder, clearly of high-quality weave.

The girl laughed. "That'll teach them who's soulbound and who's not." She swung her axe onto her shoulder with a cocky smirk.

Varron's eyes narrowed on the boy. He had seen him, somewhere before, only where? The boy glanced to the side nervously, and Varron remembered his face – only before his hair had blown unbound, shadowing his visage.

Celaeno's brat! And the fire-haired wench? Was she the Kitsune heiress who had recently married the Lord Heir? Varron's smile grew.

"Did you have to beat them all?" Stargazer wailed. "Couldn't you have let me take one or two, at least? I'm supposed to be your soulmate."

"They were insulting you, trying to take me home like that. I had to defend your honour."

"Aren't you ever going to let me defend *your* honour?"

"I'm just doing the woman's work, Stargazer." She tossed her head. "When the big boys come by, I'll let you take them."

"Come on, we'd better get back to the Guildhearst," Stargazer cautioned.

Varron restrained himself from charging ahead, from throwing himself upon them. He was still weak, still healing. And if the girl had dispatched peri mercenaries and troglodyte warriors alike for a simple proposition and a slap on the backside, he had no wish to tangle with her in open ground.

No, no he would wait. Like any predator, he would follow from a distance, and wait for his opportunity. He would judge their strengths and their weaknesses. And when the time was right, he would present his Master with several new war trophies. Not all, though, he amended. The little redbird he would keep for himself.

L'al Darhis stood over the canyon, watching her orders being carried out with a stern eye. Morden was at her side, as were his lieutenants. Legions of camp slaves, those not at work in the tunnels above them, clustered on the other side of the twenty foot deep culvert, shivering under the watchful eye of the slavemasters.

The kobold girl was dragged forward into the narrow canyon. A burly troglodyte held each arm, pulling the girl to a predetermined patch of dried ground. Two large spikes sat imbedded in the ground, a length of brittle cord around each. The men set Ciilet on the ground and lashed her wrists to the spikes; the kobold seemed too fearstruck to even struggle. Abandoning her, the troglodytes scrambled to higher ground. Murmurs spread among the slaves; the girl was better dressed and better fed since she had last been seen outside Darhis's rooms. What had the Alteri's favorite done to warrant such punishment?

Morden shot Darhis a questioning glance as the woman strode forward, holding her ornamented staff aloft. It was long, forged of an alien gleaming black metal, a deep blue gemstone set at its cap, flanked by silver rings.

Darhis set two fingers to her lips and whistled. A half-breed named Garn came out, a hellhound at his side. The crowd recoiled visibly, and even Morden's men shivered at the sight. The dusky gray beast struggled on the tight leather tether, slavering and growling. It spied Ciilet staked out on the ground and its aggression shifted from the kennelmaster to his intended prey. Murmurs of dissension built within the crowd as they realized the gruesome fate meant for the kobold maiden, but a few choice blows silenced the slaves.

Darhis stood tall, unwavering. Morden bit his lip nervously.

She nodded once to the half-breed, and he released the hound.

The hellhound howled once, an eerie, bone-chilling sound, wolf and predator bird mingled with something unearthly in its tones. With one ferocious bound, the hellhound leapt a good thirty feet, streaking down the narrow culvert towards the kobold girl, tugging feebly on her bonds, unable to take her wide eyes off the predator.

The hound sailed through the air, claws unsheathed, jaws wide. Darhis brought her staff down hard against the earth. The silver rings jangled loudly, a sweetly discordant tone.

The hound stopped, not a hair's breadth from the girl. Still slavering, growling low in the back of its throat, it sniffed Ciilet's hair, nostrils flaring, bloodshot eyes narrowing dangerously.

It struck her once, a light tap of a massive paw. She flinched, but no more.

It rubbed its head against hers, as if in a gesture of camaraderie. She murmured weakly, hardly daring to breathe.

Darhis struck the staff against the ground again. The hound turned, its amiable nature dissolving instantly. It roared hungrily, its eyes narrowing on Garn. The half-breed realized his peril a moment too late, a weak whimper escaping his lips as the hound leapt through the air, bounding towards him with lightning speed.

Garn looked up at Morden and Darhis, fury and betrayal on his features.

"Mord–" he cried, just as the hound reached him. The beast's jaws closed tightly about his neck; all present heard the deadly snap. Without a moment's pause the hound tore into the man's chest cavity, greedily devouring its kill.

Darhis whistled again, a higher pitched cry, and unseen kennelmasters, her own Alteri warriors, released the other eight dogs. Within an instant, nine furious skeletal bodies covered the remains of Garn, muzzles red with blood as they fought amongst themselves for meagre portions of the dwindling corpse. Darhis smiled softly as she watched her hounds feast. Within minutes Garn was cleaned to the bones.

Darhis stepped off the ledge, leaping into the canyon.

"Darhis!" Morden called out as she gracefully landed on the canyon floor, midway between the feasting hounds and the kobold girl. The hounds spun about, by no means satisfied by the half-breed. They streaked across the floor, four hounds shoulder-to-shoulder, nearly leaping over each other in their bloodlust. Darhis stood unflinching as they bore down on her, staff in hand.

Darhis brought the staff down on the ground. The rings jangled. The dogs stopped.

She sat down on the ground, holding out her hands as the dogs whined and whimpered, rolling onto their backs in submission, their bony tails wagging hopefully as she bestowed gracious pats to their heads.

She rose, striding over to Ciilet. With a flick of the wrist, she unsheathed her dagger at her thigh. Swiftly, Darhis cut Ciilet free, and hauled her to her feet. Darhis smiled, winking. "I told you," she whispered. "You put on a good show."

Still Ciilet continued to shiver, barely able to stand. Darhis pushed her towards the wall, and nodded to the men on the ridge above them. A rope was hastily lowered, but the slave was too weak to climb it. Darhis glared at the troglodytes on the ridge pointedly, and one climbed down to rescue the girl.

"Take care of her!" Darhis barked. "See to it that she's cleaned up and sent back to my rooms."

"I always knew you were one for bondage, Darhis!" Morden chuckled above her.

Darhis shook her staff, and three of the dogs leapt up at Morden. He backed up, screaming as the dogs nearly cleared the canyon wall, their claws digging furrows into the rock mere inches from the top of the wall.

Darhis shook the staff anew, and the hellhounds dropped to the floor, returning to her side. "I am your life and death!" she shouted to the assemblage. "You will honour me! I am your T'Jara, your Huntress!" She spun about, glaring at Morden on the ridgetop. She smiled, seeing the fear in his eyes.

She held her staff high over her head, and a cheer went up from the slaves. Her smile grew when she saw it was genuine applause, unprovoked by the whips and truncheons of the men. She closed her eyes, rejoicing in the cheers washing over her. They were hers, captives of her power, willing prisoners of her charisma.

The cheers died to a murmur, and Darhis spun about to glimpse a blackrobed figure high above the ridgetop. Everyone, including Morden slowly turned to stare awestruck at the imposing spectre. A snarl grew in Darhis's throat as she spied the intruder who had stolen her audience. She leapt up from the canyon, clearing the jump the hellhounds had failed to make. Passing Morden, she raced up the rockside, leaping from rock to rock, nearly flying up the cliff towards the spectre. With one last stride, she landed on the ledge before the man, her dagger bared.

The man lifted his gloved hand and the black mask from his face.

Darhis recoiled. "Larien?"

His skin was not longer stretched taut over a skeletal frame, left to pool in deep wrinkles about his eyes and jowls. Though it was still a little too yellowed, a little too dull, his skin was now firmer, his bone structure stronger. His dark eyes were still underlined by tired circles, yet they were no longer nearly so bloodshot. Larien threw back his cowl, and his once-colourless, thin hair was now a thick, deep silver, streaked with faint strands of black.

"You seem surprised, Darhis," Larien murmured. His voice was still gravelly, a raspy hiss, but of a deeper, more powerful pitch. "Did you really think me such an invalid?"

"Tejar," Darhis breathed, sinking to one knee.

"I see your hounds are in good training. I hope you left Morden some men, at least."

She nodded, a faint blush touching her cheeks.

He touched her shoulder, and she could still smell decay mingling with silken. "Then perhaps it is time for the hunt to begin."

Darhis's eyes sparkled hungrily.

16

The air grew denser, more cloying, as they travelled northeast through the winding spires and rambling mountainsides of the Boundary Hills. The clouds were nearly uniform now: a flat dull brassy colour, that only occasionally parted to reveal the stars behind. It was disturbing to the young peri who knew only the jewel blue clouds laced with silver and white that hung above the City Mount. Bys and Sim, however, joined by the other kobold trackers and porters, seemed resigned to the change, and paid it little heed.

Stargazer shivered astride Silverscales, his hands twisting the saddle loop. The dragon was equally uneasy with the change in the environment, and clawed at the crumbling rust-rich ground, snorting at the dust.

"Wish we could fly," Aerin grimaced, seating atop her golden dragon. "This dust is getting to Luck." To corroborate, Luck sneezed loudly and bucked his head, his bronze-red mane flying, whiskers whipping about his muzzle.

"Whisker doesn't mind." Mindrin lounged in his saddle, giving his jade dragon a comforting pat on the shoulder.

"Whisker doesn't mind anything!" Sintaka laughed. "I swear you keep that pup spiced."

"He's not spiced," Mindrin gave Whisker a scratch behind his leonine ear, prompting a contented purr. "He's just agreeable, aren't you, boy?"

"Wish we fly could too, Aerin," Shard sighed. "But we'd just be advertising ourselves to Larien."

"He'll find us anyway," Aerin grumbled. "He's Larien, after all. We might as well let our dragons stretch their legs."

"Smoke's sick of walking too," Shard sympathized.

"At least we could send a scout up in the air to survey the territory," Aerin begged. "There could be an ambush lurking just ahead of us."

"She's learned her lessons well," Sintaka smiled, looking over her shoulder as she led the party astride Ghost. "Your brother would be proud. But I think Shard's right on this one, Aerin. We'll have to go by intuition."

"Are you all right?" Stargazer asked, drawing up alongside his mate. "You seem more nervous than I am."

"I don't know," Aerin rubbed her bare arms, though she felt no chill; the air was too warm for the season, if anything. "I'd swear something's been stalking us for the past few days. This feeling – it's getting stronger the farther north we go."

Shard caught Aerin's concern; he had to admit he shared it. His nerves had been frayed already from the long travel up from Amaru and the constant barrage of imagery from the mindlock with Larien. But now he felt something more, a distinct feeling that eyes were upon them, watching them hungrily. He gazed up at the sky. The burnished clouds parted just enough for them to make out the growing sliver of White Moon. It was the sixth day of the Spider Moon.

He glanced covertly at Sim, walking along at his side, entirely at ease with the bizarre humidity and the dark clouds. *Damn him,* Shard thought deep in his mind. Why did he have to look so good in everything he wore? Just before leaving the Guildhearst Sim had traded his pristine white coat for a sleeveless black jacket and trousers far more suited to the long travel ahead. It was not enough that he looked as stunning in black as in white, but the scant tunic revealed the lean muscles of his arms, and the fabric clung to his lithe figure with his every movement. It was as if the Powers themselves were conspiring to undo the young lord.

A small creature darted in front of Ghost, and the silver dragon bucked in alarm. Sintaka cried out, holding firm to her saddleloop. "What the hell was that?" she demanded, forcing Ghost down on all fours once more. A grotesque, nude rodent bearing a vague resemblance to a hare disappeared into the rocks.

"Jack-hopper," Bys grinned with dark humour. "The Denáren equivalent of a bunny rabbit."

"Did I see *horns* on it?" Stargazer demanded.

"Can't afford to be cuddly in the wastelands," Bys explained. "It's survival of the meanest up here." He shifted in the saddle on his gray packhorse. "Mnemsyara's nearly over us," he pointed to glow of the Bluestar, hidden behind the clouds. "We'll break for a little lunch in about an hour. If we're lucky the clouds will break and she'll give us a nod – it's the last we'll see of the sun or the moons. By the time you get up to my keep, the clouds never part. So, Sim," he turned to the Onmyóji, walking alongside Smoke. "I hear you lived back when this was all forest," he indicated the dry barren mountainsides. "Is it true you knew Cimmerian?"

Sim nodded. "I don't know if 'knew him' is the right term. I met him, once or twice, during peace talks with Djedethra. He was always the one calling for continued war – we knew he'd settle for nothing less than Elória's complete destruction. But I never thought he was capable of something like the *yúgure.* He always struck me as just another lonely, sad, angry sorcerer."

"Did you see him in his true form?" Bys asked eagerly.

"The Black Griffin of Djedethra: yes, I saw it once. He was trying to impress Nikaas of the griffins' true powers. He morphed right in front of the entire assembly – instead of this peri there was a black griffin, with a full thirty-foot wingspan, standing in middle of the throne room."

"I've never seen a griffin," Shard lamented.

"No, you wouldn't have. There aren't many of them left, these days," Bys nodded sadly. "Most that do travel beyond their home mountains keep to their peri form when they're among strangers – you'd never recognize them." The wind sang through the high spires, a haunting sorrowful melody. Shard shuddered at the eerie sound, so like a woman's voice. "Alsaya's mourning," Bys murmured, making a sign against evil spirits.

"Bys," Sim asked, looking up at the kobold. "I don't suppose you've ever... but, have you heard of a kobold named Armal? He was a slave at Chalandris until its fall. From the Norashi Guild, originally."

"Armal Norashi? One-eyed? Had a sense of humour you wouldn't believe? Well, I'll be damned. Yes, Armal came to Hesperin some time after Chalandris fell. He worked with the Mantalore Guild, with mining operations up here. Good man. Married a Mantalore girl, had five kits together."

"Armal always wanted a family," Sim smiled softly. "Where does he live now? I'd like to see him again, after this is all over."

Bys hung his head sadly. "He died about thirty-five years ago. Cave-in, in a tunnel he was scouting. He always wanted to do the scouting himself, that was ol' Arm. You knew him?"

Sim nodded, a sadness shrouding his eyes. "We were... good friends. We were... in the rebellion together. At Chalandris." He said nothing further, walking ahead, his head hung in mourning.

"Strange fellow, that Sim," Bys whispered to Shard.

Shard barely heard him, his eyes on the solitary sorcerer. Good friends: lovers perhaps? Something strange flickered within him at that thought, a burning knot tight in his throat. Jealousy? He reprimanded himself harshly for it. Who was he to begrudge Sim lovers? Even if he had spent all but a hundred years of his four millennia asleep, a hundred years was a long time to be alone. He couldn't fault him for finding companionship.

He could, he *could*, a little voice screamed a moment later. He couldn't even begin to picture Sim – wide-eyed innocent Sim – with anyone, Elórian cleric or kobold slave. What did Sim feel for the dead kobold? Shard's jealousy wondered. What secret bond had they shared that he would probably never have with the Onmyóji? He realized with a pang of self-loathing that he didn't want Sim mourning for anyone else, thinking of anyone else, certainly not with a lover's tenderness.

What's wrong with me? How had he become so petty, so cruel?

He stared at Sim's back. *I love you, Sim Onmyóji,* he thought as loudly as he dared. *Can you hear me?*

Sim continued to pace alongside Bys's pony. Shard let out a sigh, either of relief or misery. It was common knowledge that one's soulmate, bound or not, could read one's thoughts if they were loud enough.

Sim turned then, looking up at Shard quizzically.

Shard? Is everything all right?

Shard was certain his entire face flushed a dark crimson. "Fine," he croaked.
Did you just call me? I thought I heard something.

"No, no, uh... do you want to come up on Smoke?" he asked. "You've been walking for nearly four hours now."

"Oh, I hadn't noticed." Sim paused a moment considered it. He showed not the faintest signs of weariness, neither in his stance nor on his youthful face. *Beautiful face,* Shard thought distractedly. Sim scrambled up behind Shard and settled back in the saddle atop Smoke's long serpentine back. Rather than slipping his hands through the saddle loops at his side, however, he wrapped his arms about Shard's waist. Shard stiffened instantly, feeling the blood rush to his face.

"Shard? Is it another attack?"

Of course he saw nothing peculiar in the gesture, Shard chided himself. He had often held onto Shard during their long flight up the Hesperin: it was a standard position for secondary riders, not the least bit unusual. Shard realized Sim was waiting for an answer and stammered: "No, not really, at least... in a way," he temporized. "Everything's been... different since the mindlock." *No bloody kidding,* his mind added weakly. When before had he ever considered sharing a saddle with another man anything but innocent? *Powers*, innocence was in short supply these days, he thought. If he had entertained any doubts that it was merely his adolescent libido daydreaming, they were disappearing by the moment. Anytime Sim came within five feet of him his heart would start racing. He swiftly regretted the invitation to share Smoke; with Sim sitting so close, practically pressed against him, he felt his very blood was on fire.

He was actively trying to undo his comrade, Shard thought, when Sim gave him a reassuring squeeze. "It's all right, Shard," he whispered in his ear. "We're all with you; we'll figure this all out soon."

"Hah," Shard laughed weakly. "Not long ago I was telling you that."

Sim voice was oddly soft, thoughtful, carrying a wealth of ambiguity. "Things change," he murmured.

"They sure do," Shard breathed under his breath.

I think I am *in love with you, Sim,* he thought again.

There was no reply, and Shard sighed again, this time with untempered disappointment.

"You can't fly!" Bys snapped in exasperation.

"Of course he can," Aerin grinned proudly. "He's an Arashi knight – well, he will be in three months, when he turns twenty-one."

"Oh, sure, you can hang in the air for a little longer than me, maybe, and maybe jump a little higher too," Bys dismissed it with a wave. "But you can't *fly!*"

"Why not?" Stargazer asked as he took small bites of his lunch of rice and barbecued meat. "Why can't you, if you put your mind to it, if you can convince your entire body of your faith? And don't tell it's just a 'long-legs' discipline

– I've heard of kobold Arashi too. It's not about skill with conventional magic – one of the greatest Arashi can hardly float a cup."

"My brother," Aerin added with a proud tilt of the chin.

"He can fight my mother to a standstill, and she's over double his age."

"So... you're saying that will enough training, and enough faith, I could fly like a bloody three-feather?"

Stargazer nodded. "You could fly now."

"If I want to fly more than anything, I could, even though I don't have a speck of floater magic in me?"

"Uh-huh. Try it."

Bys set his lunch aside, standing up. He closed his eyes, concentrating, as if willing himself to float like a sorcerer. "No," he grumbled, opening his eyes.

"Why don't you?"

"'Cause I know I'll break my leg!"

Stargazer placed his bowl and chopsticks on the ground as he rose to his own feet. He took a deep breath, then – simply pushed himself off the ground, rising into the air in an infinitely slow leap. He ascended high above, hanging in the air leisurely, his cape fluttering about him, before he dropped back to the ground. Bys stared incredulously.

Mindrin lifted his panpipe to his lips and began to play a light folk melody. Replete, Sintaka reclined alongside him, her head in his lap, her golden eyes gazing up at him with naked adoration. The Boundary Hills had lost almost all of their woodlands now, their stark hillsides coated with briars and spindly leafless trees. Only hearty weeds blossomed in the crags and crevices. To the west, the Boundary Hills abounded with deep forests, populated by the great horned deer and the furbacked wolves. But to the east, towards Dragon's Jaws, there was only wasteland.

Shard sat several paces from the rest of the party, gazing up at the few stars he could see through the cracks in the clouds. The deluge of images had ebbed and the whispers in his head had silenced, for the moment at least. Only the restlessness remained, strong as ever, causing him to pace frantically while their lunch was unpacked, manifesting itself in a little twitch he had developed in his right hand. He ate what he could of lunch, but as seemed standard of late, he had no appetite. He was exhausted, but unable to slow down, as if he rode a perpetual silken high.

The dragons rested in the shade. Whisker sneezed once from the dust in the air. A bird-like cry echoed over the rocks. "Ryyx," Bys explained.

"Shard?" Sim paced over to his side, sitting down next to him.

Shard braced himself against the rocks, shivering once. "I feel like I'm feverish," he whispered weakly. "I'm hot and cold all at once."

"Oh, Shard," he brushed ebony locks back from his face in a tender gesture.

He only loves me as a teacher loves his student, Shard sighed inwardly.

"You took in a lot from Larien, a lot more than you had expected." He lifted his hand to Shard's forehead, closing his eyes as he lightly probed the turmoil inside Shard's mind. "Most people have to train for decades to find the power you used on pure instinct. But now your mind's trying to sort it all out – you're not trained for it, you're still so young."

"I saw Terrays," Shard murmured. "In my dreams," he explained unnecessarily to Sim's awestruck expression. "You're right – she does look exactly like you."

Sim smiled at the memory. "Healers... they always have a bit of a chameleon in them. She knew a spell to turn her eyes as green as mine, if only for a few hours at a time. She'd put on one of my robes, a loose one, and go to court as me." He laughed. "Not even Daethin could tell the difference, until she'd start laughing and give it away."

"I keep *seeing* it," Shard breathed. "The *yúgure.* I hear this scream – I wonder if it's supposed to be Alsaya? And then I see it shatter... right in front of me." He moaned softly, raising a hand to his forehead, and Sim saw it tremble slightly.

"What does the *yúgure* look like?" Sim asked. Shard was slightly cheered at the Onmyóji's attempts to distract him from whatever was troubling him. If only it were so simple.

"Oh, it's beautiful," Shard smiled in genuine awe as he remembered his dream. "It's," he held his thumbs and forefingers together, overlapping slightly, "about this big, cut flat. Beautiful deep blue, full of iridescent highlights. Silver, and blue and violet, like a Hesperin opal. And I could see, not see really, but feel, this aura coming from it, like the guardian spell on your castle in the Highlands. But stronger, older, like... oh, it's almost like a memory – like a song I heard when I was a child but can hardly remember now. Old Magic, I'm sure of it. Only it seems so familiar... It's... so beautiful," he murmured, seeing it before his mind's eye once more.

"Like your eyes," Sim breathed softly.

"What?" Shard's mind snapped back to the here-and-now.

"Your eyes," a gentle blush touched the Onmyóji's cheeks. "I can see the Old Magic in them. Kemuri's right – you *do* have an affinity for it. Violet... shards of purple and blue," he continued to gaze deep into Shard's eyes. "I wouldn't be surprised if I saw a little of the *yúgure* in them."

Shard inched his face closer to Sim's, only a fraction closer, and Sim did not pull away. They stared at each other in silence for a long moment, and the outside world seemed to fall away into nothingness.

"Larien's never seen the *yúgure,*" Shard murmured.

"Mmm?" Sim asked, almost reluctantly returning to the moment.

"He's never seen it, never felt it," he explained as Sim regarded him questioningly. "Never. He's only read about it, heard about it, from spies and clerics, and a few of Ravanor's Hokabalh priests. He doesn't know what it looks like, or what it feels like to hold it in your hand. But I do. It's not my imagination! I've *seen* it. I see it in my dreams... and – and I *know* that's what it looks like. It's like I've seen it before, long ago. I don't understand it.

But I can *see* it!" He rose, staggering off.

Sim got to his feet, utterly bewildered. "Shard?"

"Hey, don't stray from camp, Shard!" Bys called out.

Shard raced across the crescent shaped valley, scrambling up the rocks. The dragons lifted their heads in unison to watch him, with the exception of Whisker, who continued to doze, purring softly in his sleep. Shard slid down the angle slope into a gully and ran across the flatlands, grimacing at the decaying sulphur clinging to the ground. His boot hit a stone and he stumbled, his arms pinwheeling to steady himself. He had no idea why he was running so furiously, only that something was calling him, and that it felt wondrous to finally answer the restlessness and run as fast as he could.

"Shard!" Sim called from the distance. A small ryyx, all scaly limbs and lizard-like swiftness, darted by, its feathered wing-like arms tucked under its belly. Shard reached the other side of the gully and caught hold of the ragged roots growing from the side of hill, clinging tightly to the roots and he pulled himself up the slope.

Sim's voice was growing fainter as Shard raced onward, barely aware of the ground behind his feet. He could feel it in the air, a whispering presence, of the same hue as the aura he sensed in his recurring dreams. Faint lines, feeble currents of magic, almost undetectable, but instantly recognizable.

His brow was slick with sweat; his breath came in ragged pants. After a desperate scrabble up a tall cliff, he found himself standing alone on a circular plateau, overlooking countless identical mountain peaks, tall and sharply pointed, their sides red with rust.

He bent over, his hands on his knees, and he drew deep breaths into his aching lungs. Straightening, he ran a hand through his hair, brushing it back from his face.

"Shard?" Shard heard Sim's voice. A few minutes later, Sim's head appeared. "What are you doing?" he demanded as he hauled himself up onto the plateau.

"I... I feel it."

"What?" Sim drew nearer. "Shard, what is it?"

"The *yúgure*. It's out there."

"You can feel it? The *yúgure's* energy? Are you certain?"

"*Yes!* It's right there!" He pointed to the east. "It's... like a smell of a perfume your mother used to wear... or the sound of song you heard once. So faint, you almost can't hear it, but you know what is it. It calls up a memory you never knew you had."

"A memory... of the *yúgure*?"

"I don't know, I don't know, but I can feel it... it's right there. Right in front of me. Taunting me."

"Shard." Sim placed his hands on the boy's shoulder. "Come back to camp. We can't do anything about it from here. We'll go to Dragon's Jaws, and we'll talk to Bys's men. If that's where they're digging we'll be there in another day or two."

Shard wavered, began to slump back against Sim. "*Dedjar no fara, ka'eri,*" Sim murmured as he gently turned the young man around.

"What was that?" Shard asked faintly, exhaustion setting in.

"Oh, nothing."

"Sounds nice," Shard murmured. He let Sim support him as they slowly walked towards the edge of the plateau. He paused, lifting his head. "Something's wrong."

Sim felt it too. "Something's coming." **Aerin, do you sense anything back at the –**

A dark blur flew in front of them, and the connection was severed instantly. The two peri stared agape at the beast that appeared to materialize out of the thin air, not five feet from them. It stood nearly four feet high at the shoulder, its dark skin stretched over a frame of pure sinew and bones. Its teeth were long, daggerlike, filling a huge maw, and its eyes glared a bloodshot crimson.

"What is it?" Shard whimpered, shrinking.

"Hellhound." Sim withdrew his katana from the scabbard at his side.

Sim? Sim? Aerin mindspoke repeatedly, a desperate sending.

"What's wrong?" Stargazer rose to his feet.

A howl, and suddenly four dark shapes alighted on the rocks around them. Hellhounds, baying for blood and completely surrounding them. *Damn it,* Aerin swore, *why did we let ourselves get boxed in like that!*

"Get to the dragons!" Sintaka shouted, already on her feet, her hand on the bullwhip at her side. Mindrin let the panpipe fall to the ground and ran towards the excited dragons. Aerin swung her axe threateningly as she backed away from the cliff where the nearest hound perched. Stargazer unsheathed the North Star from the scabbard on his back.

The first of the hounds leapt, landing on the ground next to the dragons. Without a moment's hesitation it sank its teeth into the nearest set of scales. Stargazer cried out in horror as the dog bit deep into Silverscale's shoulder. The dragon screamed, bucking in alarm, trying to throw the beast off him.

Take off! Stargazer commanded. **Silver, Smoke, Luck, take off now!**

A second hound joined the attack, throwing itself on Ghost. Sintaka uncoiled her whip, cracking it over the hound's back. The hound yelped, but continued the attack, claws digging deep wounds on Ghost's leg, jaws snapping at the dragon's neck.

Stargazer dropped to his knees, unleashing a shockwave which struck the hound hard. Ghost flew into the air, screaming and thrashing from his wounds, his right front leg mangled and bleeding. Silverscales rolled over, crushing the hound beneath him, before scrabbling up into the sky. Smoke and Luck joined them, Smoke's tail lashing out to strike the hound recovering from the shockwave. Whisker continued to cower on the ground, whimpering in fear.

Whisker, GO! Mindrin screamed, running towards it.

Whisker, take Mindrin! Sintaka ordered.

The sedate jade dragon came to life, roaring at the two hellhounds closing on him, before floating above the ground. He swept down to catch hold of the back of Mindrin's jacket, lifting him off the rock floor.

"Sintakaaa!" Mindrin wailed as the dragon carried him higher.

You're no good to us down here, bear! Sintaka apologized. She and the other peri began to form a defensive ring. Shouting inaudible protestations, Mindrin scrambled up into his saddle. The two hellhounds on the ground turned their attention to the five packhorses.

"The ponies!" Bys ran forward, his spear held high. The third hellhound leapt from the rocks, landing square on his back. Aerin attacked, her axe catching the hound on its shoulder, cutting a deep gash. The hound turned on Aerin.

"Get off!" Aerin swung the axe again, striking a second deep wound on the creature's neck. Bleeding profusely, the hound still pursued her, leaping at her unshielded midsection. Aerin went over, the hound on top of her. A searing pain gripped her abdomen and she screamed, an agonized high-pitched wail that drew an accompanying groan of agony from Stargazer.

"Hey!" Bys jabbed the hound's flank, and it turned to snap at him. The fourth hound struck Bys, forcing him down again. A blur of gold, and Luck dove to the ground, catching the hound in its mouth. Luck shook the beast fiercely before letting it drop to the ground. Crippled, the hound lay unmoving, whimpering softly. Mindrin cheered triumphantly as he watched from his vantage point astride Whisker, high above. "Stay up there!" Sintaka shouted. "Good job, Min!"

Struggling to sit, Aerin swung her axe again, striking the hound hard on the side of its massive skull. Howling in pain, the hound fell back. Stargazer dropped to her side. Dazed, Aerin looked down to see four puncture marks across her abdomen.

Sintaka moved to cover them as Stargazer pulled Aerin back from the fighting. Bys was on his feet within a moment despite his wounds. The kobolds were fighting the hounds off the horses, but two horses were already dead, and one kobold lay on the ground, unmoving. They succeeded in cutting the other horses loose, and let them run free, giving them a slim chance against the berserker dogs.

Another howl echoed off the rocks, and two more hounds joined the fray, replacing the two wounded. "Where are they coming from?" Sintaka shouted in frustration.

Mindrin! Aerin needs you! Stargazer begged.

Whisker tried to drop to the ground. Instantly a hound sprang onto the dragon's back. Whisker lashed his tail and knocked the hellhound off. Mindrin caught the semi-conscious Aerin and pulled her into his lap. Another hound sprang at Whisker, catching the dragon's hind leg as he tried to take off. Whisker wriggled in the air, and the hellhound struggled to hang on.

"Hey! Take it easy, Whisker!" Mindrin howled. "You'll shake us off too!"

At last the hellhound's strength gave way and it fell to the ground, tearing a gash in Whisker's leg on the way down.

They won't let us get to the dragons! Sintaka cried. Each time Luck or Smoke dove in an attempt to lift them to safety, the hounds would bound at them, snapping and clawing, driving the dragons back up. Stargazer leapt into the air to reach Luck as the dragon dove again. But the hounds were ready this time, and refused to lose another peri. A dog jumped up, catching Stargazer's boot and dragging him back to the ground. Silverscales circled mournfully, his flight erratic, blood streaming down from the wounds on his shoulder. Ghost snapped at the hounds, but dared not descend.

"Someone's controlling them!" Stargazer shouted. A hellhound leapt and he ducked instinctively, only to put the dog between him and the rock of the cliffside. Bys staggered to join the shrinking circle as brother and sister stood back to back against the two circling hellhounds.

"What about Shard?" Stargazer gasped.

Bys struck a hound with his spear. The wooden handle broke in half, and the spearhead remained in the hound's side, but the dog hardly seemed to notice. The kobolds raced towards him, lobbing rocks ineffectively at the dogs. Sintaka slipped her foot under Aerin's discarded axe and kicked it up to Bys as the hounds circled for another attack.

L'al Darhis smiled to herself, watching the fight in her mind's eye as she stood under the gnarled tree. She struck the staff on the ground once more, the silver rings jingling. The hunt was in earnest. She changed her vision slightly, turning her attention to her other three pups. *Excellent.*

"Why aren't they attacking?" Shard demanded as he cowered behind Sim. The three hellhounds circled them angrily, snapping and growling, but making no move to attack.

This isn't normal hellhound behavior. Something's controlling them. Sim stepped forward, thrusting his sword out menacingly. The hounds jumped back, only to return, patrolling uneasily at the edges of the plateau. They wanted to charge, he could see it their eyes. They were straining against an invisible bond.

Shard, get ready to run, Sim mindspoke.

"W-what?"

I'll try to hold them off. Take my sword and run. Try to get back to camp.

"You'll be defenseless," Shard protested.

I'll have my magic. Don't worry about me. Just run. I'll try to shield you while I can. I'll give the hounds something to think about. Hopefully, they'll go after me and let you go.

"Sim, I can't let you–"

Sim thrust his swordhilt into Shard's hand, closing his hands around the handle. Before Shard could protested, Sim stepped forward, locking eyes with the largest of the hounds. The hound yelped as a painsend jumped through the mental connection. The dog's growling grew louder, more menacing. Sim unleashed a bolt of blue lightning against the lead hound. The dog fell back, whimpering as the electricity crackled about him. The two hounds leapt at Sim, their programming overwhelmed by their instinct.

"Go!" Sim shouted as he released a shockwave, knocking the dogs back from the edge of the cliff. "*GO!*"

Shard ran. He scrambled down the cliffside, Sim's katana clutched tight in his hand. Nearly falling as he reached the bottom of the red rocks, he raced over the ground, not daring to look over his shoulder.

The hounds charged Sim in a unified wave and he cast a blastshield, knocking them hard against the rocks as the shield rose to protect him. Where the blastshield had killed a maned tiger at point-blank range, the hellhounds were only dazed, snorting and growling as they shook their heads. They were nearly unstoppable, their very cells fortified with the *yúgure's* dark magic.

They leapt again, but not at Sim, passing him by to descend the cliffside, racing after Shard. Sim cursed himself. How could he have missed it? They weren't sent to kill them. They were sent after Shard.

Shard! he called desperately. **They're coming!**

Sim– the first hound hit him on the back, forcing him to the ground. Shard cried out as he felt the creature's fetid breath on his neck, anticipating the sharp pain of the blackened fangs against his flesh. But the creature merely held him on the ground, rasping in his ear. Given the hellhound's mythic reputation, the creature's actions were almost gentle.

He tried to inch his hand closer to the discarded sword, and one of the hounds set its paw overtop warningly. He gazed into the beast's maw, filled with dagger-tipped fangs, foaming spittle dripping to the ground as it regarded Shard with a predator's hunger.

Wish I was food, don't you? Shard glared. The hound on his back growled low, its weight against Shard lifting slightly. Shard let his body lie limp on the ground and slowed his breathing. The dog's weight eased further, and Shard felt a paw nudge him. The hound stepped off his back, sniffing Shard's hair in curiosity.

Shard spun around, his hand rising, clamping hard against the beast's hard skull. The hound snarled angrily, surging against Shard's hands. He matched its fury, staring back insolently at the beast. He felt his rage rising, tumbling over itself in a race towards a flashpoint.

FIRE!

The hound wailed like a wounded puppy, bucking its head, nearly flipping over backwards as it leapt away. Shard leapt to his feet, extending his hand. The katana leapt into his hand and he raced back towards the rock, pressing his back against the cliff.

The hounds advanced angrily, but he would not let them surround him again. The smell of charcoal and burning hair hung in the air. Shard saw the leader sported two large burn marks on the side of his muzzle, shaped almost like a pair of hands.

The lead hound lunged forward, and Shard slashed at him with his sword.

It was a poorly timed blow, and it glanced off the hellhound's head. Nevertheless it drew a thin stream of blood. The second hound leapt in turn and Shard swung the katana around, striking against the dog's paw. "Don't you–" the third hound leapt and Shard drove it back. "Get back–" two hounds leapt at once, and Shard fell back against the rock hard.

"*Stop!*" Shard screamed, and all three hounds flew backwards, head over heels, sprawling on the ground ten feet away. Shard blinked in disbelief. *Was that a shockwave?* He had never been able to cast one so powerful before.

The dogs twitched their hind legs, alternately snarling and whimpering. Shard ran.

He ran across the flats until he came to a gully. At first he slowed to prepare to scramble down, then changed his mind as he heard the snarling and snapping of the hellhounds at his back. *Powers be with me.* He leapt into the air, arms pinwheeling as he closed his eyes, willing every ounce of strength into his jump. The air seemed to slow about his hair and time seemed to stand still as he hovered in the air, slowly inexorably descending to earth. The hounds fell behind him, leaping to catch him and falling short, tumbling down the fifteen feet into the gully. Shard landed on the edge of the rock wall and ran again, barely breaking stride.

"Don't they know when to die?" Bys swung the axe at the hellhound. Two of his kobolds were fighting another hound with staffs, succeeding only in driving it back, inflicting no lasting injuries. The hound Luck had attacked continued to twitch on the ground, trying ineffectually to rise, its back broken. *They should be attacking it,* Sintaka thought. *Hellhounds always pick off the weakest.* But as long as the phantom operator had the hounds under his control, they would continue to attack only the peri.

Aerin's going bad, Mindrin sent. **She's not bleeding much anymore, but she can't stay awake.** He kept Aerin's dress hiked up, pressed tight against the bite marks, occasionally slapping her face lightly to get her attention.

Sintaka's whip wrapped about the neck of one of the hounds, but the hound only used it pull the peri away from the guarded circle. She lost her hold on the whip and fell hard on the ground. The large hound with the maimed neck leapt on her back. Stargazer broke formation as well, throwing himself on the hound, driving his swordpoint directly through the beast's head. The creature screamed in its death throes, trying to shake Stargazer from its back. But the astrologer held on, forcing the sword in deeper, until at last the hound slumped to the ground, dead.

The siblings backed up, faced by four hounds advancing in a unified wave. Stargazer felt the hard rock against his back. There was nowhere left to go.

L'al Darhis smiled, a rush of adrenaline surging through her as she visualized the final attack. The hunt was at its climax. She raised the staff high over her head, ready to deliver the last command to her hounds.

"I am your T'Jara; obey me," she breathed.

Something hit her hard between her shoulderblades.

With a raw cry of pain she fell forward. The staff clattered uselessly to the ground.

Dust flew in her face as she hit the ground. She reached instinctively for the staff but a hand caught hers, twisting her arm painfully behind her back. Darhis lashed out with her legs, tripping her opponent. She rolled over, her hands reaching up to throttle her assailant. Limbs tangled with hers and her back was pressed hard against the dirt. Mischievous gray eyes glittered above her.

"Hello, pretty," Arjin tal Kitsune grinned, before covering her mouth with his own, silencing her scream of protest.

17

He leapt off her, flipping backwards, head over heels, to land on his feet under the gnarled tree. Darhis coughed, flipping herself to her feet, glaring at him with a predator's eyes. A peri, dressed in well-tailored leather huntsman's coat and trousers. He stood at least four inches taller than she, his figure sleek and insolent. He held a polished aristocrat's cane, his only weapon. His long hair fell past his waist, unbound.

"Who are you?"

"Oh, don't you recognize me, pretty?" he held his elegant cane out before him with one hand. With the other he twisted on the handle, withdrawing the long whiplike blade from its sheath. He tossed the hollow cane aside. "I'm the devil." He pointed the blade's tip at her, tucking his left hand behind his back dueling style.

Darhis sneered, unsheathing the dagger at her thigh, darting towards him with all an Alteri's speed.

He did not parry her attack with his swordstick, but instead nimbly ducked the first thrust, catching her wrist before she realized what had happened. "Oh, do better," he chided, before he forced her arm back, flipping her over onto the ground.

Darhis scrambled to her feet, throwing herself on her opponent. He parried her first thrust, then her second, moving with the speed of a cat. His reed-thin blade whistled through the air as he met every one of her attacks, first nimbly retreating like a master fencer, then driving her back, advancing with practiced ease. With each foiled attack, Darhis's frustration grew. She swung wildly at his neck, her arm trembling with rage. He merely dropped to the ground, one long leg swinging out to trip her to the ground. He then waited patiently, balancing his swordstick on his palm, until she rose again.

"Arrogant prey," she hissed, casting her dagger aside. She held out her hand and her staff flew into her palm.

"I'm no one's prey," he informed her in a silky voice.

Stargazer stared down the ring of hellhounds. The beasts hesitated, almost confused, shaking their heads and growling excitedly. They tensed, their hind legs coiled springs ready to break free. Stargazer murmured a prayer under this breath to whomever might be listening.

The first hound leapt. Stargazer flinched.

A blur of jade fell from the sky, jaws open wide. The dragon fell upon the hound, nearly swallowing it whole, rolling over on himself, his jaws closed tight onto the hellhound's head. The other hounds drew back, confused, their eyes searching the heavens for another attack.

"Whisker!" Stargazer gasped.

"That's not Whisker," Sintaka stammered incredulously. "That's Westwind."

A warcry, and a peri youth fell to the ground, his immense falchion already drawn and shining in the air. The second hound lunged instinctively, and Ceih caught it on the side of his sword, his powerful swing cutting through flesh and sinew, throwing the hound ten feet from their position. The hound landed on its side, snarling and convulsing as it tried to draw itself up. The two remaining hounds drew back warily.

"Oh, come *on!*" Ceih challenged, stepping forward, swinging his falchion wide. The wounded hound, sporting a bloodied gash on its ribs, charged him, while its companions watched. Ceih fell to the ground, letting the hound overleap him, then pivoted about, catching the hellhound on its other side, inflicting a second deep gash. The hound staggered back, eyes still locked murderously on Ceih.

The two remaining hounds considered their options carefully, before they leapt in unison on the wounded dog, each taking a side of its neck, bringing it down to the ground and tearing it open.

Ceih turned, exchanging a swift glance with Sintaka. She nodded and peri and kobold alike turned around, scrambling up the rocks in search of higher ground.

Shard collapsed against the rough ground, too weary to go on. He could hear the hellhounds circling him. He tried to rise, but his legs were too weak. He had lost track of the time he had been running, the dogs just beyond him. Now he was exhausted.

He heard Sim's voice. Was he dreaming?

"Get away from him." Energy crackled in the air and Shard heard a hellhound yip as it was struck by a lightning bolt. The other two stayed their ground.

"Shard?" Sim begged, drawing closer, his hands raised to deliver another attack. "Shard, get up. You can't stop now, Shard. Come on, get up."

"Too tired..." Shard moaned, trying to prop himself up on his arms. A hellhound attacked, pushing him back down before withdrawing to guard its quarry.

A cry above them, like a falcon calling out as it dove on its prey. Shard lifted his head and saw a streak of deep blue as Smoke fell out of the sky. She landed square on one of the hounds, knocking it over. Shard somehow found the strength to rise, and ran towards Sim. He stumbled, almost drunkenly, but his legs kept moving, and he held out his hand desperately as he drew near the Onmyóji. Sim caught his hand in his and clasped it tightly as they ran across the wastelands. They heard Smoke trill again as she dove, trying to buy them more time. Shard heard the hounds howling and snapping at her, but did not look back, keeping his eyes fixed on the path ahead. Hand in hand, he and Sim raced over the uneven terrain, aware of little beyond their breath burning in their lungs. Shard did not ask where they were running. He knew Sim had no idea either.

I'm so sorry, Shard, Sim mindspoke.

The earth opened up under them.

A brief yelp of surprise escaped Shard's lips as they fell.

Darhis swung the staff hard against the tree. Arjin leapt into the tree, grasping hold of a gnarled blackened branch. He hung there, a cocky grin on his face, before he dropped atop her, his leg extended. His boot hit her square on the shoulder, and they both toppled to the ground.

"Can't get enough of me, can you?" Arjin chuckled as he looked down at his enraged foe. He leapt back, handspringing to an attack pose, the swordstick appearing in his hand once again. Darhis held the staff aloft defensively.

"You call yourself Larien's minion?" Arjin scoffed.

"I'm no one's minion. I am a Huntress!"

"You're a joke."

With a feral scream, Darhis charged him. Arjin leapt to avoid the first strike, and his leg struck out at her unguarded hip. Darhis staggered and the blade came about again, drawing blood across her shoulderblades.

"Stop playing and fight like a man!" Darhis jeered, stumbling back.

Arjin's eyes glittered. "Careful-what-you-*wish*-for," he singsonged.

Darhis charged him again, and he seemed to phase out of existence as the staff came down. Suddenly he was standing behind her, his foot striking her hard in the small of her back. His hand caught a fistful of her hair, and he whirled her around, slamming her forehead against his knee. As she stumbled back, his leg swung out again, kicking her hard in the gut. She reeled in a daze, and Arjin backhanded her sharply across the face. Her hold on the staff slackened and she fell back on the hard earth.

"Now, wonder was *this* does?" Arjin scooped up the staff.

"You..." she hissed. She coughed, and blood was on her lips. Her eyes widened as she saw Arjin swing the staff high over his head. "*NO!*" she screamed as he brought the jeweled cap firmly down upon a sharp-edged rock.

The cap broke. The jewel cracked, and the rings tumbled to the ground. Arjin smiled triumphantly, holding up the remaining metal pole.

"I'll–" she raged incoherently, getting to her knees.

"Ohhh, scratch my eyes out, pretty," he begged teasingly.

She threw herself upon him. Arjin let her momentum push them over, and he fell back on the ground, flipped her over his head. Darhis was battered and bruised, incapable of mounting a coordinated attack. Arjin caught the fist she swung at him and threw her against the tree. Darhis coughed again, moaning as she slumped the ground.

A mournful howl echoed in the rocks. "Take it that would be my cue," Arjin picked up his swordstick, resheathing it.

"You'll never leave here alive," Darhis croaked, pulling herself to her feet.

"You're persistent," he laughed. She leapt at him and he flew into the air, letting her pounce on empty air below him. Darhis fell on the ground, cursing. She barely rolled away before Arjin's boot came down to earth, a fraction from her ribcage.

Arjin picked her up by the scruff of the neck. "Love to stay, but my boyfriend's jealous as hell. Don't forget me, pretty," he kissed her again, a rough, insolent kiss, before biting her lip sharply and throwing her back, then somersaulting up into the tree. Darhis coughed, wiping her mouth. He was already gone.

"What happened?" Stargazer gasped. One moment the hounds had been scrambling up the cliff after them, the desiccated corpse of their comrade abandoned. The next they were wailing and howling in agony, turning tail and streaking away into the mountains.

"Arjin," Ceih gloated.

The kobolds dropped back to the ground, surveying the damage. Two horses were dead, the other three lost amid the jagged landscape. One kobold lay dead as well, his limbs sprawled in all directions. Sintaka whistled and the dragons dropped to the ground, one by one. Mindrin landed Whisker alongside them, Aerin unconscious in his lap.

"Aerin?" Stargazer ran to Whisker's side. "Oh, Powers!" he choked, tears already brimming in his eyes. "She needs a healer, fast!"

Bys coughed, grimacing from the pain in his back. "Don't know where we'll find one out in this desert."

The lame hellhound continued to thrash weakly, slavering and moaning. Bys's remaining men strode over to it, spears in hand, and swiftly put it out of its misery.

Sintaka lifted the leather Mindrin had pressed over the wound. Four punctures, deep but clean. The bleeding had already stopped. It was impossible to see how much had seeped into the crimson leather. "Thank Oracle for Tiryn's blood," she breathed. "She's already healing herself."

"Where's Sim?" Mindrin asked. "His sister was a healer; maybe he can help her."

"Where is he?" Stargazer demanded frantically. "Where's Shard?"

Dead silence hung over the group, the only sound their laboured breathing and the distant whistle of the wind. Suddenly a loud voice bellowed in all their minds at once, the mindspeech as refreshing as a cool draught of springwater.

Hey, Bys. You out there, y' ol' desert rat? We just picked up two stray peri and one dragon, all scared shitless, in tunnel number eight. They yours?

Aerin heard a familiar voice, distant and muffled, at the edge of her awareness. "Yósha?" she croaked, her eyes fluttering open. She was not in the muted sunlight of the Boundary Hills, but inside a dark cavern. The air was cool and moist.

"Aerin!" Stargazer dropped to her side, clasping her hand in his. "Thank the Powers!"

"What happened? I... I was attacked?" She raised her head from the soft down bed to see linen bandages encircling her slim waist. "Ahh!" she gasped as the pain struck her, a tight stitch in her abdomen.

"Shh, rest," Stargazer lay her back down, smoothing her hair. "One of the hounds got you, remember?"

"Did I get him?" she asked weakly. Stargazer nodded. "The others?" she pressed. "The dragons?"

"Bys lost one of his men, and all his horses are gone, dead or escaped. But the rest of us are all fine. We're in a kobold tunnel; Bys's men found us. Silverscales has a gash on his shoulder, Ghost's front paw's torn pretty rough, and Whisker has a hound's tooth in his hind leg. But they've got a kobold healer fixing them up already."

Aerin blinked, her eyes still unfocused, as she listened to the faint chatter behind her in the tunnel. "Hah... must be delirious... thought I heard Arjin..."

Stargazer bowed his head, hiding his wry smile. Aerin sat bolt upright, despite the pain. "No!"

"Well, well, the little midget's finally up." Arjin swaggered over to her bedside. "Must be the healer blood in us, eh? Gimna hardly even had to stitch you up."

"*You!*" Aerin howled indignantly, leaping up from bed. Before Stargazer could stop her, she flung herself at Arjin, her hand raised to strike. But her attack dissolved into an embrace as wrapped her limbs about him. "*What the* hell *are you doing here?* Damn you! I *knew* someone was following us!"

Arjin set her back on the ground, mindful of her injuries, and Aerin continued to stare up at him, fury and admiration at once in her stare. "Does Mother know you're here?"

"She had better. We've been tracking you for the better part of a quarter-turn."

"What did you do? Sneak out of Amaru at night?"

"Aerin! You don't think Ceih and I would get left out of an adventure like this?"

"You are *impossible!* Ohhh, Celaeno's going to *kill* you when you get back!"

"She'd better not." He preened. "Saving all three of her kits – I expect to make satrap for this."

"You already *are* a satrap!" Aerin wailed.

"Really? Too many titles, I lose track of them all." Aerin threw herself at him in a second mock attack, and he swung her around with a delighted laugh. At length he set her down, shooing her back to her bed.

Sintaka huddled against the far wall of the immense tunnel, resting her head against Mindrin's shoulder. Bys was conferring with the rest of his men some distance away, while Sim and Shard stood nearby, Shard looking wan with exhaustion.

"So it was an Alteri?" Sim asked.

Ceih nodded. "Controlling the dogs with a staff, about three hundred yards from your position. Probably miniature symbiotes, or some other parasite in their brains, letting her control them. Westwind and I went to take care of the hounds while Arjin took out the Alteri. They stopped the attack as soon as he broke her staff."

"Working for Larien, I'm sure."

"Oh, I'm sure," Arjin agreed readily. "Hey, Shard, how's the magic treating you?" he gave the boy a playful slap to the backside, grinning at his flustered glare of indignation. Arjin gave Sim a lazy wink. "Hey, Sim," he purred, and the Onmyóji blushed.

"Well, I don't know what your Dynast will do to you, but I'm glad you Arashi are this rebellious," Bys announced as he approached them. "Looks like we're not going to Dragon's Jaws after all. Daav and the boys have been keeping their eyes open – thank Myrddin for us. We can take these tunnels all the way to Larien's dig site. There's a small keep dug at a crossroads of the tunnels about ten miles east. Helonsden. We can stay there tonight and go over some strategies."

Arjin moved to his dragon's side, and ran his hand over Witch's sleek metallic black scales. "How far to Wyvern's Rest?"

"Another day from Helonsden. We have a new keep we set to building as soon as we found the site of their primary digs. Thandállen. Still unfinished, but you'll like it, I think. Harkens back to the Dark Age. You ever seen a true Mantalore keep, long-legs?" He smiled when Arjin shook his head "You'll like it," he nodded. "Are the dragons up to travel?"

"Sintaka's is lame," Ceih informed him. "And Stargazer's has lost a lot of blood. But they're healing fast. And Whisker's as happy as ever, despite the five stitches in his leg. I don't want to leave them alone here – not that I don't trust Gimna, but we may need them later. We'll double up riders and let them walk alone the rest of the way. They should be fine in a day or two. We'll move out as soon as Aerin's well enough to travel," he ruled.

Bys clasped his hands. "All right, I'll see Daav about getting us some food to replace what we dropped for the hounds. Judging by the way she's shooting daggers at you two, Aerin should be fine to travel in another hour or two."

What went wrong? Larien demanded.

"The Amaru called in reinforcements. I lost my control over them," Darhis growled as she huddled under the tree, nursing her wounds. "Some swaggering dandy with a knight's training. He broke my staff. It'll take me some days to make a new one."

Perhaps I was hasty in appointing you Varron's successor, T'Jara.

"If you lose patience this quickly, I'm surprised Varron's still alive!" Darhis snapped back. "You're no fool, Larien. Who else can command hellhounds like pets? I'll get you your Amaru boy, don't worry about that. I've never lost a hunt yet."

See that your record is not broken. I would hate to see such potential shattered.

The connection flickered once, then was broken. Darhis sat up taller, holding out her hands as a whimpering dog approached her. "Ohh, puppy," she hugged his massive head. "Did that little kobold rat hurt you?" she eased the spearhead out of the dog's shoulder, smiling to see the severed arteries were already healing, the skin already regenerating. Still she cursed inwardly. Four hounds out of nine killed. Half her precious fighting force felled by arrogant Amaru and their dragons. She would have revenge for that.

She paced under the tree, stretching to the ease the aches in her limbs. The hounds whimpered, watching her intently. She had been overconfident, that was clear. She would not be so easily subdued the next time they met.

She heard footsteps behind her. Clumsy attacker, sneaking up on the rocks, his boots slipping on the loose dust. She heard a hiss of metal, a sword being unsheathed.

Varron dropped to the ground behind her, raising his sword high for a decisive strike. Darhis spun about and clubbed him on the shoulder with the remnants of her staff.

"You're pathetic," Darhis spat. "Is this what Varron Lehs has become?"

"I won't let you replace me!" Varron hissed, staggering to his feet.

"I don't *want* to replace you, you impotent shitwit!" she snapped. "Keep Larien as your Master; I've no wish to be his little pet."

"Liar! How could you reject such an offer, to be on the right hand of the Devil!"

"I am T'Jara. I am no one's slave!"

Varron swung the sword wildly at her. A hellhound pounced upon him and pinned him to the ground. "*Stop!*" Darhis shouted at the hound. It hesitated, inches above Varron's face. Darhis let it hold Varron down as she sat down on a rock beside him. "Kill me and they'll tear you to pieces. Oh, it'll be fast. But it will a hard death. You'll think it lasts forever. They'll go for the soft tissue first: the stomach, the intestines. You'll go mad from the agony before you die."

"I'll see your heart in my hand, Alteri!"

ENOUGH! Larien's voice rang in both their heads at one. Darhis winced, cursing. The mindspeech was magnified by the symbiote, and Varron howled in protest.

**I'll see you both staked to my wall if you cannot quell your pointless bickering. You are both failures, in my eyes, so take pride in your equality.*

*Now follow the Amaru dogs – separately if that's the only way to keep you both alive. But I want them found before they reach Wyvern's Rest.**

"They're underground," Darhis objected.

Then sniff out their burrowing holes. Send your hounds scouting for any signs. Even the most persistent kobold comes up for air eventually. I will hunt in my own particular fashion. We will find them before they and their kobold hordes challenge us at Wyvern's Rest.

The connection broke off abruptly, leaving the two enemies alone on the wastelands.

"Well?" Varron demanded.

Darhis tapped the hound on the shoulder and it grudgingly moved off Varron's chest. "My dogs will tear you to shreds if you defy me," she hissed warningly. "I'll not be slave to some man's heavy hand."

"I'll snap your neck the moment you seek to betray me, your puppies be damned."

Darhis smiled. "Then we have an arrangement." She looked up at the rocks, envisioning the Amaru crawling through the hidden tunnels with their kobold allies. She licked her lips, tasted the coppery blood. *Run while you can, "pretty,"* she sneered. *I'll have your hide sure enough.*

18

They journeyed through the wide tunnels, at times descending deeper into dark rock, at others rising until the air grew hot and Stargazer was certain they could see cracks in the ceiling letting in the brassy daylight. Slowly, the dragons grew more conditioned to walking through the gloom. Glowlamps were set in the rock at wide intervals, but the peri's wide eyes soon adapted to the darkness of the kobold tunnels. Occasionally they would see miners at work, pushing carts of minerals along the corridors.

Aerin stirred sleepily in her saddle, leaning back against Stargazer for support. Gimna the kobold healer had changed her bandages one last time before they had set off, and the party was cheered by her rapid recovery. Still she was exhausted from blood loss, able to do little more than sit half-reclined astride Luck.

Sintaka shivered, her head bent, her eyes cast on the textured leather saddle. Mindrin massaged her shoulders gently. "It's all right," he assured her. "Just keep your head down. There's plenty of air, don't worry."

"Cave-fright?" Bys asked. Mindrin nodded as Sintaka continued to avert her eyes from the tunnel ahead. "Mmm, happens with some peri. You're doing fine, Sintaka," he encouraged. "The tunnel never gets tighter than this. We'll be at the keep in an hour at this rate." He walked alongside his men, their heads bowed in mourning for their lost comrade. "We'll dance for Zhan tonight, don't worry," he reassured them.

They passed through a junction in the tunnels. A recently begun tunnel was being dug at a forty-five degree angle to the main corridor. Kobolds silently huddled around the large dark red creature sliding across the floor. It looked like a immense circular-shaped slug, with a fleshy head perched at the front of its gelatinous body. Stargazer thought he caught sight of two tiny vestigial arms hanging limp against folds of flesh.

"Is that a burrower?" Stargazer asked as they passed.

"Yep," Bys nodded proudly. "Rock munchers. They're a headache to breed and expensive to raise, but they're the bones of our mining operations. Their brain and eyes are up in their heads, there, but they're all mouth underneath.

They secrete enough acid to eat their way through any rock, and their favorite food is dull, unrefined stone. They hate gemstones, and gold and silver give them indigestion. It's the perfect partnership. And we little folk are all about partnerships."

Aerin wrinkled her nose. "They don't smell very good," she murmured.

"You get used to it."

Aerin fell back against Stargazer. "Rather not."

"I know what you mean," Stargazer agreed softly. "I can't wait to see the sun again. The *real* sun, without all these clouds."

Shard stirred in the saddle, his head against Sim's shoulder. Sim guided Smoke while Shard slept behind him. Shard lifted his head briefly. "Sim..." he murmured, yawning softly.

"Go back to sleep, Shard."

"Sorry..." Shard let his head fall back to Sim's shoulder.

"Don't be. You need your sleep."

"I owe you," Shard mumbled, before he fell back asleep.

The dance for Zhan, the fallen kobold, continued late into the day. The largest chamber of the keep, as large as the throne room in Amaru, was filled with kobolds of the Mantalore guild, all celebrating the life and honouring the death of their guildmate. The flames of the large central pyre burned high, and the combined voices of the miners rose high in mournful song. From their rooms high above the central chamber, the peri watched the ceremony, spellbound.

"Heard of the kobold funeral dances," Sintaka murmured. "Never seen one before."

"They never let outsiders see them," Mindrin breathed. "We're lucky."

The kobolds danced around the pyre, tears streaming down their faces as they sang the wild songs of the Boundary Hills. The howl of the furbacked wolf and the cry of the golden eagle combined in their melodies; the scream of the dying deer and the whistle of the screechowl rose with the ancient songs.

"Beautiful," Sintaka whispered, awestruck.

Several roasted birds slowly turned on the spit inside the fireplace, and bowls of stew cooled on the table in the peri's chamber. No one seemed particularly hungry. "We can't save the world on an empty stomach," Ceih attempted to rally the troops. He picked up a bowl and blew on the thick stew to cool it further before digging out a hearty bite with the flat wooden spoon provided. "It's fresh, at least," he offered.

"That's not necessarily a good thing," Mindrin objected, turning from the balcony. To Ceih's questioning look, he smiled weakly. "We're a little far from civilization for that to be three-feathered quail." He pointed to the avians turning over the fire. Arjin, in the midst of testing his own bowl of stew, set his spoon down abruptly.

Ceih merely shrugged and swallowed another heaping spoonful. "It's good," he confirmed, scooping a third spoonful. Arjin shot him a disdainful look.

"Bar-*ba*rian," he scoffed. Stargazer held up his hand to silence the room as Sim shyly emerged from the room above the main chamber. He sat down in the armchair across from Sintaka, and Stargazer moved to his side.

"How is he?" Stargazer asked as the Onmyóji two-spirit rested his head in his hands.

"Sleeping... somehow I think Aerin is getting a better rest than Shard will find tonight." He hung his head sadly. "His mind's racing, I can't make it slow down, no matter what I try. It's in our blood." Sim looked up. "What's wrong with us?" He glanced about the room, meeting the eyes of all the questioning peri. "Our bodies can live for hundreds, thousands of years. But our blood runs so hot, we burn out within a fraction of that time. We can't sit still! Kobolds take nearly a century to mature to adulthood – peri are grown by twenty. It's insane. It makes monsters like Larien who'll raze an entire continent to the ground just to stay strong and healthy a moment longer. And it makes children like Shard whose own power can kill them at emergence."

"Shard will be fine, I'm sure," Sintaka offered encouragingly. "He's always run a little faster than the rest of the world. I'm sure he can outrun whatever demons Larien has on his tail. He's an Amaru after all. We're tougher than we look."

"Yeah, yeah!" Ceih announced, his voice trembling in spite of himself. "Come on... let's – let's have something to eat, huh?"

Slowly the Amaru rose, hardly cheered, and moved towards the waiting meal. **How bad is it?** Stargazer asked Sim as the Onmyóji eased himself from the chair.

I honestly can't say, he admitted. **I've never met anyone like Shard. But we have to find the* yúgure *shard and end this as soon as possible. No matter what powers he has, he's only a kit. He can't keep this pace for long before his body starts to suffer for it.**

Shard drifted in and out of dreams. Whenever he was conscious enough, he was aware of the tight aches in all his muscles, a testament to his long run from the hellhounds. He felt drained in all possible ways. Almost. Still the restlessness tugged at him, and he ran in his sleep.

The *yúgure.* How could the others not feel it, when all he could hear, all he could sense was the dark magic's deep pull?

He opened his eyes to find himself on a misty white plain, alone, surrounded by shifty fog that seemed to shimmer with hidden colours. He turned around, calling for help, but he moved as if drugged, his motions slowed, his voice slurred.

He heard two swift claps, like the sound of smart boots against marble, and he turned to see a figure robed in black staring down at him. Tall, slender, face completely obscured by a black shroud.

"Who are you?" Shard demanded.

The figure raised a gloved hand, pulling the cloth down about his neck.

Shard found himself staring into a stately peri's face. He was handsome, or he would have been, in a stark way, were it not for the coldness in his face. It penetrated everything, from his dark stare to the tightly drawn lines about his terse smile.

"Shard," he spoke calmly. "Dynast Celaeno's little boy." He strode forward, his robes floating about him, the clouded edges disappearing into the smoke. "We meet at last, face to face... as it were," his smile tightened further.

"Larien," Shard breathed. "You look good. And able to cast yourself this far, able to invade someone else's dreams."

"I will only grow more powerful. Your Onmyóji was premature in declaring me an invalid, I assure you."

"'You're hopeless Larien,'" Shard quoted. "'Death.... what hope is there... only *yúgure*. I'll never find it. Damn fool... not in time. Hopeless.'"

Larien's eyes widened.

"I know you're living on borrowed time, Larien," Shard challenged. "You don't have the *yúgure* yet. And you'll die without it."

"You think you can find it before me?"

Shard said nothing.

Larien circled him hungrily, much as the hellhounds had. "You're an interesting specimen, do you know that? A little boy with the magic of an ancient. Pity your body's too frail to handle your own magic, eh?" He drew closer, pinching Shard's chin, forcing his face up. "You can feel it, can't you. It pulls at you, draws you nearer. I can feel it too, but not nearly in so many colours, so many facets, as you do. You're a rarity. Or should I say an aberration." He tugged Shard closer. "You know where it is don't you? Tell me," he whispered fiercely. "Will I find it in Ravanor's Treasury?"

Shard swallowed hard, caught in Larien's stare. "Yes," he breathed.

Larien smiled.

"But Sim and I will stop you before you can use it."

"Fool. You think you stop me? I have survived the *yúgure* blast, the Rebellion at Jaridan, the countless wars and crusades of the Dark Age. I've lost count of the failed assassinations, the wasted assaults on Chalandris."

"You think you can never die, Larien?"

"Who ever said peri need die?"

"You can't live on death," Shard protested.

"It has served me well in the past."

"The Dark Age is over."

"I'll see it return." Still smiling calmly, almost benevolently, his hand shot out and clamped tight about Shard's windpipe. "Remember this, little one? Do you see yourself back on the rooftop?" He tightly his grasp, and Shard coughed, his airway blocked. Shard wrapped his hands about Larien's wrist, trying to free himself, but the sorcerer would not relent. "No more confines, no more frailties."

First... through Varron's body, now... through telepathy. Can't... you ever... do anything yourself?

Larien tightened his grip on Shard's throat, and Shard felt his vision blur as he was lifted from the ground. He struggled to draw breath, to free himself from Larien's grasp. But his strength was failing. His eyes slid closed as the pressure in his lungs mounted. He wanted no more than to rest, to make it stop.

"*Larien!*"

A blur of white materialized from the clouds, and a peri darted out of the aether, aiming a kick at Larien's head. Shard was released, and he collapsed to the ground, gasping for breath. Fighting the starbursts in his eyes, he sat up, focusing on the figures on the ground. Larien was struggling to rise, muttering assorted curses in long-dead tongues. A peri crouched on the ground, dressed in a long white kimono.

"Sim?"

The peri stood, unsheathing a sharp katana. "Did you think you'd win so easily. Did you think I wouldn't stop you?"

"*Damn you!*" Larien howled. "This does not concern you!"

"Your logic escapes me." The peri advanced calmly.

Shard scrambled to his feet. He stared in awe at the peri, looking all the world like Sim Onmyóji. Yet the eyes weren't Sim's; they were a vivid turquoise.

"Out, harridan!" Larien held his hands across his chest like a barrier, then cast his arms out to unleash a blastsheld. Terrays merely closed her eyes, tipping her head back as the energy hit her. It tore away at her body. Pieces of her kimono fluttered away into the smoke. The mists swirled about her dissolving body.

"Aren't you tired of this, Larien?" she demanded, stepping forward from the smoke. Her kimono was torn to shreds, now a scanty shift that bared her limbs and revealed her lithe, leonine figure. "You know you can't defeat me. You can't even push me back anymore. I gain more ground every day."

"What?" Shard stammered.

"Shall we dance again?" Terrays raised her sword threatening, point aimed at her foe. She crouched in a defensive posture. "Leave here, Shard. It isn't safe."

"Leave? How?"

Larien spun about, a lightning bolt lashing out and striking Shard. With a cry Shard staggered back, dropping to one knee. "He is mine. Keep to your own battles, wench, and leave your brother's pets to me."

"Your battles are my battles. You saw to that long ago. Who are you to handle the shard?" she accused viciously. "You were no Cimmerian at the height of your power, and even Cimmerian misjudged the *yúgure.* One-fifth of the crystal is just as powerful and five times as unstable. You'll destroy the world like Cimmerian did, and you'll die with it."

"Then I will risk death! What is life but an eternal war against death?"

Terrays sneered. "You wage eternal war against *life!*" She turned back to the terrified boy. "It's time to go, Shard," she called. "This battle you can't fight."

"The boy stays!" Larien objected.

Terrays lowered her katana slightly, her features taking on a sad expression. "Tell Sim about me," she implored. "Tell him to stop Larien, no matter what. Set me free."

"He'll die before you can reach him," Larien threatened.

Terrays sprang forward like a cat, racing through the mist towards the boy. Larien pivoted, casting a powerful blastshield. Shard flinched as the energy rippled through the air towards him. From the corner of his eye, he saw Terrays leap towards him, her katana held high over her head. Shard screamed, his hands going to up shield himself as Larien's energy wave and Terrays's weapon descended as one. Terrays reached him a hair's breadth before Larien.

"Shard! Shard, wake up!"

Shard sat up in bed with a start, his eyes wide, his breath racing in his chest. "What! What–" He sat in his bed, surrounded by Sim, Stargazer and Mindrin.

"It's nearly noon," Mindrin stammered. "You've been asleep for hours. No one could wake you."

"Larien... it was Larien."

Sim cursed under his breath.

"Tried to kill me, tried to stop me. He knows I can sense the shard, the *yúgure*. He knows I'll try to stop him. He knows my magic's growing. He tried to kill me. Almost did... Terrays," he breathed.

"Terrays?" Sim demanded. "Terrays, what about Terrays?"

Shard's eyes drifted closed again. "No – no, you don't," Mindrin shook him roughly. "You're not going to sleep again."

"Terrays?" Sim pressed.

"She was there..." Shard murmured. "I saw her. She's there... with Larien."

"What do you mean?" Sim demanded. He took Shard's shoulders and shook him. His voice trembled and his eyes were blazing with emotion. "What do you mean, you saw her."

Shard smiled faintly. "She's not dead... Sim. She's alive... with Larien. In that... that place. She told me to tell you..."

"What? Tell me what?"

"Stop Larien, no matter... no matter what it..." his eyes dropped closed and he fell into sleep once more: a deep, dreamless sleep that at last brought him rest.

Shard awoke again in the late afternoon. Again he sat bolt upright in bed, gasping for breath. Sim was sitting in a chair on the far side of the snug room. When he saw Shard awaken he was at his side in a moment.

"Shard? Are you all right?" he asked, dropping down on the edge of the bed.

"What time is it?" Shard asked, running his hands through his hair, over his face.

"Nearly five. You've slept all day."

"I... I suppose we're not... moving on to the next keep."

"No, not today. Tomorrow."

Shard slumped back into bed. "Sorry... sorry for wasting our time."

"Shh," Sim smoothed his hair. "We'll stop him, don't worry. Shard... I don't want to press you. But... please, my sister? What did you mean, you saw her?"

Shard smiled wanly, shaking his head. "I don't know. I can't understand it. But... she was there, in the dream with me. She said.... Oh, I can't remember... it's all so faint. Ahh!" he sat up again as the pain in his head throbbed. "I can't remember!" He looked up at Sim, his eyes pleading. He took Sim's hands in his, fumbling as he placed them over his temples. "Mindlock with me."

"What?"

"It's the only way... to make sense of it. I can't. I'm too young – my mind can't figure any of it out. You can. Please, Sim. I need to make sense of this."

Sim bit his lips, shifting his fingers on Shard's temples. "I don't... I haven't done many of these..."

Shard smiled faintly. "I trust you."

Sim stared deep into Shard's eyes, emerald meeting amethyst, as he peered into Shard's soul. Almost instantly Shard could feel Sim in his mind, only the faintest presence, like a distant mindspeech. Swiftly though the sorcerer's presence intensified, and Shard felt the distinctive signature of Sim's thoughts, his emotions. Calm, ordered, with the illusion of peace of mind. But underneath Shard could sense the turmoil within the Onmyóji, the pain and the loneliness masked by centuries of training and magic-induced sleep. He felt Sim sifting through the pained imagery in his mind, trying to make sense of the countless thoughts.

At first Shard resisted on instinct, unused to the invasion, accustomed only to ordinary mindspeech and the mental exercises his father taught him. This mindspeech with Sim was far more intense, driven by a far older magic. His consciousness tried to withdraw at first, surprised by the touch, but at length he relaxed, albeit reluctantly. **Sim...?** he asked, still hesitant.

It's all right... Sim's awareness drifted deeper, methodically slipped past the barriers Shard's consciousness tried to erect against the invading presence, slowly deciphering the flurry of images much as Shard had deciphered the combination to the guardian spell. Shard felt the restlessness within his mind slowly ebb, replaced by a growing sense of confidence and calm. Overlapping images gradually separated, indistinct feelings and emotions suddenly growing clear. The whispers were pushed back into his deeper subconscious, and the screams at his ear were stilled, quieted to hushed voices. The discordant choir slowed to a recognizable melody. For the first time in days, Shard released a low sigh of relief, his mind clear at last.

Where the first touch had been disturbing, unexpected, now Shard found it natural, comforting, this second voice in his mind, this companion presence at the edges of his soul. His defenses relaxed further, and he could feel Sim everywhere, his presence surrounding him, like a warm protective shield. He could sense more of the Onmyóji now, his pain, his sorrow, the dulling apathy of thousands of years' sleep, the fear of stepping out of his shell and the illusion of peace it provided. Years of pain and loneliness muted by sleep, worn down and eroded into living death, simply to survive. Shard felt the courage and strength it had taken him to step out, to accept the pain anew and experience the hope of a new life. He felt Sim's continued hesitation, the voice in his head urging him to withdraw, to sleep again before life only turned on him once more.

Terrays's face appeared before them both, sad, distant, contemplative. Her lips did not move, yet they heard her speak in their minds.

Who are you to handle the shard? You know you can't defeat me.

Your battles are my battles. Shall we dance again?

Tell Sim. Stop Larien, no matter what.

You're hopeless, Larien.

Terrays? Sim asked.

Stop Larien.

Set me free.

The image of the *yúgure* flashed before their mind's eyes, a glimmering blue jewel, its inner light illuminating its countless facets. **I can see it,** Sim whispered. Shard felt him reach out, extend his hand towards the opal, which now shattered into five pieces, four fading away into blackness, one diamond-shaped shard remaining against the velvet darkness.

Who are you to handle the shard?

You know you can't defeat me. Your battles are my battles.

Larien...

Set me free.

She's there, Shard whispered. **I can see her.**

Sim nodded, his eyes caught in the *yúgure's* pull, drawn deeper into the vision, drowning in the shard's magic. **Shard... can you see it?**

Shard reached out himself, trying to touch the pulsing jewel. He sensed Sim drawing closer, their two souls pulled in towards each other, united in the quest for the ancient jewel. A desperate yearning stretched out towards the *yúgure* shard, and Shard's own presence behind it.

Their hands touched the shard at once, the jewel rippling like water, dissolving into nothingness, letting their hands seep through. Their fingertips brushed, briefly, and a blinding.light appeared, as if to drive them back. But instead of repulsing, this new spell only drew Shard in deeper, immersing him in a startling new awareness, assaulting his dizzied consciousness. He could feel Sim everywhere now, an all-pervasive presence, saturating his uncomprehending mind. He sensed the Onmyóji's fear, his lonely longing, his searching soul, reaching out to Shard's consciousness.

Fear flared within him. Could Sim read him so easily? Was his mind laid out like an open book before the sorcerer? Powers... did Sim know?

He pulled abruptly, his own consciousness withdrawing back into itself. Almost instantly Sim withdrew as well, the spell broken in a sudden flash.

"I'm sorry," Shard murmured, closing his eyes against the bright lights blazing in his head. He was lightheaded, nearly overcome. It occurred to him that the entire encounter had lasted but mere moments.

"No... no, I shouldn't have," Sim stammered, holding his hand to his forehead. "I didn't mean to – are you all right?"

"I'm fine," Shard nodded. "Don't be sorry. I asked you to."

"Terrays..."

"Where is she? What does it mean?"

"She's... there. With Larien. I... I don't understand it."

"What... what if the souls of the destroyed aren't snuffed out," Shard ventured tremulously. "What if they are in limbo, trapped... with the ones who destroyed them."

A shudder ran through Sim. "Trapped... with Larien. For four thousand years?" Another, fiercer tremor raced through him and he doubled over, convulsing with nauseated horror.

"Sim!" Shard leapt up, putting his hands on his shoulders.

"Terrays... I could feel her. Terrays... she's alive – in him, in *him*, for all these years?" He rose from the bed, clutching his stomach as he bent over.

"Sim!" Shard leapt out of bed, hurrying to his side. "Here," he held Sim's shoulder, easing him down into the chair. "Just keep your head down."

Tears were streaming down Sim's face. He bent over, hugging his knees, whispering his sister's name. Shard knelt on the ground beside him. "I thought she was dead..."

"She... she is. She's been dead all these years. But her spirit lives."

"Lives... in Larien's mind, a slave? A slave to *him!* All these years! All these years he's held her hostage – fed off her *soul!* What... what do we do?"

"We stop Larien," Shard spoke with a confidence he did not feel. "And we set her free."

19

A distant rattle of a cave-in resonated through the tunnel. Luck bucked in alarm, nearly casting Aerin and Stargazer to the ground. "Whoa, Luck, steady!" Aerin yelped, hanging tight to the saddleloops as Stargazer's arms tightened about her in reflex, digging into her wound. Sintaka shuddered, turning to hide her face in Mindrin's shoulder.

"Damn it, the whole tunnel's going to cave in!" she wailed. "I just *know* it!" Her soulmate could only hold her close, warily scanning the tunnels for signs of stress.

Smoke and dust spilled into the main corridor as the rattle grew fainter. The two kobold scouts came racing back down the narrow tunnel, panting for breath, their young faces pale with terror. "Well?" Bys asked as he stood before the train of restless dragons.

"Hellhounds," the girl, Zara, gasped out. "Three of them, large, wiry. They saw us the instant we surfaced. They moved like lightning, practically flew on top of us before we knew what was happening."

"We barely had time to collapse the entrance," her companion, Zayl, stammered.

"*Chiga*," Bys cursed. "They're good. They're tracking us. They'll sniff us out every time we surface. Damn. At least we can reach Thandállen safely."

"Are you sure?" Ceih asked grimly. "They're determined."

Bys shook his head. "No one will find Thandállen. It's newly dug, a fully armed kobold keep. They might dig at every steam vent and fumarole and whine at every crack in the rocks, but they'll never reach us. Not unless they lead a full scale attack. And my men are ready for that."

They pressed onward, passing small clusters of working kobold miners and their burrowers. The air grew warmer even as they descended deeper underground. Shard stripped off his greatcoat and his black jacket, rolling up the sleeves of his thin white shirt. Stargazer fussed with his braid, trying to keep his heavy hair off his skin. Aerin slumped back against her soulmate, bored and restless.

The tunnel grew less regular, natural stone formations taking the place of smooth burrower-dug walls. The dragons lifted their heads, whiskers twitching in anticipation. Aerin sat tall in the saddle, raising her head to catch sight of the road ahead. Sulphur wafted in the air, carried by the winds through the cave chambers. Yellows and reds stained the cave walls. Mineral flowers bloomed in the cracks along the rock.

"We're getting near," Stargazer stated. Luck shook his head in confirmation.

Shard sat tall as well, wrinkling his nose at the smell of the hot springs.

The tunnel arched downwards, then terminated abruptly in a dead end. Smooth rock blocked their way ahead.

"Where are we?" Arjin demanded, leaping off Witch's back. "You said this was Thandállen."

Bys held out his hands, stopping them from advancing any further towards dead end. He knelt down on the ground, his hand rising to his temples as he closed his eyes is concentration. Silence reigned in the tunnel.

"What's he doing?" Aerin whispered.

"I think he's sending," Stargazer whispered back. "Kobolds can mindspeak, but it takes more out of them than it does us."

For a moment there was only silence. Then, slowly, a sound began deep below them. Like gears slowly winding, machines coming to life. The peri frowned, looking down at the rock floor, listening at the noise grew. Bys stood up, stepped back. The rock floor in front of them began to contract, sliding under the terminus wall. Arjin and Shard ventured forward tentatively. Below the false floor, a cyclopean staircase unraveled in a corkscrew.

"You peri," Bys scoffed. "You look for magic walls, guardian spells, illusory fields. You'd never think to look for a plain old trap door. Shall we?"

Shard and Arjin remounted their dragons, spurring them down the staircase. Once the last of the kobolds at the party's flanks passed through, the false floor slid back into place. "This is the first lock. We've another one at the bottom of the staircase, and two more doors. Each of the subsidiary tunnels has two independently controlled locks. We're no lovers of flashy magic, but our mindspeech is essential here. All the locks are controlled by three master kobolds in the operations room. No one gets in or out of Thandállen without their knowledge. We have security that could teach you Amaru a thing or two."

"I've sent word ahead to call in the men from our outposts around Wyvern's Rest," he informed them as they snaked deeper underground. "We'll have our war council together by suppertime." He glanced back at the peri on dragonback. "We have some wonderful hotsprings down there. Just the thing to wash off the dust." He grinned. "Enjoy it while you can. We've got a lot of work ahead of us."

"Ohh, heavenly," Aerin sighed as she sat immersed to her shoulders in the hot, mineral rich waters of the pool. The cave ceiling arched high above her, stalactites dripping from the rock in rippling patterns. The cavern was huge, rivaling the great hall in which she had been wed. Countless multicoloured pools bubbled up from veins of boiling water below, the hot steam rising in swirling colours towards the ceiling. Mineral fragments and veins of crystal glittered in the dark walls, scattering the light of the glowlamps.

Aerin slid herself under the little six-inch waterfall spilling off from the pool above her, letting the water flow over her shoulders. "How are you doing, Aerin?" Arjin called from the pool above her.

"This is just what I needed!" she shouted back. Her regenerative powers had already reduced her livid wounds to four reddened dimples. The mineral laden waters only furthered the healing, easing the painful chafing of the bandages, flushing the wounds clear of infection. She ducked her head under the water, rising a moment later, brushing her hair behind her ears.

"I'd swear we were at the Smoking Waters, at Amaru," she glanced over at Stargazer, shaking his hair free of his braid, dipping under the water himself a moment later. He emerged grinning, his hair hanging over his face in heavy tendrils. Aerin smiled bittersweetly at the sight. "You'd never think we were going to war tomorrow." She rose from her underwater perch, wading through the water to join him. Smiling softly, she brushed his hair back from his face. "When did it get this complicated, Yósha?" She pressed her forehead to his, and kissed him tenderly.

"Sintaka?" Mindrin asked, sitting down next to her. They were perched on an outcrop, overlooking the hot springs. Aerin and Stargazer shared one pool, while Ceih and Arjin splashed in the adjacent one. Sim and Shard were nowhere in sight, possibly already with Bys inside the main keep's walls. Neither of them seemed in the mood to relax.

"Mm?" she looked up, a wan smile on her face. "Hello, bear," she tried to summon some cheer, and failed. She leaned against his shoulder, her expression miserable. "Sitting in these caves like rats," she grumbled. "I'd rather be out in the forests, with the sun on my back."

She felt Mindrin smile; his delight brushed the edge of her awareness. "What?" She sat up, seeing his pleased expression. "What are you so happy about?"

"I..." Mindrin shrugged. "I like it – you having to lean on me." When she frowned, he explained: "It's not always easy, you know, being soulbound to the Heiress of the Known World – who, incidentally, can throw me over her shoulder like I'm a feather, and whose favorite combat move is the *neck-snapping* kick!" He laughed lightly. "I know it sounds terrible – but it's nice to know you're not some infallible avatar, that I can look after you sometimes."

"Oh, Min," she smiled bittersweetly, touching his cheek. "You don't think I take you for granted, do you? I'm no avatar. You know I couldn't do a thing without my shadow." She leaned against him with a weary sigh. "I'm glad you came. I could really use some of your cheer right now."

Mindrin sat back, pulling back his jacket to reach a pocket inside his coat. He withdrew a small seed, faded yellow with a dull olive stripe surrounding it. As Sintaka watched, bemused, he carefully tucked the seed under a patch of damp moss, dotted with beads of condensing moisture. "What are you doing?" Sintaka asked.

Mindrin lay his hand overtop of the moss, closing his eyes as an enigmatic smile touched his lips. A warm glow of gold shimmered low to the ground, and tiny roots sprouted through the moss, taking hold on the rock. A green sprout appeared from the moss bed, growing taller and thicker before Sintaka's eyes. Leaves unfurled from its thornless stalk, and buds blossomed from the stem. One of the buds opened up, revealing a beautiful red flower, shaped like a paper lantern, a faint phosphorescence pulsing within.

"Have a flower," Mindrin smiled innocently. "A flower always makes me feel better."

Sintaka smiled softly, bending low to inhale the lantern rose's fragrance.

"Now," Bys unrolled the map on the table. The kobold lieutenants stood close, while the taller peri gazed over their heads. The parchment showed Wyvern's Rest, a large cluster of stylized mountain peaks, surrounded by red circles denoting encampments of Larien's armies. Forming a semi-circle from the southwest to the north, the Mantalore kobold forces were marked in blue.

"We've been building our forces since the early summer," Bys explained. "Scouting posts gave way to better keeps. Thandállen was just a lookout station two months ago. And ever since I spoke to Kemuri I've been sending kobolds up from Outpost to fortify our positions." He smiled tightly. "We're ready to take back what's ours.

"Now, it's about eight miles as the eagle flies to Larien's main encampment, here," He pointed with his worn stub of a pointer. The kobolds clustered tighter under the dull light of the warm glowlamp hanging overhead. "On the north flank of the mountain we're now calling Wyvern's Rest. They're burrowing in from the north face – I suppose to avoid the death traps Ravanor's was rumoured to have built. Knowing my history, I'd have to say that's the smartest way. Reconnaissance shows their digs are ordered, well thought out. Its a kobold leading them in there. Probably a Mantalore, at that." The faces at the table turned grim. Bys nodded. "You know what we do to deserters. To ferals."

They nodded, their expressions cold.

"What do they do to deserters?" Stargazer whispered.

"You probably don't want to know," Aerin whispered back.

"Daav, Merkh, Siurn. What's your status?"

"I've two thousand men at our post here, at Fallon'ser," Merkh pointed at the northmost blue circle with a stubby finger. "Siurn, two thousand more, here," he indicated a circle just north of Thandállen.

"And a full contingent here," Daav confirmed.

"Tunnels?" Bys asked.

"They've caught a few of our scouts; we always lose a few," Siurn sighed. "But we can get most of our men within half a mile of their camps, if Myrddin's with us. From there, it's open ground. We can surround them at night, take them by surprise. What're their forces compared to six thousand trained

Mantalores?"

"They're led by Larien," Ceih observed. He said nothing more, his point clear.

"He could be at Wyvern's Rest already," Arjin mused.

"He is," Shard stated. "I felt it. He's there, overseeing the operation, ready to take the *yúgure* the instant they break through. We can't risk a direct attack until we know what's become of the shard."

"He's right," Sim nodded. "Even if Larien isn't holding it high over our heads as we attack, we can't run into battle knowing the shard's loose somewhere. You don't charge a warehouse stockpiled with blackdust."

"So what do you do then?" Merkh shot them a dark glare over his shoulder. It was clear what he thought of peri opinions. "Sit around like slovenly long-legs? *Pèr ta su!*"

"We need to find the *yúgure,*" Shard decided. "I need to know where it is. I have to get to it before Larien does. When I have it, then we attack."

"Oh, and what, boy? You'll sniff it out like bloodhound?" Merkh taunted.

Shard's reply was swift, hollow. "Yes."

"Enough. Shut it, Merkh. You're no Guild Chief."

"Neither are you, Bys!"

"I'm the Mining Overseer of all Hesperin, of all the guilds," Bys snarled, his cheerful child-like demeanor dropping in an instant, his light, boy's voice dropping to a dangerous growl. "I'm the one who decided whether your ass fries or not. And that *boy* is our expedition leader, chosen by Lord Kemuri himself. Now shut it and *listen* for once, or you won't get even your ass out of the trenches!" He cracked his pointer down hard on the table's edge in emphasis. Merkh flinched visibly.

"Now," Bys tucked the pointer under his arm. "Shard's right. We little folk don't know a thing about mucking about in long-legs' magic. If he can sniff out the *yúgure,* then he can do much that we Mantalores can't. Shard, do you have a plan?"

Shard looked to Sim questioningly, and the Onmyóji nodded his encouragement. "I need to get closer to Wyvern's Rest," Shard spoke. "The south side, it doesn't look too protected. Am I right?"

Bys nodded. "Larien's forces are centered on the north and the west. We've had clashes with his scouts before. But the south side of the mountain, it's nothing more than a few guards, one or two small war camps filled by no more than twenty troglodytes each."

"Can you get me there?"

"The Valley of Warlords," Bys traced the slim canyon with his pointer. "I can put you just across the valley tomorrow morning if you'd like."

Shard nodded. "I'll take a small team. Um," he glanced around him. "Stargazer, for council, Sintaka and Aerin for protection, and..." his gaze fell on Sim briefly, before he reluctantly looked away. "Mindrin," he decided. "He's... he's good at reading ambassadors' duplicity: I was thinking he would make a good lookout. Anyone charging us is bound to have strong emotions;

an empath would make the most sense." **Sorry, Sim,** he added silently.

I understand, Sim nodded. **You'll be in enough danger without an Onmyóji at your side like a beacon to draw out Larien. Just take care of yourself.**

Shard smiled, no longer caring how lovestruck he seemed. "I will," he whispered.

"Nice room," Sim nodded thoughtfully. Shard had to agree. After the comfortable but decidedly small accommodations at the Guildhearst in Outpost and the Helonsden Keep, the chambers Bys had provided for them in Thandállen seemed like a palace. The room was dimly lit by the suspended glowlamps, its expansive size enhanced further by the large floor space, the bed, table, dressing cabinets and couch all far against the walls. Tapestries hung on the bare walls, adding colour to the room, complementing the rich cushions and trailing cloths arranged over the bed and the small couch. It would have been a windowseat, Shard thought, had there been any windows nearly a quarter-mile underground. There was even an adjacent bathroom, rather than modest facilities found only down darkly lit corridors.

"Looks more like a guest room in Amaru's palace than a military keep," Sim continued.

"Is your room this nice?" Shard asked.

Sim nodded. "Maybe not as nicely decorated, but then you are the expedition leader." Shard tossed his greatcoat on the bed, then unclasped his jacket. His rubbed his neck, stretching to ease the muscle cramps. "Here," Sim moved behind him, placing his hands on his shoulders. Shard stiffened instantly only to relax a moment later as Sim gently massaged his sore shoulders, the faintest healing glow easing the tension in his muscles. A soft sound of pleasure slipped Shard's lips before he could stop himself.

"Oh, that's better, thanks," he murmured swiftly, moving away, his muscles clenching tight once more.

"I... I should go," Sim said, stepping back. "You've a long day tomorrow; I shouldn't keep you up."

"No," Shard objected. "Please, Sim. Stay a while? Stargazer's already gone to bed, and I doubt he wants me calling on him." His cheeks flushed slightly as he sat down on the bed. "He and Aerin are newlyweds, after all. Me... I don't think I could sleep a wink. I could use someone to talk to."

"All right," Sim nodded. He moved nearer, lowering himself into the nearby chair. "What should we talk about?"

"I don't know. Tell... tell me a story," Shard decided at last, stretching onto the bed. "About Elória. About the Lady Alsaya. About Old Magic, about Oracle. Anything. Recite something. I just want to hear a friend's voice."

"All... all right," Sim agreed. "Um... long ago, before there was land, before there was sky or stars, before there were Powers, there was only Darkness. And then the First Fires sprang alight, and burned the sky with their magic. And they were the Powers Insubstantial, the source of all life, of all magic.

And from the Powers came Oracle, the Avatar, the child and master of the Powers. And Oracle... harnessed the Powers, and brought order to the chaos of the First Fires." Sim glanced over at Shard to see him lying on his back, his hand folded over his chest, his eyes turned to the ceiling, his gaze distant.

"And she made the Seven Worlds, and layered them one above the other, from the infernal Underworld, where the First Fires still burn, to the Overworld, where Oracle reigns over Elysium. And she made the sun, Mnemsyara, and the three moons, to bring light to the worlds, and she set them up... up in the stars. And she made the Well of Stars, to be a portal between the worlds, so that the dead could find their way to the stars that shine over all the Seven Worlds together. And then Oracle made the peri, and the kobolds, the troglodytes and the griffins, and all the creatures and set them within the Seven Worlds. And she did not try to contain the Powers to her Overworld, but let them flow free, to keep all worlds united as one through the binding currents of magic. And that Old Magic Oracle first used to unite the Seven Worlds still flows to this day, ready to be tapped by those who possess the powers of old. And... Shard? What comes next? Shard?" He looked to his side and saw Shard lying still on the bed, his eyes closed in sleep.

Sim smiled softly, rising from the chair. He gently slid Shard's greatcoat off the bed and lay it on the chair. Lifting one of the heavy woolen blankets folded at the foot of the bed, he drew it over Shard's slim frame. "Sleep well, *ka'eri*," he murmured softly, stirring Shard's hair.

He turned and left the room, gently closing the door behind him.

Shard opened his eyes briefly, a quizzical smile touching his lips as he pondered Sim's gesture.

He rolled over on his side, tucking his arm under a full pillow. His mind swam in confusion. The mindlock had helped to some extent. The furious din of Larien's thoughts, that had been somewhat quieted. Even Terrays's incessant whispers had been stilled, for the time being at least. However, an entirely new set of images had taken their place. The echoes of Sim's presence rang in his head at all hours. He felt as if someone had dealt him a blow in the stomach; a hollow ache rose within him to join the unbearable tension rebuilding in his aching muscles. He felt as thought he were dangling on a precipice, denied safety and a clean death all at once. To suddenly be exposed to such depths of another's very being, to know them as one's own soul, and then to be wrenched back – it was a psychic torment that instantly burned at his synapses.

Ka'eri...

He let his eyes fall closed, struggling to find some peace in a dreamless sleep.

Larien sat in his simple black throne, his eyes focused on an unseen plane behind his closed eyelids. Silken shimmered about him, its cinnamon scent rich in the air. He stirred restlessly under his dark robes. The illusion was becoming harder to maintain. Even as he could force his flesh to regenerate, it weakened his spirit immeasurably. If he didn't find the *yúgure* soon, he would have little more fight left within him.

His hastily erected throne room lay inside a large tunnel Morden's emaciated burrowers had already sucked clean of rock and dust. Above him he could hear the sound of pickaxe against rock. The smell of burrower acid clung to the walls. Before him, on a little table, lay the most priceless of the treasures Morden had harvested from the antechambers. A jewel encrusted scepter lay alongside a golden jewelry box filled with flawless diamond pyraglyphs. Next to the box sat a foot-long scorpion made entirely of golden wire. And these were just the first. Each day, each hour, uncovered more and more breathtaking wonders. Yet none of them mattered. All that counted was the *yúgure*.

It was indeed most vexing, this latest turn of events. Varron and Darhis had yet to flush out the kobold rabble. The Mantalore dogs could be under him at that very moment. Cursed creatures: their lack of magic made them almost impossible to trace; they were like rats, like flea-infested vermin. Sim was equally impossible to trace: four thousand years had taught the upstart bastard more than a trick or two. Shard still lived, still drew breath. And now the interfering Onmyóji knew. He *knew.*

Victory seems a touch more distant now, does it?

"Silence."

Sim has been trying to kill you for four millennia because he thought you destroyed me. He condemned you to four centuries of living death, and existence in a corpse's shell. Now he knows the truth. That I was denied the simple bliss of nonexistence to serve as your unwilling soulmate all these years. That you drained my soul to fuel your rise to power and made my lifeforce a slave to your whims. What will he do to you now, I wonder?

"Silence! In no more than three days Morden will break into the main vault. There inside Ravanor's sarcophagus, I will find it. Then Sim Onmyóji will be food for the vermin and his little boy with him. And you, my Alsaya, will have your simple bliss soon enough."

He rose, staggering out of the throne room, anxious to escape the smell of silken. Swathing his face behind his dark veil, he forced himself to stride calmly, as a leader should, as he stepped out into the dim light of the Denáren twilight. The troglodytes and kobold slaves bowed in abject submission as he passed them by.

Rising up the rickety ladders and gliding through the dark corridors dug deep into the mountainside, he ascended towards the starless sky, then dropped deeper into the mining shafts cleanly sucked out by the monstrous burrowers, then carefully chipped straight by the pickaxes of innumerable kobolds. Three dead slaves, worked past their breaking points, lay in a corner, awaiting the troglodyte sweepers to cart them down to the pits. They had once fed the hellhounds. Now they were simply burned, the smell of their charred corpses serving as a reminder to all slaves of their eventual fate.

Slaves cowered in the shadows as he swept by, as ominous as a spectre-guard of Níst. He delved deeper, passing antechambers picked clean of all wealth. Arriving at a fork in the corridor, he took the left passage, bypassing the roughly hewn steps leading down to the tomb of Habradar, which was still being excavated. More wealth to be uncovered, to fuel his future campaigns. But it would have to wait. The *yúgure* was all that mattered.

He turned into a long, narrow shaft cleanly hewn that led him downwards on steep, slim steps. It was not one of Morden's recent digs, but the old tunnel Ravanor's Hokabalh priest had used to escape after entombing his body with the sacrifices. Once Habradar's tomb antechamber had been uncovered, it was easy to calculate the location of the escape shaft.

He seemed to walk forever, through the darkened tunnels, until at last the sound of digging drew louder and the stench of burrower saliva grew pungent in the dim lighting.

MORDEN! Larien bellowed, taking pleasure that the mindspeech would ring with added pain in the mind of a half-breed.

"The Master graces us with his presence."

He found Morden seated on a rock ledge, watching the digging continue in the thin shaft below his dangling feet.

"How does the work progress?" Larien hissed.

"Quite well, quite well. Has Darhis come back yet?"

"Enough of your trifling infatuations. The Treasury. When will I have it?"

"We have it already," Morden chuckled. "Look at it, Larien. You're standing on the exit shaft of the Hokabalh clerics. It's only a matter of time until–"

"A matter of time, a matter of time, I grow weary of that reply! You parrot it like an imbecile, a trained beast. I want the Treasury. Not the antechambers. Not the priest's exit tunnel. I want my hands on Ravanor's sarcophagus."

"Why? You have enough wealth for all possible campaigns you could want to finance from what we unearthed, minus my cut of course–"

"Silence!" Larien caught the man's shirtfront, whirling him off the ledge, holding him high over the black shaft. In the struggle the thin veil drawn under his eyes fell away, revealing his face. Morden shivered as he hung over the void. The wrinkles were retreating under Larien's eyes, his skin growing flush with new life. His hair had regrown thick and full, its silver sheen replaced by inky black. Yet his breath still smelled of death and decay. "Your incessant whining about your price, about your money, about your reward. My concerns are *vastly* beyond your apelike comprehension! So be kind enough to grant my this favour and *shut it* about your payment, and *all the whores* we could buy with this money. Now stop sitting around preening like a dandy and *get to work!* I want to smell the stench of Ravanor's still decomposing *corpse* by tomorrow night!"

"Tomorrow night?" Morden stammered. "Isn't that a little premature?"

"It had better not be, if you want to live long enough to enjoy those strumpets your reward will purchase!"

Leaving Morden shaken and newly-motivated, Larien stalked back out of the tunnel. He growled at the slaves, sending them back into their shadows.

No more excuses. No more delays. He would have the *yúgure* before the full moon.

He would have it...

He *would!*

Or all was lost.

20

They crouched low in the tunnel as they listened to the gears shift beneath them. The first of the locks opened and they hurried up the winding staircase. "Remember," Shard called as they stumbled up the steps. "No mindspeech, unless it's necessary. It's a long shot, but I want as little magic around us as possible. Larien might never hear us if we paced outside his room, or he could pick up on any stray thought we have. Try to stay focused."

"Right," Sintaka nodded, eyeing the tunnel walls warily.

"Stay close. As soon as we're out on the flats, let's find cover. Stargazer, I want you ready to cast a shield whenever we need one. Aerin, Sintaka, keep your weapons up. Mindrin, pretend we're in the middle of court and the ambassadors of the other provinces are circling like buzzards."

"R-right," Mindrin stammered.

They reached the landing of the circular staircase, and waited nervously for the last lock to open. The gears wound slowly, and the false wall before them retracted, letting the dull brassy light of the Denáren Wastes spill into the tunnel. "Go," Shard whispered. Aerin led the charge, her axe clenched tightly in her hand, her machete slung over her back. Stargazer followed, his spyglass tucked into his tunic's belt. Shard and Mindrin followed, Sintaka protecting the rear.

"Thank Oracle we're out," Sintaka breathed.

"Not much of a sight," Mindrin frowned as they advanced. Dry sandy earth and lava stones mingled with the rusted rocks beneath their feet; long black creeper vines tangled over the ground. A lone spine-backed armadillo sunned itself on a warm rock. Something large and black scuttled into a crevice and Mindrin averted in his eyes in horror.

Aerin bounded over the jagged rocks, ducking under a heavy overhang and huddling in the shade. "Glass," she held out her hand as Stargazer joined her. Before them lay a thin dried riverbed, the earth parched and cracked, stained with minerals. Steam vents blasted roiling smoke into the air. Across the riverbed the stark mountain peaks rose into the dense clouds. "There," Shard pointed to the second highest of the mountains, almost exactly opposite their location. "That's Wyvern's Rest." He glanced down at the mountain's base. "Looks like a small encampment there. Aerin?"

"Got it," Aerin murmured. "Three large tents; I count... seven, no, eight troglodytes. Big ones – you should see the horns on them, even the women are built like battering rams. And one or two peri on patrol. There could be as many as thirty, given the tent size."

"Mindrin?"

Mindrin crouched deep in the shadow, his eyes half-closed as he held his hands to his temples. "Nothing yet. Background noise... no one's happy over there. But nothing near by."

"What about you, Shard?" Stargazer asked.

"The *yúgure*'s somewhere here," Shard nodded. "But... ah, I can't narrow it down." He closed his eyes, frowning with concentration. "It's like trying to find a whisper in a crowded room. I need to get closer. Sintaka?"

Sintaka sprang from their shelter, taking the scouting position. She whistled once, a sound easily mistaken for a bird's call. Aerin handed Stargazer back his spyglass and they slipped out from under the rock's shade, scrambled down the leisurely sloping valley's edge.

"I hate to say it," Aerin breathed. "But... do we know how to get back to our tunnel? Everything looks the same to us."

"Don't worry," Stargazer assured her. "I've got a fix on it. It's just up that ridge there."

"If we have to bolt, follow Star," Shard ordered. He patted Stargazer encouragingly on the shoulder.

"We're getting close to the riverbed," Sintaka said. "You want to go closer, Shard?"

"Over there." He pointed to a ledge about twenty paces from the boulder. "Let's go."

They darted through the yellowed sunlight, keeping low to the ground, avoiding the larger golden patches of the light where the clouds were thin and let Mnemsyara's light through. Sintaka checked the ledge, then dropped out of sight. Shard followed a moment later, his greatcoat's hem brushing the ground as he bent to look over the ledge's jagged boundary. A shelf rested against the rock wall, the slope having eroded sharply, or crumbled away during a flashflood. Below them the slope grew steeper, a fifty-foot wall leading down to the flatland of the dried river.

"Cover me." Shard knelt down on the rock, his coat sweeping about him. He bowed his head, letting his face grow emotionless in deep concentration. Aerin and Sintaka crouched on either side of him, ready for an attack. The Kitsune heiress shifted her hands on her axe handle repeatedly, while Sintaka drew an arrow from her quiver and nocked it in her longbow.

"How's your aim, sister?" Stargazer asked, unable to keep the nervousness from his voice.

"Kestrel's own student," Sintaka dared a faint gloat. "If she can teach her soulmate's son – a *scribe!* – to shoot down the moons, she can teach me to take down a hellhound."

"Mindrin?" Aerin asked. "How is it out there?"

"Angry, restless, generally still," he replied. "The entire plains seem coated in a slow simmer."

"You're doing great, Mindrin," Sintaka reassured him. "You can close yourself off as soon as Shard's found the *yúgure*."

"Remind me never to complain about the ambassadors' indigestion again," he smiled lightly. "They're like kittens compared to this place."

Stargazer looked from Mindrin's pained expression as he continued to sift for enemy presences to Shard's expressionless trance. "Glad I'm not an empath," he murmured. "I'll take astrology."

"What do the stars say today, brother?" Sintaka asked.

"Wish I could tell you." He looked up at the featureless sky with a forlorn expression. "Can't wait to see blue clouds again."

"Something's coming," Mindrin's indigo eyes snapped open.

"Where?"

"Not sure. But I can feel it. Anger, bloodlust... and something more. Frustration. Desire. Vengeance. And it's getting stronger."

Aerin's hands tensed on her axe. "Shard?" She glanced over her shoulder. "Hey, Shard? You still with the land of the living?" Shard knelt unmoving. "Shard!" she hissed under her breath. "Wake up!"

I can feel it, Shard mindspoke, defying his own edict.

"Something's coming, Shard," Aerin whispered tersely. "Come back to us, come on. It's time to get back to the tunnels."

Wait. I can* feel *it.

"Do they know we're here, Mindrin?" Sintaka asked. "Are they just guard patrolling at random?"

"Oh, they know," Mindrin whispered fearfully. "That or one of them had a very *bad* night with his mistress last night!"

"Shard!" Aerin snapped. "We don't have the time for this. We have to get back to the tunnel!"

Wait. This is my only chance. I can* feel *it, Aerin. It's right in front of me.

"Keep looking, Shard," Stargazer whispered, much to Aerin's look of horror. "We'll cover you."

Larien's getting close. He's digging... furiously. I can feel his anger. He's afraid too, he's afraid he'll die before he finds it. He's taxing his powers to their limits to keep his appearance, to keep his physical strength... he doesn't want to lose face – he knows he'll lose everything if he loses face now.

"Shard!"

I can see it...

Stargazer he threw his hands up impulsively. The shield snapped into place as the whistle of an arrow cut through the air. The arrow, aimed for Sintaka's neck, was deflected high above their ledge.

"They're coming!" Mindrin shouted.

A hellhound soared through the air, its face contorted in a scream of feral rage. It lunged at Mindrin, only to bounce off Stargazer's shield. The psychic recoil struck Stargazer hard, and he fell back as the hellhound was tossed aside. Sintaka waited for the next onslaught, while Aerin abandoned her vigilance to hurry to her mate's side.

"Don't leave your post, Kitsune," Sintaka warned, her eyes sweeping for enemy movement. She couldn't even hear the first hellhound. Surely it wasn't dead. Stargazer was just a kit, incapable of casting a shield that powerful.

"Star!" Aerin helped him to sit up. "Are you all right?"

Ignoring her own warning, Sintaka turned from the ledge outcropping to glance at her brother. "Is he all right?" she asked, relaxing her grip on the bow slightly. Shard continued to kneel in his trance.

Something hard struck Sintaka square between the shoulders. The arrow flew wild, barely missing Mindrin's crimson hair, and Sintaka fell to the ground with cry. Aerin swung around to confront the adversary, but the axe was wrenched from her hand and she was twisted about. Sintaka had another arrow nocked and ready, but it was too late.

Varron Lehs stood before them, holding Aerin before him as a living shield. He locked one muscular arm about her neck, tightly constricting her throat, while he wrapped another about her waist. "Don't try anything now," he hissed in a threatening voice. He tilted her head slightly, regarded Aerin's terrified visage. "And you were the one they took a bite of, eh, little bird?" he tightened his arm about her waist, and Aerin winced in pain.

"Oh please, please, please don't hurt me," Aerin whimpered, her hands ineffectively clutching at his arm. "Star?" she gazed across at him pleadingly.

"I expected more life out of you," Varron sneered disdainfully. "Now..." his eyes swept the crowd coldly. "Is the boy dead, or just sleeping?"

"He's in a trance," Stargazer explained.

"Dreaming of the Master's shard, no doubt. Well, then he can tell the Master where to find the shard once my reinforcements come. And you all will stay right here, unless you want to see your little redbird bleed."

"Oh Powers, no, no, no, please no!" Aerin wept. Her hands slipped from his arm, her fingers lightly brushing the edge of her medallion. Stargazer backed up instinctively. Puzzled, Varron tensed.

Aerin screamed, a high-pitched, glass-shattering wail. The focusing crystal glowed fiercely and Varron howled as the pain echoed within his mind, magnified a thousand-fold.

Aerin held out her hand, her terrified demeanor collapsing in an instant. The axe clattered once on the ground, then flew into her hand. She drove the claw-foot hard into Varron's stomach, then leapt free and swung the axe around, aiming a blow for his neck. Varron sprang for safety, and the axe came down on the ground inches from his feet. He kicked out, and his boot struck Aerin in the gut, knocking her back.

"Darhis!" Varron screamed as he darted back from Aerin's axe. Mere heartbeats later a hellhound flew over the outcrop, tackling Aerin's shoulder and forcing her to the ground. She landed, screaming with indignity, next to

Shard. The hellhound bumped against him, but he did not stir.

"No, you don't," Aerin caught the head as the hound lunged for her throat. She braced her feet against the beast's belly and kicked her legs up, propelling the hound over the edge of the shelf. The hellhound was on its feet in an instant, but so was Aerin, and the axe came down hard over the hound's skull as it howled a warning.

"No, you don't, you inbred little *shit!*" Aerin shouted, bringing the axe down over the creature's head again, and again, until she at last heard bone crack.

"Behind you!" Stargazer shouted as a second hound dropped to the shelf. He cast a shockwave and the hound was repelled backwards. "Shard!" he shouted, shaking his brother's shoulder. "It's time to go! Shard!"

Not yet... I can see it, Stargazer. Wait... just a minute more!

"We don't exactly have a minute!" Stargazer shouted as he raised another shield to protect Sintaka as the hound leapt for her unguarded shoulder. Sintaka fired an arrow; the hellhound twisted away, and the arrow lodged in the beast's ribs. The hound barely flinched.

"Shard!" Aerin shouted as she swung her axe wide. Another hound dropped to the ground. Mindrin hid behind Sintaka as she prepared another arrow. They were barely keeping the two dogs back, and if a third attacked from the other side, it would only be Stargazer's sword that would keep it off Shard and Mindrin.

"Shard!" Mindrin begged. "Please, we have to go, now!"

Aerin kicked out at a charging hound. Her heavy boot struck the beast hard in the teeth, and she brought her axe down over her head a moment later. The hound leapt back, yelping, barely avoiding the stroke.

Shard's eyes snapped open, a ghost of a smile touching his lips. "I found it," he breathed.

"Let's go!" Mindrin hauled him to his feet. "Sin! Aerin! Let's go!"

"Down!" Sintaka ordered. They dropped off the shelf, skidding down the rolling hillside, rocks and pebbles scattering under their feet, dust clouds kicking up in their wake. A howl and they heard the hounds on their trail. "Go, Stargazer!" Sintaka shouted. "We'll follow."

Yips and yowls sounded behind them as a hound lost its footing and rolled down the slope all the way to the riverbed. Stargazer darted ahead, leading the way as they scrambled laterally along the slippery hillside. Mindrin nearly carried their dazed leader while Aerin circled warily like a sheepdog on the edge of the flock. Sintaka guarded the rear, throwing her bow over her shoulder to unfurl her bullwhip.

"This way," Stargazer climbed up over the burnished rocks onto the plateau. By now the first of the hounds had caught up with them. Aerin shifted her axe to her left hand, withdrawing the machete from her backscabbard with her right. She swung both threateningly, and the hound backed away tentatively.

"Two ridges to go!" Stargazer shouted.

"Why did we get so far from the tunnel?" Sintaka despaired. "Back, you!" She cracked the whip over the ground, and another hellhound darted back.

"I found it," Shard whispered.

Varron was on the run now, in pursuit. The full four remaining hellhounds were on their tail, swiftly gaining ground. Stargazer felt the air burn his throat as he pushed an extra ounce of energy from his legs. Shard stumbled, still lost in the after-effects of the trance, and Mindrin lifted him up high. A hellhound flew through the air and Aerin swung the machete high over her head, bringing the blade down over the dog's ear, before swinging the axe against the hound's head. The axe hit off balance and only stunned the dog, but Aerin did not care, resheathing her machete as she ran once again.

"Damn it, damn it," Sintaka swore over and over, her mantra as she ran over the broken ground. Mindrin made no effort to the hide tears of exertion and fear. Another hound leapt, and they dropped in unison. The hound sailed over them, landing on the ground, ready to strike anew. Sintaka cracked the whip over its back, once, twice, screaming for the party to go on without her. She kicked and whipped the hound, beating it back as its howls of rage turned to those of fear and pain.

Another howl rent the air, and a second hound landed on Sintaka's back, its jaws snapped at her shoulder. Sintaka did not fall, only stumbled, and rammed her fist hard into the dog's eye. She twisted her hand in the tender eyesocket, before she encircled the hound's head with a muscular arm and threw it bodily over her shoulder. The second dog struck the first, and they snapped at each other, distracted.

An arrow whistled, and Stargazer held up his hand, creating a brief faltering shield to reflect the arrow inches from Shard's head. Still the boy hardly noticed what was going on about him. "Who's shooting?" Mindrin screamed.

Aerin caught sight of another figure, fleetingly on the rise. A woman, maybe, or a slender youth, holding a gnarled staff in one hand, and a one-handed crossbow in the other. She could give it no further attention; the hounds were nearing again.

"There! Go down, now!" Stargazer commanded, and they leapt down over the ridge. Aerin recognized the outcropping they had first sought shelter underneath. Vines laced across their path, nearly tripping them. **Open!** Stargazer commanded. **It's the Amaru long-legs! Stargazer! Open!**

They could see the rocks where the false wall had once retracted into the earth. The tunnel was still closed. It would take time for the gears to swing the first lock open. The hounds snapped at Sintaka's ankles.

OPEN, damn you! Stargazer nearly screamed at the wall, pounding on the door. Mindrin set Shard down, turning to see Sintaka racing towards them, two hounds on her tail. She had lingered too long behind them, and she was still fifty paces away.

"Get behind me, Mindrin!" Aerin shouted as she raced towards the iron-red slope. "Come on, Mindrin, what are you doing!" she demanded as Mindrin stumbled past her, stepping out onto the open plain. The first hound reached

Sintaka, tackling her to the ground, pushing face her into the mat of black creeper vines.

Mindrin knelt on the ground, touching his hand to the dry earth.

"*Mindrin!* Get up from there!"

He closed his eyes, concentrating, letting his magic flow along the ground. The vines rustled once, then rose up from the ground like dancers, encircling the hounds neck, pulling the fighting creature off Sintaka. Another set of vines tangled the second approaching hound, pinning it to the ground. Sintaka did not look back, did not search for her lost whip, but ran over the ground towards the rocks.

Stargazer could hear the gears slowly creaking to life. Too slowly. He pounded on the rocks, bruising his fists on the stones. "Hurry up, damn you!" he shouted.

The rock wall began to shift. Stargazer roughly forced his dazed brother through the widening crack. The hounds began to break free from the vines. Varron was gaining ground, appearing now over the rise. The door continued to open gradually. Mindrin was pushed through. Aerin leapt in, followed by Stargazer and Sintaka. The door opened wide, and then began to slide closed, just as slowly. "Come on, come on," Stargazer prayed. The dogs were getting close. Aerin pushed Mindrin and Shard back deeper into the tunnel. The door rolled closed as the first of the hellhounds reached the tunnel gate. A gray muzzle thrust its way in, then withdrew as the lock slid into place.

"Back in the rat's hole again," Sintaka moaned. "Powers, I miss the Vastwood."

"Keep going," Stargazer breathed. "They'll probably seal this tunnel up, now that Varron knows where the entrance is."

"You mean blow it with blackdust," Mindrin gasped.

"Come on!" Aerin pushed them further down the tunnel, down the staircase. "We won't be safe for sure still we're inside Thandállen's walls. Shard?" she asked, as she passed him. He continued to lean against the wall, his greatcoat dusty, his eyes distant and clouded. "Shard? Are you all right?"

"Where..." he breathed.

Aerin chuckled weakly. "You don't have the faintest idea what just happened, do you?"

He smiled faintly, hardly seeing her. "I found it."

"Come on," Aerin offered him her shoulder. "Sim's waiting to see you."

"Sim?" Shard asked as they crept down the staircase, the sound of the hounds scratching outside the rock wall.

"Yeah, remember him?" Aerin teased lightly.

Aerin? Shard asked weakly. **Can I ask you something?**

Sure, she replied, puzzled. **What's wrong?**

You speak the Old Tongue, right?

Yes. What is it?

What does* ka'eri *mean?

Aerin frowned as she helped him down the stairs. *Ka'eri? *Well... it means* *'beloved.' Literally translated it means 'my heart's mate.'**

"Heart's mate," Shard breathed.

Why? Where'd you hear that, anyway?

"Oh, in a poem somewhere... something that just came to me," he murmured. A little sphinx's smile came to his lips as he leaned against his friend, letting her help him further down the tunnel. He felt lightheaded, buoyed by an exhilarating euphoria. His eyes drifted closed, and he did not see the knowing smirk that touched Aerin's lips.

Shard stood at the low-topped table where they had discussed strategy only the night before. Had it been only yesterday? His mind reeled. So much time had passed since then, since even his morning awakening. It was not yet ten o'clock in the morning.

"I have a plan," Shard spoke hesitantly.

"Oh, the boy has a plan," Merkh chuckled.

Shard glanced at the faces around the table, all smiling encouragingly. Arjin, Ceih, Sintaka, Stargazer, Aerin, Sim: all were watching him intently, waiting to hear his words.

Sim. *Ka'eri.*

Shard smiled warmly at the Onmyóji. But there was a sparkle in his violet eyes that gave Sim pause. **You're smiling like someone with a secret.**

More than one, Shard thought, keeping it soft enough that Sim could not hear it.

"I know where the *yúgure* is," Shard spoke. "I know where to find it, how to get to it. It's all laid out in my head, like a map. Put me on the plains with a pack of fighters and I'll home in on it like compass seeking north."

"All right," Arjin grinned. "Let's go."

"No," Shard shook his head. "You and Ceih are going to Fallon'ser."

"What?" Arjin demanded. "Are you cutting us out of the action?"

"You'll get all the action you could want. Once I have the *yúgure,* you and Ceih are going to lead the combined kobold forces against Larien's men." He saw the look of surprise on their faces and continued. "You and Ceih will go north with Merkh and Siurn to Fallon'ser, and assemble the troops. Tomorrow night I'll take a small team in to get the *yúgure* shard and take it to a safe location. As soon as we have it secured, we'll send you a mindspeech, and you'll attack Wyvern's Rest. Strip it to the ground."

Ceih nodded smugly. "I'm ready for that."

"Wait, wait, wait," Merkh spoke up. "I don't know about Siurn, but I know *my* men won't think much of being led by an arrogant long-legs aristocrat."

Arjin narrowed his gray eyes dangerously. "Do you have any idea who I am?"

"Oh, sure, sure, you happen to have famous parents. But this isn't the High Court of Hesperin. Don't think you can lord your blood over us up here."

"You know, I don't think I like you. Little dwarf."

"How's the Overworld up there, gawky?"

"Just what are your qualifications to lead us into battle," Siurn asked politely.

Arjin stood tall, thrusting his chest out proudly. "The Garvas Rebellion in 197. Garthan Raiders at Brox Lideyrn in 208. Uprising in Catishar country in 212. Siege at Faradan in 265."

"You fought at all of those battles?" Merkh demanded.

"I *led* them," Arjin said pointedly.

"I don't believe you. Upstart dandy like you, you probably cowered behind your Mama Kitsune or your woman there," he gestured to Ceih, "and let the real warriors do all the work – hey, *hey!*"

Arjin took hold of the back of his tunic and plucked him off the ground as if he weighted no more than a feather, holding him up to his eyelevel. Merkh kicked and swore, pummeling Arjin's shoulders and kicking his legs, but the knight did not so much as flinch. He simply stared at him coldly.

"What are doing? Hey, put me down, ya queer bastard! *Bys!* Tell him to put me down!"

Bys merely chuckled, trying ineffectively to conceal his broad smile.

"Come on, you geldings, help me!" Merkh squealed to his men. They hung back uncertainly. Merkh continued to fail and scream for help, looking everywhere but Arjin's intent stare. At length Ceih laid his hand on his soulmate's shoulder.

Arjin dropped Merkh.

"Enough of this!" Bys ordered, still smiling despite himself. "Shard. You were saying?"

Shard repressed his grin. "Well... well, Arjin and Ceih will stay at Fallon'ser. Leave after supper tonight. You've got all of tomorrow to get your attack plans in order. Around midnight tomorrow night you should get the signal."

"One day's not much time," Ceih objected.

"We can't afford to linger. Can you do it?"

Ceih and Arjin exchanged glances. "Yeah," Ceih nodded. "We can do it."

"Then be ready to attack starting at ten in the evening tomorrow night. I don't expect to send the call much later than one or two in the early morning. We'll take them in the night."

"Who'll send the call?" Arjin asked.

"Aerin. She's your sister, and she'll be the strongest voice in your head – excepting Ceih, of course. No matter what might happen to us, she'll be the one whose mindspeech will reach you the clearest."

"No matter what might happen..." Aerin murmured. "Hardly encouraging."

"You think you can find the *yúgure* shard?" Bys asked.

"Don't worry about that. I can feel it like a beacon, even from down here. Just get me up to the surface and I can lead you right to it."

"It's buried deep in the mountain."

"They built tunnels to put it there, didn't they?"

"Can you find the old passages?"

Shard nodded. "I think so."

"I think we're forgetting something," Merkh interrupted. "Larien. He's digging in there right now. My scouts sent back a full report not an hour ago: the slaves used to slack off a little during the night; since yesterday they've doubled their shift loads and worked a full twenty-four hours. Larien must be making the last push into the Treasury. How do you know you won't be too late tomorrow night?"

Shard shook his head. "I'm not worried."

"Why not? He must be almost through if he's digging this hard. How do you know you won't walk right into him tomorrow night? What – what do you know that Larien doesn't?"

A slow smile spread across Shard's features.

21

Someone had provided Mindrin with an ocarina, and he perched on the rocks above the table, whistling an old folk tune. A kobold girl brought out a large glass bottle to the table, taking care not to stumble. "Sapphire wine, straight from Shal Emis," Bys announced as he popped the cork and began to pour a small amount in each of the large kobold mugs. "Hardly our standard fare, but I think the occasion calls for it."

"Come on, Min!" Sintaka called, and Mindrin bounded from the rock, hurrying to her side. Bys continued to fill the bottom of each of the wooden mugs, and the fragrant aroma of sapphire wine rose above the table.

"Let's toast the greatest victory, or the greatest fiasco we Mantalores will ever have," Bys raised his mug. The eight peri followed suit. "To... life and death, old friends and new enemies. To beginnings and endings... and... to dances and lovemaking," he finished. "Let's bury the bastards and go home to our beds!"

"*Taka su!*" Arjin swore as they brought their mugs together.

"You'd better get going," Aerin said after she drained her mug. "I think Merkh was ready to leave an hour ago."

"Merkh needs an enema," Bys laughed. "But you're right. We've gone over the plans all we can here. It's time for you to take them to the kobolds up at Fallon'ser."

Arjin and Ceih finished their wine, then turned reluctantly as their comrades gathered about them. They all wore bright smiles, intending the goodbyes to be brief and the reunion imminent, but they all knew the spectre that hung over them.

"Take care of Sintaka," Ceih told Mindrin, patting him on the shoulder. "You're a Tora, an *ani* to the end. Don't forget that, kit. Sintaka," he turned to his matesister. "Take care of Mindrin. Bring my brother back."

"Hey, Shard," Arjin paced over to him. "You look out of place here."

Shard nodded, painfully conscious of how he stood at the fringe of the gathering. "Leader's curse, I suppose." He glanced over at Sim, who was straying from the other peri as well. Arjin caught Shard around the neck and dragged him back to the group.

"Come on, Shard. Leaders don't stand alone." He propelled Shard towards Sim. "Keep an eye on him, huh? His mother will roast me over a slow fire if anything happens to her little one." Shard felt as if his cheeks were on fire. He only hoped he didn't look too foolishly contented to be handed over into the Onmyóji's care.

"Well, will we see you again in Amaru after this is all over?" Arjin asked good-naturedly. "Or will you be disappearing off into the mist once the *yúgure's* safe in Shard's pocket?"

Shard looked up at the Sim hopefully, and under the scrutiny Sim smiled shyly. "No, I'll meet you in Amaru, Arjin. Powers forbid I force you to live without the pleasure of my company," he added wryly.

"Why, Sim," Arjin tittered with mock bashfulness. He proceeded to wrap the Onmyóji in an affectionate headlock before proceeding on to Mindrin and Sintaka. Sim blushed, casting Shard an embarrassed smile.

"Did you mean that?" Shard asked softly. "About coming back to Amaru with me – with us?" he amended.

"Of course I did," he ruffled Shard's hair lightly. "Where else would I go?"

Ka'eri, Shard thought tenderly, making little effort to hide his smile.

"And remember to always guard your right side," Arjin said to Sintaka. "You still let that one slip sometimes. Stargazer," he turned to the heir, biting his lips as he tried to compose an appropriate farewell. "Stargazer... oh what the hell," he began to turn away, only to wrap his hand about Stargazer's braid, pulling the astrologer into a passionate embrace.

"Arjin!" Aerin screamed, rushing to free her soulmate as Arjin continued to kiss him hungrily. "Get off!" She and Ceih together managed to pry the knight away, Ceih gently leading the blushing heir to the sidelines, Aerin beating her brother mercilessly about the shoulders until the blows dissolved into an affectionate embrace.

"Remember, keep your sword up, don't let your arm drop," Ceih warned the boy sternly. "You can bluff a warrior once, an imbecile twice. More than that and you're only fooling yourself. You'll be a great Arashi once you let yourself. And remember, if you ever get stuck," he turned Stargazer around to face the Kitsune children. Aerin threw her head back, laughing loudly as Arjin caught her up in his arms, swinging her about. Ceih smiled warmly. "Just remember what you're fighting for."

Shard stretched in his armchair, his boots up on the brick wall surrounding the huge fireplace. In his hands lay a kobold book called *The Mark of a Leader,* closed and unread. He imagined Bys had slipped it into his room: a little motivational reading before the big push. He was too restless to read. Every time he opened a page his eyes raced ahead over the words. He would close the book again in frustration after reading no more than a few garbled lines. Too many thoughts weighed heavily on his mind. The *yúgure's* siren song still tugged at his mind. Larien's lust for the shard continued to echo in his head. He could see Terrays in his mind's eye, her features an eerie duplicate of Sim's. Sim...

He got up from the chair, casting the book aside angrily. He began to pace, his hands laced together behind his back. *Ka'eri*. Teachers did not call their pupils "my beloved." Brothers did not call each other their "heart's mate." Shard stumbled as he paced. What did he do now? What could he say to Sim? He knew he was supposed to be relieved now, yet everything seemed doubly complicated. Even as he was walking on air he seemed to be sinking.

He hurriedly undid the clasps on his black jacket and tossed it to the floor, untucking his white shirt and rolling up the sleeves. The room was freezing cold and boiling hot at once. The fire was slowly dying, and the night chill was already blanketing Thandállen. Shard hardly noticed.

Sim, Sim, Sim, he chanted miserably. Why did he make his life so complicated? Sim was only three doors down. All that was needed was one loud thought, not even a mindspeech. One damned *thought* was all it took.

This is no way to be going to war!

He threw his hands up furiously, stamping his foot on the ground.

A knock rang against the wooden door.

Shard jumped.

"Shard?" Sim called, opening the door a crack. "Can I come in?"

"Sure, sure," Shard nearly squeaked in his surprised delight. He was grinning like an idiot, he knew it. Sim stepped into the room and Shard's smile fell. Sim's face was a mask of concern and worry. His eyes were clouded and distant, much darker than usual.

"Sim?" Shard asked. "Are you all right?"

"How do I look?" Sim asked grimly.

"Not the best I've seen. Worried. We all are."

Sim nodded. He pressed his back to the door and discreetly turned the lock. "Ever since Arjin and Ceih left with their kobolds everyone's been quieter. They bring a lot of life with them. Let's hope they can rally the kobolds as well as they can rally us."

"Arjin's the son of one of Hesperin's national heroes. Merkh notwithstanding, they'll follow him to the Underworld and back. Hey... hey, did you know he and Aerin are both a quarter-kobold?"

"You're joking!"

"No, really. On their father's side."

Sim laughed. But his smile evaporated as suddenly as it appeared.

"Is everything all right? You seem... I don't know... worried over something else. Something... more."

"I have a lot on my mind."

"Tell me," Shard gestured to the brick wall. "Maybe it will make you feel better."

"Maybe," Sim moved over on the ledge. Shard knelt on the floor at his feet, gazing up at him, concern welling in his eyes.

"What's wrong?" Shard asked in a faint voice as Sim averted his eyes, sorrow written across his every feature. He touched Sim's knee like a suppliant. "Tell me."

Sim laughed, a faint, bittersweet laugh. "Oh, Shard," he ruffled the boy's hair once again. "I've... just been thinking about what you and Arjin were asking. Whether I'd be returning to Amaru."

"You're not going to change your mind are you?" Shard asked desperately.

"No, no, of course not," Sim reassured him swiftly. "No, it's just that I got to thinking about it, afterwards." He looked down at his black-gloved hands, and slowly began to remove them in his slow deliberate manner.

Shard never failed to find it entrancing.

"I was thinking about Armal. You heard about him?"

Shard nodded. "The kobold from Chalandris. Your lover." He had not meant the word to come out sounding so accusing, but his jealousy had betrayed him. Sim blinked once, questioningly, before he began to laugh.

"My lover? What made you think that? No, no," he chuckled at Shard's innocent misunderstanding. "Armal and I weren't lovers. We were just good friends, that's all." His smile shifted as he remembered fondly. "Good friends." He glanced down at his bare hands. "He... he asked me to stay with him and the others, I told you that, didn't I? He and the others were ready to make me one of them. Do you know how rare that is, Shard? Kobolds will mingle freely with peri now, but to actually invite them to join their guild – and to me, who grew up when kobold and peri were often at war – it was an incredible honour. But I turned it down. I went back to the Highlands. Armal and I had known each other for three years. He called me brother. But I just couldn't stay in that world. It was too painful to live, even among friends. But now, now I'm awake, I'm alive, and I'm promising to go back with you to Amaru, and... what? Be Tiryn's apprentice? Work with Galen in the libraries, sorting out old manuscripts? And... I'm looking forward to it, Shard. Before, each time I went into a fight, either in the tavern I had visited to catch up on my current events, or in Chalandris itself... I never really thought about the 'after.' Everything was a suicide mission in its own way. But now I'm thinking about the after. I" – he laughed in disbelief – "can't *stop* thinking about it."

Shard swelled with pride in the Onmyóji for his revelation. But he did his best to hide his wide smile, saying instead: "Something must have changed a great deal since Chalandris–"

"It was you, Shard."

Shard fell silent, his eyes wide at such a revelation. "You," Sim repeated at Shard's expression of disbelief. "I..." he laughed again, nervously. "Oh, Shard," he took Shard's face in his hands. "I've been in love with you since the moment I first laid eyes on you."

Shard stared at him incredulously. "I know, I know," Sim nodded, withdrawing his hands. "Hardly what you were expecting."

Sim loved him? Ever since that first night?

"And I know nothing will ever come of it. I accepted that long ago, Shard. Don't worry: I won't try to seduce you. I know you... that someday soon you'll fall head over heels for some palace girl, and I'd never try to interfere in that. You deserve whatever happiness you'll find, and I know you'll find it soon. You're too... *alive* to be denied it long."

Shard continued to blink, his mind crawling to comprehend. *Sim loves me*, he repeated over and over, never quite daring to believe it . He struggled to keep his breathing regular as he felt his heart race, beat so fast he feared it might explode in his chest. Was it all a dream? Or another psychic hallucination of Larien's invention? Sim mistook his mounting exhilaration for unease, and continued swiftly:

"You're probably wondering why on earth I'm telling you these things. I don't really know myself, to be honest. But we're going to war tomorrow – we don't know how easy it will be to actually get the *yúgure*, or how many of Larien's guards we'll trip over in the process, or if the *yúgure* will be stable or if it will just explode in our hands the minute we find it."

Shard felt dizzy; he could feel the floor spinning beneath his knees. He feared he might black out, or else spontaneous combust right in front of the Onmyóji. Something deep inside him was screaming, and he did not know how much longer he could contain it.

"And – I just thought – I wanted you to know. In case anything happens. Anything at all. It's selfish of me, I know, leaving all this on your shoulders just so I can get a good night's sleep. But I wanted you to know – and know that should by some miracle everything turn out all right, I'll never ask to be anything but your good friend, or try in any way to–"

Shard snapped. He rose up on his knees and swiftly covered Sim's mouth with his own, silencing him with a light, tender kiss.

Almost as swiftly he sank back to the floor. Sim stared down at him in disbelief. Their eyes searched each other's desperately, looking for any sign, any faint clue. Shard could see Sim's thoughts fly through the same overwhelming flight as his own had moments before. Shard could no longer force his lungs to draw breath slowly and regularly. His heartbeat was surely an audible din.

Sim raised his hand slowly, hesitantly. He touched Shard's cheek gently, and the touch trembled; whether it was his hand or Shard who shivered neither of them knew. Shard kept his eyes locked with Sim's, his breathing growing erratic as he could not keep up with his furious pulse. He could hear the blood rushing through his head. Surely Sim heard it too. He felt ready to pass out.

Sim's fingers lightly glided up Shard's cheekbone, brushing against his skin before tangling themselves in Shard's shimmering black hair. Shard's eyelids slid closed as he unconsciously pressed his cheek against Sim's hand, unsatisfied with a feather touch.

Gently, Sim drew Shard nearer. Their lips met again. Suddenly shy, Sim began to draw back, but Shard pressed closer, covering Sim's lips once more.

Shard stood, taking Sim's hands in his and drawing him to his feet as well. Sim watched him closely, doubt in his eyes. "I should go." He began to step away, but Shard gently drew him back.

"Shard?" A light furrow touched his brow as he regarded the boy with a confused expression.

"Don't go," Shard shook his head again, a slow smile spreading across his face. He slipped his hand around Sim's neck, fingers lightly twining in his hair. Sim resisted slightly, and Shard kissed him again, only the faintest brush of lips, a reassuring caress.

"This can't be a good idea," Sim murmured, but already he was returning the embrace. He raised his hand to Shard's shoulder as if to push him away, but he soon clenched the thin shirt tightly.

"We could all die tomorrow," Shard argued, taking a step back towards the bed.

"All the more reason not to," Sim protested, stumbling after Shard. "What – what if we don't die?"

Shard smiled warmly. "Then we won't die," he murmured meaningfully, kissing Sim once more. *I love you,* he thought again, a distant, distracted thought, and Sim's fingers tightened in the fabric of Shard's shirt, as he deepened the kiss impulsively.

He felt he was floating in another dreamscape. Shard forgot all about Larien, the *yúgure* shard, Terrays; everything but the Onmyóji he held in his arms. He could scarcely remember the war that awaited them, the search for the *yúgure* that would unfold in a mere twenty-four hours. Sim's lips slipped from Shard's own, brushing across his cheekbones, lightly lipping at his earlobe.

Shard's hands dropped to the hem of Sim's black tunic. Sim stepped back, raising his arms over his head as the shirt slipped off, falling to the floor to join Shard's rumpled jacket. Shard shyly ran his hands down Sim's chest, before a smirk touched his face and he gave Sim's ribs a merciless tickling.

Sim caught Shard, pinning his arms to his side as they both laughed. "You had it coming," Shard protested between laughs.

"Bitch," Sim returned the insult affectionately, burying his face in Shard's neck. Shard's white shirt fell aside a moment later.

They tumbled wordlessly into the large sleigh bed. Their clothing fell to the floor to join their previously discarded garments, and they rolled under the heavy furs and woolen blankets to ward off the night chill.

He felt Sim in his mind again, like the mindlock at Helonsden. Only now the sensation seemed doubly intense. At first it was only a whispering presence, much as before, and Shard's own mind stretched out in reply. For a time it was no more than a mindspeech, a simple pleasure, and inwardly, Shard laughed in delight. He heard Sim's own laughter echoing in his mind as the Onmyóji bent his head and kissed him once more.

His senses seemed heightened, even as the outside world seemed to dissolve into the gray-white mist of the dream world. He was acutely aware of the warm kobold bedding under his skin, the intoxicatingly soft pillows beneath his head. He could hear the wind blowing through the fireplace chimney, a faint whistle from the surface, high above Thandállen.

He ran his hands through Sim's hair, drawing him even closer, kissing him deeply.

He felt Sim's consciousness grow stronger in his own mind, ably slipping past Shard's untrained mental defenses. Before Shard was even aware of it, the psychic bond was heightened once more. He could feel Sim's calm presence, the comforting mask he wore over the darker, restless emotions within him. Shard felt his loneliness, the emptiness that had gnawed at him ever since Terrays's death. Sim's sorrow washed over him in waves, almost overwhelming him. Yet under it Shard sensed something else: mounting hope, a reborn vitality, hesitantly emerging, unsure of its own strength.

Almost at once the foreign presence intensified exponentially, and Shard's mind reeled at the sudden invasion. Suddenly it seemed Sim's distinct presence had infiltrated every reach of his mind. His own individual consciousness rebelled furiously, even as Shard delighted at the experience. This was more than a sending, more than a mindlock. Not even the violent psychic assault with Larien had reached such a depth. He was too young, too undisciplined to withstand such telepathy. What was this? He felt as if his very soul was being invaded.

Was this soulbinding?

"Shard?" Sim whispered, nuzzling his neck.

Soulbinding? Shard thought, his mind reeling.

Sim lifted his head, blinking, concern in his features. **Oh... I'm sorry,** Sim stammered. **I didn't...**

Soulbinding, Shard thought, a dizzy rush nearly overwhelming him.

Shard... I didn't mean... I thought you...

Shard surged upwards, kissing him.

They sank back into bed. Briefly arrested, the intrusion of Sim's presence continued, only Shard no longer viewed it as an invasion. His mind's defenses relaxed gradually, mental barriers falling aside. He felt the Onmyóji's distinct thoughts blending with his own. Shard did not flinch from the new wave of sensation; instead he reached out to it. Falteringly, his own soul stretched across the mindlock, calling out to Sim's. He feared a guardian spell to unlock, but he touched Sim's mind to find his defenses already cast aside.

A flurry of images bombarded his senses, even as he saw nothing but Sim's deep emerald eyes above him. Countless whispers assailed his consciousness even as he heard nothing but the Onmyóji murmuring Elórian endearments. He saw his own memories spring up before his mind's eye, dimly realizing that they weren't his own after all. But he was drugged, intoxicated, no longer caring for anything beyond his Onmyóji.

Was that Elória he saw before him, all green forests and spacious palaces?

He could smell the seashore of Amaru; he could hear the wind whistling over the Bay of Jade.

Alsaya stood on the ramparts of Elória, her long golden hair floating on the breeze, her expression yearning, mourning.

The air was heavy with the smell of the death as the Wastelands lay smoking with the *yúgure* fallout.

The shard flashed before their combined vision, calling out to them again.

Can you see it? he asked tremulously... or was it Sim who spoke? He could no longer tell.

The maelstrom spun faster, senses blurring, images combining, as Shard's consciousness stumbled to keep pace. A flood of sensation threatened to drown him as he touched the entire scope of Sim's life experiences. The world seemed to collapse in on itself, time slowing down and speeding up at once, hurtling towards a conclusion. He clung to Sim fiercely, dizzied and drunk. It was going to kill him, he was certain. No one could withstand such an onslaught, having an entirely different soul grafted flawless onto one's own. Yet he did not fight the pull, but let the current draw him in deeper.

Everything blurred, accelerating furiously: his mind, Sim's, there was no longer any distinction. Their souls were no longer some finite presence, contained and separate, but something greater. The whirlpool spun faster and faster, collapsing in on itself, a reeling runaway sensation.

Until a single moment, less than a heartbeat, that seemed to stretch forever. For a mere instant in time all final barriers were battered down. For an instant there existed only one soul, newly created. Shard caught his breath as the world seemed to catch fire.

Time resumed all of sudden, and the tenuous connection dissolved immediately, the maelstrom gradually tempering itself into nothingness.

Shard leisurely floated back to awareness. The restlessness was gone, he realized dimly. The ambition, the frustration, the rush of adrenaline forever denying him rest, all were washed away. Not even the prospect of the *yúgure* could rouse him. He drifted asleep, his head pillowed on Sim's shoulder, lulled into dreams by the Onmyóji's fingers lightly twining in his hair.

22

The wall gave way and Morden tumbled forward, collapsing atop the kobold slaves beneath him. The kobold cried out at the blinding brightness that assaulted his eyes. Lifting a hand to shield his eyes, Morden frowned at the overwhelming glare of gold.

Gold!

Morden stumbled to his feet, stepping over the backs of his workers as he limped into the large chamber which had opened up. "Light!" he shouted. A slave brought in a glowlamp, and Morden's eyes dilated in wonder as the light gleamed off an almost solid wall of gold.

"Holy Myrddin, Aurin, and Chaiya," he gasped. He found himself in a small crawlspace between the wall and the gold statues, peri in form, but nearly double life-size.

His jaw agape, Morden found a gap in the massive gold monoliths and squeezed through, glowlamp in one hand, his other against the hilt of his dagger. Through the tiny passage, he nearly tripped over a tangle of freshwater pearl strings littering the ground in front of him.

"Powers...." He stood before a massive room, easily thirty, forty times the size of the lush antechambers he had broken into before. A dozen steps led down from the thin border around the room where he stood. He saw identical golden statues, depicting a powerfully built peri archetype, bordering the entire chamber. Below him, in the main chamber, he could make out the silhouettes of heaped jewels and immense boxes of rare wood, concealing greater treasures.

"Light!" he barked. "I need light. Call Larien. Tell him we've broken through." He was too dazed to trust himself to mindspeech. He let the glowlamp fly, and it rattled down the steps, its sphere of glowing light coming to a stop at the bottom of the steps. The light set off countless blinding rays of gold from various statues. The entire room seemed to be gilded from top to bottom.

Slaves hastily set glowlamps on staffs throughout the room. Larien wrung his hands impatiently as terrified kobolds gingerly stepped closer to the immense double doors at the far end of the room. "Don't worry, Master. Just checking for deathtraps. We'll soon have Ravanor's sarcophagus for you," Morden gloated.

Larien continued to wring his hands, rubbing his ring repeatedly. It was one in the morning – but then who was he, who never slept, to complain about the hour. All that mattered was the *yúgure* shard. Soon he would no longer need to fear the passage of time.

The slaves waved an all-clear and they proceeded ahead. Paths had been created in the dazzling wealth long ago; Morden wondered if they had any significance, if an aerial view would reveal a strange pattern. To one side they passed a small wooden pagoda, doubtlessly concealing immeasurable wealth within. At the other a life-size silver griffin perched among the golden drekks, its gilded wings outstretched for flight.

The slaves shoved the huge double doors inward, and they continued into a second chamber, perhaps twice the size of the first. Still larger statues, scraping the fifty foot ceiling, stood sentinel within the second chamber. A large reflecting pool sat in the center of the room. It still held water. Floating candles, all long extinguished, bobbed on its surface. As Morden drew nearer he saw a mosaic pebbled on the bottom. A well-muscled peri man, presumably Ravanor, wearing nothing but a slim silk wrap across his lap, sat in a woodland attended by half-naked peri strumpets. Morden smiled. Ravanor knew his priorities.

He looked up to see the second set of double doors. Six figures hung in the gold frames, three to each door. Morden frowned as they drew nearer. Women, it appeared. The slaves nodded that the way ahead was clear, and they moved toward the doors.

Morden recoiled as they drew nearer. Statues of peri women, exquisitely carved, naked and gilded like all the figures in the chamber. But they were twisted in various poses of agony, their arms extended up in pleading gestures, their faces contorted in grimaces of unbearable pain. The outer two were placed with their backs outward, their limbs placed as if they were struggling to climb the door to escape some horrid fate. The inner two held their arms out, as if begging for their lives.

It occurred to Morden that they weren't statues.

"Ravanor's six consorts," Larien breathed, his face warm with satisfaction.

Morden shuddered.

Larien pushed the doors open, and they gave easily. Morden gave the women one more cautious glance before he followed. They pressed into the final chamber, oddly small and snug compared to the two antechambers. Ten skeletons lay on the floor, their clothing rotted, their limbs stretched out pleadingly where they had fallen three millennia before. A huge bird's claw carved out of ivory rose up from the ground, holding an immense marble sarcophagus. Ebony carvings held up the domed ceiling. Curtains of gold chain hung as wall tapestries.

"This is it," Morden whispered. He glanced at the three other doors, all smaller than the main one through which they had entered. "Those must lead to the other treasure vaults. Can you imagine how much this is all *worth?*"

Larien was not listening.

"At last," he strode over to the claw. A thin set of steps lead up one of the talons, and Larien nearly flew up the stairs to stand at the slight landing that rested on either side of the sarcophagus.

Morden slipped up beside him. "Well... hmm, this could be a problem." He examined the heavy marble lid, four feet wide and nine feet long. "I'll get one of the boys to bring in something to–" A low roar built in Larien's throat, and he caught the edge of the lid, flinging it aside as if it were made of straw. The marble cracked in five large pieces on the floor below. Underneath lay a coffin of pure gold. Larien tore its cover with the same ease, only this time his grimaced with pain at the exertion, and his hands trembled afterwards. Within the gold coffin was one of pure platinum. Larien ripped the cover away, screaming with the effort it took. Morden slid back, wrapping his hands around one of the talons as his face paled with fear.

Within the platinum coffin lay a mummy, wrapped tightly in linen bandages, arms closed over the chest. A solid gold mask inlaid with countless precious stones covered Ravanor's face. Tiny amulets were tucked in the bandages. A tiny jewelry case carved of ebony lay between the wrapped hands.

"There it is," Larien breathed. "*Yúgure*."

"*Yu*-what?" Morden asked. "You don't mean..."

"Ahhh," Larien reached into the coffin, prying the box free from the hands. He heard the bones snap as he forced the bandaged hands to free their prize. "The legends spoke true," he murmured, holding the box up to the hand. It was the length of his hand, thin and shallow. Larien closed his eyes reverently as he opened up the box. He opened the case, gazing down hungrily.

It was empty.

A shudder ran through Larien, and he heard a choking sound deep within his throat. The box was empty, holding nothing but three-thousand-year-old dust. He stared incredulously at the case for long moments, cold sweat forming about his eyebrows. At last he found his voice. "It's. Not. Here. It's... not... here...."

"Larien?"

An explosion of laughter broke free inside his mind.

A tic appeared by his left eye.

"Not... here...." He shook the box. "Where is it? Why isn't it here?"

"What, Larien? What isn't there? Larien?" he touched the man's shoulder, and Larien surged back, throwing him off the claw's landing onto the ground below.

The laughter grew, silvery, mocking.

"*Why?* Everything was right!" he howled. "The location, the layout, everything down to the slightest detail! Why isn't it here?" He threw the case to the ground as if repulsed by it. "*Where is it?* Why isn't it *here?* You know, *don't* you?" He tipped his head back, roaring at the ceiling. "*You!* Cimmerian's whore! You undead *bitch!* Where is it? Where did you hide it! *Terrays!* I won't be beaten like this! You know, don't you? You know where it is!"

Morden scuttled back, his face blanched in mortal fear.

The laughter rose higher and higher, rich with scorn and unholy delight.

"Terr-*rraayy*-aasss! I won't let you hide from me! I won't let you defeat me like this! Damn you: damn you, your brother, and that infernal Amaru *whore* of his! I will have it, curse you! You can't keep it from me! Can you hear me, Terrays? I won't let you! Damn you! Do you hear me? *Do you hear me?*"

"I like your wings," Sim murmured, tracing the outline of a feather down the small of Shard's back.

"Yeah?" Shard asked, glancing over his shoulder before burying his face back in the down-filled pillow. "Wondering how far down they went?" he teased.

"Something like that," Sim smiled softly. He lightly traced another feather, then bent his head and pressed his lips to Shard's skin. He kissed his way up Shard's spine, burying his face at the nape of his neck.

"I can feel you," Sim breathed. "In my head." He chuckled softly. "Can't get you out. Is this soulbinding?"

Stargazer said it was strongest for the first day or two, Shard explained, **when... when I asked him why he was always so distracted the day after.**

"How can we fight a war like this?" Sim asked helplessly. Shard shifted on the mattress, rolling over. "Hey," Sim protested softly as he rose.

"Hey, yourself," Shard returned as he gazed up at him. Sim smiled, sinking back on his elbows. He kissed him softly, then shifted on his side, taking Shard's hand in his.

"*Ka'eri,*" he murmured, placing a tender kiss in Shard's palm. "My heart."

Shard snuggled closer, then paused. He propped himself up on one hand, tilting his head to one side as he lightly brushed Sim hair back. "What?" Sim asked with a confused smile. Shard kept his expression grave with scrutiny a moment longer, then broke into a broad grin. "*What?*" Sim asked again.

"You *do* have points to your ears," Shard declared in delighted awe. "Little tiny ones," he traced his fingertip along the edge of his ear. Instead of curving down in a smooth ellipse, the tip of the rim rose into an almost indistinguishable point, easily overlooked or dismissed. "Never even noticed them before." A little cat's smile touched his lips. "My own two-spirit," he murmured contentedly, darting forward to give the delicate point a teasing nip. The action caught Sim off-guard and they both fell back in momentary surprise, laughing. Shard looked down with momentary surprise at the Onmyóji who now lay beneath him. He tried to affect what he imagined was a lady-killer's smile, only to burst into embarrassed laughter. Sim, too, was laughing, unable to contain his delight.

Slowly, they both sobered, their eyes clearing. "Beloved..." Sim breathed, idly fingering a strand of his hair. For a moment their smiles faltered as the reality of their situation returned. A flutter of fear danced in Shard's eyes and something inside him snapped.

"Don't you dare die on me!" Shard hissed fiercely. "Don't you *dare* go on some suicide mission against Larien!"

Sim only shook his head, smiling softly again. "Don't worry, *ka'eri,*" he assured him gently. "We're going back to Amaru after this." To Shard's satisfied smile he added, "After all, I promised Arjin."

"We can't disappoint Arjin, can we?" Shard agreed, his smile growing.

"Some have tried, few have lived," Sim teased. He considered a thought for a moment, narrowing his eyes at Shard. "We could get married," he suggested.

"No, we couldn't!" Shard exclaimed, drawing back, and Sim laughed that he had hit a sore spot. "There is no way in hell I'm putting on a kimono and standing around like a sacrificial doll just to appease the Matriarchs' passion for useless ceremony!"

"You're such a slob," Sim ruled.

"I am not!" Shard sat up indignantly.

"You *are!*" Sim propped himself up on his elbows.

Shard caught up one of the pillows and brought it down over Sim's head. For a moment Sim reverted to elder Onmyóji sorcerer and gaped in utter shock before the adolescent boy regained strength and he sat up as well, picking up his own pillow and beating Shard with it. Laughing, the two pummeled each other mercilessly, until the delicate linen of Shard's pillow gave way over Sim's head, ripping loudly down the center. It sprayed them both with white feathers as they collapsed back to the bed.

"Well," Shard struggled to sober himself, thankful for the strong kobold walls surrounding them. He would hate to have to explain himself to prying ears outside. He glanced back at Sim, wiping a tear of laughter from his eye.

"This is no way for an Onmyóji sorcerer to act," Sim protested softly. He looked up at Shard, smiling fondly. "You're positively determined to destroy an old man's reputation."

"Stop calling yourself that," Shard objected, drawing closer. "Sleeping doesn't count. You're only eighty-one; just a kit. Just like me," he murmured, silencing any further objections with a long kiss.

"Just like you," Sim whispered dreamily, drawing him closer once more.

"What are you thinking?" Shard asked. They had both grown silent as the morning wore on and they reluctantly rose to dress for the long day ahead. No one had come to fetch them yet, but there was enough work awaiting them without falling behind schedule.

Sim pulled his sleeveless shirt over his head. Straightening it, he gave Shard a gently wry smile. "You tell me."

"Terrays?" Shard asked as he slipped his black jacket over his rumpled shirt.

Sim nodded, his eyes downcast.

"We'll save her, don't worry," he assured him. "Nothing will bring her back to this world," Shard admitted sadly. "I've only heard of the Oldest magic restoring life to the dead, and even that, I think – it's just mythology. But we can free her from Larien's hold. When he dies her spirit will be able to cross over. I'm sure of it."

"I wish I could destroy him," Sim cursed. "Do to him what he did to Terrays."

"Then you'd just be like him," Shard reminded him gently. "All his cruelty would be yours. You'd only destroy yourself."

"I know," Sim nodded, averting his eyes for a moment. He turned back to Shard and smiled tenderly at the boy's fumbling attempts to button his jacket. "Here," he straightened the high collar and fastened the top clasp at Shard's neck. He laughed softly. "Your hair's a mess," he reprimanded, giving Shard's tousled locks a swift finger-combing.

"So's yours," Shard whispered back. The Onmyóji chuckled helplessly; he settled Shard's locks into something approximating order, then pressed a quick kiss to the bridge of his nose.

"I'll be fine, Shard," Sim assured him. "Just take care of yourself out there; don't worry about me."

Shard smiled bittersweetly. "You know I will."

"I know," Sim nodded, reluctantly moving away. He picked up the black gloves, still sitting on the rock wall where he had left them the night before. His face appeared heartbreakingly young and vulnerable as he sadly cast his eyes down to the floor. Shard hung back, longing to comfort him, yet suddenly feeling shy and uncertain.

Sim stared at his gloves a moment, before he tugged them on swiftly. He looked up at Shard, his eyes ancient and timeless again, the Onmyóji shield cast under their penetrating stare. Shard gazed at him pleadingly, as if to will the shield to dissolve, to will Sim the child-sorcerer to return. But he knew it would only hurt the Onmyóji in the long run. The shield was the only thing that had kept him alive for so long, and he needed it to survive the last phase of the mission. Extremes would doom him; if he were to confront Larien and the *yúgure,* he needed his detached focus.

Shard nodded in understanding. "Ready?" he asked, his voice little more than a whisper.

Sim nodded back. All of a sudden there was little to say.

It was late at night, the kobold waterclocks revealed, yet the air that slipped down through the cracks in the rocks was hot, dry and acrid. Aerin bit her lip, her shoulders heaving as she struggled to slow her breathing. Sintaka stared ahead intently, her hand at her side against her new whip; it was kobold design, longer and thinner, but she was fairly confident she could wield it just as well.

Shard met Stargazer's eyes in the gloom. The young astrologer looked just as terrified as Shard felt. Impulsively Shard crossed the scant distance between them and crushed his brother against him in a fierce hug.

**We haven't seen enough of each other the last few months,* he apologized.*

We'll fix that when we get back to Amaru.

I'm sorry I missed your wedding.

Stargazer set Shard back, smiling. **Don't be. If you hadn't, we could still be in Amaru getting fat while Larien stole the shard out from under our noses.** His smile shifted slightly. **And you wouldn't have found Sim.**

"You know?" Shard breathed, blushing fiercely.

Stargazer laughed in his mind. **Everybody knows. It'll take a stronger will than you have to hide a soulbinding.**

The lock creaked open, and the brothers reluctantly turned to view the tunnel open up before them. Bys and his retinue of ten kobold warriors were the first to advance, followed by the peri. All advanced with weapons drawn, expecting an ambush the moment they stepped out onto the surface. The air burned their throats and stung their eyes. They waited uncertainly as the lock behind them closed, a security precaution. Even if Varron and the remaining four hounds charged them, the kobold controllers could still blow the tunnel and save Thandállen. The thought that they were surrounded on all sides by blackdust did little to help their already plummeting spirits. Mindrin looked as if he would become sick to his stomach, his face white, sweat beading his brow.

The last door sank away and they ran to escape the claustrophobia of the tunnelway. Shard struggled to swallow the knot in his throat as the change in pressure sent a gust of acrid air into his face. He scrambled to his feet outside the tunnel. Already the lock was sliding closed behind him. The Mantalores were taking no chances.

The sun had set and only the filtered moonlight illuminated the barren plains, in a ghostly orange glow. The air should have been cold, but it was as warm as ever, stagnant and decaying about them. Shard shivered; he felt as if he was wading through death itself.

"You realize we're going to find the thing that did this," Sintaka whispered into the silence. A collective shudder followed her pronouncement.

"Let's go," Shard spoke, hoping his voice sounded more confident to the others than it did to him.

They hiked down the plateau edge parallel to the dried riverbed, the sand scraping between their boots and the iron-red rocks. Already they had passed the place where Varron and the Alteri's hellhounds had attacked. Soon they crept by the small tent city. It appeared deserted.

"Larien's taking everyone to the north side of the mountain," Shard said.

Proceeding east, they mapped the rim of the riverbed. They fell into a line, two figures wide, the kobolds at the rear, the warrior peri leading. Some glanced at their surroundings, others stared at their feet as they walked. Shard kept his eyes focused on their destination, a large mineral cone just visible against the steep rock behind it on the opposite side of the riverbed. Indistinguishable from the rest of the mineral formations – save from the kaleidoscope of energy he could see arcing about it.

"Shard?" Sim asked. "How are you doing?"

"Fine... as fine as I can be," he whispered back.

Sim drew alongside him, his hand brushing Shard's encouragingly. Shard gave the gloved hand a grateful squeeze.

"Uh... Shard?" Aerin asked. "This is probably the question I'm not meant to ask but... what are we going to do with the shard once we've got it? We wrap it up tight in spinner's web and take it back to Amaru, but then what? Just bury it in one of the vaults?"

"We can't do that," Sim shook his head. "Not even the best men can keep this secret. When the words spreads every army will be besieging Amaru to get it. Destroying it would be just as dangerous – look what its last outburst did." He gestured at the surroundings.

"Then what do we do?" Stargazer asked.

"There is a spell, a very old one, for draining focusing crystals. It involves dismantling the crystal's matrix. But it's like defusing a blackdust keg. One wrong move and we're all dead. Once we get the shard back to Amaru, we'll try the spell. I'm fairly confident that the Dynast, Kemuri, Shard and I working together, could drain it. We'll take a ship out to sea – that way if it goes wrong the Continent won't suffer as much."

Stargazer watched Shard's reaction closely. No less than a quarter-turn before, Shard would have protested that he was unsuited to such an important and dangerous task. Yet now he almost did not seem to hear, his eyes still focused ahead. And the closer Shard drew to the *yúgure* the stranger his behavior grew, as though the crystal's energy were a drug to the young boy.

They walked until they were parallel to the large mineral cone, then Shard turned, leading them down the gently eroded slope. The hillside was generally stable, and they reached the riverbed flatlands with a minimum of scuffling and swearing. Shard stumbled once, tripping on his coat hem when he recovered, but his face registered no sign of comprehension. Sim steadied him, but Shard hardly noticed.

The riverbed was dry and cracked; occasional steam vents blasted superheated gas into the air. Chemical and bacterial stains laced across the exposed rock. They picked their way carefully, wary of any loose ground that might give way to reveal a scalding hot spring. The wind drifted over them, producing the distinctive mournful song. The kobold guards muttered scathing curses against the land. Mindrin's teeth were chattering, not from the cold. "How are you holding up?" Sintaka asked softly.

"I...am... sick of being a walking malevolence detector! I'm a court empath! I'm trained to tell whether ambassadors are cheating at card games!"

Stargazer felt for him. Even he could sense the painful electricity in the air, crackling at his hidden senses. For a trained empath like Mindrin it was surely torture. "Let's... let's play a little game," he suggested. "Everyone think where you'd like to be right now."

"Child's games," a kobold sneered.

"What else have we to do?"

"I'd give anything to be back in Hesperin with my family," Bys offered. "There's a lovely little restaurant in the High Town where I'd take my wife. They make the best roast three-feathered quail – a fixed-menu six course meal, each plate better than the last."

"Oh, I can't wait to get back to Amaru," Sintaka spoke up. "Take Ghost to the Vastwood, find a nice tree to climb, get up in the open air, sit back, and watch the moons rise."

"I just want to be with Spark again," Mindrin sighed miserably. "She never falls asleep without one of my bedtime stories."

"Love to be back in the school," Stargazer smiled wistfully, "studying astrology with Galen and Jax. I'd even practice ancient tongues right now."

"To be in a locked room with my soulmate," Aerin decided. "Any locked room."

Sim smiled at that. "I know what you mean," he murmured softly, and Shard blushed, coming out of his dream haze for a moment.

Alsaya's voice sailed over the valley again, like a wraith's wail. The game was swiftly forgotten, and they hiked across the river flat at a faster pace.

The slope leading to the north side of the river was dustier, giving way under their feet. Cursing inwardly, they struggled to ascend as quietly as they could. Mindrin sensed no approaching guards, yet he was first to point out the background chaos of the Wastelands clouded his perceptions. It could be a loud swear uttered in the heat of the moment after tumbling down a mountainside, or nothing more than a whisper of sand that might betray their presence. With a ragged gasp Shard hauled himself onto the stone table above them. A sneeze sounded below him on the cliffside. "Sorry," he heard Mindrin whisper.

Sim reached the top and Shard held out his hand for him, pulling him to the shelf. Sim smiled, brushing the dust from Shard's hair; the rust-gold dust had dulled his shiny locks to a flat black. A moment later Aerin appeared. Shard caught hold of her gauntlet and hauled the light-boned girl onto the rocks.

"Is that it?" Aerin frowned at the cone, twenty feet high and about eight around the base. The light cast the white silica in a pinkish light, and maws lurked in the shadowed cracks.

"Can't you feel it?" Shard asked dreamily.

"Hey," Aerin gave his shoulder a nudge. "Don't you go blacking out again. If the hounds come back you're pulling your weight, Shardseeker."

"Shardseeker," he considered softly. "That... has a ring."

They moved back from the ridge, allowing the kobolds to haul themselves up in turn. The mournful howl of the wind faded in the distance and an eerie silence pervaded. It seemed to Shard a very leaden silence.

He crept towards the mineral cone, his eyes still clouded, but with greater clarity than he had before. It didn't overwhelm his senses anymore. No, now he was used to the call of the *yúgure*. He glanced back over his shoulder to see the last of the kobold scramble to his feet, coughing under his breath as his comrades brushed the dust from his back. "There," Shard pointed, breaking into a measured stride towards the cone. As Stargazer and the others hesitantly followed they could see what appeared as a shadow cast by the cone was in fact a gap in the sharp rock wall of the mountainside.

"In there," Shard breathed.

They walked behind the cone, smiling fleetingly at the slight shade it offered, before slipping between the two spires. It was a narrow entrance, and they turned sideways to fit, but upon entering, the natural corridor opened up into a little hollow. Tall fifty foot spires enclosed them on all sides, and before them the bulk of the mountain rose high into the air in shambling, crumbling columns.

A hot spring bubbled before them, the steam rising high in a continuous column, the dark water churning in the center, gentle waves lapping against the silica crust rimming the pool. A stunted tree, long since calcified, stood as their only companion.

"This way," Shard edged around the hotspring, finding a second pathway in between the tightly packed rock crests. Sim and Stargazer exchanged worried glances then followed accordingly. Slowly the way opened up into a wide corridor, as the electricity in the air mounted. Behind him he heard a cry and a scuffle of feet.

"I can't..." Mindrin gasped, his hands to his head. "I can't go on like this."

"It's all right," Sintaka soothed, helping him straighten. "Close it out, Mindrin. You've done enough." She shot a glance up at their leader, but Shard continued onward, caught in the siren's song.

They climbed higher, ascending a plateau above the first tier of spires. They stood on a rise overlooking a long trench that appeared to be a dried riverbed. Torrent tributaries from the times of flooding during the Dark Age. Some hardy lichen and clingmoss eked out a living on the dusty floor. "Dragon's tracks," Aerin breathed, and Stargazer nodded. In the ominous stillness of the night it did seem like a deep furrow made by the claw of a mythic dragon.

Across the trench stood a barren wall. Yet Shard stared at it with a furious intent. Before anyone could stop him, he flew over the chasm with all the training and purpose of an Arashi knight, and raced up the pebbled rock to lay both his hands on the rock. He swiftly sank to his knees, pressing his forehead against the rock. Sim raced down the trench and up the other side, hurrying to his soulmate's side. Aerin frowned, chewing on her lip. Bys and the other kobolds could only wonder.

Shard knelt with his hands and head against the rock, the occasional shiver through his body the only sign of life. Sim paced about him worriedly, but did not interfere. "What's he doing?" Sintaka whispered at length.

"I think he's unlocking a guardian spell," Stargazer guessed.

Sintaka crossed her arms. "I didn't know he could do that."

"Neither did I."

A low hum was felt first through their feet, then in their eardrums. Like an old organ coming to life, it slowly grew in volume and pitch. It rose higher and higher, until the peri winced in pain, though the kobolds heard nothing. It echoed like a psychic scream in their minds, until Shard let out a ragged cry and the rock wall before his hands dissolved in a shimmer of light.

All shaking their heads and wiping the tears of pain from their eyes, the peri stared in awe at the perfectly carved doorway that now stood before them. Ancient runes and pictographs lined the three-framed door, a huge griffin of the Ravanoran standard looming over the doorway. The kobolds continued to stare in complete bewilderment.

"The Treasury of Ravanor," Aerin was the first to recover her voice.

"He broke the seal," Stargazer marveled.

Shard raised his head, giving his lover a faint smile. "It's in there. *Yúgure,*" he murmured before he collapsed to the ground.

23

Shard recovered his wits swiftly, and a plan was hastily formed. Mindrin was too exhausted to serve as a lookout, and no one knew what shockwaves the breaking of the seal had set loose. Larien could already be on his way. Bys and his men stood guard at the entrance, too superstitious to enter the tomb. The door would have to remain open, as it seemed Shard was the only one to control it. If he wasted his powers to close it there was no guarantee he could open it once more. Already the boy was severely drained psychically, his eyes clouded even as his limbs were filled with renewed strength. Swiftly lighting a single glowlamp, the peri proceeded into the tomb.

They were soon swallowed up by gloom, Bys's diminutive silhouette fast disappearing behind them. The glowlamp was only enough to light a small distance in front of them, and the tunnel walls were set so far apart they seemed to be walking in empty space. At length the light revealed a grand staircase leading under a second, heavily ornamented archway.

They proceeded up the steps slowly, cautiously. Sintaka lifted the glowlamp high and caught sight of several dark shapes scuttling into a lateral crack in the wall. Cobwebs hugged the walls and corners. Ravanor's legacy had become food for spiders and cockroaches.

Passing under the archway they found themselves in a frescoed chamber, the path ahead branching off in three directions. A constant trickling drip could be heard. Shard tiptoed up to the strange little ledge which seemed to line the chamber. It was in fact a miniature aqueduct, with a clear liquid running in a little trench along the wall. He sniffed it carefully, and coughed at the rich smell of kerosene.

Kerosene?

**FIRE!*

He darted back as his stare set the kerosene afire. Within a moment the glowlamp was unnecessary as the aqueduct raced with flames and the entire chamber was bathed in light. They could now make out the frescoes of griffins and tigers and fantastical creatures, and the clear three-way intersection before them. Feeling the dust-covered floor ahead with her toe, Sintaka eased up to the crossroads. The lights continued down all the walls. The path to her left continued a ways before branching off at another intersection. "A maze."

"Which way do we go?" Mindrin squeaked, betraying his fear.

Silence fell, the only sound the distant hum of wind through a fissure. The wrong path could mean a fast death down a bottomless pit, or a slow death forever lost in Ravanor's tomb. "I know," Shard spoke at length.

They shared worried glances. No one could say they trusted Shard's judgement completely, given the tremendous stress his psyche was under. But they had no other option, nor could anyone say Shard's hunches had proven false so far. "Lead on," Aerin waved her head, trying to sound encouraging.

Shard guided them down the right-hand fork. They continued down one corridor for a time, then turned left. A right, a left, and two more rights, and they were completely lost, even Sintaka's sense of direction gone. Shard alone seemed confident as he walked in a dream haze, homing in on the *yúgure's* call like a pigeon returning to its roost among the jasper forests.

Another right; straight, then left, then straight again; two more rights, and three swift successive lefts. Aerin began to feel dizzy, spinning about every few seconds at the sound of an imagined foe. Mindrin was beginning to look distinctly nauseous once more as his anxiety overwhelmed him. They passed a skeleton, bleached white by invisible parasites. Sintaka paled as she contemplated her own possible future – a slow death lost in a claustrophobic maze. Someone's boot cast a flickering shadow and Stargazer and Aerin both jumped.

The maze ended abruptly, the tunnel emptying into a larger chamber. Only one doorway lead out, a strange blue light visible within. Probing the threshold for hidden traps, they cautiously proceeded into the next room.

They all caught their breaths at once at the beauty of it. It was a huge blue crystal, six feet across, suspended high above their heads. The firelight in the miniature aqueducts was reflected by several polished mirrors in the corners of the room, to best illuminate all the facets of the gem.

"Why waste this much care for tomb robbers?" Stargazer marveled.

"This is Ravanor," Aerin ruled grimly. "You remembered the history lessons with Galen. Certain death was his favorite art."

"This is the decadence of the aristocracy," Mindrin chuckled weakly, circling the crystal. "Nothing better to do than pay artisans to decorate your death-traps."

Sim looked around. Two doorways, one on either side of the crystal. The fire did not extend down the tunnels, and they loomed darkly, black holes for the mistaken looter. "Shard? Which way?"

Shard frowned. "I can't say for sure. The call, it seemed to be all around me. The... the left... I think," he decided, clearly little more than a faint guess. They all exchanged skeptical looks, then nodded in agreement. One at a time, Sintaka leading, Sim bringing up the rear, they proceeded into the left passageway.

"Is that... is that light?" Stargazer asked, squinting into the gloom. A faint white glow could be see ahead. "I'd swear that's daylight."

The tunnel opened up and they passed a black passageway continuing ahead, interrupted by several shafts of light falling on the cave floor. "Huh, must be doing it with mirrors," Sintaka mused. "You won't hear me complaining."

Shard picked a little pebble from the ground and sent it skipping across the floor. They waited for the trap to strike, yet none came. Shard bent down. He slowly moved his hand forward, until his palm was coated in white light. Nothing happened. Sintaka slapped him on the back. "See? Come on, let's go."

"All right. But let's stay out of the light where we can. Just in case." Shard threaded his hands behind his back, gathering his greatcoat behind him as he picked his way across the floor. At length he reached the shadows on the other side.

Sintaka followed, and the others each took their turn dancing about the patterns on the floor. They relaxed further as each member slowly made it across to the shadows. It seemed there was no trap.

A scream, a hiss of metal, and Shard and Sintaka both leapt back as a scythe swung across the cave before them. Sintaka screamed and Aerin joined her on instinct. A still-decaying body had been impaled on the curved spear, and the swinging motion dislodged it. It collapsed to the floor, its head snapping from his body, the leathery mummy's skull rolling over onto Shard's boots. He leapt back, disgusted.

Sintaka shuddered. Mindrin burst into nervous laughter. Aerin wobbled on her feet, as if almost fainting. The scythe at last ceased to sway, and they carefully edged around it in turn.

"Some heroes we make," Shard murmured as they continued down the darkened corridor. The tunnel looped to the left, and they turned with it. "Whatever happened to courage under pressure?"

"What courage?" Mindrin hissed. "Only cowards here."

"At this rate I marvel we're still in control of all bodily functions," Aerin coughed. "Fuck courage under pressure. I'll be glad to get out of here with a clean dress."

Their path merged with another at a fork in the tunnel and they rejoiced at a glimmer of cool light ahead. "Wait a minute, isn't that..." Aerin began.

Their spirits fell. They had doubled back on their own trail. They stood inside the Blue Diamond Room once more.

"Right archway then," Aerin decided, and they all gritted their teeth, crossing the floor to enter the second tunnel.

The floor before them was tiled, lined with square-shaped bricks. They bore assorted pictographs inscribed in the Hokabalh tongue. Sintaka frowned, examining the tiles. "Why do I think this isn't some well-meaning decoration?"

"What do you think happens to you if you don't step on the right tile?"

Mindrin wondered.

"More to the point, which ones are the right tiles?" Aerin asked.

"Well..." Sintaka edged closer to the first of the flagstones. "I suppose there's only one way...." She eased her foot out onto a stone tile. "Maybe..."

"No, Sintaka, wait!" Aerin called out as the woman's foot touched the stone. The tile sank slightly under her weight and Aerin and Shard leapt out in unison, catching her about the waist. They yanked her back, an instant before a bright orange flame spurted out from the wall. The flame flared all the way to the far wall, the heat driving the peri back. From the far wall it ricocheted under magical influence, bouncing like lightning back and forth until it formed a burning net across the flagstones. After several agonizing seconds, the flames died away. Stargazer coughed from the lingering smoke.

"Powers, what were you thinking?" Aerin gasped. Sintaka merely shivered, still in shock. Aerin eased her down to the stone floor and Sintaka drew up her knees against her chest.

"Didn't think...." she murmured. She stared up at the wall. Now that she knew where to look, she could see the tiny pinholes along the wall. Each stone had a corresponding jet waiting to discharge a pressurized flame on the unwary peri. Doubtless nearly every flame would be reflected to form the deadly net.

"Even the worst traps have a failsafe." Stargazer frowned at the stones before them. "Something in case the Hokabalh came back. Some of the stones must be safe to step on."

Sim shifted on the balls of his feet, looking over their heads. "Maybe there's a code? A phrase? Aerin?"

"I don't know, I don't know. Ravanor wasn't one for... for proverbs or poems. And... you – you write things in Low Hokabalh – the phonetic alphabet. High Hokabalh is only for titles, and seals. You never write anything substantial with it."

"Maybe we're only meant to step on one pictograph," Stargazer suggested.

"Umm... Arashi, sword, knight, warlord, um... that one means something like... the light after the dusk," Aerin pointed out each glyph. "Flight, master, dueling, combat, war, to cut, to kill."

"What's that one?" Stargazer asked, pointing to a crescent moon followed by three curved lines.

"Faith," Aerin translated. "And there's breath, meditation, agony, the... the awakening after death..."

"They're all to do with combat – Arashi fighting," Shard mused.

Faith, Stargazer realized.

He stepped forward, and Aerin and Shard cried out at once, raising their hands to stop him. He landed on the Faith glyph, already wincing in dread. The rock held firm. No flames spurted from the wall.

"*Yósha!*" Aerin gasped. "You could have killed yourself!"

"How did you know?" Sim demanded.

"Mother said being an Arashi is all about having faith." Stargazer was grinning now.

"Remember what I said about having a clean dress?" Aerin demanded.

"Come on, *Aeoren,*" Sim helped her to her feet. "We shouldn't waste any time."

Shard staggered to his own feet a moment later. Stargazer had already hopped onto the next tile. "The crescent with three waves," he explained. "Don't step on any other."

They slowly made their way across the floor, picking their way from stone to stone. At one point Shard stumbled once, nearly triggering a burst of flame. But he recovered, and the flame-jet did not activate. Within moments they were all assembled together once more on the other side of the glyphs. Aerin's anger against her soulmate gave way instantly and she smothered him in a close embrace. Their reunion was short-lived, for Shard began to advance again, and Sintaka urged the others to follow. "Shard?" Sim called. "Don't go on ahead."

Again the tunnel curved, and they all knew what would happen long before the blue light reappeared. With a sick feeling in the pits of their stomachs, they returned to the Blue Diamond Room.

"Did we take a wrong turn back in the maze?" Stargazer asked.

"I can feel it," Shard insisted. "It's right... all around me. Above me, encircling me. It's right here!"

Mindrin looked up at the crystal, narrowing his eyes. The others slowly followed suit. "Aerin?" Mindrin asked. "Would a psychic scream do it?"

Aerin closed her eyes, her hands closed over her focusing crystal. A hum built within her, radiating outward. The peri edged back, wincing at the crackling electricity in the air. Aerin's lips parted, yet the scream did not emanate from her throat but from her soul. The peri backed up, their hands clenched over their ears.

The blue diamond shattered, reduced to powder. The peri ducked as the crystal dust rained down around them. Aerin let her arms fall slack at her sides, staring up at the gaping hole where the crystal had hung. Another tunnel, leading directly up into the mountain. Mindrin took Sintaka's whip, and after a failed practice attempt that sent Aerin running for cover, cast the whip high enough for the tail to wrap around one of the metal posts that had held the crystal braced in the ceiling. He tugged on the whip, ensuring it was fixed. "I'll go up ahead," he offered cheerfully. "That way, if something goes wrong, you've only lost a gardener."

"Mindrin!" Sintaka snapped in outrage.

"Just kidding," he grinned as he pulled himself up. "Besides, this'll help get me back in shape. After all that time around the gardens, I'm soft as a kitten."

"*Back* in shape?" Aerin murmured in disbelief, staring at the flexed muscles in his arms as he hauled himself up with practiced ease. Stargazer swatted at her hair.

"It's clear," Mindrin called down after a moment. "I think... hey, there are rungs up here: like a ladder. We can climb up easy. I think I see light up at the top."

"Go ahead," Sintaka urged. "I'll take the rear." When Stargazer gazed at her questioningly, she nodded. "It's all right. It feels less cramped at the back. Go on, I'll be fine."

They swiftly followed Mindrin, pulling themselves up the whip. When the others were already in the shaft, Sintaka followed up the ladder rungs, replacing her whip at her hip as she held the glowlamp's handle between her teeth. She cast her eyes high up the cylindrical shaft to see the faint glow of a reddish light. Black silhouettes were cast by her comrades ascending above her. She closed her eyes, taking a deep breath to slow her racing pulse. Shifting the lantern to her right hand, she ably pulled herself up the rungs with her left. A soft whistle of wind descended around them as air slipped through a fissure somewhere in the vast cave network. All listened intently for the shift of gears or the crackle of an imminent trap, yet they climbed the metal rungs easily.

"Where are we now?" Sintaka asked as Stargazer helped her up onto the floor. Shard knelt on the floor, his hands on his forehead as he struggled to catch his breath.

"Shard?" Sim asked. "Can you go on?"

He nodded weakly. "It's so loud," he whispered faintly. "I can hardly keep it out." He drew in a deep breath, then let Sim help him to his feet. "I can go on now," he nodded, his eyes sparking as if in a silken high.

"I'd swear he's spiced," Mindrin muttered to Aerin. She nodded grimly. "Let's get him out of here and that shard in spinner's web as soon as we can."

They followed Shard down the large hallway, Sintaka hurrying ahead to take the lead with the glowlamp. Aerin shivered, rubbing her arms. It was cold deep inside the cave now.

"How are you doing?" Sim asked softly.

Shard seemed to sway as he walked. "I'm... I'd swear I had drained too much of Taki's cheap brew."

"Stay with us," Sim whispered urgently. "You're coming back to Amaru with your mind in one piece, remember? You promised to show me this kingdom of yours."

"Amaru..." *It's Spider... it won't snow until Mystic... if then. Did it snow in Elória for you, beloved?*

Yes. Terrays and I used to fight in it.

Star and I would build snowforts. Arjin and Ceih would help us.

Why are you thinking of snow, ka'eri?*

"I don't know," Shard admitted honestly. They came to a fork in the road. "This way," he pointed to the left.

The tunnel continued forever it seemed, before opening into another chamber. "What is that?" Sintaka pointed to an altar against the wall. It was pure gold, holding unlit candles. Atop it sat the graying skull of a gargantuan crocodilian beast. The creature's limb-bones and claws were arranged on either side of the altar. A winch of some sort appeared to decorate the wall.

"There are no doors out of here," Stargazer mused. "Is this the way to go, Shard?"

"I'm sure of it," Shard nodded. "I can feel it! It's above us somewhere."

"I wonder..." Stargazer put his hands on the handle of the winch and turned it once in experiment. A rough creaking sound and the chain Sintaka had failed to note anchored to the crocodile's skull was drawn taut. The upper jaw rose, hinged, revealing a new door.

"I'll be a spiced troglodyte," Sintaka smiled, peering through the opening the jaws revealed. It was small, but easily large enough for a peri to crawl through. Stargazer secured the chain, locking the winch to hold the jaws open. Sintaka lifted the lantern to reveal a great empty chasm ahead. Faint light, bluish and indistinct, perhaps the result of still-functioning glow crystals, ringed the far wall of the immense pit before them. She could see no floor below her. A creature's rib cage, turned upside-down to line its belly, led upward, like a ladder, a bridge to some unseen destination. She craned her neck about to see a second rib cage descending from a second backbone above.

"I'd swear it's a leviathan," she murmured. "But they're only mythology. Looks like we're meant to climb up there. Looks pretty dangerous, but I don't have any other ideas? Anyone?"

"I repeat that I'm a *court empath!*" Mindrin protested as they slowly climbed through the large cage. He kept his eyes fixed on Sim's legs before him, refusing to look into the blue abyss below him. "I'm not meant for this sort of thing!"

"You think I'm made for this?" Sim chuckled softly. "No one's enjoying this."

"At least we're out in the open air again," Sintaka smiled.

"You *like* this!" Aerin cried.

"Yeah, well, each to her own. You're the court's baby, I'm the Alteri amazon."

"I still can't believe they made you an honourary T'Jara."

"I can!" Mindrin insisted.

Shaking her head, Aerin crawled from rib to rib, following Stargazer's movements, careful to avoid any stress points in the ancient fossil. Ahead of Stargazer, Shard led the pack at a slow pace. Nearly two hundred feet below, a fast-moving river wound its way through the vast cave chamber. "I'll never understand that whole Alteri passion you've got in you. This is hardly the same as camping in the Vastwood, Sin–" she reached forward for the next rib. The bone gave way and she fell forward. The ribs beneath her crumbled under the sudden impact and she screamed as she spun in the open air. Sim shouted her name and Stargazer spun about in the cramped space, throwing himself down on the bones regardless of the risk, casting his hands out to her. Aerin groped wildly for his arm, and by luck more than skill her hand fastened claw-like around his wrist in a death-grip. Instantly he had both hands about hers, holding her fast. "Aerin?" he gasped.

"*Chiga-a-a*," she let the oath escape her lips in a slow breath as she stared down at the void beneath her swinging legs. Bits of broken calcified bones continued to rain around her, drifting down towards the cave floor.

They reached the top of the bone ladder without further casualties, though Aerin needed to sit down for a good ten minutes to recover her wits. They stood no longer within carefully crafted chambers, but a natural limestone cave, surrounding by clusters of stalagmites and scattered bones of animals. They appeared to be beasts of burden: sacrifices to Ravanor's ghost. How the Hokabalh priests had gotten an entire stable of creatures so high into the mountain baffled them.

Shard led them down a faint path through the graveyard. Occasionally they passed a large carved statue of a guardsman, standing watch over the ghosts of the sacrifices. A fat carrion rat scurried for cover as the peri approached. "What do they eat?" Mindrin wondered.

"Each other," Aerin quipped. "Consider it economy."

Suddenly the pain begun, a sharp cry of agony and fear blazed in all their minds at once. Their legs buckled and they staggered, reeling from sudden vertigo.

"Bys! They've been attacked."

"I can't feel them anymore!"

"It's Larien. He's found us."

"We have to go back, we have to help them."

"We can't!" Shard snapped, angry all of a sudden. "We have to go! *Yúgure*. I can feel it. We're so close. We have to get it, before Larien catches up with us."

"He's right," Sim agreed.

"What about Bys and the others?" Sintaka demanded. "We can't leave them."

"We can't help them," Mindrin realized grimly, his expression hollow, empty. "They're already dead."

They ran up the ascending path, no longer checking for booby traps or hidden doors, aware only of Larien on their trail. The pain in their minds had ebbed, confirming Mindrin's conviction. If any of the kobolds survived, they were too far gone to mindspeak. Even if they could will themselves onto the plain, they would be too late to help their friends. They could only run higher and deeper into the mountain.

They reached the top of the interconnecting cave chambers and entered the artificial tunnels once more. But the tunnels were rougher, stalactites littering the ceilings. Still the path led upward, and soon they were out of breath. The corridor angled upward sharply, and they scrambled over slick clay still moist after three thousand years. The path grew flatter, the floor wider. Damp air surrounded them; dew coated the walls. They slowed to a fast walk, eyeing the walls with suspicion. Strange little cavities, vaguely circular, peppered the slime-slick rocks.

"Why is it so moist in here?" Stargazer asked.

"I swear I can hear water running," Mindrin frowned.

Sim stumbled on a rock and suddenly whistles of pressurized wind bit into their flesh, shooting at them from both sides as hissing blasts fired from the cavities in the wall. Someone cried out, the peri fell into disarray, their hands clamped over their bowed heads. Acidic gas? Poison-tipped needles?

Stargazer tripped, falling flat on his face as his comrades ran on. Raising his head he searched for some sign of projectiles and found none. "It's all right!" he shouted, staggering to his feet as the wind continued to buffet him. "It's only wind!" he called as he pursued the others. Belatedly he realized the peri must be acting exactly as they were meant to. What might they run into in their confusion? "Stop!" he shouted, rounding the bend to catch up with them.

Too late they heard him. Leading the party, Shard's foot hit a hidden trigger and the entire floor moved, swinging up on ancient gears. A large circular panel swung up and over, and the peri screamed, each disappearing one after the other down the trap door's shaft.

"Aerin!" Stargazer raced to reach them, but the revolving trap door swung back into place on its hinges, and the metal lock clacked back into place. The hidden panel now appeared part of the mottled floor once more. Stargazer sank to his knees, trying to find the edge of the trap door, pinching his fingers as he tried to raise the tightly locked cap. But the trigger had locked and the trap door would not budge.

He slowly rose. They were all gone. He was all alone now.

Larien was coming.

Stargazer turned to the corridor ahead, racing down the tunnel floor, in pursuit of the *yúgure* shard.

24

Aerin screamed as she slid down the slick tunnel, free-falling before a sudden splash of cold liquid stung her flesh. *A water trap!* her mind reeled as the current sucked her under the river's surface. She could no longer tell which way was up, for the bubbles were churning about her at a dizzying speed and the current was whipping her around too fast. Her lungs burned for lack of air. She kept her eyes open despite the sting the water dealt them, searching for her comrades. Mindrin's mop of crimson red hair appeared briefly, brushing against her cheeks fleetingly before he was gone.

Stargazer! Mindrin! Anyone? she called vainly, knowing her mind was in too much chaos to send clearly.

Shard fought against the current, sinking deeper into the river. He hit the rock bottom hard, his feet scraping against the rock for purchase. With a herculean effort he forced himself upward. He broke the surface for a moment, long enough to see the low-hanging ceiling just above his head, before the current whirled him under again. He was sinking, unable to remain afloat. It was the greatcoat, he realized. He kicked and fought in the water, but the current was wrapping the leather about him in a confining straightjacket. Screaming into the water, a flurry of bubbles blinding him, he managed to shake one arm free from the coat. He twisted in the water and the other sleeve slid away. The black coat disappeared below him.

He could no longer touch the bottom. The river was too deep. He was tossed like a leaf, bobbing and sinking. His head hit a rock and he cried out, swallowing water. **SIM!** his mind screamed as he felt himself sinking deeper under the water. **Help me!** he begged. Starbursts exploded before his eyes as blackness began to creep in at the edges of his vision. He thought he felt Sintaka's mind calling out, but he could not be certain. He sank deeper, his limbs dead weight, his mind growing dark.

A hand caught him by the collar, hauling him upward.

He broke the surface painfully, coughing and gasping. He gazed through his limp strands of hair to see Sim's face briefly, before the current drew them both under once more.

Aerin kicked hard against the river, breaking the water's surface. She drew in an explosive breath and dove under, kicking with the current, her arms out at her sides to steady herself. Surfacing again, she felt something catch hold of the axe strapped to her back.

She twisted about to see Sintaka wedged in a corner, taking refuge behind a darkened figure. The Heiress was almost unrecognizable, her silver hair obscuring her face, her body twisted to fit in the crevice. Aerin threw her hand out and Sintaka caught hold, pulling her out of the current. Aerin gasped in horror, swallowing water; a leering skeleton perched behind Sintaka, its arm held high, bearing a scimitar. It took Aerin a moment to realize it was only a statue, the bones coated in gold.

You... all right? Sintaka gasped.

Where are the others? Aerin asked as she tried to position herself behind Sintaka.

"Don't know," Sintaka pulled herself up on the skeleton's outstretched arm, trying to get a better view of the churning river. Another skeleton was arranged half-under the water, as if a dead man was trying to claw himself out of the deathtrap.

"Do you see light ahead?" Aerin frowned. It seemed that she could make out a distant light, like the shine of glow crystals reflected off gold.

Sintaka strained higher and the skeleton's arm snapped off at the elbow. Still clutching the forearm, Sintaka tumbled into the current, pulling Aerin with her. Within moments the elder warrior was swept away; Aerin groped in vain for her hand, but Sintaka disappeared under the waves. The current pushed Aerin onward, and she struggled to right herself in the water. She kicked and paddled furiously, as the water drew her towards the growing light.

The floor rose up and the water churn in a set of swift rapids. Aerin hit a rock and was sucked under into a whirlpool. She swiftly lost sight of the surface and held her breath as she tumbled over the rapids. The water rose and fell in a waterfall and Aerin went head over heels, her limbs flying in all directions as she splashed into the catch-pool below.

Coughing and sputtering she splashed at the surface, swimming blindly towards the water's edge now that the current had ebbed away into gentle lapping waves. She groped for land, her eyes red and burning, her vision blurred. Her hand found rock and she hauled her shoulders onto land. Coughing and moaning in pain, she lifted her head.

Her breath caught in her throat.

Before her glittered an uninterrupted wall of pure gold. Piles upon piles of it were heaped all around her, filling the cave chamber to the ceiling. The still-burning glowlamps revealed gemstones and scepters, bolts of rare silk and ivory sculptures. Golden skeletons were arranged everywhere in various poses, their bones gilded and enameled. At her side Shard and Sim rested against the pool's rim, staring at the sight in sheer awe. Mindrin was already staggering to his feet, gathering his tunic about his midriff, wringing the water from its hem.

Stargazer! Yósha? Are you there?

Aerin! Thank Oracle. I"m still in the tunnel. I never fell through. Where are you?

Follow my thoughts. Aerin glanced to her right to see a little mineral bridge leading over the river as it arced around the room. A gaping hole signaled the start of another corridor, two golden skeletons standing watch on either side. **I think the tunnel leads right here. Keep following it. I'll guide you if you get lost.**

Aerin struggled out of the water, her limbs aching with the strain of swimming, her legs shaky. A loud splash behind them and Sintaka landed in the pool behind her.

"Are you all right?" Aerin called. "Sintaka?"

Sintaka surfaced, coughing and swearing, her hands pushing her hair from her face. Shard dragged himself out of the water, stumbling to his feet. "We've found it," he gasped, ripping open his jacket as if it was suffocating him. "It's here."

"Shard?" Sim climbed onto the rock. Mindrin took a step to follow and collapsed, his legs giving out. Crawling to the nearest box sitting on the ground, he cracked it open, his jaw dropping at the sight within.

"Pyraglyphs," he picked up one of the tiny pyramids, holding it up to the light to inspect its sides. "Flawless diamond pyraglyphs. Do you have any idea how much these are worth?"

"Aerin! Shard!" Stargazer burst through the entryway, out of breath.

Aerin advanced towards the center of the room, following Shard as he limped onward. Even she could feel it now, a wealth of energy focused within the room. As if their own life-forces were amplified beyond measure. It acted like a narcotic on their souls, dulling senses and clouding minds. She glanced about her. Mindrin continued to stare at the diamonds in the jewel-box, entranced. Sintaka stood as if a statue, in the process of wringing out of her hair, her eyes unfocussed as she stared up at the ceiling. Sim was struggling to his feet, staggering after his soulmate.

Shard wove through the clusters of artifacts and riches, hardly noticing the wealth about him. Aerin hurried up to his side, followed closely by Sim. The rush of water could be heard once more, and they realized the river flowed around the chamber before disappearing underground once more. Before them the wealth fell back, revealing bare ground, covered in places by beautiful woven silk rugs, their longs tassels splayed out across the ground. A plain wooden bier lay in the center of the chamber, devoid of ornamentation. Atop it lay a body; not a mummy, but a decaying skeleton, its long robes worn to tatters hanging off its ribs, its skin and muscles reduced to yellow scraps of desiccated flesh clinging to its bones. Its hands were clasped over its breast, as if in deep sleep.

"Ravanor," Sim breathed. "Don't step on the carpets, Shard!" he called out.

"Why not?" Aerin asked.

"If they're what I think they are, you don't want to know."

Shard continued to advance blindly, his eyes sparkling as he beheld the shard Ravanor continued to clench in his bony fingers. The light of the glow crystals shone off the opal's many facets, lapis and emerald twinkling alongside amethyst. Aerin and Sim halted abruptly, as if repulsed by an invisible field. But Shard moved forward, his hand extended towards the gemstone.

"Is... that it?" Aerin breathed, knowing the answer already. Sim nodded slowly.

Shard halted at the edge of the bier, staring down at Ravanor's corpse. The *yúgure* lay against his breastbone, less than the length of Shard's little finger. A faint light seemed to ripple through the shard, completely independent of the glowlamps. The air surrounding the bier was charged, ionized.

Shard's fingertip brushed against its cool, smooth surface, and he stiffened, as if a shock raced through him. He threw his head back, his eyes closed at the intense sensation. "Shard!" Sim called from the threshold. He pushed against the barrier, but could not breach it. Shard moaned softly, his head shaking furiously against the magic, before his neck snapped rigid once more. His eyes opened for the briefest of moments, and Sim and Aerin both shuddered. His pupils were gone, and it seemed the exact shimmering hue of the *yúgure* shard was echoed in his empty eyes. Then his eyelids slid closed again and he shuddered once more as another wave of current raced through him. With a shaky breath, his legs gave way and he sank to his knees, his hand still closed over the shard. By now the others had joined Sim and Aerin at the threshold, watching in mute horror as Shard continued his communion with the *yúgure*. A low hum began in the ground, pushing them back from the threshold. The energy barrier around the bier grew fiercely, rising and shimmering as it momentarily became visible. The peri staggered back, repulsed further as a mounting bubble of magic assaulted their hidden senses. Just as swiftly it died away, softly and gently without explosion. Aerin swatted at the air before her, confirming that the barrier was gone.

Shard slowly pulled himself to his feet again. He opened his eyes and they were cool violet once more. "It's all right," he insisted, and when he spoke his voice was clearer, lucid once more. Aerin realized her own drugged torpor was gone as well, the veil lifted from the room.

"What happened?" Stargazer demanded frantically.

"I... I was joined with it, I think," Shard explained. "I felt – I can't describe it. It almost overwhelmed me – I had to empty nearly my entire mind to accept it. Shudder to think what Larien might have done in the same situation. But I think we've reached an understanding now." He reached for the shard, carefully pried Ravanor's right hand off the gem. With a crackling sound, the hand released its death-grip, and Shard forced the arm to straighten, laying it down against the bier's surface. He smiled down at the *yúgure*.

"Shard, be careful," Sim called.

Shard lifted the *yúgure,* wincing in anticipation of a new attack. All let out a collective sigh of relief as Shard lifted the stone to his face to stare in wonder at the shimmering surface of the focusing crystal. "Ahh," Shard smiled, taking a step back.

Ravanor sat up with an unearthly howl, desiccated arms lunging out to grasp the intruder. His head snapped alert, empty eye sockets glowing red, lower jaw dropping wide in a hellish expression. Shard screamed, and the others joined him.

Shard leapt back from Ravanor's grasp, tripping over his leg and falling back against a pile of drekks. Ravanor twisted to regard the others, arms outstretched. Then the parched ligaments gave way and the skeleton was no more. The inanimate bones clattered to the ground.

Sim raced to Shard's side. The boy was shivering. "Shard!" he hugged Shard tightly. "Are you all right?"

Shard nodded and Sim helped him straighten. He shook the excess moisture from his jacket, then removed the shimmering silver mail from inside his inner jacket pocket. He shook out the spinner's web, and, placing the *yúgure* against it, carefully wrapped the slick magical cloth around it. "Let's get out of here," he spoke grimly, slipping the wrapped shard back in his jacket pocket, already clasping his jacket closed once more.

"I couldn't agree more!" a voice boomed loudly in the confines of the small room.

They spun around, hands on their weapons, to see a tall figure cloaked in black standing at the foot of the mineral bridge. Straight-backed, strong, he slowly advanced across the bridge as the first of his companions appeared in the doorway – a large troglodyte, his tawny skin laced with battle scars, one of his spiraled ram's horns broken in half.

"Larien," Sim breathed. "He's regenerated."

Larien clapped his hands together in a slow sarcastic rhythm. "Isn't Ravanor one for surprises? Two treasuries in one little mountain. Well, this is a fine chase you've led us on! I must congratulate you on finishing my task for me. But surely you did not think that the rampant flow of energy your breaking of the seal released would go undetected by one such as I."

He stepped onto the chamber floor, and his growing army of troglodytes swiftly moved to flank him. Another man appeared in the doorway, a short, heavyset man, clearly a kobold half-breed.

"And you almost escaped with the shard in your keeping – I congratulate your skill and cunning. But I'm afraid I've searched for too long to be foiled by a pack of children." A scornful smile touched his lips as he regarded Mindrin cowering behind his soulmate. "Who are you, then?" He observed the youth's golden tattoo and the fine scrapes and cuts on his pale hands, so unused to hard work. "A little courtier, perhaps? The Dynast's pet? You are out of your element, I think."

The peri backed up defensively as Larien advanced slowly. The trog guards held back, their large fleshy hands tensing expectantly on their weapons. Stargazer drew the North Star, and Aerin unslung her axe from her back.

"Now, give me the shard," Larien held out a hand that still seemed perhaps a little too slender, too long-boned. "And I promise you a swift death, relatively painless, much like the ones we gave your little friends below."

Aerin lunged forward, her face contorted with anger, and Stargazer swiftly drew her back. Sintaka's hand tensed on the handle of her whip.

"You can't have the *yúgure*," Shard spoke, edged back, sliding around the funeral bier. "Listen to me Larien!" he called desperately as the sorcerer advanced and the peri fell back once more. "You can't handle it. It's too strong for you. Just to touch it is to risk annihilation. I was barely able to empty myself enough – only because I've felt it before, because.... because I somehow knew what to do. Listen to me! Had I touched the *yúgure* only a turn ago, it would have killed me – turned my own restlessness, my own rebelliousness against me."

"If a little child can hold the shard in his hand then so can I," he dismissed. "Cimmerian was a maelstrom of rage and frustration, yet he harnessed the *yúgure* to do his bidding."

"The *yúgure* was intact then, more stable. Please, Larien, listen to me!" he begged, backed up further. "Hear my thoughts – I'm not lying. It's too dangerous. Try to use this crystal and you'll never live long enough to see your new empire. Terrays knows I'm telling the truth!" Shard challenged, and Larien's expression flickered for a moment.

"Lies. Of course you fear the *yúgure* in my keeping – you know I alone have the will to master it."

Shard motioned to his friends and they began to retreat towards his position. Larien gestured once and the guards charged forward, their weapons drawn.

Aerin met the first trog, swinging her axe high. The trog leapt at her, underestimating her size and skill, and she brought the axe down hard against his shoulder, angling the blow to his neck. With a squeal the trog collapsed to the ground, a splash of dark blood coating the axe blade.

The next trog hung back, wary, and Sintaka sprang forward, striking him in the head with a high-flying kick. As the trog went down Sintaka unfurled her long whip, cracking it as the next guard rushed to help his comrade. She slipped her wicked dagger from her hip-sheath and drove it hard into the beast's neck. He threw Sintaka off his shoulders and she bounced back, catching herself on a handspring.

The third trog lumbered through the maze of gold coins to cut off the retreating Mindrin and Stargazer. Brandishing his greatsword high above his head, the trog charged. The North Star met the attack, and Stargazer parried the blade aside. With an agility that belied his size, the trog pressed, and Stargazer fought furiously to keep his ground.

Larien advanced calmly against Shard, who cowered behind the bier. Sim leapt up onto the bier, casting a shockwave against the tyrant. Larien waved his hand and a shield snapped up to deflect the spell. "Star! Sintaka!" Shard shouted. "Come on!"

"There's no escape," Larien vowed. "I will not be denied."

"Sim!" Shard called as the Onmyóji threw himself at Larien, his sword drawn. Larien parried each furious stroke with his bare hand, the shield's aura shimmering about his skin.

Sintaka cast her whip about a trog's neck and leapt up; swinging on the whip, using her body as a counterweight, she yanked the trog to the ground. She aimed a fierce kick at her felled adversary, intending to snap his neck. The trog caught her ankle and cast her aside. Stargazer ducked under the wild thrust of a trog's greatsword and thrust the North Star upward, impaling his foe. Larien parried Sim's thrust and struck him in the chest, the shockwave propelling the Onmyóji backwards. Sim hit the bier hard. Stargazer and Mindrin retreated to his side; Mindrin helped him to his feet as Stargazer assumed a defensive posture against Larien.

"Pointless," Larien sighed. "To think a pack of gangly youths could stand against me." His arm snapped back to arrest the downward stroke of the axe as Aerin charged from behind. He bent slightly, throwing the Kitsune heiress, axe and all, over his shoulder.

Shard huddled behind the bier, shivering. He cried out as strong arms wrapped about his torso, pinning his arms to his chest.

"I've got him, Master!" Morden cried out, lifting Shard to his feet. Shard struggled and fought against the kobold, but they were of a height, and the man's bulk made him a superior opponent to Shard's slender frame. "I've got the boy!"

"Don't you touch him!" Stargazer flew onto the bier. Morden held a hand to Shard's chin, pinching it tightly.

"Ah-ah, move and I'll snap his neck. I only need the shard, not the boy."

The limping trogs were assembling behind Larien. "Seize them," he sighed in a completely disinterested tone. The guards charged.

Shard slapped both his palms down on Morden's fleshy thighs. *"Fire!"* he shouted.

Morden howled as sudden flames sprang from Shard's palms, scorching his pants and burning his skin. He staggered back, releasing the boy, and Shard spun around, aiming a kick for the center of the kobold's chest. Morden gasped, the air knocked from his lungs, as he stumbled over his own feet, tripping over the trailing edge of the carpet.

"The carpet!" Sim shouted in the distance as Aerin danced around a similar rug.

"The carpet?" Morden frowned. Strange, he felt lightheaded, as if the ground were lurching underfoot. He glanced down at the scarlet and gold rug on which he stood and the blood drained from his face. The silk threads rippled and contorted like a living being; already his legs were swallowed up to his calves. He tried to move forward and he fell.

"Larien!" he howled. He could just see the sorcerer sneer with contempt on the other side of the fierce battle. "You!" he called out to Shard. The living carpet had devoured him to the knees, and as he struggled forward the carpet only tightened its grip, dragging him back. "Help me!" he wailed to the terror-struck peri. He could no longer feel below his waist, his ribs. "Please!" His arm was yanked under and he extended the other one out in a desperate plea as the numbness crept up his shoulder to his neck. With a howl of terror Morden Mantalore was sucked into the carpet, the shimmering threads swiftly resuming their former, innocent texture.

"Time to go!" Stargazer shouted, leaping down to help Shard as another trog appeared out of the piles of gold. Aerin kicked her own troglodyte onto a carpet and he growled and grunted in his native tongue as he was swiftly swallowed.

"Where do we go?" Mindrin demanded, scrambling over the bier as a trog's blade nearly struck him.

"In there!" Shard cried, pointing to the river. Before Stargazer could stop him, he leapt into the river, disappearing under the current. Stargazer hesitated a moment, before resheathing the North Star and shoving Mindrin into the river. **Everyone, in the water!** he cried before jumping into the fast-running river as well.

Shard caught a swift breath of air before the water drew him under. He fell through the tunnel, the river sweeping him into darkness. The water threw him against rocks and over rapids. **Stargazer? Sim?** he called. His head broke the surface and he saw the tunnel branch off into two tunnels. The water coursed to the left, and had deposited a silica barrier half-covering the right-hand tunnel. Shard tried to right himself to turn left with the water, but the river threw him against the silica crust, and it crumbled. The water changed course abruptly, sweeping Shard down the right-hand tunnel.

Larien sighed miserably, staring at the fast flowing river. All but one of his trogs were dead or incapacitated. Morden was gone, and the peri had escaped down the water.

"Go... down there," his remaining guard said in heavily accented Common.

"Your abilities of perception astound me," Larien sneered.

"*We*... go down there?" he asked hesitantly, grimacing at the water. It was common knowledge that trogs were terrible swimmers.

"What an original idea." Larien took hold of the troglodyte's shoulder, shoving him into the river.

With a roar the water dissolved the eroded clay that had covered the old tunnel. Shard exploded into the open air of the Denáren Wastes, the water pushing him down the old dried-up channel. He spun in the air, riding the crest of the wave. At length he surfaced in the river. His hand brushed against the wall of the riverbed and he held on tightly, fighting against the fierce current.

He hauled himself onto the rock, and his heart sank. They were outside Wyvern's Rest, out in the valley where they had left the kobolds. On the banks of the newly reborn river lay their allies, the Mantalore kobolds. They lay sprawled on the ground in various positions, blood spread on the ground beneath them. A tall man stood guard over their bodies, a long sword swung over his shoulder. When he caught sight of Shard, he advanced towards the boy.

Varron Lehs.

"Shard?" Stargazer struggled up the rock. He caught his breath at the sight of the fallen kobolds.

"We meet again, it seems," Varron brandished his sword. Stargazer crouched before Shard, the North Star drawn. "Not you again," Varron sneered. "I had hoped it would be your little redbird."

Varron laughed as the astrologer's eyes turned dark with fury, pleased with the effect of his taunt. Stargazer leapt into the air, delivering a kick to Varron's head. Varron lifted his sword to block the next thrust and their blades sang in the night air. Varron bounded high above and Stargazer spiraled into flight, meeting his sword blow for blow. Unseen by the astrologer, three feral peri guards appeared from the concealing shadows, their eyes pinned on the groggy Amaru youths.

Sim staggered to his feet to feel the air shimmer with a surge of powerful magic. He raised his head and saw Larien materialize into being on a distant rock outcropping. *He can phase now,* Sim realized in horror. Even without the *yúgure*, he was a formidable foe.

"You like my handiwork?" Varron nodded to the slain Mantalores as he charged Stargazer again. Stargazer leapt to land on the sword's blade itself before vaulting off the whistling blade to careen through the air. He landed behind Varron, throwing the North Star at him like a spear. Varron parried the attack and Stargazer called the sword back to hand. "Nothing compared to what I'll do to your little Kitsune doll," Varron laughed. Stargazer sprang at Varron's head.

Sim leapt at Larien, a kick to the shoulder felling him. Sim withdrew his katana, plunging it to Larien's chest. Larien's hands came up and caught the blade a mere inch above penetration. Sim shoved down on the sword-hilt, but Larien's bare hands held the sword above him.

"Do it," Larien taunted. "You're better than this, Onmyóji." Sim withdrew the blade and stabbed again. Again Larien caught it. "*Do it, whelp!* End an old man's suffering. Cast a shockwave through the sword. Electrify me with the blue lightning *I taught you!* Rip my soul from my heart and destroy me! Condemn me to eternal unrest and your precious sister to oblivion!"

Sim's face blanched and Larien smiled. "Yesss," he hissed. "Send her to that dark place she was meant to visit four thousand years ago. Cast her from her last foothold of existence and snuff out her soul. Don't you see, you foolish boy? You can't set her free! She's already gone. You can only deliver the final blow."

"You're lying!" Sim swore, shoving harder against Larien's hands. Blood trickled down Larien's fingers, but he would not yield.

"You know I'm not. Did your little whore tell you everything would be all right? You know the world better than that, Onmyóji. I live and she endures.

Kill me and she dies forever."

Don't listen to him, Sim! he heard his own voice call to him.

"Do it," Larien taunted.

Terrays?

Please Sim! Kill him! Let me go!

"Yes, Sim. Let her go. It's what we both want."

Terrays... you're alive...

No, I'm not. Please Sim! Don't keep me like this any longer.

"*DO IT!*" Larien screamed.

SIM! Terrays begged.

"I can't," Sim's hold of the sword eased.

"Fool!" Larien cast the boy off him effortlessly. The shockwave threw Sim hard against a rock. Larien caught Sim around the neck, wrenching him to his feet. "You know, I thought about taking your soul," he revealed. "You were always such a lovelorn little wretch – a few honeyed words and I could have had you in the palm of my hand. Maybe with your enhancing power coursing through my veins I could have cast a spell to match your sister." He lifted Sim off the ground. "But you were always too weak," he sneered. "Terrays was always the superior prize." He threw Sim brutally to the ground. "Let her endure then, as my slave, until I use the *yúgure* shard to cast her from my mind forever!"

Aerin fought one of peri guards, while two others had cornered Sintaka and Shard against a rock. Stargazer battled Varron, neither giving ground. Mindrin had been left, forgotten, at the river's edge; no one wanted to waste time on so obviously unworthy prey. From his vantagepoint he saw Larien advance on Sintaka and Shard as they battled, unaware of the approaching enemy. "Sintaka! Shard! It's Larien, he's coming!" Mindrin shouted across the din of battle.

Sintaka leapt up, spiraling in the air, catching the guard's neck between her ankles. A twist and he was flipped to the ground. Rising gracefully, she drove her boot against his throat, snapping his neck in one kick. "Come on," she held out her hand to Shard, and they raced across the ground.

"Where are we going?" Shard demanded as he hurried to keep pace.

"Anywhere but here," Sintaka snapped back. "You've still got it?"

"Yes," Shard nodded.

A shimmering wind whipped over the ground and a cinnamon scent wafted in the air. Sintaka skidded to a halt as a black shadow phased into existence before her. Larien gestured and Sintaka was raised bodily into the air by a whistling blue wind. Shard ran on, seeking higher ground.

The static energy constricted about Sintaka in brilliant bands, and she cried out in pain. Larien tightened his hand in a fist and Sintaka rose higher from the ground, writhing helplessly in the energy cage. Larien waved his hand aside and Sintaka was thrown against the rocks. The cage broken, Sintaka collapsed, unconscious.

"Shard!" Sim ran up the hillside.

Shard raced across the ground, blindly running among the spires, scrambling over the loose earth. A hand caught his shoulder and he was spun about to stare up into Larien's empty eyes. Shard raised his hand to fight, and Larien's hand tightened on his shoulder. A sharp pain radiated towards his neck and Shard's body went numb. His speech slurred, his eyes hazing over, he collapsed against Larien's shoulder. Larien tore open Shard's jacket, revealing the *yúgure* snug in his pocket. "Time to go, little one," Larien sneered, throwing his cloak over the boy. A shimmer and they both dissolved away into the energy wind. **Varron!** a call rang out in the air.

Stargazer charged Varron, his sword raised high. Varron merely spat on the ground with contempt. As Stargazer reached him Varron phased out of sight. With a feral cry Aerin felled the last of Larien's guards, and a strange silence fell over the plain.

"Shard!" Sim called out as he reached the boy's last position. The last of the elemental smoke had faded away into the stagnant air, and all that remained of Shard was a dark blue clasp torn from his jacket.

25

“Sintaka!” Mindrin knelt at his soulmate’s side. She moaned weakly, and he was relieved to see that the blow to her head was not serious. He sat down, cradling her head in his lap as he waited for her to recover.

“Failed...” she murmured weakly. “Lost him... lost my brother...”

“We’ll get him back,” Mindrin brushed her bangs from her face. “You just get better first.”

“Bys?” Aerin knelt over the fallen kobold. “He’s still alive!” she shouted. “He’s still breathing!” Somehow, Bys lived, hovering in a coma on the edge of death. A long gash streaked across his midsection, yet if he received help swiftly, he might recover.

“Sim!” Stargazer raced up alongside him. “Aerin needs you.”

“He’s gone.” Sim stared emptily at the patch of ground where Shard had stood only minutes before.

“Sim!” Stargazer took his shoulder and shook him roughly. “You’re both healerkin, and you’re a two-spirit. If you lock with Aerin you could heal him.”

“He’s gone,” Sim breathed.

“Aerin needs you. She can’t heal Bys without you. He’ll die in minutes without your help.”

“I can’t, I can’t,” Sim wept, shuddered, stamping his foot on the ground. “He’s gone, Stargazer, he’s gone!”

“Hey!” Stargazer wrenched him about to face him. Sim stared at him in shock. “He might be your soulmate but he’s my brother. Don’t think I’m not terrified for him! But he’s alive, Sim. Bys won’t be much longer – or does his life not matter as much?”

Suddenly he stopped, disgusted with his own impulsive words. “I’m sorry, Sim. I didn’t mean.... We’ll get him back,” he vowed fiercely. “We’ll go to Chalandris Keep and get him and the shard back. Now go help Aerin heal Bys!”

“Yes, yes, of course, I’m sorry,” Sim nodded, regaining his wits. He hurried over the ground to join Aerin as she knelt over the kobold. Swiftly taking up a position across from her, he took her hands in his, placing them over the bloodied wound. "Just concentrate, *Aeoren,*" he instructed. "Think of healing Bys. I'll help you."

Aerin nodded, closing her eyes as she pressed her hands against the kobold's cold flesh. She mumbled a short and irreverent prayer to Red Moon as she began to extend her senses around Bys's broken body.

Shard? Sim called one last time. There was no answer. Reluctantly he closed his soulmate from his mind, concentrating only on the patient, willing his and Aerin's latent healing powers to emerge and radiate outward from their joined hands.

For the longest time she floated in a surreal world, the outside forgotten, aware of nothing but her own powers, which had previously seemed so faint, hardly worth notice. It seemed like hours – days – later when Aerin recovered her senses. She was bolted back into awareness with a shock that caused her body to jerk in a protesting tremor. Her eyes snapped open and she stared deep into Sim's in complete wonder. He smiled sadly, the only joy he would allow himself. He lifted her hands from Bys's body and Aerin stared down to see the bloody gash had healed to a glossy pink scar. Bys convulsed in an explosive shudder, and he drew in a ragged breath before collapsing to the ground once more, lost in a deep coma. But it was a healing sleep, one from which he would emerge once his body had replenished its strength.

Sim rose, staggered away from the kobold, turning his face from Aerin's. Dimly she remembered – Shard; Shard was gone, taken by Larien to Chalandris Keep.

"Aerin," Stargazer dropped to the ground next to her. "Is he all right? Are you all right?"

She nodded faintly. She was exhausted, her soul depleted in the effort it had taken to affect a healing. Then she remembered the last duty she had to perform. She eased Stargazer's hand from her shoulder as she bent over Bys's body. She closed her eyes, willing her tired mind to life once more. She reached out, her spirit flying over the mountain range separating them, calling out to her brother.

Arjin...

The reply was swift. **Is it time? Do you have it?**

Yes, she lied. **But...**

We're coming! he snapped impulsively, and she knew he had already deciphered the truth. She could never bluff him.

No! she cut him off. **You're playing the part Shard wrote for you.**

Aerin, what's wrong? You sound so weak.

A lot has happened, she opened her eyes to look down at Bys's pale face. His features gave him the look of a peri child. She could almost forget that he was twice Arjin's age.

Then it's time? he asked once more.

Aerin's eyes darkened as she surveyed the corpses littering the ground:

Larien's fallen allies and all the kobolds she had been unable to save. **Do it!** she spat, with the venom of a long warrior heritage. Countless deaths at Larien's camp would do nothing for the ghosts of the fallen Mantalores, but it would at least ease her heart somewhat.

The connection to Arjin faded as swiftly as it had been forged, and Aerin found herself back on the hard rock of the wastelands once more. She looked down at Bys, then at her axe, lying forgotten on the rock. Stargazer was pacing above her. Sim had sunk down on some adjacent rocks, his head hung in sorrow.

"All right!" Aerin called out, snapping them from their grief. "Let's get Bys back to Thandállen. His healers will know what to do for him. We need to get our dragons back."

"Why?" Sim asked in a defeatist monotone, his face empty of all emotion.

"Because we can't very well walk to Chalandris Keep, can we?" she demanded hotly, her Kitsune temper flaring to life. She rose, hefting her axe. "You don't have the monopoly on vengeance any longer, Onmyóji. We're going to get Shard back, and that damned crystal too. And we're going to make Larien sorry he ever crossed paths with us."

Sim shook his head, his eyes filled with terror. "He's Larien. I couldn't even defeat him when he was half-dead. Now he has Shard, *and* the *yúgure*. What can we do against that?"

"What else can we do?" Stargazer asked. "Give up now and let Larien blow us all to the Overworld while he's trying to figure out the shard?"

Sim turned away. "I will stop Larien," he decided softly. He glanced back at them. "Larien's right. You are only children. You shouldn't waste your lives fighting him."

"Hey," Sintaka objected as she limped towards them, Mindrin supporting her. "Don't you call us children. You might be from before the Dark Age, but I've spent more years up and around than you have. And I've seen my share of things outside the City Mount, trust me."

"Do you have any idea what is means to go up against a fully regenerated Larien?" Sim demanded hotly. "Why should you all die in a battle you can't win? I'm the only one left standing who can fight him. I..." he averted his eyes. "I could have killed him – only minutes ago – I didn't. Now he has the *yúgure* and Shard in his grasp. I have to stop him, with my life, if need be."

"And leave Shard alone not a full day after soulbinding?" Stargazer demanded. When Sim turned away again the astrologer spun him back roughly. "Do you think Shard wants you to kill yourself out of guilt and defeat? You said you wanted to come back to Amaru with us when this is over, right? Being an Amaru means sticking together through everything. It means faith in your companions. Maybe we aren't Arashi Masters or Onmyóji sorcerers, but Shard is our family, and so are you, and we aren't going to sit back and let you kill yourself on some suicide attack."

"Then it will mean your deaths as well," Sim argued.

Stargazer shook his head vehemently. "Only if we believe that going in.

And then Larien's already won."

"You're too young to be so committed," Sim sighed mournfully.

"Who ever said idealism was a curse?" Stargazer argued.

"We're wasting time," Aerin argued. "Bys needs a warm bed and a kobold healer. And every minute we're wasting Larien's got *both* shards and is doing Powers-know-what to them."

"Let's go!" Sintaka insisted.

"He'll be expecting us," Sim protested, but the defeat was gradually draining from his face. His eyes widened, beginning to glitter with a mad sort of hope.

"That just makes things more interesting," Aerin grinned the reckless Kitsune smirk as she swung the axe over her shoulder.

Shard slowly drifted back into his body. He became increasingly aware of the aches and pains in all his limbs, specifically a tight constricting itch around each wrist. He opened his eyes and found himself in a dark stone chamber. He sat on the floor, his back propped against the cold rock wall. His jacket was gone, his white shirt ripped and tattered. His arms hung above his head, manacled, thick chains fused into the wall.

"Awake at last, I see," a familiar voice taunted.

Shard lifted his head further to see Larien watching him from the shadows. Slowly he tried to rise, pushing himself by the heel of his boot. "What do you need me for?" Shard demanded as he druggedly rose to his feet, lowering his sore arms. "You have the shard. I'm just a kit – worthless to you."

"When we first met, I might have believed such self-deprecation. But you've touched the shard, you've been made one with its aura." Larien advanced slowly, his dark cloak fluttering about his legs as he moved. "Strange... that a mind so undisciplined, so young, could align itself so flawlessly with the *yúgure* itself." A hand shot out, clenching about Shard's chin, forcing him to look up into Larien's eyes. "I know what you are," he hissed low. He stared deep into Shard's eyes, initiating a tremulous connection. "You're a key. A being fused of such Old Magic as to align itself perfectly to the power of the *yúgure* shard. I wonder how such a creature came to be born. But you're right – you are worthless to me now that you've served your purpose."

"You're afraid of me," Shard realized.

Larien drew back in horror. Shard continued to stare up at him, holding the frail mindlock. "I could destroy you."

"What is this?" Larien growled, but the fear fluttered in his voice.

"Fight him, Terrays!" Shard called.

Larien backhanded him across the face and Shard fell back to the cold stone floor. The ruby ring scraped a bloody cut on his cheek. "You're finished, Larien!" Shard shouted. "Even now the best Arashi knights of Amaru are leading an attack on Wyvern's Rest. You'll lose everything you gained there."

"Fool!" Larien snapped. "Do you think I care for the material wealth of Ravanor? Let the Amaru claim it. It will all be mine soon enough."

"All your men will die. All your slaves will be liberated."

"Slaves! Hah! I shall have the world as my slave. You blind little child," he mocked, retrieving the *yúgure* shard, still wrapped in spinner's web, from one of his cloak's many little folds and pockets. "This, *this* is all that matters. I wanted you to see this," he smiled. "My awakening. It's only fitting you should be the one to witness it."

Shard leapt to his feet, lunging for the gem. But the chains held him back.

Larien unwrapped the shard, until it lay in his hand, only the thin spinner's web separating it from Larien's bare palm. "Larien, don't!" Shard cried as the sorcerer snatched the *yúgure* up in his left hand, his bony fingers clenched around its sharp edges in a death-grip.

Larien instantly roared in intense pain, his body jerking and twitched as currents of powerful energy raced up his nerves. He fell to his knees, then dropped on one hand, his limbs convulsing in erratic spasms. Shard tried to reach him, to tear the *yúgure* from him, but the chains would allow him no ground. "Larien!" Shard shouted over the loud banshee wail that reverberated inside both their minds. Larien was coughing, his eyes bulging wide, a slick overcoat of black iridescence racing across his eyes, clouding his pupils. Electricity sizzled in the air, crackling and popping all around them. Shard struggled and swore, but could not reach him. A wind raced through the dungeon, shimmering like a slick rainbow, striking Shard and driving him back to the wall. The wail grew louder, fiercer.

Shard looked up to see Larien slowly rising on one knee with a roar of fury. The multi-coloured glow continued to whip about him, yet now it fed him rather than weakened him. He forced himself to his feet, his face contorted in an unearthly howl. As another powerful tremor raked his body his cloak fell to the floor, revealing his new, stronger body under his black robes. His arms thickened to fill out the loose sleeves; his fingers grew stronger clasped about the crystal. A new colour swept his face, giving him a new vitality. He drew a strong breath and his ribcage expanded with the energy of a young man.

The wind settled about him and Shard stared up at the newly reborn sorcerer. The last vestiges of his weakened state had left him and he stood tall, an embodiment of destructive malevolent energy. His face was that of a man in his first few centuries, handsome perhaps, but in a hard, unyielding way. His eyes flickered once more with the *yúgure* hue, then resumed their cold dark colour.

"Now do you see?" Larien asked softly. He laughed, a steadily rising sound. "And you, Terrays?" he roared. "Do you see? Hah, but how can you now? Can you still hear me, bitch? Strange, I cannot hear you!"

Shard cowered against the wall.

"Yes, fear me, you little abomination," Larien hissed. He wrenched Shard to his feet by his hair. "See me!" he commanded. "See the power you thought would consume me! But I shall consume *it* – I shall consume the entire world to feed this hunger!"

"Then you don't need me anymore," Shard whispered.

"You're wrong, little one." He threw Shard back to the ground. "You still have a part to play. You're my ransom pawn," he laughed. "My live bait with which to catch an Onmyóji. Were the threat of mass destruction not enough – and I don't think it is – the threat to his precious soulmate will surely be enough to entice him back here!"

"You have no guards," Shard shot back. "You emptied Chalandris to feed Wyvern's Rest. There's no one here but you and Varron. You think that's enough to stop an Onmyóji sorcerer?"

Larien recoiled at Shard's powers of telepathy. "Read my mind as you can, you know I need no guards. What's a child Onmyóji against the keeper of the *yúgure* itself? Not even the bitch of Elória can stand against me!" he reached down for the ring, ready to rip it from his finger.

It didn't budge.

Shard laughed out loud, unable to contain himself.

Larien kicked him. "It's only a matter of time, you little brat, before she *has* to bow down!"

Shard huddled against the cold wall, warily examining the sorcerer.

"Only a matter of time," Larien muttered, turning away, rubbing the ring's surface.

"T'Jara, T'Jara," a troglodyte screamed as he raced into roughly hewn chamber carved into the mountainside. He froze in the doorway, staring at the large bed in the corner. A wide-eyed kobold girl slowly sat up from the furs, clutching the bearskin to her breasts. Moments later Darhis herself rose, her short hair tousled about her face.

"*What* is that racket out there?" she demanded icily, her gray eyes glaring with murderous intent.

"We are under attack," he growled in his native tongue, gnashing his fangs. "Mantalore kobolds. Hundreds, thousands!"

"Get out!" Darhis snapped. She sprang from the bed, hastily dressing. "Hardly unexpected," she grumbled, lacing up her tunic. She should have known the dogs would strike as soon as Larien left. She turned her eyes on the kobold wench shivering in bed. "You wish to go back to your people?" she asked, not unkindly. "Go," she gestured to the door with the spear. When the girl blinked apprehensively, Darhis allowed herself the faintest smile. "Go," she offered encouragingly.

Ciilet sat taller, shaking her head. "I stay with my T'Jara," she protested.

Darhis blinked, uncomprehending at first. She gave her captive a tender smile, and touched her chin lightly. "Stay here then. Pack up a few things. If we win, we'll break open a bottle of that hog-man's sapphire wine. If not, we'll head for the forests."

Darhis continued to dress, barely taking the time to lace her boots as she bolted down the corridor leading into the night air. She caught her breath as she broke onto the open ground. Already fires were raging on the lowlands beneath the ridge, where the slave quarter was kept. Braziers had been knocked over and torches set to the tents. Countless kobolds swarmed like locusts, battling the guards below, some already beginning to climb up the shambling hillside towards the high camp.

"You!" Darhis bellowed, catching a skinny peri youth as he raced by. "Why was no alarm sounded earlier? Why was I not woken?"

"I don't know, I don't know," he wailed.

Shorts-staining child, she scoffed. "Idiots! Why are there fires burning out there? How could you fools let them get so close?"

"They... tunnels! All over. Too many to count! They came out... everywhere! Can't pinpoint – too many!"

"Shut up," she backhanded him across the mouth, her rough gauntlet drawing blood. She stared across the mountainside, her eyes raking the hills for some sign of a pattern. In the chaotic light of the burning fires she could hardly make out her men from the Mantalores. The freed slaves surely ran wild, adding to the numbers of aggressors. How in the Huntress's name had so many kobolds appeared? The hounds had been sniffing the rocks every day, searching for the telltale musk of a kobold or the acrid smell of blackdust. **Larien!** she called desperately. **Larien! Where are you?**

There was no answer. Darhis stared in disbelief a long moment before she realized it was not because she was locked from his mind. It was because he was not longer at Wyvern's Rest. He was no longer in the Boundary Hills.

"*Chiga!*" she cursed. "*Igatin tantal!*" she shouted to the skies. "Hold the lines!" she cried out in the air, her piercing voice echoing in the sprawling valley below. "They're only kobolds, you fools! Do you want to lose your treasure to mere vermin!"

The battle raged on. There seemed no clear victory. The trogs and the peri along with the kobold slavemasters rallied at all ramps and stairways, repelling the invaders, but the Mantalores rose like a tide.

Darhis bent down and laced up her boots. The Treasury was not her trophy. No Alteri cared for material wealth. The thrill of life was currency enough. She had two options, then. To retreat and steal into some faraway cave with her remaining hounds and that charming little kobold girl, or to stand and fight what could well become a lost cause. Truly, there was little reason to fight. These were not her people. She could easily pocket enough gold to sustain her until she found useful employment.

She saw two blots against the dusky sky, swooping and diving. The clear serpentine outlines of dragons. Kobolds did not fly dragons. A feral growl rose in her throat as she remembered her humiliation on the wastelands. What would she bet that one of those riders had a mane of long auburn hair?

With a wild warcry, she caught up her spear and charged headlong into the fray.

26

Arjin tal Kitsune surveyed the battlefield beneath him as he drove Witch into another steep dive. The dragon lunged at the fleeing troglodytes, her claws raking along their backs, her jaws snapping at a fleeing miner. She took to the skies once more, allowing Arjin an aerial view of the battle under his direction. Corpses littered the dusty lowlands, some Mantalore kobolds, some Denáren troglodytes. The sky was haloed in angry red and oranges as the fires burned out of control, devouring worn slave tents and makeshifts outposts. Only moments before a spark had touched a powerkeg of blackdust, rocking Wyvern's Rest in a vicious explosion. Like tiny ants, the silhouettes of kobolds climbed the mountain itself, the high camp their objective. Screams and warcries echoed in a myriad of languages and dialects. The battle was going well, he decided smugly. He looked over his shoulder to see Ceih sending Westwind plunging on a large tent, the jade dragon's claws tearing the canvas roof from its wooden frame. It was like Brox Lideyrn all over again.

He howled in the air as Witch soared high above the carnage in a wide arc. It was the wild battle cry of the old Kitsune knights, the dreaded sound of the Dark Age wars. He caught sight a large gathering of trogs trying in vain to mount a catapult against the still advancing kobolds and the soaring dragons. Drunk on a heady rush of battlelust, he urged Witch to dive again.

"No one screws with a Kitsune," Arjin vowed as Witch plunged, her limbs outstretched. The trogs scattered and Witch landed atop the catapult, her strong jaws snapping the beams in one sound bite, her claws raking deep furrows in the frame.

Arjin laughed as Witch bucked, preparing to take to the skies again.

Something tackled him. He never held the saddle-loop and was knocked bodily off his dragon. He tumbled to the ground, rolling over to rise swiftly. A warrior-woman knelt before him, her spear outstretched threateningly. Witch, already fifteen feet above the ground, circled warily, waiting for her master to leap back astride her. It was an easy jump for an Arashi warrior. But Arjin held his ground.

"Fly away, Amaru?" Darhis taunted.

Arjin waved Witch to assume a higher circling position. **Wait up there,** he mindspoke, adding audibly. "This won't take long."

"I am Darhis," she announced with a ritual nod of the head. "Born of the L'al Tribe of the Great Forests; Mistress of the Hunt; Stalker in the Darkness; T'Jara of the Alteri."

Arjin quirked an eyebrow. He gave her the same flamboyant bow he gave the conservative Matriarchs. "Arjin, Red Knight of Kitsune; Satrap of Kistu'ker; Overlord of the Castle Highlands; formerly Heir-to-the-Kitsune-house-until-my-little-kit-sister-was-born; Death-to-all-proper-Matriarchs-and-incidentally-their-husbands; So-well-bred-I'm-*inbred!*" He gave her a second sweeping bow, leaning on his swordstick. "And possessor of – by unanimous declaration – the best legs in *all* Amaru."

"You mock me," Darhis sneered.

"Wouldn't dream of it," Arjin's demeanor turned deadly serious as he unsheathed his long blade with a flourish of the wrist. He slowly circled her, his blade pointed at her throat. "Shall we continue your lesson?"

"Hah!" Darhis charged him, knocking his blade away with one blow, pivoting to face him as she brought the butt of the spear's shaft against his head. Arjin appeared to stagger with the blow, only to weave to the side. He caught up his swordstick, spinning about to inflict a thin cut across her collarbone.

Darhis swung the shaft around, but Arjin was no longer there. She barely had time to draw it back to guard herself before he reappeared again, delivering a sharp kick to the small of her back. Darhis staggered forward and Arjin appeared at her side, bringing her head down on his knee.

Darhis thrust the spear-shaft forward like a quarterstaff, and Arjin parried with his swordstick. "Want me all to yourself?" he taunted as they danced back and forth in their own circle, the rest of the battle passing them by.

"No one humiliates me and lives to boast of it, least of all an arrogant Arashi knight."

"Oh," Arjin ducked a wild stroke, then parried the next attack. He lunged forward and Darhis swiftly spun into a defensive stance as he pushed her back. Whip-thin blade met hard wood over and over, their strokes too numerous to keep track of. "I'm sorry, you seem to be mistaken." He let her drive him towards an overturned ox-cart and backflipped on top of it as her spearpoint narrowly missed pinning him to its side. "I'm not an Arashi knight." He leapt from the top of the cart and his boot struck her in the face before she could free her spear to guard herself. He threw his swordstick high in the air as he handspringed out of spear's reach. Flipping high above her, he caught the swordstick in mid-air before landing back to the ground. "I'm an Arashi *Master*."

Darhis hurled the spear at him in frustration. While he ducked to avoid it, laughing at her temper, she charged him, delivering a flying kick to his jawbone, before locking her leg about his neck and forcing him to the ground. She stood, driving her foot towards his neck. Arjin caught her boot and threw her to the ground as well.

The battle fires waned and raged anew as successive waves of Mantalores and mercenaries attacked and withdrew. Occasionally a fight would intrude into their circle and be swiftly dispatched by either combatant with a swift knock-out blow. Darhis drove him back towards the burning tents; Arjin forced her towards the slope of the mountain. At times they fought brutally, drawing cuts and inflicting deep bruises with murderous rage; at time their fight turned almost playful as they traded blows in challenging postures.

"You... fight well, for an arrogant city dog," Darhis gasped, wiping the blood from her nose and lip as she lunged with the large mace she had appropriated from a fallen troglodyte.

"Aren't too bad... yourself," he whirled her around to propel her into a metal torch. Darhis caught herself against the metal, instantly pivoting back to meet his next blow. "For an Alteri sword-for-hire," he spat, catching her hand as she tried to club his shoulder. Darhis swung her leg out and tripped him. Arjin collapsed to the ground, narrowly rolling away as the mace came down on the parched earth a fraction from his ribs.

Darhis chased him through the wreckage of a collapsed lean-to. Arjin fell under an abandoned tower-shield propped against some timbers as the blade struck metal, then kicked the shield. Darhis leapt back to avoid being pinned by it.

Mere moments seemed to stretch forever as each pounded the other with their best moves. Witch glided overhead, circling occasionally, completely bewildered. Darhis unearthed the full extent of her Alteri heritage, while Arjin countered with the wealth of Arashi training. Each time they found themselves at a standstill. Darhis leapt up, treading air to deliver a flying kick to the head. Arjin blocked her leg and threw her to the ground. Darhis inflicted a long cut to Arjin's thigh. Arjin struck her hard across the shoulder-blades with his swordstick. Each time they were never able to score more than a glancing blow.

"I'm going to... win," Arjin gasped raggedly, wobbling on his legs.

"I... know," Darhis breathed, shifting uncertainly. She cast a swift glance behind her. Arjin had backed her up towards the nearly sheer cliffside below the high camp. "A... good hunter... knows when the chase has ended," she declared. She took a step forward, her expression dizzied. "The hunt is yours..." she gave a little bow, lowering her weapon.

Arjin slowly lowered his own swordstick, nodding his assent.

Before he could blink she was in front of him, moving with lightning speed. She elbowed him hard in the gut while at the same time flicking out her thigh-dagger. A short sting to Arjin's scalp and she was gone, handspringing backwards to vault high into the air. She landed on a ledge twenty feet above, a long auburn tail hanging from her clenched fist. Arjin stared up at her in horrified wonder, his hand slowly rising to his scalp where she had snipped the lock of hair.

She tossed the dagger down to him in a conciliatory gesture, then ran up the ledge and scrambled to higher ground. Reaching a ledge where the battle had already passed, she saw several abandoned knapsacks leaning against the rock wall; gold glittered at the seams, clearly the result of workers secretly hoarding their own cuts from the Treasury. Perhaps she wasn't entirely without need for monetary recompense, she decided, throwing a bag on her shoulder.

She looked down at the battle. The troglodytes had rallied their forces and were pushing the kobolds back. Perhaps they would triumph, perhaps not. Either way she had no reason to risk her life now that the hunt had ended. She thought of the three remaining hellhounds, conditioned to obey her will, the delightful kobold girl patiently awaiting her return, and the cool shade of her forest home.

A true T'Jara knew when to cut her losses. Every hunter knew when to go home.

Sim squinted in the misty air, trying to remember the landmarks of the Denáren Wastes. Smoke flew high over the ground, Luck and Whisker close behind. Ghost, fit for flight once more after his long sojourn underground, flew beneath him, glad to be out in open air once more. Silverscales, still weak, flew riderless at the back of the party while Stargazer shared a dragon with a different riding partner every few hours. It was nearly sunrise now.

They had flown without rest since midnight, when they had left the still comatose Bys with the Thandállen kobolds and taken to the skies. The glow from the battle at Wyvern's Rest lit up the night skies, and a heavy cloud of smoke doubtlessly still rose far behind them, out of sight. They could not afford to think of the battle. All that mattered was Shard.

"I would kill Larien myself if I could," Aerin had vowed at sunrise several hours before.

"So young to think of killing," Sim had murmured, and Aerin had sat tall in her saddle.

"I'm a Kitsune. We are warriors born. We aren't murderers, but we never flinch from eliminating the enemies of Amaru."

"I almost wish you could, myself," Sim had sighed. "I don't know if I will be able to, when the time comes."

"Why?" Stargazer had asked. And Sim had told them about Terrays.

Now they soared over open flatlands, the land below dotted with geysers and hotsprings. Black rock lay over the red in recent lava flows. Stargazer sat behind Sim in the saddle, letting Aerin ride Luck alone. They would not reach Chalandris before dusk. Aerin had slept in her saddle for a few hours before sunup, and Mindrin dozed now, slumped over his arms against Whisker's back. It was all they could do, thankful that they could go at least three days without sleep if needed before weariness took its toll.

"I'm sorry about your sister," Stargazer whispered over the wind, for the third time that morning.

"I should have accepted it by now," Sim murmured. "Four thousand years, I should be able to let go."

"No, no!" Stargazer exclaimed. "Don't accept it. Don't ever accept death! It's only one step away from welcoming it. And *oblivion!* If there's any way we can still save her soul from it–"

"No," Sim shook his head. "I can't hesitate again. I lost my chance before and we lost Shard."

"You can't blame yourself for that! To kill your sister's soul with the same blow..." he paused considering it. "Maybe – maybe Larien is lying. Maybe killing him will set her soul free to go to the Overworld. That's it, Sim – he's probably lying, manipulating your weakness and trying to throw you off guard."

"No... no it makes sense. She was meant to be destroyed when he killed her – yet she survived, inside him. If he dies, so does her soul. She told me to do it. She told me to kill her."

"But there has to be some way to–"

No, Stargazer, Sintaka interrupted. Stargazer turned to look back at his sister, surprisingly somber as she sat astride Ghost. **Let it go, Yósha,** she mindspoke. **You can't save everyone. Were it me in Terrays's place, I would seek oblivion in an instant to stop a monster like Larien. I know you would too.**

Stargazer said nothing. "You've a good heart, Stargazer," Sim patted the hand about his waist. "I can see why Shard worships you like he does." He could sense the astrologer's blush behind him. "No... Sintaka's right. There's no other way."

"Maybe there is no such thing as true oblivion – how can anything that existed be completely destroyed," Stargazer offered in consolation. "I'm sure no matter what happens some part of her will go on."

"Thank you," Sim nodded. "Ohh, I don't know how I can do it. Maybe Larien will destroy himself with the *yúgure* or cast Terrays's soul out to the outer world before we get there. A coward's way out."

"You're no coward, you're a brother horrified at the thought of having to hurt your sister," Stargazer told him. "But if she has to die – if there's no way to save her soul, I know she'd rather be released at your hands than Larien's."

"I know," Sim agreed. "Thank you, Yósha. You're a good brother." He lifted his eyes back to the horizon. "That's the Fist of Namanthis – I remember it from my days in Elória. We can make to Chalandris before sunset if the dragons can last that long."

We'll need a plan before then, Sintaka cautioned.

Aerin straightened, stretching her arms high above her head before she reached down for her waterskin and took a long draught. **I've got a notion... needs a little fleshing out.**

"Tell us," Stargazer shouted over the wind, twisting in the saddle to look back at her.

Shard shivered against the wall. They had moved him up from the dungeon early in the morning, disturbing his fitful sleep. Now he slumped chained to the wall of what had once been the main antechamber to Larien's throne room. Above him, over the crumbling staircase, he could hear Larien's agonized groans. He was still assimilating the *yúgure's* power, and the energies released with each attempt crackled in the air.

He should be hungry, he realized. He hadn't eaten in nearly a full day. In the parched air of the Denáren Wastes, he should be dying of thirst. But he felt nothing, no pain, no aches, only a deep weariness. Someone had placed a bowl of water in front of him, but it was salty, mineral-laced, and he left it alone. His shirt hung in tatters from his shoulders, but he felt neither heat nor cold anymore.

He raised his head as Varron paced before him, chewing on a loaf of dry bread. Varron's stare glittered with malicious glee. Shard narrowed his eyes. "Do you think you're impressing me?"

Varron lashed out his foot, overturning the water bowl. Shard hardly flinched as the water splashed in his face. "You're right to be scared," Shard told him. "You're nothing to Larien. Maybe you were once, but you've failed too many times to be anything more than a liability. Once he's finished assimilating the *yúgure* you'll be nothing but dead weight."

Varron shivered at how easily the boy read him. Swiftly he masked his unease in a veil of bravado. "Am I supposed to be intimidated by you?" He caught Shard by the back of his collar, lifting him from the ground then let him fall once more. "A little queer gelding, too weak to put up a fight!"

"Enjoy it," Shard nodded to the loaf of bread in his hand, "while you can. Larien will turn your entire body inside-out before the quarter-turn is up – just to prove he can."

Varron kicked him in the head. Shard collapsed to the ground. The man sneered again, turned on his heel and marched away.

Shard winced as he heard Larien cry out once more. It was at such moments that his heightened senses could hear *her*, barely at the edge of awareness, her soul crying out in pain as she battled tirelessly to keep herself sane. The *yúgure* was killing her.

Fight him, Terrays, Shard implored. **Just a little longer. Sim's coming. Hold on, for just a little longer. Then you can rest.**

It was the early afternoon at Wyvern's Rest. Most of the fires had burned themselves out, yet a few continued to kindle and flare up in isolated patches on the scorched earth. Once again the tide of battle turned in favour of the exhausted Mantalores. Ceih scrambled up the rocks towards the few plateaus and ledges where the troglodytes and peri had concentrated their defenses.

"Come on!" he shouted as he reached stable ground, brandishing his falchion high above his head. "*Cshekka mendko grast illay grenla su!*" he urged in Kobold. The Mantalores surged up over the crest in a frenzied wave. The first of the trogs raced forward to confront them and swiftly fell under the brunt of the attack. "Come on!" Ceih leapt over the bodies of the fallen, chasing Larien's retreating men. "We'll have the Treasury before nightfall!"

he proclaimed on a rush of adrenaline, swinging the five-foot blade of his sword wildly at an charging foe.

"It looks so quiet," Mindrin breathed. "I can't believe *that's* Chalandris Keep."

The sun was slowly setting in the western sky, colouring the Denáren Wastes a deep blood red under the clouds. A light wind brushed over the peri as they stood on the tall rock outcropping. Chalandris Keep stood on a similar shelf to the north, seeming little more than a small set of dilapidated ruins, a quarter-mile away.

Aerin lowered the spyglass, handing it back to Stargazer. "It looks pretty empty from here. It would make sense if he sent all his men to guard Wyvern's Rest. I'd wager he's only got himself and Varron in there."

"Chalandris could hold three thousand men in the main keep, and four more in the caverns beneath it," Sim told them. "But I think you're right, Aerin." He sat down on the ledge, letting his legs dangle off the edge. It was nearly two hundred feet to the floor beneath his feet, and the shelf on which Chalandris rested was at least twice as high, the rock wall sheer and slick. He closed his eyes, reeling from the vertigo.

"Sim?" Aerin asked.

"Bad memories," he breathed. He lifted his head.

"Do you think he knows we're here?" Sintaka asked. She glanced at the dragons, now lying low against the rocks, completely exhausted.

"Maybe," Sim shook his head. "Maybe not. He only has eyes for the *yúgure*. I can barely sense him... or Shard. The..." his voice almost broke, but he recovered swiftly. "The energy unleashed by the *yúgure* is like a shield, blinding both sides. I... broke into Chalandris from the north-east, four hundred years ago. He'd expect me to try again. We could go up from the west, but he'd expect that too. We could double back..."

"'You can bluff a warrior once and an imbecile twice,'" Stargazer mused. "I say we go up from the south, right up the sheer rock face."

"That's suicide," Sintaka frowned. "Unless you have a hell of a plan."

A faint smile touched his face. "I've got a notion."

"Dragons," Varron declared, looking up at the sky. Five dragons: one jade, two silver, a golden and a blue, soaring high overhead. Even with his spyglass, he could barely see any riders. "They're very high up, Master. Scouting, maybe."

It doesn't matter.

"Can you sense where they are, what they're planning?"

No... it does not matter, I said. Bring the boy to me.

"You... you can't sense..." Varron frowned. "What do you mean, Master?"

Fool! Do you think I feel anything but this... how many times have I told you only the shard matters? Bring me the boy. Wherever the Onmyóji filth is hiding, he'll come soon enough.

Varron scowled as he strode over to the semi-conscious boy. Shard raised his head as Varron roughly unshackled his right wrist, threading the chain out of the metal pin. "Didn't he used to tell you everything?" Shard asked, raising an eyebrow. "He has everything he ever wanted now... what does he need you for?"

"Up!" Varron yanked him to his feet, dragging him up the stairs.

Sim... Shard called, but as always, he felt nothing but the dizzying mask of the *yúgure*'s energy haloing Chalandris Keep.

Mindrin gasped, sweat streaming down his face in a thin rivulets as he continued to concentrate. Behind him Sim knelt with his hand over the nape of the gardener's neck, willing him added energy to fulfill his task. At length Mindrin collapsed into Sim's arms, looking up at his handiwork. What had begun as three tiny scalervine seeds had sprouted into a complex network of vines and leaves, anchored in the tiny fissures in the rock. The ladder stretched four hundred feet to the top of the sheer rock face, strong enough to bear their weight.

"Up you go," Sim helped Mindrin to his feet. "You're a good grower, Min."

"Well... Dynast has a lot of gardens to tend," he gasped, wiping the sweat from his brow.

"Varron's still watching the dragons, I'll bet." Aerin secrued her axe over her shoulder. She started up the ladder as soon as Sim and Sintaka confirmed its strength. Stargazer followed; Mindrin was then helped to start up the ladder while Sim and Sintaka brought up the rear. "They should circle around a few times then head east, as if we're going to go in the same way Sim did during the rebellion. If Chaiya's with us they won't know what hit 'em." Aerin reached the top of the wall and scrambled over the crest, disappearing out of sight. Stargazer began to climb faster, eager to catch up and have her within sight once more.

"Don't hurry," Sim warned as loudly as he dared.

Stargazer straightened on the ground, staggering away from the ledge and the dizzying vertigo. He raised his eyes and looked up at Chalandris Keep, a series of crumbling rust-red fortresses. It seemed completely deserted, inhabited only by ghosts. Aerin was wringing her hands, trying to keep from drawing her axe prematurely. Behind him he heard Mindrin pull himself over the ledge.

"Let's go, huh?" Aerin asked nervously.

Stargazer nodded. The long flight to Chalandris, interminable a short time ago, now seemed far too swift a span. What could children do against the ghosts of Chalandris?

All too soon Sim and Sintaka appeared as well, dusting the thin film of earth from their clothes. They exchanged mute nods and turned, hiking up the slope to the first of the structures. A boundary wall ran around the edge of the keep. It was mostly for show, once kept in pristine order, now a crumbling ten-foot structure. Large blocks of volcanic stone lay littered at a break in the wall, and they leapt up the stones like a staircase. The top of the wall formed a parapet from which guards could look down the slopes of the rock shelf. But no one was left to stand watch, and they swiftly reached the platform above the wall.

Aerin staggered the minute she hit the stone, her hands rising to her head to block out the sudden wail that assaulted her hidden senses. Stargazer followed, and suffered the same shock the moment he crossed the threshold of the decaying parapet.

"What is it?" Aerin asked, shaking her head as her senses slowly grew adjusted to the new environment.

"It's the *yúgure,*" Stargazer explained as he helped Mindrin to his feet. The empath was dizzied from the sudden overload to his weakened mind, wobbling uncertainly on his legs. "Larien must be trying to assimilate it," Sim breathed. "It's putting out enormous energy. Little wonder there was a shield up around the keep."

"And we're inside it," Stargazer realized. "We've got to hurry. Mindrin, are you well enough to try it?" The gardener nodded, and Sim walked up to him, placing his hands on Mindrin's temples.

"I'm a light touch, don't worry," he offered to Mindrin's worried expression. The gardener stiffened as a wave of energy ran through his body. As swiftly as it began, the mindlock ended, and Sim stepped back. Mindrin was unsteady, his expression dazed, but he was still standing, his eyes relatively clear.

"Go," Sim commanded the others. "Now that he can sense us, Varron will be after you."

"I'll keep it up as long as I can," Mindrin said, tapping his forehead lightly. "With any luck, Larien will think you're still with us."

"Four against one," Aerin said confidently. "We'll give Varron the best decoy he's ever seen."

The party of four raced along the parapet. Sim turned and eyed the highest spire of the decrepit keep. Larien's ego was too great to allow him to reside anywhere but the throne room. Taking a great breath, he closed his mind as much as his fear would allow, raising a shield around his emotions. If the plan worked, Larien would sense the empath's residual thought patterns and believe Sim was running towards the main gates with the others. He only hoped Larien was as drunk with the *yúgure's* power as that. Mindrin was a brave youth, but his empathic skills were very limited compared to what Larien could unleash if he suspected a deception.

Trying to muster the Onmyóji calm that had kept him alive so long, Sim began to climb the crumbling rocks.

"Your friends are coming for you," Larien gloated. He paced back and forth in the throne room, his long black cape brushing the ground with each step. In keeping with his new youthful physique, he had adopted the dress of the old warlord of Chalandris, a form-fitting black suit decked with silver jewelry and decorative body armour. Only a few quarter-turns ago Larien had been a decrepit old man bent over with age. Now he looked no older than his mid-twenties, a tall, frighteningly powerful man, his strength evident in his strong bones and his penetrating stare. Shard wondered with a wry laugh whether the *yúgure* would reduce him to a babbling one-year-old within a few more days. Such ill-timed humour was the only way to keep the fear from overwhelming him.

"Ah... the front gate. How predictable," Larien mused. "They are right to assume few guards stand in their way." **Varron! Intercept. Do what you will with the Amaru brats, but save the Onmyóji for me.** He glanced down at Shard, shackled to the wall, his right hand free and rubbing his sore arm. A long day of fretting with the manacles had left him with chafing red rings about both wrists.

"Think Varron's up to handling five?" Shard asked. "He hasn't exactly been up to performance standards lately."

"You are right in that, pup. And you're right – I will dispose of him soon enough. Ahh... Varron was a great convenience to me at times... but now I fear I'm outgrowing his dull-witted company."

"And that symbiote in his head makes sure he'll never survive your displeasure."

"The best slaves are those who know their place. You could learn from Varron – ah well."

"Do you think we'll let you keep it?" Shard nodded to the shimmering crystal flake in Larien's gloved hand.

"Don't you understand, you little nuisance?" he spun back on Shard. "You're already dead. You lost this battle before it ever began!"

"Then why are you still afraid?"

"I fear nothing!" Larien picked him off the floor, shaking him roughly. "Don't think you have the power to stop me, you little wretch. Whatever you have within you is nothing – nothing compared to this!" He shoved the *yúgure's* flat surface against Shard's forehead and the boy hissed at the sudden pain. "You see?" he advanced, pressing the stone harder against his flesh. "You are nothing to me now, you little fool!"

Shard slapped both palms against Larien's face, glaring up at him determinedly. Larien howled at the immediate invasion of his mind. He pressed the *yúgure* harder against Shard, but the boy only seemed to draw further energy from it, his nails digging thin furrows in Larien's skin as he intensified the mindlock.

Fight him, Terrays, he called out to the fading presence. **I know you can do it!**

Larien found sudden strength and tore himself away from Shard's grasp. He staggered backwards, hissing as he rubbed the ten tiny spots of blood from his face. Shard collapsed on the floor.

Furious, Larien lifted a large termite-eaten timber that littered the floor and hurled it in Shard's direction. The boy saw the wood fly towards him and raised his hands to mount a feeble shield.

A whistle cut through the air and out of nowhere a sword appeared, impaling the wood only a foot away from Shard and sending it clattering away. The katana remained fixed in the wood for a moment, then vibrated and twitched before flying back across the room to its owner.

Shard and Larien both turned to see a slender figure at the window.

"Sim!" Shard cried out in profound relief.

Larien snarled, holding up the diamond-shaped prism threateningly.

Sim charged.

27

Sim flew across the chamber with the speed of an Arashi Knight. Before Larien could draw power for an attack Sim leapt at him, delivering a sharp kick to his chest. Gasping, Larien went over, the *yúgure* flying from his hands and clattering across the room to the far side of the chamber. Sim raised his katana high then thrust it down at Larien's chest, but the man's reflexes were too swift, and Larien erected a shield over his body. Sim's blade hit the shield and the recoil knocked him backwards. He fell against the throne itself, before tumbling to the ground.

"Cunning strategy," Larien rose. "Did you mindlock with another, let someone carry your thought imprint while you slipped up around the back? But it will buy you nothing." He unleashed a power stream of blue lightning, and Sim's hands snapped up to defend himself.

"Sim!" Shard raced to reach him, but the chain about his left wrist snapped him back several feet short.

Sim lunged for the *yúgure*, catching it up in one hand. He instantly screamed as if burned, and the crystal dropped back to the floor. "You see," Larien chuckled. "It serves me now."

"Sim!" Shard fought with the unyielding chain. "Cut me loose!"

"Touch him and he dies," Larien shouted. He narrowed his eyes at the Onmyóji. "We finish this now, boy... if you want to keep your pet alive."

Sim held out his hand and the sword leapt into his palm. "No, Sim!" Shard called. "He's too powerful!"

But Sim was already summoning a whirlwind of energy about him, and Larien held his hands together, gathering a ball of fierce magic. Shard yanked on the chain helplessly, trying to reach the combating sorcerers.

"Can you feel it?" Mindrin asked as they proceeded down another abandoned corridor within the keep. Cobwebs gathered in corners and occasionally a rat would dart by, squeaking its disapproval of the outsiders. A smell of decay and rot assaulted them around each corner.

"What?" Aerin asked.

"Sim and Larien are fighting."

"We should go help," Stargazer fretted.

"We'd only get ourselves into trouble, and Sim too," Sintaka warned. "That's his fight. We have our own. Keep your eyes open."

"What would Mother say if she knew a Kitsune heiress was posing as bait?" Aerin wondered aloud.

They came to a fork in the road. The right-hand arched doorway lead down another set of corridors, while the left expanded into what must have been an old banqueting hall. A rusted pot still sat over a long extinct fire pit, and splinters and slices of wood littered the floor. Above them the ceiling was vaulted, shadowed by decaying rafters.

"We're being watched," Aerin breathed.

"Which way?" Stargazer asked.

"More open ground to the left, more escape routes to the right," Sintaka said. "I say the right."

"You're probably right," Stargazer waved her ahead, and Sintaka and her soulmate stepped over the threshold, proceeding down the right-hand corridor.

The moment Mindrin stepped through the archway they heard the rattle of a chain rasping against stone. Aerin leapt back as a wrought iron portcullis fell down from the arch, closing the right-hand passageway. "Sintaka!" Aerin peered through the bars of the portcullis. Sintaka and Mindrin were trapped on the other side. "Hang on!" Aerin called, pulling at the gate to make it rise. But it would not budge, blocked at the top or else thoroughly imbedded in the floor.

Something swung down from the rafters, kicking her in the chest. Aerin cried out, falling back against Stargazer as Varron Lehs dropped down from the shadows.

"I'll deal with them later." With a hiss, his sword was unsheathed, pointed at the two young warriors. "You first."

Stargazer and Aerin backed up into the old banqueting hall, Varron slowly advancing towards them.

"Aerin! Stargazer!" Mindrin called through the immovable gate.

"*Chiga,*" Sintaka cursed. "Come on, we have to find another way around."

"We could get turned around, or ambushed," Mindrin protested as he ran after her.

"Better than do nothing while my brother and matesister get carved up. This way!"

"Sintaka! Now you'll get lost!"

Varron brought the sword down against the stone as Stargazer leapt away, somersaulting in midair. Varron shifted his focus to Aerin as she moved in to defend Stargazer. His moves were trained to perfection and anger only increased his focus. He parried each blow of the great axe, before lashing out a leg and knocking Aerin aside. Instantly Stargazer was back, and the motions of combat were repeated once more. Varron seemed to grow more powerful and more tightly focused with each glancing blow struck by either youth, and exhaustion only seemed to inspire him further. Aerin was thrown to the ground, skidding up against the remnants of an old wooden table. Stargazer leapt up in attack and Varron flew to meet him. They soared together to the ceiling, before chasing each other down the wall back to the ground.

He fights like an Arashi, but with none of the training, Aerin thought as she scrambled back to her feet. She flew through the air, her axe already descending in a powerful downward swing. Varron kicked Stargazer aside and swung his sword about to meet the blow. The sword vibrated in a high-pitched hum, but held against the strike. Aerin instantly stepped back, swinging the axe over her head for a blow to the neck. Varron met it, and every consecutive move. Stargazer was back, and soon Varron met each of their blows. For all they tried to strike in unison, Varron was able to evade their every attack. They tried to corner him against the wall, but he overpowered them and maneuvered the combat back into the open hall.

Energy of blistering intensity whipped about the throne room, forcing Shard against the wall for safety. Sim and Larien were nearly lost in the cocoon of magic enveloping the center of the room. Occasionally a burst of newly released energy would collapse the envelop and Shard could see them, if only for an instant. The *yúgure* lay forgotten in the corner; Larien had already assimilated enough of its power for the moment.

Sim was gaining ground, pushing Larien back with steadily mounting attacks. The elder sorcerer resorted to further defensive actions as shockwaves and blue lightning assaulted him at once. He howled, throwing his arms up over his chest to deflect the energy. A stray bolt struck the *yúgure* and the crystal hummed as it spun about on the floor.

"The shard!" Shard shouted over the din of combat.

Sim moved to block Larien's path, putting himself as a shield between the sorcerer and the shard. Enraged, Larien found his strength anew, letting mounting waves of energy flow from his hands. Sim's hands flew in a flurry of motions as he sought to block the magical attack.

Shard huddled back against the wall, turning his back to the fighting as the wind screamed. *Insanity!* They were dueling not *five feet* from the unstable crystal shard! Any stray burst magnified at the right angle could destroy all of Chalandris Keep. Yet if Sim couldn't keep Larien from getting his hands on the shard again, the energy unleashed could make the Winter of a Thousand Years seem little more than a bad season.

"Sim! Over here! Give me the shard!" he called loudly.

"Move and he dies!" Larien warned.

Sim struck Larien with a shockwave, then spun about and caught the shard. The pain seared his senses, but he held it long enough to throw it across the room. The shard skid over the dusted floor, coming to a halt a few feet from the boy. With a roar of pure rage, Larien cast a wide arc of blue lightning at Shard as the boy lunged for the *yúgure*.

The lightning reached him as his hand closed over the *yúgure*. A shield rose to deflect the energy and the lightning scattered in all directions.

Sintaka reached another fork in the corridor, and skidded to a halt as her mind raced to calculate her location. She was now completely lost in the labyrinth of the keep's architecture.

"Shard!" Mindrin gasped. "Sintaka, this way," he took hold of her arm, tugging her to the right. "Shard and Sim need our help!"

"What about Aerin and Stargazer?" Sintaka asked, unwilling to sacrifice one brother for another.

"We'll never find them in this maze. But I can feel Shard. He's just above us. Come on, Sintaka! If Larien wins that battle it won't matter what happens to Stargazer and Aerin."

Aerin tripped Varron, her leg overturning him to the ground. She brought the claw-foot of the axe down on his leg hard and he howled, thrashing on the ground as the metal sunk deep into his flesh. Aerin twisted it viciously and kicked at his head. But a sudden rush of energy flowed through his limbs and he caught her foot, twisting her away. Aerin snapped her head and Varron recoiled from a painsend amplified by the crystal pendant. Stargazer was upon him in a flash, but already Varron was ready. His reflexes were only growing faster, his strength increasing with each wound he received. Madness blurred his bloodshot eyes.

Stargazer fell hard against the ground, dazed and wounded, a thin stream of blood tricking past his eye from a glancing blow by Varron's sword. Varron leapt off the ground, backflipping onto the balcony above as Aerin flew after him. She struck his face hard with the butt of the axe and he roared at the pain. His body shivered once and he looked back at her, his eyes burning.

It's the symbiote. The more powerful Larien gets, the more powerful Varron gets. Apprehensive, Aerin began to back away. He sensed an advantage and pressed it, swinging his sword for her hair. Aerin ducked away, shifting her axe from side to side as she backed up along the balcony. A small set of steps led up to the next storey, and Aerin hesitantly considered a retreat. Varron rushed her and she swung the axe over her head. He caught her axe handle and forced her back against the wall, slamming her against the brick. With a gasp as the air left her Aerin released her axe, falling to the ground. Her hand touched her crystal as she prepared another painsend; before she could mount a defense, Varron kicked her in the head.

"Aerin!" Stargazer shouted, feeling her pain.

Varron picked her up and threw her from the balcony. Stargazer dropped the North Star and raced towards her. He barely caught her before she struck the ground, and they both collapsed to the cobblestones.

"Aerin!" Stargazer looked into her unconscious face for any sign of life. A trickle of blood stained her hairline. He slapped her cheek lightly hoping for some reflex, but she lay unresponsive in his arms.

Varron leapt to the ground. A sharp kick to Stargazer's shoulder and he fell back. Varron caught Aerin's wrist and lifted her from the ground only to let her drop to the cobblestones once more. "Pity. I had expected more out of her than that." He raised his sword, pointing it at Stargazer. The youth scrambled back, his hand extending for the North Star. The sword skittered across the ground to fly into his palm. Varron gave Aerin's leg a little tap of his boot. "Limp as waterweed. No good to me now. Ah well, perhaps when she wakes up to see your corpse littering the ground and your scalp hanging from my belt, I will get a little more fight out of her. Pity, you can't live to see what I'll do to your precious little redbird." He turned Aerin onto her back, his hand sliding appreciatively down her leg.

Stargazer snapped, the last of his hesitation overwhelmed by sudden anger. A shockwave shimmered in the air around him, then flew out at Varron, throwing him back against the far wall. Varron barely had a chance to raise his head before Stargazer was upon him, the North Star whistling downward. Varron parried, pushing the Amaru youth back. Varron kicked out and Stargazer blocked the blow with his own leg. They danced about each other, trading frenzied blows, the air surrounding them ionized with furious magic.

Shard slowly rose to his feet. He glanced down curiously at the manacle surrounding his wrist. "Fire," he whispered under his breath. A little burst of sparks dissolved the lock and the shackle fell to the ground.

Larien flew across the room, hands outstretched. Shard raised his arms before him and a shield repulsed Larien with all the force of a shockwave. Yet Larien held his ground, and the energy whipped around the room, holding Sim at bay.

"What's going on?" Mindrin whispered at the base of the steps.

"Was going to ask you that," Sintaka murmured.

The shockwave dissipated and Sim sprang forward. Sintaka watched spellbound as Larien spun around just in time to see the Onmyóji attack. The sorcerer was slammed backwards, past Shard, against the wall beneath the open windows of the throne room.

Larien looked down at the sword burrowed in his chest, pinning him against the wall. Sim kept his hands tightly clenched on the swordhilt, his eyes locked with Larien's, his expression one of amazement.

"Sim! Get back!" Shard shouted as the energy wind began to whip about the two sorcerers. Sim stared in horror as no blood welled from the wound. He looked back at Larien to see the man's eyes completely clouded with the colours of the *yúgure*.

Larien threw his hands out and Sim was propelled backwards. Larien wrenched the sword from his body, tossing it to the ground. He took a step forward, his eyes reverting to their original colour, his lips curling back in a snarl. He shrugged his shoulder, letting the cloak fall. Something sharp struck him below the collarbone and he flinched, more from surprise than pain.

"You," he hissed, seeing Sintaka standing at the head of the stairs, another shuriken in her hand, her arm tensed to let it fly. He yanked the metal barb from his shoulder, tossing it aside. Sintaka threw the second shuriken, and Larien snatched it out of the air a full arm's length from his body.

"Get down!" Shard cried. A rippling shockwave sprang out from Larien's body, striking everyone at once. Sintaka fainted instantly. Sim and Shard were forced to the ground, their shield incapable of deflecting the energy.

Mindrin started forward, and Larien waved his hand, as if to swat away a fly. The shockwave cast Mindrin across the room like a rag doll.

"Don't you see?" Larien caught Shard's hand, yanking him to his knees. "I have already assimilated enough energy to counteract any feeble resistance your mind might offer me, no matter the amplification of the *yúgure*. Now, if you'll *please!*" he wrenched the shard from his hand.

Shard shot up, clasping his own hand over the *yúgure,* interlacing his fingers with Larien's. The *yúgure* amplified the mindlock, and within moments their minds were linked.

"Shard..." Sim crawled across the ground to reach him, but the energy net continued to hold him against the floor. Sintaka moaned weakly, her hands against her forehead as the shield pinned her against the top step. Mindrin lay in a heap against the far wall, unconscious.

Varron howled in agony, staggered backwards. Stargazer knew the battle was going in their favor; Larien was in pain, and Varron was receiving the recoil along the symbiote's nerves. Stargazer advanced on the warrior, driving him back against the wall. But then the symbiote tightened about Varron's brain, delivering a fresh burst of energy to his limbs. He threw Stargazer off him, and the astrologer handspringed backwards.

"You think–" Varron roared, and his voice was distorted, a faltering bass ripple coursing through it. His sword had dropped to the floor, and he ignored it, raising his hands. A golden glow began to pulse about his clenched fists.

Forgotten, Aerin's body jerked in a faint convulsion.

Varron unleashed the blastshield, his body shuddering at the energy the symbiote channeled through it. The blinding gold wind obscuring Stargazer from view an instant before the brick facing of the wall exploded in a shower of dust. Varron stepped forward, hands clenched anew, as he peered through the clearing dust. Where was he?

"Hey!" Varron looked up for the source of the cry a moment before Stargazer's boot struck his face. They both crumpled to the ground; Stargazer lost his hold on the North Star and again the sword slid out of reach.

Varron leapt to his feet, black ink flickering before his eyes as the symbiote forced further magic into his cells. He raised his fist high, only to take a hard blow to the jawbone. As he reeled, Stargazer aimed a kick to his chest, then another blow to his face. Unarmed, he pummeled Varron with every technique of Arashi hand-to-hand combat. The man staggered and faltered, unable to recover long enough to fight back.

He ducked a wild punch to the face and caught Stargazer's belt, seizing his leg in the other hand and hurling him across the room. His hand shot out and a long arc of lightning coursed towards the fallen youth. Stargazer pivoted about, and a crackling blue aura rose around him, deflecting the electricity surge.

Stargazer swung his arm about as if cracking a whip, and the energy arced out in a chain, lashing Varron across the chest as he stared incredulously. He collided against the far wall, his shirt bearing burn marks, the scent of scorched fibers lingering in the air.

Stargazer leapt at him, energy already wrapping about his hand in preparation for a second assault. Varron's head snapped up and a shockwave struck Stargazer, neutralizing the attack. Varron lunged at Stargazer, tackling him as he staggered from the shockwave. His fingers clenched in Stargazer's jacket, transmitting a painful shock of energy. Stargazer fell to the ground, kicking Varron, flipping him over his head. Instantly the astrologer was on his feet, the lightning whip rematerializing in his hand. Varron squared his shoulders for another charge, but the lightning cut a swath across his chest, stunning him.

His eyes now almost uniformly black with the energy overload, Varron called the North Star to his hand. Stargazer advanced, blue lightning haloing him. Varron roared, springing for the astrologer. Metal met magic, and the sword deflected the lightning, sending it searing across Varron's thigh. Wild on the silken rush from the symbiote's erratic commands, Varron hardly noticed. He checked Stargazer's shoulder, then rammed the handle of the North Star against the youth's jaw. His ankle hooked around Stargazer's leg, and he forced the astrologer to the ground. As Stargazer tried to rise, Varron kicked him in the chest. He swung the sword high over his head, his face contorted with a leer of bloodlust.

A feral scream echoed in the confines of the hall. Varron looked up in horror; he saw the boot a moment before it struck his face. Stargazer glanced up, dazed, to see Aerin and Varron collapse together.

She pummeled him viciously, her golden gauntlet cracking against his face, drawing blood. Her knee dug into his thigh-wound until he howled and trashed in agony. Varron surged forward and she leapt off his chest, bounding backwards. He lunged at her and she ran up his body, stepping off his shoulder to spring high in the air. With a banshee's cry she held out her hand and her axe flew from the balcony, whistling in the air as it spun towards her.

She caught it in midair. Varron pivoted about to see her dropping towards him, her tattered skirt fluttering about her legs. He screamed, a strangled, anguished sound. The axe swung about in her hands, slicing through the air. Aerin alighted on the ground, swinging her axe to her side. Varron's head tumbled to the ground a moment later. With a dull thud, his body followed.

Aerin slowly turned, her eyes wide as she stared down at Varron's severed head. His expression of horror and realization was frozen on his features. Her breast heaving with ragged breaths, she turned to Stargazer, slowly propping himself up on his elbows.

"You couldn't let *me* handle him?" Stargazer demanded, nearly manic with dizzied relief.

"Sorry, Yósh," she breathed, still gasping for breath. "Kind of... got carried away."

Larien howled in the white dreamfog, the recoil of Varron's death burning in his every nerve. The *yúgure* seemed to augment the pain as it did the link with Shard. He seemed to dissolve within the dreamscape, his consciousness on the verge of blacking out.

Mustering all his strength, he reconstituted his dream image, standing on the misty plane anew. Opalescent lightning bolts raced through the sky, and the clouded shifted on a whirling wind.

Shard stood before him, his clothes spotless and pristine, a long black coat hanging from his shoulders. "How can you be here?" Larien hissed furiously.

"I don't know," Shard replied honestly. He looked up at the lightning coursing through the clouds with genuine awe. Larien sprang forward and Shard spun around, staring intently at the sorcerer.

Lightning crackled about the elder magic-wielder, eating away at his flesh. Roaring, Larien snapped his head, sending energy racing in turn at Shard. The boy held his ground, his hands clenched at his sides, his violet eyes wide. He winced, expecting a shock, yet the energy flew over him.

"You think you can beat me?" Larien roared. "You little child! You think you know anything about fighting, about war, about life and death? You might have the power to wield the shard, but only I have the soul!"

"You're wrong," Shard stated. His voice was calm, though he shivered in fear and uncertainty.

"To hell with you!" Larien raged, throwing his arms out as he cast a blastshield. Shard waved his hands and the golden lightning crackling about him diverted the energy.

"What do *you* know about life and death?" Shard demanded over the storm, his voice trembling with anger. "What do you know about *life?* Your life is nothing but greed! You killed Terrays to feed your hunger. You spent your entire reign killing everything you could! You're worse than Cimmerian, worse than the *yúgure*. You're a cancer!"

"*You think you know me? You think you know what it is to fear death?*"

"I do now," Shard nodded, shuddering. "I suppose I have you to thank for that."

"Abomination!" Larien screamed. He hurled a volley of blue lightning at Shard. It was deflected, arcing away to the right long before it reached Shard's shield. "*You!*" Larien roared as he saw Sim step out of the mist. The Onmyóji was clad once more in his flowing kimono, his sword in his hand.

"Sim," Shard nearly swooned with relief, his mind reeling. The two-spirit continued to stare at Larien, dark intent shimmering in his eyes. Slowly, Shard turned back to the cornered sorcerer as well. Larien's wall of shielding rage was beginning to crumble now, and open fear was spreading across his features.

"What?" Sintaka murmured weakly, rising to her knees. The shield had dissipated somewhat, yet she could rise no further, held in place by invisible tendrils about her arms and legs. Shard and Larien stood frozen in the center of a spiraling energy wind, their hands locked in combat. The *yúgure* pulsed like a blue-tinted lantern rose at the heart of the storm. Sim knelt on his hands and his knees at the edge of the wind. At first she thought he was immobilized as well, but then she saw him creep ever closer to the battling sorcerers.

"Sintaka!" Mindrin called from where he sat, pinned against the wall. The wind rose, a tangible whirlwind of glowing filaments. Sintaka was forced back onto her stomach, flattened against the ground.

"*Noo!*" Larien wailed as the combined energy of the two sorcerers rose around him, burning his flesh in a hailstorm of searing bursts. He struggled to erect a shield about him, but the magical assault was unwavering. "How can you be here?" he demanded of Sim. "Weak-willed *child!*"

"You've always underestimated me, Larien," the Onmyóji declared. The wind whipped his robes about him, the trailing edges of the kimono dissolving into the mist. The assault rose in pitch and Larien bucked and twisted within the magic field.

"I will not be beaten!" he thrust his arms out, repulsing the magic. "I have touched the *yúgure*. I am one with it!"

Sim and Shard held their hands out, casting a second wave. Larien staggered under the blow, his shield beginning to fail. "What are you doing?" he raged, fear in his voice. "Get back!" he roared, unleashing a blastshield. "You cannot stand against me! Kill me and the *yúgure* will shatter! Will you destroy the world?"

"Would we leave you alive to destroy it yourself?" Sim countered as the stream of energy flowing from his hands intensified exponentially.

"You cannot do this to me!" he raged. "How can you do this to me?"

"That's what you've never understood about us, Larien," a cool voice drifted from the clouds. Larien stared in horror as Terrays stepped out of the fog at his left side, her tattered kimono fluttering about her slender limbs. "You've never understood the conviction that's kept me alive within you all these years. You've never understood the will that drives me, that drives the others. We *care,* Larien. It gives us the strength to fight, forever, if we need to. But then how could you understand? You care for nothing but your own hunger."

Larien swung his arms over his head, harnessing the crackling energy like a whip, hurling it around to cast it squarely at Terrays. She didn't even flinch as the current flooded over her harmlessly.

"The *yúgure* isn't a wellspring of silken to be tapped," Terrays sneered.

Larien roared, unleashing another burst of energy towards her. Raw magic washed over Terrays, burning her garments, yet she stood tall, unaffected.

"You know in the end the ones who care will overthrow you. You see nothing but your own failings, your own mortality. We see so much more. That's our power, Larien. Our vision, our faith."

"Your feelings?" he spat. "Your *love?* Is that what you'll say next, harridan?"

Terrays's face turned cold, ruthless. "I am *so* tired of hearing your voice."

Larien drained his own defense reserves, casting all the power in his cells at the woman, unleashing a shockwave of brutal intensity. Sim and Shard both staggered back at the burning aura the charge carried about it.

Terrays stiffened. She tensed and convulsed, doubling over and collapsing to the insubstantial ground. A slight wolf-like smile touched Larien's face as he watched her thrash in agony.

"Terrays!" Sim shouted over the roar.

Terrays knelt on the ground. Her back appeared to ripple, as if something under the skin was thrusting upward. Two large growths pulsed under her skin, ripping the white fabric of her dress, pushing up against her skin. Rivulets of golden blood began to flow down her back as the skin itself tore under the pressure, the ichor evaporating the instant it touched her flesh. Terrays bucked once, throwing her head back, and a pair of large white griffin's wings burst from her back, haloed in steam.

Terrays rose to her feet, the last tatters of her dress falling away. She closed her eyes, flexing her wings once, and the feathers wrapped about her slender body before rising above to shade her head. "You see?" Terrays turned to Larien. "You thought the *yúgure* would feed you. But every pulse, every touch of magic flowed to me as well."

Larien released the last of his reserves, summoning all the anger and fury he could, unleashing it in a powerful blastshield. Terrays moved forward steadily, her hands raised to block the energy. Sim advanced, lightning crackling about his blade. Shard walked steadily towards him, his eyes set on Larien. "Damn you!" Larien shouted, pure lightning lancing out from every inch of his body. The energy wind howled around the four sorcerers, tearing away the dreamscape, darkening the clouds to an angry steel-gray.

They leapt together, striking as one. The magic current flew from Sim's sword, cutting through Larien's shield. Terrays flew at him on her griffin wings, blue lightning cast from her hands. Almost blinding energy radiated outward from Shard's frame. The wind rose faster in a deadly whirlwind, drawing them together into a blinding sphere of energy.

Larien's magic surged out in deadly attacks that had felled countless peri in the past, magnified beyond all reason by the *yúgure*'s magic. Shard, Sim and Terrays countered with their own inborn magic and determination. The glowing sphere expanded, then condensed, collapsing in on itself. Larien howled in fury and cheated ambition, four thousand years of frustration released in one last final attack.

You cannot! Larien screamed, his last denial.

FIRE! Shard commanded.

The entire dreamworld caught on flame, circling in towards Larien in towering bonfires. Larien howled as his flesh caught flame.

Terrays leapt through the flames, her wings alight as she drove her sword into his side.

Sim thrust his flame-wrapped sword under Larien's ribcage, sinking it up to the hilt.

Shard lunged at Larien, punching his hand through his chest.

With a gasp, Shard was jolted back to the material world. He knelt in a half-rising posture on the ground, locked in combat with Larien. His left hand was still clasped over Larien's, closed over the shard, but his right arm was thrust into Larien's body, punched through armour, flesh and bone. Blood welled from the gaping wound, already evaporating in the evening air.

"Destroy... me..." Larien hissed, his eyes clouding over. His head dropped back, burning blood trickling from the corner of his mouth.

Shard stared awestruck as the hum began, resonating outwards from the *yúgure*. Larien dropped back as if on his knees, yet his lower legs were already beginning to dissolve. Shard gripped his fingers inward to find he held something invisible in his hand. Slowly he opened his hand and felt a soft wind whisper against his fingers, floating away.

"Shard?" Sintaka asked, slowly rising to her knees once more.

Shard looked down at his left hand. The *yúgure* was pulsing rapidly now as the hum increasing in pitch. He looked back at Larien's face, growing paler and faded with each moment, as if the colour was burning off his skin.

"Shard!" Sim shouted, struggling to his feet. The hum had become a high-pitched wail, and the energy wind was already rising from the ground again. Shard felt hands grasp his shoulder, wrenching him from the death-embrace. He was hurled aside, shoved to the ground. A moment later a deafening silence assaulted their hidden senses, and a roar of energy wind raked across their bodies, flattening the peri to the ground.

"Shard, *ka'eri*," Sim whispered fiercely, hugging Shard to him as the currents tore through the room. Shard buried his face against Sim's neck, shuddering as the last of the wind begin to die down. Larien destroyed? No matter how well deserved, a peri's destruction was seldom without repercussions. And what of Terrays, cast into oblivion with Larien's death?

"Look!" Sintaka called. Slowly Sim and Shard rose and turned back to the remains of Larien and the *yúgure* shard.

A faint blue glow continued to pulse over the ground in an opalescent sphere. Nothing remained of Larien save for his discarded cloak. Tears dotted Sim's cheeks as he contemplated his sister's fate. But then the energy began to dissipate, and a form could be seen stretched out on the ground. The glow lifted, revealing a young woman.

She lay on the stone floor, naked, motionless. Her short dark hair was ruffled, disordered; wispy bangs and fluffy tufts before her ears framed a young face. Her left arm lay arced high over her head, while her right hand was clenched against her shoulder in a fist. A ruby ring hugged her finger.

Sim stared incredulously, frozen at the sight. A tremor shook his shoulders, but he could not move. The young woman shivered on the cold floor, stirring slightly. She lifted her head, slowly opening her eyes. Sim was shivering now, clenching his fists tight at his sides to keep from bolting. Still he could not move, could not hope, until she focused her turquoise eyes, her expression pleading.

"Sim?" Terrays whispered, her voice breaking.

Sim raced to her side. He caught up Larien's cape, draping it over her back. Slowly, gently, he helped her to sit up, arranging the black cloak about her to keep the evening chill off her skin. Terrays inhaled in a gasp, so unused to the act of breathing. Her eyes slid closed and she collapsed against her brother in complete exhaustion.

"Who..." Sintaka inched closer.

"Terrays!" Sim framed her face, tilting her head back to stare into her eyes. He gazed in disbelief as she gave him a weak smile. He laughed and wept at once, hugging her to him fiercely, kissing her forehead, crying against her hair. He held her out again, still not convinced, only to weep with joy and clasp her close once more. "Terrays, Terrays," he sobbed with relief.

Shard smiled softly, unmoving, unwilling to intrude upon the reunion of brother and sister.

Terrays pulled away from Sim, wincing in pain as she raised her right hand, still clenched in a tight fist. Faint streams of dark blood trickled down her wrist. Sim laughed breathlessly at the sight, hugging her against him once again. "You're alive," he whispered fiercely. "You're not dead, not gone."

Terrays smiled to herself, shifting against her brother. Shard slowly advanced, kneeling down next to the twins. Terrays looked up, meeting his eyes. "Thank you," she breathed, her voice a weak whisper.

Shard reached out, gently helped her unfold her fingers. Terrays winced again as her hand slowly opened. The *yúgure* lay in her palm; she had clenched it so tightly, its sharp edge had cut into her skin. But the crystal flake was not what is once was. Where before it shone with all the hidden radiance and countless facets of a Hesperin opal, now it was a shiny opaque black, like an obsidian spearpoint.

"It's inert," Terrays whispered. "We don't have to worry anymore." Closing her fist over the *yúgure* shard once more, she fell back against Sim, who drew her close. Shard looked over at his soulmate and they shared a weary smile. Shard turned to see Sintaka limp over to help Mindrin rise to his feet. The timid empath seemed half-dead with fright.

"Is it over?" Mindrin gasped. "Are we safe now?"

Yósha, Shard called out and grinned in pure joy when he heard the swift response, nodding to Mindrin. He turned back to Terrays, dozing lightly in her brother's arms. "But I wouldn't call it over," he finished softly.

28

Arjin let loose a loud howl that echoed off the surroundings. Ceih laughed at his soulmate's excess – this time well earned. He looked down from the topmost rock ledge on which they stood, sweeping his gaze over the burnt and blood-stained battlefield below. It had taken them an entire day of bloody fighting, but at last they held Wyvern's Rest. Corpses littered the field below, the wagons circulating to collect the bodies, Mantalore and enemies, to be burned in the evening air. A chain of prisoners wove over the ground: the Mantalores leading their captives underground. Most of the trogs had committed suicide before Wyvern's Rest fell; their captives were mostly peri and kobold. From what he knew of their honour code Ceih knew those kobold prisoners would *wish* they had killed themselves once the Mantalores finished with them.

"It's ours!" Arjin shouted, casting his arms out as the cry bounced off the mountain crests. "Treasury of *fucking* Ravanor!" He spun around, staring down at Ceih with an intense expression. "Treasury of Ravanor. Wealth of the Dark Age. On Amaru land. On the Dynast's allotted *bride-price!* Do you know what this means?" he demanded, skipping down the mountainside.

"That our kingdom suddenly became the richest land in the entire Aetherworld by a factor of *hundreds?*" Ceih asked politely.

"That we have to ask for raises," Arjin decided, jumping to land on Ceih's outcropping. "Ohhh, I *love* you!" he declared, spinning Ceih around and kissing him passionately. He left Ceih reeling as he skipped down the mountain, practically turning cartwheels.

"Yeah, I know," Ceih murmured wryly. He kicked up his falchion, swinging it over his shoulder. He strode down the mountain pathway, contentedly smiling at a job well done.

They sat on the rocks outside Chalandris Keep, looking out over the Denáren Wastes, the land dusky in the evening light. The Bluestar had just set, and the hidden moons warmed the wastelands from above the shading clouds. Sintaka had kindled a little fire with the sticks she could salvage. Mindrin snuggled against Whisker's leathery hide, dozing softly. Terrays leaned against a rock, dressed in a makeshift robe stitched from Larien's cloak. Sintaka had lent her a pair of soft moccasins, but they were a little too big for her, and she kicked them about her feet, enjoying the strange sensations of touch after four millennia of limbo. She ran her hand over her fingers, exploring the many bizarre nuances of a body she had forgotten. Shard lay in Sim's lap, resting his head on his shoulder. The Onmyóji kept his arms locked about him, as if terrified to lose him.

"So the *yúgure* is neutralized?" Aerin asked.

Terrays glanced down at her lap, where the shard rested alongside the ruby ring. "All the energy it took...." Terrays picked up the shard, running her fingertips over its slick surface. The shard had left a faint diamond-shaped imprint in her right hand; time would tell whether it was permanent. "It drained the *yúgure* of almost all its power. What's left is trapped, encased under layers of inert crystal twenty times more powerful than spinner's web."

"What will we do with it?" Aerin wondered.

"I'd like to keep it, I think," Terrays mused, turning it over in her hand. She glanced up. "You know, if this shard survived the other four are probably out there somewhere."

Mindrin's eyes widened. "I wish you hadn't said that," he whispered.

"Well... if these shards only pop up once every four thousand years..." Aerin mused. "I'm not going to lose sleep over it. So, what do we do now?" she asked, warming her hands over the campfire. "Gift-wrap Varron's head and send it to Auntie Seiren via royal messenger?"

"We could stay the night here," Stargazer offered as Sintaka bound the wound on his arm. "Head back to Thandállen tomorrow. We should probably take it easy on the poor dragons. We can take two days to go back to Wyvern's Rest."

"Or go back to Amaru directly from here," Sintaka suggested. "Meet up with Ceih and Arjin back in the city. We have the luxury of time now."

Mindrin slowly inched towards the campfire, rubbing his sore shoulders. "Let's go back to Amaru. Can't wait to see Spark again."

"To Amaru," Stargazer agreed. "Can't wait to see Mother again."

"I don't want to sleep in the keep," Terrays stated vehemently. "I've slept too long under that roof."

"We can sleep under the stars..." Stargazer smiled. "And the clouds," he added with a wry smirk.

"There must be some food in Chalandris – I saw Varron devouring some bread this afternoon," Shard offered. "We should have enough to get back to Amaru in style." He shifted in Sim's arms, wrapping his arms about his waist.

Terrays quirked an eyebrow, smiling wickedly. "Finally got around to it, I see."

"What are you talking about?" Sim asked, his eyes narrowed.

"I was wondering if you two were ever going to soulbind," she chuckled.

"Was it that obvious?"

"Yes," she replied honestly. Shard chuckled softly at that, and Sim's puzzlement grew.

"What? Could everyone tell?" he asked.

"Yep," Aerin nodded matter-of-factly. Stargazer blushed, nodding as well. Shard sat up, now blushing fiercely as he wondered how obvious his lovesickness had truly been to his family. Sintaka shrugged and Sim's face fell in astonishment.

Mindrin hesitantly raised a hand. "I didn't," he offered in consolation.

Shard and Sim exchanged mildly horrified glances.

HEY! Amaru! a voice called out, touching at their edge of their minds, loud and exuberant despite the vast distance separating them. **We did it!** Arjin shouted. **We got it. The Treasury is all ours!**

They all smiled with relief and delight, but found themselves too weary to reply. It did not sit well with Arjin, and he pressed in irritation: **Hey! Didn't you hear? The Treasury. The bloody Treasury! Do you have any idea how much money our Dynast just won herself? There isn't a number invented to describe it!**

That's nice, Arjin, Aerin replied.

Hey, hey, did you get it? he asked worriedly. **Is everything all right?**

Yeah, Aerin nodded. **Yeah, we got it.**

Arjin's presence retreated, doubtlessly confounded beyond belief at their seeming apathy. Sintaka and Stargazer exchanged glances. "We just became rich," she told him, a wry smile on her face.

"Richer than before?" Stargazer asked in mock unconcern.

"Jaxa always said she wanted Kishca's crown jewels," Shard mused.

Terrays set the ring down on the ground, letting her fingertips linger over the jewel for a fleeting moment. Her face twisted in a sudden mask of anger. She raised a large block of volcanic rock and brought it down over the ring. Its magic drained, the ring powdered under the blow, leaving only a glittering dust. Satisfied, Terrays sat back with a long sigh.

"Hey," Mindrin pointed up to the clouds. "Look at that."

They all turned their faces up to the sky. The clouds shifted, parting, and a slim fissure had developed between their mottled red surface. A black scar cut across the clouds, letting in the first glimpse of starlight the wastelands had seen in four millennia. They all stared up in silent awe at the few silver specks twinkling through the clouds: the trailing edge of the Well of Stars. Stargazer slowly rose. "This calls for something," he decided in a distant voice. "I feel like flying," he nodded resolutely, turning from the campfire and striding towards the edge of the rock ledge.

"Star! Wait for me," Aerin called after him, scrambling to her feet.

Shard rose as well, gently disentangling himself from Sim's embrace. Stargazer reached the edge of the ledge and stepped forward, spreading his arms at his sides as he fell over the chasm. "Star!" Aerin laughed, racing after him.

Shard walked to the edge of the ledge, gazing down at the four-hundred-foot drop to the lowlands below. Stargazer slowly glided on the air currents, his arms out at his sides like bird's wings, his face tipped to the rushing wind. Aerin chased after him, tucking her arms to her side as she spiraled through the air with all the control and precision of an Arashi Master. They rose and fell on the updrafts, free as birds, reluctant to return to the earth. They passed through a steam cloud and disappeared from view only to reappear a moment later: two distant figures, one silver, one red, spreading their arms to control their descent to earth.

Shard turned, glancing back at his soulmate, sitting next to his sister, the Onmyóji twins staring into each other's eyes like lovesick kits. Sim looked up to meet his soulmate's gaze and Shard bit his lip to repress the guilty smirk as he peered over the edge. Sim and Terrays laughed together, and Sim nodded towards the cliff encouragingly.

"Shard... you're not thinking – Shard!" Sintaka shouted as Shard spun about, stepping out into the open air. Her admonishments were soon drowned out by the whistling wind. Shard felt the air catch him, guiding him out over the wastelands. No longer a sorcerer, just a little kit again, he cast his arms wide against the updrafts. Laughing with sheer joy, he closed his eyes and tipped his face to the air, riding the wind down to the valley below.

ISBN 155212789-3
9 781552 127896